Praise for WATCH ME by Angela Clarke

'*Watch Me* sees the return of Nas and Freddie from *Follow Me* and goes further into their past and the guilt it has left them with. Fast paced and full of excitement, it's hard to know where each chapter will take you in this thoroughly unpredictable ride. It kept me gripped and I cannot wait for the third instalment to see what happens next.'
Katerina Diamond, author of *The Teacher*

'*Watch Me* is another zinging thriller in this social media crime series from Angela Clarke. From Snapchat to doxing to revenge porn, each turn of the page will make you reconsider your Internet life, and will definitely leave you worrying who's watching you. Smart, sassy and totally on point, following Nas and Freddie's investigations are a must.'
Sarah Pinborough, author of *Behind Her Eyes*

'The clock is ticking in Angela Clarke's excellent new novel *Watch Me*. DS Nasreen Cudmore and her friend Freddie Venton receive a chilling message via social media – they only have 24 hours to save the life of a young woman. Who has taken her? The answer lies online but the deeper they delve the more dangerous the situation becomes. Someone is watching their every move. Creepy, clever and unnerving; you won't ever want to log on again.'
C. L. Taylor, author of *The Missing*

'Starts with heart-pounding suspense; and the excitement intensifies throughout.'
Sharon Bolton, author of *Daisy in Chains*

'I loved this! An utterly addictive, gripping thriller.'
Robert Bryndza, author of international number one bestseller *The Girl in the Ice.*

D1023653

'Stylish, pacy and packs a bruising punch.'
Sarah Hilary, author of the DI Marnie Rome series.

'A sharp, punchy, fast-paced thriller, that will keep you hooked
until the very last page.'
Casey Kelleher, author of *Bad Blood*

'Fast, feminist and sharp as a knife. Just ripped through *Watch
Me* by Angela Clarke and recommend you do the same. If you
dare.'
Anna Mazzola, author of *The Unseeing*

'Clarke drags you into the dark world of the internet in this edgy,
tense, social-media thriller. You'll hold your breath, as you turn
pages at speed to find out the next twist in a world filled with
complex characters who are wonderfully vivid, with real depth
and warmth. I for one can't wait for the next book in this series.'
**Rebecca Bradley, author of the Detective Hannah Robbins
Series**

'An utterly compelling, brilliantly plotted tale that expertly ramps
up the tension and drags the reader in as the pages turn and the
clock ticks down.'
Neil Broadfoot, author of *All The Devils*

'Ingenious, fast-paced and full of dark wit. This is crime writing
with attitude.'
Mark Edwards, bestselling author of *Follow You Home*

Praise for FOLLOW ME by Angela Clarke

'Written in the sharpest style, the story races along, leaving the reader almost as breathless as the heroine – but there is a verve to it that is impossible to resist … Clarke is certainly someone to watch'
Daily Mail

'A very contemporary nightmare, delivered with panache'
Independent

'Freddie is a magnificently monstrous character'
Saturday Review, BBC Radio 4

'Clarke has made an appealing flawed female lead who'll make immediate sense to readers who enjoyed Rachel in *The Girl on the Train*. An invigorating cat-and-mouse game, with a dark and filthy wit that deliciously spikes the regular drenchings of gore'
Crime Scene Magazine

'Slick and clever'
Sun

'Set in a London of East End hipsters, Tinder hook-ups, and internships, this tongue-in-cheek tale explores murder in the age of social media'
Sunday Mirror

'A chilling debut'
Hello

'*Follow Me* is compelling, a proper page-turner'
Emerald Street

'Angela Clarke brings dazzling wit and a sharp sense of contemporary life to a fast-paced serial killer novel with serious style'
Jane Casey, author of the Maeve Kerrigan series

'In *Follow Me*, Clarke creates a completely compelling world, and a complex heroine. Freddie is refreshing and fascinating – a credible addition to the crime canon and a great alternative for anyone who has grown frustrated with the male dominated world of the whodunnit. *Follow Me* is literally gripping – the tension levels were forcing me to clutch the book so hard that my hands hurt!'
Daisy Buchanan, *Grazia*

'A fascinating murder mystery and a dark, ironic commentary on modern social media'
Paul Finch, author of *Stalkers*

'Gripping, darkly funny and feminist, I loved *Follow Me*'
Caroline Criado-Perez

'Pacey, gripping, and so up-to-the-minute you better read it quick!'
Claire McGowan, author of *The Fall*

'Smart, fast paced, fresh and frightening. *Follow Me* is a gripping debut'
Rowan Coleman, author of *The Memory Book*

'*Follow Me* is a well written, taut, absolutely fascinating and scarily good crime novel that is too true to life … It will certainly make you look at social media and Twitter in particular with the utmost scepticism and horror. Outstanding! Clearly the start of a wonderful series, superbly written. I definitely want more'
Ayo Onatade, *Shots* magazine

WATCH ME

Angela Clarke is an author, playwright, columnist, screenwriter and broadcaster. Her debut crime thriller *Follow Me* was named Amazon's Rising Star Debut of the Month January 2016, long listed for the Crime Writer's Association Dagger in the Library 2016, and short listed for the Dead Good Reader Page Turner Award 2016. *Watch Me* is the second instalment in the Social Media Murder Series. Angela's memoir *Confessions of a Fashionista* is an Amazon Fashion Chart bestseller. Her play, *The Legacy*, enjoyed its first run and rave reviews at The Hope Theatre in June 2015. She hosted the current affairs show *Outspoken* on Radio Verulam for six months in 2014, and has appeared on the BBC World Service, BBC Radio 4, BBC Three Counties and more. Her journalist contributions include: The *Guardian*, *Independent Magazine*, *Daily Mail*, *Cosmopolitan*, and *Writing* magazine. In 2015 Angela was awarded the Young Stationers' Prize for achievement and promise in writing and publishing. She volunteers with Womentoring, and the RSA Meet a Mentor scheme, and others, to help encourage and support marginalised artists into the industry. A Fellow of the Royal Society of Arts, Angela lives with her husband and far too many books.

You can follow Angela @TheAngelaClarke

Also by Angela Clarke

Follow Me

ANGELA CLARKE

Watch Me

The Social Media Murders

HarperCollins PUBLISHERS
Since 1817

This novel is entirely a work of fiction.
The names, characters and incidents portrayed in it are
the work of the author's imagination. Any resemblance to
actual persons, living or dead, events or localities is
entirely coincidental.

AVON

A division of HarperCollins*Publishers*
1 London Bridge Street,
London SE1 9GF

www.harpercollins.co.uk

A Paperback Original 2017

4

Copyright © Angela Clarke 2017

Angela Clarke asserts the moral right to
be identified as the author of this work

A catalogue record for this book is
available from the British Library

ISBN-13: 978-0-00-817461-3

Set in Minion by Palimpsest Book Production Ltd, Falkirk, Stirlingshire

Printed and bound in Great Britain by
Clays Ltd, St Ives plc

All rights reserved. No part of this publication may be
reproduced, stored in a retrieval system, or transmitted,
in any form or by any means, electronic, mechanical,
photocopying, recording or otherwise, without the prior
permission of the publishers.

MIX
Paper from
responsible sources
FSC www.fsc.org **FSC™ C007454**

FSC™ is a non-profit international organisation established to promote
the responsible management of the world's forests. Products carrying the
FSC label are independently certified to assure consumers that they come
from forests that are managed to meet the social, economic and
ecological needs of present and future generations,
and other controlled sources.

Find out more about HarperCollins and the environment at
www.harpercollins.co.uk/green

Dedicated to Laura Higgins

*and to all those who work tirelessly to help and advocate
change at www.RevengePornHelpline.org.uk*

Prologue

She gets off the bus one stop early, opting to take the muddy back path over the busy main school gate. She could slip in unnoticed. A lie, but the greasy, stone-spiked, mouldering leaves and dog-wee-splashed track give her a few more seconds of cover. Mum doesn't believe she's sick. But she is. A heavy, squirming bacterium has multiplied inside her, thousands of poisonous sacs settling in weighty pockets of flesh. They could see it. They could sense it. She'd never be accepted. She knew that now. Adults say it's because she's clever: what a joke! It's because she's defective. *Malformed.* A broken pot which has bulged and cracked in the kiln. Her stomach is looped and low, her breasts sagging boulders pulling her down. The tops of her thighs burn through her straining tights. She can feel the welts forming: raw blisters on the skin. There's a comfort in the pain: *penance.* Wincing, she thinks of the restraining hands. Pushing her down. She strokes the bruise on her arm, and tries to blot out what happened next.

In the schoolyard two girls, younger than her, patent record bags slung over their shoulders, giggle. Their voices drop as she nears them. Why would they be bothered with her? There's a shout from a group of year seven boys, she looks at the asphalt when she sees they're watching her too. What's going on? Her heart drums a warning in her ears. Gripping the strap of her school bag tight, she walks faster, almost running by the time she reaches her locker. The hallway and stairs teem with students, her year, the years above and below, a hundred eyes greedily turned on her. Someone shouts: 'Slut!' Her cheeks burn. Sweat pools under her arms, her breasts, her back, choking wafts catching in her throat. What's happened? Anxiety surges through her. Her fingers slip as she enters the pin code for her locker. They're waiting; the air is tense with expectation, and the joke she's not in on. She steps back as she opens her locker, fearful something'll burst out. What she sees is worse. Photos have been slid into the locker through the sides. *Her with her shirt unbuttoned. Gelatinous mountains of breasts. Her skirt round her waist. Knickers pulled down.* With clumsy hands, she tries to stuff the pictures into her bag. To cover them. To cover herself. They skitter across the floor. Panic fizzes like sherbet through her, foaming into her eyes. Falling onto her knees, desperate to hide them, she scrabbles for the photos as they slip and scrape across the vinyl.

'Nice minge!' a boy shouts. They're all laughing.

'Whore!' a girl calls. Another spits at her. Jerking back to avoid it, her bottom bangs into the locker behind. A fresh wave of laughter. There's a tight, jeering knot of friends around the spitting girl. All she can see are leering, cackling faces. Vicious monkeys that flood the stairs, swarm through the hallway. Someone waves the photo in the air. Another boy pretends to lick it. They all have it. She's pinned, skewed like a caught butterfly, displayed for all the world to see.

Inside, the sacs rupture, and she's washed in a wave of black. Her heart breaks.

Chapter 1

Friday 11 March

20:00

Melisha Khan stared at the message on her phone. An image. Words. A timer. *You've got six seconds to view this*. Her school uniform felt like it was tightening, her white shirt compressing, her striped tie snaking around her neck. Her mind scrabbled for normality. *Five seconds*. Her hand shook. Her fingers didn't respond.

Four seconds. Her eyes spun off the words on the note and ricocheted round the room.

I can't go on…

Pages of highlighted French GCSE notes fanned around her feet. Her laptop upended. *Three seconds*. A stain of red nail polish spread on the floor.

I can't live in fear…

Melisha tried to form a sound. Her lips were lax, useless, dull. Inside her a voice screamed *this is important*. Do something. Anything. *Two seconds.*

This is the only way…

Melisha thought she was mature. Had it all sussed out. She felt the cold reality now. Cotton-wool wraps, safety, childhood, were stripped away. She was raw. Alert. Adult. This was the moment she grew up. Her eyes fixed on the words, the sentences. The note came into focus:

As I type this I feel calmer. I'm doing the right thing. It's a relief. I can't go on after people find out. It's disgusting. I've let down my friends, family, teachers, everyone. Only those who've seen will know why. I can't live in fear of it coming out. All the lies are finished. Mum, Dad, Freya, Gemma, I screwed up. I can't hurt you more. I love you. It's time I fixed the mess I made. This is the only way. I promise you all you're better off without me. I know you'll feel sad reading this, but I know that'll be over soon. The pain will fade. Your tears will dry. You'll live happy lives. I love you. Now it's time to go. I'll be dead within twenty-four hours of you receiving this note.

One second. From deep inside the command grew, forcing its way up and out of her, juddering her whole body. 'Mum!' she screamed. And the photo vanished.

Saturday 12 March

20:01

His bike sped through the wood, jumping the tree roots which pushed through the muddy ground like bony fingers. His brother's bike light, lower and slower, turned birch trees into streaks of white in the dark. The wind whipped back from him. He was flying. Fifteen minutes till curfew.

A flash of orange caught his eye. *Treasure.* He skidded to a halt as the path gave way to a grass clearing, grey in the gloom.

His brother shouted behind him. 'We're late!' Nose and cheeks pink from the cold, he didn't want to get in trouble. 'Whose bag is that?'

'Dunno.' He kicked at the handbag with his toe. 'Looks like a girl's.' There were folders and books in the top. He laughed, teasing, 'Maybe she's shagging someone!'

'Gross!' His brother's small face screwed up.

'Let's take it for Mum.' He knew he'd freak. Stealing was naughty.

There was no squeal. His brother didn't answer. He looked up at him, he was pale. Eyes wide saucers. Mouth like a goldfish.

'What?'

He gulped as he pointed behind them. His arms shaking. Turning was like watching a replay on his computer game. Slow mo. Behind them, five, maybe six big steps away was a girl. Lying down. Curled up. His ears went weird. Like whistling. Her forehead was on the grass, face turned towards them. She had pretty yellow hair. It was cold out there. He stepped towards her.

His brother whimpered – 'No!' – his voice whiney. He made a sound like their cat did when it had a fur ball.

He took another step. Her eyes were open. They were black like a doll's. He jumped. Thought he might pee himself. Gripped his trousers. 'She's dead.'

'I want Mummy,' his brother cried.

'She's dead.' He stumbled back, treading on his toes. Fell over his bicycle. This was real. He had to protect his brother. He was the eldest. He grabbed for him and the bike. 'Go. Get going!' Tears burned his eyes. He wanted Mum. He wanted Dad. Scrambling, he pulled his own bike up. The metal was ice in his hands. 'Go!' he shouted as they pedalled. Faster. Faster. Looking back he saw her lying in the moonlight. Her dead black eyes watching them.

Monday 14 March

13:27

From: FreddieVenton@gmail.com
To: GStrofton@NHS.net
Subject: Hello

Hey Nurse Strofton!

Long time no hear! I saw Nasreen Cudmore a few months
ago. We ended up working together. You might have seen
it on the news? Bit crazy – hunting a serial killer!! She said
you were a midwife. That she'd seen you a few years back.
So I thought I'd look you up. I found you on the hospital
website and had a guess at your address – there looks like
there's a standard format. Hope this doesn't bounce back!

Well, this is weird. After all this time. It's taken me weeks to write this. And I call myself a journalist – ha! I've been taking some time off actually. I had to have an operation, needed a bit of time to recover. But that's not really important. I'm writing because I wanted to say sorry. My therapist thinks it might help to go back and apologise to those I feel I've hurt. Can you imagine that? Me with a counsellor! What a London twat I am! But the truth is I am sorry for everything that happened back then. I was just a kid, and there was some stuff going on with my parents. Not that that's an excuse. I'm sorry. I hope you're okay. I want you to be happy.

If you ever fancy catching up for a drink or something, I'm staying back with my parents right now. They're still in Pendrick. Your hospital's only thirty minutes away according to Google Maps. Let me know… For old time's sake?

Cheers,

Freddie x

From: GStrofton@NHS.net
To: FreddieVenton@gmail.com
Subject: Re: Hello

Never contact me again.

Chapter 2

Wednesday 16 March

09:05

Sergeant Nasreen Cudmore had never been hungover before. A slight headache, sure. Nothing a paracetamol wouldn't fix. But this morning her body was rebelling. Her mouth felt fur-lined, like the inside of an over-worn Ugg boot. The insipid March sunlight burned her eyes. She'd escaped the nauseous sway of the tube to pant along Victoria Tower Gardens, veering right and away from Millbank and the Thames, perspiration seeping into her collared shirt. Her long black hair, washed hurriedly, clung damp and freezing against her neck. She wasn't a big drinker at the best of times, and this certainly wasn't the best of times. Moments from last night ignited in her memory. *Fingers ripping at shirt buttons. Loosening belts. Her hands on his warm skin.*

The yellowing art deco chunks of the secure building that housed the Met's Specialist Crime and Operations units came into view. Only the presence of concrete car-bomb barriers, dressed up as flowerbeds, distinguished it as anything other than a normal Westminster office block. DCI Jack Burgone had head-hunted Nasreen to join his specialised cyber and e-crime Gremlin taskforce after her involvement in a high-profile murder investigation last year. Eight weeks into her new job, and the rest of the now four-man team still didn't seem thrilled to have her on board. DI McCain, who preferred to go by the nickname Chips, had raised his salt-and-pepper eyebrows upon meeting her. After twenty-five years of exemplary service in the paedophile unit, eight of those under DCI Burgone, Chips had been looking to take a less active role. But Burgone had persuaded him to join the newly conceived Gremlin unit. They'd been joined by DI Pete Saunders – a vain, ambitious thirty-five year old who liked to remind people of his achievements both in and out of the job. Saunders took great delight in pointing out others' shortcomings. Especially Nasreen's. In the two years since it'd been formed, the triumvirate Gremlin unit had overseen a number of successful ops, including the apprehension of the founder of underground drugs website Lotus Road. DCI Burgone was the force's golden boy: dedicated, focused and well connected from his days at Eton, he'd shunned a job at a government boardroom table in favour of real results on the frontline of the force. And Nasreen was the newbie who'd got drunk in the pub. Way to go, Cudmore.

At twenty-four, Nasreen had spring-boarded from the graduate fast-track scheme, and landed a promotion to Detective Sergeant. Fast. She'd worked hard, and sometimes at great personal cost, to get where she was, but her age, her skin tone, and what she'd been told were her good looks had left her dogged by accusations of favouritism, tokenism, or worse. Not being able to hold a drink in front of her colleagues was not going to help.

9.07 a.m. She was late for the morning meeting. She'd never been late before. Ever. It was the second thing she'd done for the first time in the last twenty-four hours. She was never going to have a one-night stand again, either. Licking her dry lips she caught a taste of *him*. Shame burst through her body in a fresh wave of sweat. They'd sense it straight away. Chips and Saunders knew she was out of her depth in the team, and she'd played right into their hands. Idiot. Could she call in sick?

People, officers and civilian support staff were streaming past now. Her feet felt as though they were moving of their own accord. Marching her forward. After the total fool she'd made of herself, and consumed by burning embarrassment, Nasreen's need to people please still overrode everything else. Swiping her ID card, she hurried into the lift, pulling her hair into a ponytail and scraping under her eyes for stray mascara. The email she'd sent was seared onto her mind. Too little, too late.

This morning's meeting was to cover the case they'd been discussing in the pub last night. Several glasses of red in, and after a busy day during which she hadn't managed to grab lunch or dinner, the details were hazy. Did it involve going into a school to talk about e-safety? Saunders had suggested that might be a suitably non-challenging role for her. She'd laughed, but it hadn't been a joke. It was something to do with social media; she scrolled through her phone. A little yellow square with a white ghost on it denoted the newly downloaded app. Snapchat – that was it. It was something about school kids sending messages via the app. Was it bullying? Used to always being prepared, Nasreen hated floundering for answers. It was one of the reasons she was good at her job: she liked to know why,

13

liked to ask questions, put things, and people, where they belonged. Uncertainty was what life gave you; order was what you made with it.

Opening the Snapchat app, an unread message from yesterday appeared: a photo of Saunders's chiselled face grimacing at her, his manicured stubble casting a five o'clock shadow over his skin. Cartoon dog ears and a tongue added to the surreal effect. A timer in the corner of the photo wound down from eight seconds, after which the image would disappear. If only she could do that with last night. Snapchat's USP was that images or videos were only viewable for a time dictated by the sender. Then they vanished. You couldn't see them again. Why? Some people – other people – sent sexy photos of themselves to lovers. A glimpse of her lacy peach knickers crashed through her head. And black boxer shorts. Hair flopping forwards into those penetrating blue eyes. Lips on lips. Skin on skin. The lift door opened onto the spotless, cream-walled, grey-carpeted corridor. Her floor.

Chips looked up as she let herself into the designated meeting room. He had a kindly, line-riven face, and the red, mottled cheeks that come from a career spent indulging in Scotch on the difficult days. Like Father Christmas, if Santa had spent years locking up sex offenders. A paper bag split open to reveal a bacon roll – with a bite taken out – was on the chair next to him. He knew how to handle his hangover, as he knew how to handle his drink. He would never lose control like she had.

'You're late, Cudmore.' The tap of Saunders's biro against his silver chain-link watch rang through her like a gunshot. He sat with one ankle resting on the other knee. His pumped biceps were barely contained by his starched pale blue shirt.

She felt scruffy. 'I'm sorry, I… The train…'

'Let's get on with it, shall we?' DCI Burgone spoke softly. She

14

feared she might laugh. Burgone's black hair had been forced into waves of submission. Whereas Saunders might be considered ruggedly handsome, Burgone was beautiful. He had an elegance to his features and a confidence in his movements that highlighted his patrician nature. His nickname in the force was Jack the Lad, a knowing joke given that he was a consummate pro, and anything but flashy. Nasreen grabbed the nearest chair, looking away from her boss's questioning gaze.

Who'd left the pub first last night? The whole floor had been out to welcome the new receptionist, Lorna. Anyone could have seen them. Superintendent Lewis was explicit about relationships between colleagues: *not on her watch*. It was instant transfer. If anyone found out, Nasreen would be gone. She'd only said yes to the first glass because she was irritated no one had organised welcome drinks for her. And then it all went wrong. She'd left him sleeping under the duvet, mortification powering her home. Frantically sending that email. *Damage control.* Still drunk. She was zealous at stamping on accusations she'd slept her way to the top. If anyone said anything suggestive she told them where to stick it – loudly. She avoided being alone with male colleagues in social situations. If there were two of them left at the bar, she'd head for a group or call someone else over. Nothing that could fuel the fire. And now what? She'd poured petrol all over it and handed round the matches. Her career was smouldering. If only she could work out who knew what.

The DCI opened the file on his desk. 'Thank you all for coming in this morning.'

'Urgh,' said Chips. 'I feel like I've licked a badger's arse.' Nasreen thought she might be sick.

'Thank you for that delightful image, Chips,' the DCI smiled. 'As discussed last night, we've had a request from the Hertfordshire

15

Constabulary for some educational support. A fifteen-year-old girl from St Albans took her own life after sharing her suicide note on Snapchat.'

Suicide? She must have missed that bit when she was at the bar. Nasreen hated suicide cases. Especially teen suicides. Abruptly, she felt like she was fourteen again. Hearing the phone ring late at night. Her parents waking her to say her friend Gemma was in hospital. That she'd slashed her wrists. That the note blamed Nasreen and her best pal, Freddie.

'The photo of the typed suicide note was circulated among her friends and sisters, and primed to vanish after six seconds.' The DCI's voice dragged her back to the present. He held up a printout: a photo of a typed note, overlaid with a text banner. 'The local force didn't have access to it at the time of the investigation, but what we assume is a screenshot copy of it has been leaked from someone and is being shared online. Several parents have contacted the school to say their children have been sent the note over WhatsApp. The local force and the school are worried.'

'The Werther effect?' Nasreen had read a lot of suicide research.

'The what?' Saunders looked amused.

'Copycat suicides,' said DCI Burgone. 'With well-publicised cases there are often suicide clusters. It's called suicide contagion – a real and alarming syndrome.' Chips tutted and shook his head, as if this sort of thing could be discouraged with disapproval.

'Schools and communities are particularly susceptible to the phenomenon,' Burgone continued. He sounded like a newsreader from a bygone broadcast; it was reassuring, and one of the reasons the press loved him. His handsome face was made to be on camera. 'The detail of how the suicide note was sent hasn't made the news yet, and we'd like to keep it that way. It has spread across social media, and the school are worried in case anyone else tries to take their lives, emulating Chloe Strofton.'

Nasreen's head snapped up. *Strofton.* Her pulse quickened. Coincidence? Had she misheard the name – hungover, tired, and wired from everything that had happened in the last twenty-four hours?

'The local force has requested we go in and chat to the pupils,' the DCI was saying. 'It'll be a good PR exercise for my funding budget. It's a standard approach: try to stem the sharing of the note. Reinforce the inherent dangers. Tell the young people they can talk to us or their teachers if they have concerns. We're seeking to nip this in the bud quickly.'

'I'm pretty sure Cudmore volunteered last night,' Chips grinned. 'She's closer to the kids' ages. They won't want to hear from old lunks like me and Pete.'

'Speak for yourself!' Saunders reached a powerful arm down for the vitamin drink at his feet. 'But I can't be doing with kids. Not the maternal type. Isn't that why we got her in?' He was watching for her reaction.

Nasreen kept her features placid. Did he know? 'What was the name?' Her voice sounded strangled, she coughed to cover it.

'Someone needs to rehydrate.' Saunders took a glug from his drink. She concentrated on looking at her phone, as if she were about to type notes.

'Strofton. Chloe Strofton.' DCI Burgone looked at his paperwork. 'Aged fifteen. Parents Deborah Strofton, forty-six, and Robert Strofton, fifty-two. Two sisters: Freya Strofton, thirteen…' It felt like Nasreen had plunged into freezing water. It filled her ears, her mouth, her nose, her eyes. She knew what was coming. 'And Gemma Strofton, twenty-three.'

It was her. Gemma. The girl that had changed Nasreen's

life. Chloe had succeeded where her older sister Gemma had failed. She had to say something. She knew the victim, or at least she had known the victim's sister eight years ago. She opened her mouth. A blast of remembered anger, fear and sadness hit her, ripping jaggedly through time. She could see herself, lying on her single bed in her pink-painted bedroom, fourteen years old, sobbing. Desperate to make it better. 'I'll take the case, sir.'

DCI Burgone nodded. 'Good. A young woman – like Chips says, you'll have more chance of connecting with these kids.'

Young? Was that what he thought of her? And he'd said *woman*; did he agree with Saunders? Had she been brought onto the team as a female officer to deal with the emotional stuff after all? He smiled, and she stared back into his eyes. The same eyes she'd stared into last night.

Chips and Saunders were gathering up their stuff, Saunders groaning and stretching his arms out as he stood. Nasreen had a new email. He'd replied. Her chest constricted. Everything raced past her: the wine, the email she'd sent, Gemma, Chloe, DCI Jack Burgone's lips on her.

To: NCudmore@btinternet.com
From: JonathanBurgone@police.uk

We need to talk.

Those four little words never signalled anything good. They heralded the end of relationships, disciplinary actions, bad news. Saunders was back in his blazer, Chips was headed for the door. Looking up she caught the DCI's eye: static shot through her. She couldn't breathe; she could only think of what he tasted like, what he felt like, how he'd made her feel. He'd talked to her, listened to what she'd had to say. Or she thought he had. Was it a trick of the alcohol? Had she wanted to believe he thought she was smart? He could've just been being polite to a new member of his team. But when they'd stood outside the pub, laughing in the rain, she'd seen it in his eyes: lust. He'd felt the connection too. She couldn't be on her own with him here in the office. Not yet. She needed to get things straight in her head. She stood, knocking her chair into the table behind. She walked fast to catch up with Chips as he and Saunders reached their open plan office, aware the DCI was just behind her. Her phone beeped. At first she thought it was an echo, but the others' phones all sounded at the same time. A cacophony of beeps.

'What the?' Chips frowned. 'Which one of you silly buggers is sending Snapchat photos now – I thought we'd had enough of that last night.'

Saunders grimaced, turning his phone over in his hand. The DCI pulled his from his suit pocket. Now was not the time for PPI insurance junk mail. Nasreen swiped the screen of her phone and it opened on her new Snap. It was from a number she didn't recognise. Time to change her security settings. The timer in the top right-hand corner was ticking down. *Six seconds, five seconds.* It was a photo of a typed note, overlaid with a text banner. Nasreen's breath caught in her throat.

'Holy shit!' Chips said.

'Is that another suicide note?' Saunders asked. 'How the hell did they get my number?'

'And mine!' Chips grunted.

Nasreen scanned the words, the name at the bottom: *Lottie Burgone.* 'It's my sister's number.' The DCI frowned. 'Is this a joke? Did one of you send this?' He glared at her.

'No.' Nasreen looked round. They were all shaking their heads. Alarm flickered in Saunders's eyes. She looked at the photo:

19

A pointless opulent life leads you onto nothing.
I can't go on. Lottie Burgone

'Get her on the phone – now. Call her, Jack,' Chips was saying. Nasreen stared at the words in the caption that overlaid the note:

You have 6 seconds to read this and 24 hours to save the girl's life.

Her brain crackled. This wasn't a wind up. This was a threat. Her fingers flew. *Four, three, two...* She screenshot the image, taking a photo of it half a second before it disappeared forever.

Chapter 3

Wednesday 16 March

09:31
T – 24 hrs

'I'm calling the number.' Saunders had his phone to his ear. 'Straight to voicemail. It is her number, yeah, your sister's, sir?'

'Yes. My phone recognises it. I don't understand... Why would she send this?' The DCI was holding his phone in both hands. Nasreen thought he was shaking it, then she realised he was shaking.

'Do you have another contact for her, sir?' Nasreen reached over her desk for the landline.

'What's her address?' Chips ran round to his computer.

'She lives in Greenwich. She's a student at the university,' DCI Burgone stuttered.

'Undergraduate?' said Nasreen. 'How old?'

'Sociology. Eighteen. She'll be nineteen next month.'

Three years age difference to Chloe Strofton. A similar demographic. Young teenage woman. Student. Could she have seen the fuss around Chloe's suicide online? Was this a contagious suicide attempt? 'Any other telephone number, sir?'

'Zero, two, zero, three…'

Nasreen wrote the number down as the DCI said it.

'That's her flat number.' He blinked. Held his mobile to his ear. Nasreen heard the tinny sound of the girl's voicemail message. 'She lives in halls. There are five other flatmates. All girls. I think. I usually take her out for dinner. We meet at the restaurant.'

'I'm sure there's some innocent explanation,' Chips said. 'The lassie or one of her pals mucking about.' Nasreen saw Saunders give him a look. The line rang in her ear.

'Does she have any history of mental illness, sir?' asked Saunders.

'No, of course not,' snapped Burgone. 'Sorry. I know you're just… following procedure.' The words sounded cold. Callous.

Saunders cleared his throat. 'And does she have any history of trying to harm herself?'

'No. She's happy. She's really into running. Fitness. This isn't her. She wouldn't…' His face paled. 'I'll send her a WhatsApp message. Sometimes it's easier to contact her that way.'

The phone at the other end of Nasreen's call was picked up. A woman – young, breathless, anxious – answered. 'Lottie?'

She had been waiting for her call. Lottie wasn't there. Had this flatmate received the same frightening Snapchat? Nasreen's stomach fell away. 'This is Detective Sergeant Nasreen Cudmore. Is Lottie – Charlotte…' She looked at the DCI; he nodded his affirmation. She tried to keep her face neutral. 'Is Charlotte Burgone there, please?'

'Has something happened to Lottie?' The girl sounded panicked.

22

'Can I ask your name, please, miss?' She looked straight ahead at her computer, away from the DCI.

'Yes. Sorry. It's Bea. Beatrice Perkins. I'm Lottie's friend. Her flatmate.'

'And is Lottie there, Bea?' Nasreen felt the eyes of the room on her. Chips had paused from typing on his computer.

'No. She's gone. I mean, she went for a run this morning. But she never came back. I tried her phone but she didn't answer. And I got this weird Snap. And oh god – have you found her? Is she okay?' The girl's words fell over themselves – fast, frantic. Nasreen looked up at DI Saunders and shook her head.

'I'll get on to the university.' Saunders picked up his phone.

'Christ.' The DCI was staring at his mobile. 'She hasn't picked up the WhatsApp message yet. It says she hasn't seen it. But if she's running then…'

'And at what time did she go for her run, Bea?' Nasreen noted the times on her pad – the timeline of a missing person.

'Six a.m. She always goes at the same time. She's a morning person. Dani – our flatmate – she saw her leave. She was up to get to the library early. She's got coursework due.' The girl was babbling. They'd need to speak to the other flatmate. 'Lottie always wakes me when she gets back. She's always back at seven thirty. Always. But she didn't come back today. I didn't realise until after nine. I slept through. I missed my lecture.'

'Does Lottie run alone?'

'Yes. No one else can get up at that time each day. She's a machine,' Bea said. 'I mean in a good way. Oh god. This is awful.'

'Take a deep breath for me, Bea, you're doing great.' Nasreen kept her tone even. 'Does Lottie ever go anywhere else straight from her run? The library? Another friend's perhaps? A boyfriend's?'

'No. She comes home to shower. She wouldn't go anywhere

23

else before that. She likes her hair to be done.' Bea sounded small, far away. Nasreen wished she could put her arm around the girl.

'And has Lottie been upset about anything lately?' She knew what she was asking, in front of her boss, in front of Lottie's brother.

'No! She wouldn't kill herself! She wouldn't!' Bea's voice wavered and smashed like porcelain on kitchen tiles.

Even those closest to suicide victims don't always suspect that anything is wrong. 'Is there anyone else there with you, Bea? We may need to send an officer to come and speak to you.'

'Dani will be back soon. She should be. Oh god. Lottie wouldn't do this. She wouldn't.'

Nasreen looked at her watch. 'You're doing great, Bea, just a few more questions. So the last time any of you saw Lottie Burgone was at six o'clock this morning?' *When I was coming home from sleeping with her brother.* 'So she's not been seen for the last three and a half hours?' It wasn't normally a priority at this stage, but Lottie had sent a suicide note. As far as Nasreen knew, DI Saunders and Chips had never met Lottie Burgone, and she certainly hadn't. Why would she send a suicide note to all their phones? How would she have their numbers? *You have 6 seconds to read this and 24 hours to save the girl.* Her gut contracted. This sounded more like a ransom note.

'We haven't seen her since then. I should've woken up earlier. I should've gone to look for her.'

Nasreen looked at Chips as he picked up his handset. 'I'll get onto the local force,' he said. 'Get some eyes on the ground.' His voice was gruff, focused.

'Bea, I'm going to need a list of all Lottie's friends, boyfriends, anyone she's been hanging out with recently. Do you think you can do that?' Nasreen asked.

Bea Perkins took a big breath in. 'Yes.'

'Thank you, Bea.' Chips was now onto the Greenwich force. He gave her a nod. 'Bea, we're going to have someone with you very shortly to go through that list. They'll be in uniform. In the meantime, I'm going to give you my number here and my mobile as well. If you hear from Lottie, or think of anything else before my colleagues get there, call me immediately. Have you got a pen?' She heard the girl rummaging in the background, imagining the chaos of a student bedroom. This girl shouldn't be doing anything more than worrying about her classes today. She gave Bea the number.

'I've put in a request for some floaters.' Chips was talking as if it was just another job. As if they weren't talking about the guv's sister. 'We'll run a cell site check on her phone, see if we can pinpoint where she was when that message was sent.'

Burgone nodded.

She wouldn't interrogate him, but they needed to get as much information as possible. The DCI hadn't seemed to blink for over a minute. Chips stood awkwardly, unsure whether to offer a pat of comfort to his boss and friend. DI Saunders was on his own phone at the other end of the office, his back turned to them, his voice low, rolling out the plan. Nasreen spoke gently. 'Is there anywhere else she might go, sir? Friends from home?' She didn't even know where Burgone was from. 'A boyfriend's? What about your parents'?'

'Oh god – Mum and Pa.'

Nasreen flinched at the affectionate term. Under normal circumstances, that would have earned a gruff laugh from Chips. It was like seeing something soft and intimate, and Nasreen didn't want to intrude further than they had to. Burgone seemed to summon strength from inside, his face taking on its usual self-assured expression.

'Our parents are in the South of France. I'll call them. She doesn't have a boyfriend. That I know of. I've met some of her uni flatmates – Bea, who was on the telephone to Cudmore, and another, Dani. They're nice girls. I doubt they've had any involvement with the police before. I don't know about the others she lives with. Before college Lottie was a boarder at Bedales, I think she's still in touch with some of the girls from there.' Worry lines fanned out from his eyes. 'She spends a lot of time on social media, particularly Instagram – she has a number of sponsorship deals.'

'Sponsorship for what?' Was Jack's sister famous? Had he ever even mentioned his family to her? This felt all wrong: she should have been finding out about him casually in a pub over dinner, not during a criminal investigation.

'Companies, mostly sports ones, I believe. They send her products and pay for her to feature them on the site.'

'She's famous?' asked Chips. Burgone didn't respond.

Nasreen wanted to know what the DCI's sister looked like. 'Which brands?'

'I'm not sure. My mother will have a list, she helps Lottie do her accounts.'

Saunders was walking casually over, hands in his pockets, as if strolling in the park. Did he know something already? Something from his phone call? Or was he just acting calm, trying not to distract the DCI? Her brain automatically ran through the questions and connections she would draw if they were talking to anyone else. She woke her desktop and searched for Lottie Burgone and Instagram on Google. Chips and Saunders were standing behind her, Saunders's citrus aftershave enveloping them all. The DCI was pacing.

'There.' Chips pointed at the first search result.

Lottie's account opened on the screen; she was called

LottieLondoner. Her profile picture showed the same classic bone structure as her brother, but instead of his short, dark ruffles of hair, Lottie had long blonde tendrils that hung around her tanned face, her cheeks still soft like a child's. She was thin, and very toned. There were countless photos of her in yoga positions that Nasreen knew, from the odd class she'd taken, took time, dedication and real strength to perfect. She must spend hours exercising. Could someone who's flooded with endorphins be a credible suicide risk? Lottie's account was full of taut, tanned skin: acres of it. The scoop of a traps muscle bisected by a bright green vest strap; the slice of a shoulder blade highlighted by a peach racerback; a hewn stomach under-scored by tight, pale blue leggings. At no point was Lottie naked or even provocatively dressed, but as she scrolled past photos of her doing handstands, legs split apart, knees bent into right angles, her torso bending backwards, Nasreen felt there was something sexual about them – even if the girl wasn't conscious of it. It made her uneasy. This job had a way of making you view everything through the cynical eyes of society's undesir-ables. There was Lottie on the beach. In the park. In the gym. And a number of photos of food: white plates of brightly coloured fruits; sliced avocados; and Lottie smiling and sipping green juice through a pink straw. *Perfection.*

'Athletic lass,' Chips said.

'I have those protein shakes.' Saunders sounded impressed. Burgone hadn't come to look at his sister's page.

'Yeah, but you can't stand on your head, can you,' Chips said.

'I can do the splits,' he said. It was a ludicrous mental image. He shrugged. 'I did a lot of gymnastics when I was a kid.' Subject closed.

Nasreen tried not to smile at the idea of alpha-male Saunders in a leotard. She hadn't made it to spin class this week, and, she thought guiltily, she'd had cereal for dinner three out of the last four nights. Along the top of the screen were the account's stats. Lottie had posted 2,253 times. 'She's got 24,000 followers?' Incredible!

'Has she?' Burgone smiled to himself, as if he expected no less of her. She swallowed the lump forming in her throat. Chips was frowning.

She clicked the first image: Lottie in the park, balancing on one leg, the other stretched back and up, like an arabesque. She was laughing, her hair falling forwards in soft waves around her face. It had 340 likes. 'She has fans,' she scrolled through the seventy-seven comments:

> @**Boinggirl** Beautiful hair!
> @**Reasontolive** Lottie I love you. I don't know how you do it! <3 <3 <3 Please follow me back!!!
> @**CarlyAngel86** You're such an inspiration. Thank you for sharing the real you.

Why would a girl with a seemingly perfect life kill herself? And why send the suicide note via Snapchat? And why to them? *Tell us where you are, Lottie. Tell us how to help you.*

Nasreen looked from the sunshine of Lottie's Instagram account to Burgone. He didn't meet any of their eyes. She longed to tell him everything was going to be all right. But she didn't. Training and experience taught you not to make promises you couldn't keep – not to a victim's family. And that's what he was now. No longer the guv. No longer in control. Jack Burgone was on the wrong side of the investigation.

Chapter 4

Wednesday 16 March

10:15
T – 23 hrs 15 mins

Burgone had gone for some fresh air after calling his parents; they'd heard nothing from their daughter since they'd last spoken to her two days ago. She'd seemed fine. *Normal.* That word you always watched for. The thought of anything happening to either of Nasreen's younger sisters physically hurt her. What had it been like to make that call? Chips or Saunders should have spoken to the family, listened for the telltale signs of tension, lies swimming under the surface, but it didn't seem right. This was the DCI. It was *his* family. *His* missing sister.

Superintendent Lewis had told Burgone he was to take a back seat now. Chips and Saunders were managing the investigation.

Nasreen looked at her watch. She had been ignoring her bladder for the last thirty minutes. She didn't want to leave her desk until they'd located Lottie, but she couldn't hang on any longer. The hoped-for phone call that stated this was all a terrible mix-up hadn't come. Grabbing her phone and her handbag she stood up.

'Where you going, Sergeant?' Saunders's voice rang out over the room.

Nasreen stared at him. *Are you really doing this?* 'Just popping to the ladies'. If that's all right?'

He turned his chair so his knees pointed at her, the navy fabric of his suit pulled taut. He nodded his angular face at the empty cups of water and coffee on her desk. 'You better not be too hungover to do your job properly, Cudmore.'

Nasreen felt her face colour. Was he testing her? So much for trying to rehydrate. Chips didn't look up. 'I'm fine. Sir.'

'Fine isn't good enough,' Saunders snapped, whirling his chair round to face his desk. 'We have a reputation of being the best of the force, and I'm not having you dent that on my watch, Cudmore. Pick it up.'

A wave of disbelief passed over her – did he expect her to ask for permission to go to the bathroom?

Without turning around, Saunders barked. 'Get on with it then!'

Nasreen let the door swing shut behind her. How dare he talk to her like that? They'd all hit the ground running on this one. The superintendent had authorised ten floaters: four here at the office, six out in Greenwich. No questions asked when it was one of your own. Officers from Greenwich West were questioning Bea and Lottie's other flatmates. Tracking down her other friends, shaking students from their beds, from others' beds. The thought she wasn't doing everything she could to help Burgone made her feel sick. Burgone wouldn't think that, would he? That was just Saunders posturing, surely?

30

There were two floaters ahead of her in the hallway, and with a sinking feeling she recognised the hunched shape of DC Morris. She'd met him on her first day here and found him to be odious. Rather than doing his actual job, he preferred to use his time collecting leverage, real or fabricated, on nominals and colleagues. He was a terrible choice for this investigation, but needs must and one more person, even one as insidious as Morris, was better than none. Walking beside him, her ginger hair pulled into a tight bun at the nape of her neck, was DC Jan Green. Nasreen knew little about Green, except that she was sorry the pale, freckled woman had got landed with Morris.

'I bet you it's a wind up.' Morris's voice was a low rumble that threatened to break into a laugh. 'A spoilt brat who's not getting enough attention – you know the family's minted, right?'

'I hope the guv doesn't overhear you discussing his sister,' Nasreen said. They jumped and turned to face her.

DC Green's eyes were wide, and up close Nasreen could see they were a pretty almond shape. The constable recovered quickly, tucking her hands behind her, standing to attention. 'Sorry, ma'am.'

Morris, a good ten years older than Nasreen, remained slouched. 'It's no secret Little Lord Fauntleroy was born with a silver spoon.'

Nasreen glared at him. 'I wouldn't keep DI Saunders waiting. You don't want to get landed with the CCTV tapes.' This was everyone's least favourite job, and Nasreen knew Saunders disliked Morris's whiney demeanour.

'Must be nice to just open your legs when you want to skip all the work, hey, Cudmore?' Morris opened and closed two fingers in front of her, his face a mix of lechery and disgust.

Nasreen knew she wasn't unreasonable to look at. It was why she tied her long hair back at work. Glancing at DC Green's boxy tan trouser suit, she wondered if she too opted to dress androgynously for efficacy. Could Morris have seen her and Burgone last night? No, he would have been more graphic. She kept her voice quiet, edging it with threat. She'd learned that from Saunders. 'We have a missing eighteen-year-old girl. Get your mind out of the gutter, your finger out your arse and get on with your job, Constable.' DC Green dipped her chin, but Nasreen caught the smirk. Morris's eyes were full of hate. 'Get on with it!'

It wasn't like Nasreen to pull rank, but Saunders had got to her. If she needed to prove her commitment to this case then she would. The nearest ladies' was two floors below, so she chose the stairs over the lift to get her thoughts straight.

In the bathroom she looked in the mirror for signs she'd given anything away. Apart from the shadows of the late night under her eyes, she looked normal. Alone for the first time since she'd arrived at work, she let her face fall, and the strain of holding it up hit her. The Morrises of the world didn't normally rile her. There'd be time to get her head straight later – possibly a lot of time, if Burgone let her go from Gremlin – but for now she had a job to do.

The door to the ladies' opened behind her. She straightened, brushing at a stray hair that had come loose from her ponytail. Lorna, the younger of the two receptionists, walked in. Her brunette hair was curled back into a sophisticated chignon and held in place with a lavender butterfly grip that somehow managed to look both naive and winsome. A new hire, and at the tender age of nineteen, Lorna's recent arrival on the staff had caused mass hysteria among Nasreen's male colleagues. There'd almost been a fight over who would get to buy her a pink Prosecco first when she'd come to the pub. The girl dipped her delicate pointed chin to her pastel V-neck sweater. Nasreen couldn't imagine wearing such girly clothes to work. But then she couldn't imagine mouse-like Lorna being trained in hand-to-hand combat. They may work in the same building, but they had very different jobs.

'I didn't realise anyone was in here.' Lorna sounded petrified.

She smiled hello, feeling guilty for her ungenerous thoughts. The girl was hovering, fiddling with an ornate ring, as if she were plucking up the courage to say something.

'You okay?' Nasreen asked.

A pale pink blush rose on her cheeks. 'I just wondered if there was any news on DCI Burgone's sister?' Bad news travelled fast. 'He's such a lovely man.'

Nasreen felt a stab of jealousy, though she knew she was being ridiculous. Burgone had been nothing but his usual charming self to the receptionist. And, to give them their due, neither Saunders nor Chips had said anything inappropriate about her, or to her, as far as she knew either. They may have their reservations about Nasreen's suitability for the team, but they weren't based on her gender. Which was some comfort, she supposed. The girl was still twisting her ring. She didn't want to worry her. 'We're pursuing a number of enquiries, Lorna.'

'If anyone can find her you can, Sergeant.' Lorna bit her lip.

Nasreen was taken aback; she'd hardly spoken to the girl before. It must be the Burgone effect: Jack the Lad strikes again. She was simply caught in his reflected glory. 'We're a good team.' She thought of Chips and Saunders's varying degrees of hostility towards her. Well, they *could* be. *Had* to be.

Back in the office, Burgone was at a desk in the corner, typing as if he could force answers from the rattling keyboard. She looked away before anyone caught her staring at him. Saunders was on the phone. DC Green had settled at a desk to the right and was shifting through files; she gave Nasreen a weak smile.

Nasreen paused by Chips, who was pinning a smiling photo of Lottie to the incident board.

'Dani, the other flatmate, confirmed Lottie was wearing this gym kit when she went out this morning.' He tapped the picture.

Lottie was in a matching set of Aztec-patterned pink and purple leggings and bra top, with a coordinating hoodie over the top. On the right breast of the jumper were the initials LB. Nasreen recognised the costly brand as one she lusted after herself, waiting until items went into the sale before she could afford to buy them. 'Was it a freebie?'

'Yup. Hence the lass has a photo of it on her site. Handy for our door to door.'

You couldn't ask for more than a recent photo of a missing person wearing what they'd last been seen in. Lottie documented her whole life online. It wouldn't take much for someone to work out her routines.

Nasreen kept her voice low; she didn't want Burgone to hear. 'Do you think we're looking at a suicide risk or foul play? The wording of the message – *you have twenty-four hours to save the girl's life* – sounds like a threat.'

'Aye, I wondered that.' Both of them kept their eyes forward, as if they were in a covert investigation – *undercover* in their own office. 'Us all being sent the message, it feels wrong.'

Nasreen girded herself to say the name of the first victim, not to let it carry any other significance. It was a sad coincidence she was Gemma's younger sister. That's all. 'Are we sure the other girl – Chloe Strofton – took her own life?'

The investigating force couldn't have known a second suicide note would be sent via Snapchat and that a second girl would soon be missing. Nasreen thought about the messages, the public nature of circulating the notes on the app. The infamy that was now spreading online.

34

'The coroner declared she did,' Chips said.

'I'd like to take a look at the case notes anyway – see if anything jumps out?' Chips nodded his agreement. Two wasn't a pattern. They could simply be looking at a copycat suicide, in which case the priority would be to find Lottie before she harmed herself. Would Lottie also copy the method Chloe had used to take her life? She wasn't looking forward to reading how Chloe had died, but she had to do it. The press was good about keeping details out of the public domain, especially when minors were involved, but if Chloe's suicide note had ended up on social media, then what other information might also have been leaked?

Saunders hung up and grabbed a ringing phone before the DCI could, his movements strong and swift. 'Saunders speaking.' He pulled his pad close to write notes. *News*. She froze, as if taking another step might break the fragile safety net that protected you before you knew the truth. 'Yes. I see,' Saunders was saying. 'And can you confirm where that was?' *That?* A deliberately innocuous word. Her stomach contracted. *Please don't be a body.* Burgone was gripping his desk with both hands. Green kept her eyes down.

'Yes.' Saunders's tapping foot betrayed his anxiety. 'Let me know when the lab have the results. Rush job. Orders from the top: this one's priority. Any issues and they answer to me.' His pen vibrated across the page. 'Yes. Thanks.' Laying his pen down, he carefully replaced the receiver on the cradle. He turned to face them slowly, resting the tips of his overlong fingers together. It felt like the room was holding its breath. His eyes met Burgone's gaze. 'A top matching the description of the one we believe Lottie was wearing when she left her flat this morning has been found on West Grove Lane.'

'Does it have her initials on it – LB?' Hope sounded in Burgone's voice.

Say no.

'Yes. It looks like it is her hoodie.' Saunders flexed his fingers, giving them time to absorb the words. Nasreen caught Green's eye. Her face had grown paler under her freckles. 'There are also signs of a struggle where the top was found. The SOCOs are on their way to the scene now. We'll confirm if it's Lottie's and see if we can lift any other DNA from it.'

'A struggle?' the DCI repeated.

Chips was leaning against the incident board, his thick arms folded over his chest, a troubled look rumpling his fleshy features.

'There are scuff marks on the ground,' Saunders said. 'And the top has been partially torn.'

The words were out before Nasreen could stop them. 'So she's been abducted?' Saunders shot her a look of disgust, and Nasreen didn't dare look at Burgone.

'We don't have enough to assume that yet.' Chips's maturity lent his words a much-needed level of reassurance. 'But we can't rule it out either. Let's find out if there's any cameras on West Grove Lane. See what the door-to-door teams turn up.'

Saunders nodded; Nasreen did too. Having things to do, a structure, helped.

'Cudmore, look at the other lass's file: see if you can find any link between the two girls.' He was authorising their earlier conversation, making it open. Chips's tone softened to talk to Burgone. 'Might Lottie know Chloe Strofton, guv?'

Burgone looked startled, as if he'd forgotten they could see him there. 'Not that I know of. The girl was schooled locally in Hertfordshire. I can't see how their paths would have crossed. But they could've met online?'

Social media had changed the way people socialised: your pool was no longer restricted to people you met in real life. The job had made Nasreen wary: she'd closed the scant accounts she'd had the day she started at the College of Policing. She couldn't imagine meeting up with someone she'd met online, but she knew plenty of people did. Especially those her age and younger. Perhaps Lottie and Chloe had met?

'If Lottie's internet-famous, then we have other motives to consider,' Saunders said. 'Let's check if there was anyone acting odd online, as well as looking for potential links to the Chloe Strofton case. Someone else may have borrowed her Snapchat idea.'

Burgone's face was pained. Chips rested a hand on his shoulder. 'Why don't you get some air, lad? Keep you clear headed, hey?' More than colleagues who'd worked together for a number of years, they were friends. This hurt Chips as much as it did the DCI. Nasreen turned her attention to the paperwork on her desk to give them privacy, not looking up as Burgone left the room, but feeling his every anguished step. It was just gone 10.30 a.m. Lottie had been taken against her will. They had twenty-three hours to find her: the clock was ticking.

Chapter 5

Wednesday 16 March

10:35
T – 22 hrs 55 mins

Opening the file, Nasreen sharply inhaled: there was Chloe Strofton. If there had been any doubt she was the younger sister of Nasreen's old school friend, it was gone now. The smiling selfie, taken in happier times, showed that pretty Chloe had the same blue eyes and pinched chin of her older sibling. But instead of the curly, mousey hair that Gemma had, Chloe's was long and wavy, streaked with blonde highlights. Now would be the time to mention she knew the family – or used to know the family. Nasreen should say she recognised the girl from the photo. Keeping quiet about a personal connection to a case was a bad idea. What would her colleagues think if they knew she'd bullied a young girl till she'd tried to kill herself? They questioned and arrested teens regularly enough that her young age wouldn't matter. They'd see her as a bully. She'd be lumped in with the likes of Morris. Nasty, tainted. She could imagine Chips's revulsion. If he didn't use the personal connection to the case to get her removed, Saunders would use her past, her failings, to get rid of her. He would drum her out of the team. And Burgone, the thought of him knowing what she'd done... Her skin prickled with the shame of it. It didn't matter what she'd done since, or who she'd become: that one stupid, cruel mistake had tainted her. If she told them she knew the Stroftons, she'd be off the case. But if she kept quiet, she could find out who did this to their daughter. This was her chance to make it better.

Sleeping with Burgone had been an error of judgement. She'd let her own desires get in the way of the job and look what had happened. Burgone had acted rashly too. They were both to blame, but she couldn't help feel it was she who'd jeopardised their careers. That she was responsible for threatening the Gremlin taskforce. What had happened with Gemma had taught her she couldn't let her own selfish needs override another's. This was her chance to atone for those mistakes. Nasreen looked at Burgone's empty chair, his dark cashmere overcoat hanging lopsided from the back. More than anything she wanted to help him.

Chloe Strofton's last forty-eight hours had been unremarkable. She'd spent the day at Romeland High School, after which she'd told her parents she was staying at her friend Melisha's house. Instead she disappeared. She was picked up on CCTV boarding a bus from near her school in St Albans to Hatfield, getting off at the Galleria shopping centre just after half past four. A camera then picked her up once more inside the shopping centre. She wasn't seen again until her body was found in Wildhill Wood, a number of miles away, at 8.30 p.m. the next day, following an anonymous tip-off from a male caller. The Snapchat of her suicide note had been sent at 8 p.m. the previous night. Did the wood hold personal significance to Chloe? Why had the caller not left his details? People used wooded areas for all kinds of insalubrious pursuits: drug taking, underage drinking, illicit rendezvous. She made a note to call the officer at Hertfordshire Constabulary who'd worked on the case, and ask his opinion.

Photos from the scene showed Chloe Strofton's small body on the forest floor, curled into child's pose. Her arms and face were a dark purple from hypostasis – where blood had pooled post mortem. Her veins made a blue marbling pattern in her skin: *petechiae within hypostasis.* Nasreen had seen bodies like this before: a drugs overdose. The pathologist had noted that the girl's body showed no indicators of previous drug use. Chloe Matilda Strofton was fifteen years old, 5'4", and weighed 105 lbs. At her time of death the following substances had been found in her blood stream:

- Morphine (free) of 370 ng/ml
- 6-monoacetylmorphine of 16 ng/ml
- Codeine (free) of 15 ng/ml
- Alprazolam of 34 ng/ml
- Amphetamine of 22 ng/ml

Next to the body, along with her school bag, were a blue plastic wrap and a 1cc syringe. No spoon, no cotton wool, lighter or any of the other drug paraphernalia you might expect to find from cooked heroin. Chloe had prepared the syringe elsewhere. Or someone had prepared it for her. Over-the-counter drugs, or even prescription drugs, and alcohol, were easier to source. As were razor blades and the materials you could use to hang yourself with. Chloe hadn't copied her older sister's failed attempt.

The investigating team hadn't requested to look at Chloe's computer; Nasreen would have liked to know what her search history was. How had a fifteen-year-old girl from a middle-class area, with no known history of criminal activity or drug use, ended up forty-five minutes from where she lived, dead from a heroin overdose?

Nasreen had worked on the case of a twenty-three-year-old mother who'd overdosed and suffered pulmonary congestion like Chloe. She'd asked the pathologist at the time if it would have been quick – the woman's toddler had been in the flat and she didn't like to think of him seeing his mother in agony. The pathologist confirmed that in cases of pulmonary congestion, the victim would quickly enter a comatose state, dying relatively soon after from lack of oxygen. Chloe's death would have been fast and painless. That was something. She didn't like to think of the girl on her own in the woods, frightened, in pain, with no one to help. Perhaps the bright Chloe, predicted As and A*s in her GCSEs, had researched her options and chose this as an *easy* death? Chloe would never sit those exams now, never turn sixteen, never go on to have a job, or a family of her own. A life over, all too soon.

The rap of Saunders's pen on his desk raised her and Chips's attention. The DI pointed at the phone cradled between his shoulder and his ear, and mouthed, 'Cell site hit.' A signal from the phone had been picked up! Nasreen couldn't suppress the flutter in her stomach: this could be good news.

DI Saunders was nodding, writing down what he was being told. 'Okay. Yup. We'll let the SOCOs and the tech lads see if they can find anything on it. Anything at all. Keep me updated.'

That didn't sound so promising.

Saunders turned to face them. 'The phone was ditched, not far from the spot where the hoodie was found. A young lad found it on the way to school, pocketed it, and apparently turned it on during his first break.'

Compromised DNA.

Chips threw his hands up in front of him. 'Where were the parents? Did they not notice their kiddie picking up a bleeding phone?'

'Apparently his eleven-year-old brother walks him in,' Saunders shrugged. 'Latchkey kids, I guess. What you gonna do?'

If only someone else had spotted it first – though most people would instinctively pick the phone up, regardless of whether they planned to turn it in or keep it. The boy had inadvertently disturbed the scene, delayed them finding the phone, and more than likely compromised any forensic traces on the device. And the discovery possibly had bleaker implications. 'Are we sure it was ditched, rather than dropped during the struggle?' Nasreen asked.

'The kid says it was switched off when he found it. And it was further down the road. He thinks.'

Chips snorted.

'So the perp sent the Snapchat message and then switched the phone off before dumping it?' she asked.

'Possible,' said Saunders.

That implied they knew what they were doing. Whoever had taken Lottie was savvy enough to know not only that the phone was trackable, but that it'd be trickier to trace if it was switched off. It gave them a head start. 'Whoever took her must have incapacitated her fairly fast,' she said. 'If she was screaming and drawing attention, you wouldn't want to hang around to fiddle with the phone would you?'

'No,' Chips frowned. 'The SOCOs said there were signs she'd put up a fight.'

'We have to consider the possibility that whoever took her has already killed her,' said Saunders. His jaw was set; he looked thoughtful rather than sad. Nausea rippled inside Nasreen.

Chips was sitting on the edge of his overcrowded desk. The papers he was holding in his right hand were creased under the strain of his fingers.

'If they've already killed her, why send the message about us having twenty-four hours?' said Nasreen. She couldn't be dead.

'I don't know what their game is,' Saunders replied. 'But there's been no ransom demand. And because they've ditched Lottie's phone, we have no way of initiating conversation with the kidnapper.'

He was a sage investigator, and even though she knew what he was saying was right, she was glad Burgone wasn't around to hear it. Even if Lottie's parents were rich, and it sounded like they were, it took days to raise a large sum in cash, not twenty-four hours. No ransom delivery also meant they couldn't mark notes, or hide a tracker in the money. And with no communication from the kidnapper, they didn't have anything they *could* trace. Nothing that would give away where Lottie was being held. What was this about if it wasn't about money?

'We could be looking at a personal motivation: revenge for someone the guv put away? Maybe they have no intention of negotiating. Or returning her.' Saunders seemed to read her thoughts.

'That's just a hypothesis.'

'You know we have to consider all the scenarios, Chips,' said Saunders, raising his eyebrows at his colleague.

'She's the guv's sister, Pete. We're bringing her home.' *No discussion.* His line rang and he answered gruffly. 'McCain.'

Nasreen tried to smile at Saunders, but she couldn't muster it. Neither of them wanted to contradict Chips, but the implications were clear. They were *all* thinking it. Saunders pushed his hand back through his hair, pulling the skin on his face taut. She could see the grooves of his skull, a reminder of how little really stood between you and someone who wanted to do you harm. Though, with his fast movements and limber strength, she'd put money on Saunders in most fights.

What about Lottie? She'd kicked out, fought hard enough to rip her hoodie. She was in physically great shape, strong and lean in the photos, though Nasreen would have preferred to see a few more cheeseburgers on her Instagram feed. She looked like a fighter. Sometimes just that will to survive was enough. Nasreen had seen it in her colleagues. In victims of terrible crimes. In her friends. But even the strongest will could be extinguished by another. Someone had wanted to take Lottie, and they had. They'd also threatened to kill her. Would they execute that plan as well?

Chips ended his call and headed for the incident board. 'Lottie went for a run every day at 6 a.m. She's picked up on the campus CCTV camera about five past the hour, heading towards Greenwich Church Street.' He was filling in the details on the timeline as he spoke.

'Any cameras on West Grove Lane?' asked Saunders.

'No joy,' said Chips. 'It's largely residential. But the university have cooperated fully. As they should: PR nightmare for them, a student going missing. Their in-house security are going through their recordings with the Greenwich lads. They've got a snazzy digital set-up, so they've been able to match Lottie's expected movements on campus with the relevant footage.' Chips was scribbling in black marker as he spoke.

'Everything they have should be double checked.' Saunders

stood next to Chips as he copied notes from his pad. 'We'll get Morris on it.'

Good, thought Nasreen. *Serve him right.*

'There's a camera at the offie on the corner – here.' Chips tapped the map of the Greenwich area they'd unfurled alongside the board. 'But it's trained on their back door and side alley. It points away from that end of the road.'

They tensed as Burgone cut in from the doorway. 'Idiots! There'd be more chance of people coming at them from the front.' How long had he been there? What had he heard? The muscles in his face twitched, his lips a thin line from pressure. Saunders, his back to the DCI, frowned and rested his hands in his pockets as if he were worried what else they might do.

'Which way was she going?' asked Burgone.

Chips moved stiffly, unsure whether this was the right thing to do. 'We can see her on the university's camera here and here, heading along this road,' he said, indicating the relevant area on the map. A yellow highlighter marked her flat, the road where she was picked up by the camera, and then the spot where the hoodie had been found. There were countless roads between the two points. It would take hours to find, watch, and scan tapes from all those roads, even if they put multiple officers on it.

'Yesterday she returned to her flat at the usual time of 7.30 a.m., made smoothies for her and her flatmate Bea, showered and was at lectures for 9 a.m.' Chips flicked through his notes. 'We can see her on the campus camera again, crossing the quad and talking with friends before going into her lecture building. She returned to her flat at 1 p.m. Dani reports seeing her collecting a folder for a later class. Again she's seen chatting to friends on the campus. She was home just after 6 p.m., working in her bedroom on coursework. Bea and Dani then both saw her when she came out to make her dinner in the shared kitchen: chicken and vegetables.'

'That's her favourite,' Burgone said forlornly. Lottie was meticulous about her diet and exercise: it structured her time. Her body was her tool – like a model, she earned money from it. She was dedicated and worked hard; attributes she shared with her brother.

Chips pushed on. 'According to her flatmates, she seemed fine. Possibly stressed about her coursework, but nothing concerning.'

'Then where is she!' The DCI slammed his fist onto the desk in front of him. Chips's breathing was audible. Saunders frowned; he saw emotional outbursts as weakness. 'Sorry. I just…' Burgone stopped and stared at the photo of Lottie that Chips had pinned to the incident board. He turned, and walked out.

Nasreen couldn't stand by and watch him hurting like this.

Saunders arched an eyebrow at her: 'Do you think now is the ideal moment to go for a fucking stroll, Cudmore?'

Her cheeks flamed. Everyone could hear him. 'No, of course not.' She caught hold of her heart, pulled it back inside and locked it down.

'*Of course not*,' Saunders parroted in a high and squeaky voice. Nasreen clenched her teeth, fighting to not let her anger show. 'Sit the hell back down and get on with your job, Sergeant.'

Did he know she'd been following Burgone or was he just taking his frustration out on her? Green caught her eye and pulled a sympathetic grimace. Nasreen tried to get her thoughts in order. She didn't need to give Saunders any more reasons to pick at her.

The photos of Chloe Strofton and Lottie Burgone showed blonde, attractive, young and seemingly happy girls. And yet they'd both, apparently, sent suicide notes via Snapchat. Could

Chloe's death be related to Lottie's? Had the police investigating her alleged suicide missed something? Nasreen laid out a printout of Lottie's note on her desk:

A pointless opulent life leads you onto nothing.
I can't go on. Lottie Burgone

And the banner overlaying the note:

You have 6 seconds to read this and 24 hours to save the girl's life.

She pulled out the printed screenshot of the Snapchat note Chloe had sent and laid it on the desk next to Lottie's. Across Chloe's note – which was much longer than Lottie's – was a similar banner:

You have 6 seconds to read this, and 24 hours to find me.

First person. *Different*. Both of the notes were printed, typed, in what looked like Times New Roman, on white A4 paper. Chloe's note looked like it had been folded in half, and then in half again, crinkled, perhaps from being put in a pocket? She flicked to the photographs of the scene where Chloe had been found. Yellow evidence markers marked her orange school bag, which was more like a stylish leather handbag you might see a businesswoman carry than the scruffy rucksack Nasreen had had at school. Both Chloe and Lottie were fashionable, concerned with their appearance. *A pointless opulent life*. She looked at the zoomed-in version of Chloe's suicide note:

47

As I type this I feel calmer. I'm doing the right thing. It's a relief. I can't go on after people find out. It's disgusting. I've let down my friends, family, teachers, everyone. Only those who've seen will know why. I can't live in fear of it coming out. All the lies are finished. Mum, Dad, Freya, Gemma, I screwed up. I can't hurt you more. I love you. It's time I fixed the mess I made. This is the only way. I promise you all you're better off without me. I know you'll feel sad reading this, but I know that'll be over soon. The pain will fade. Your tears will dry. You'll live happy lives. I love you. Now it's time to go. I'll be dead within twenty-four hours of you receiving this note.

Chloe Strofton

What was disgusting? And what would others know? She flicked back through the statements gathered by the local force. They hadn't had the note at that point; a copy had only been turned in when it started circulating online last week. Interviewing the family, friends, teachers etc., they all seemed to give the same impression: Chloe had gone from being a happy, confident girl, often fond of being the centre of attention, to withdrawn and quiet over the last couple of months. There'd been a break-up: a boyfriend, William Taylor, sixteen, also at Romeland High. Everyone put it down to the usual ups and downs of teen love. She'd never been prescribed antidepressants, or been diagnosed with any mental health issues. Nasreen frowned. Someone had missed something: didn't the teachers notice that something was awry? Or her parents? Mrs Strofton was a solicitor and Mr Strofton was a GP. They were good people, who had been through a lot over the years – Mrs Strofton had been ill, not to mention everything that had happened with Gemma. There could be more illness, trouble at work, financial worries, countless things that might mean you didn't spot the warning signs in your own daughter. And they would regret that for the rest of their lives. Losing a child was one of the worst things she'd seen people go through in this job.

She read over the note again, mouthing the words. There was something odd in the rhythm of it. Stilted. Was that a reflection of the girl's troubled mind? She'd used her full name to sign off. Typed. Like Lottie had. She flicked her eyes between the two notes. And then she saw it. Her heartbeat slowed. The sounds of the office peeled away like falling petals. Everything was crisp and clear. The letters sharp, elevated from the printouts. The first letter of each line of Chloe's note, and the first letter of each word in Lottie's note, spelt the same word: Apollyon. *The destroyer.* The name of a serial killer who'd tweeted clues to his next victim. Nicknamed the Hashtag Murderer, Apollyon had been caught by Nasreen and her old school friend Freddie. Her blood ran cold. *Chloe Strofton: younger sister of Gemma Strofton – Nasreen and Freddie's best friend at school. Lottie Burgone, the younger sister of Nasreen's boss.* Nasreen looked up as Chips pinned a photo of Chloe Strofton on the incident board, alongside that of Lottie Burgone. *Nasreen was the link.* The empty chair of DCI Burgone, askew, flung backwards, a flag of his desperation. His sister was missing. Taken. And it was her fault.

Chapter 6

Tuesday 15 March

11:00

'And how does that make you feel?' Amanda, tight grey curls hugging her face, tipped her head to the side.

Freddie Venton stopped looking at the framed counselling qualifications on the boxy magnolia walls and stared at the woman. 'Are you taking the piss?'

'What makes you ask that, Freddie?' Amanda's hands rested on her notes like primed mousetraps.

'Bit of a shrink cliché.' It smelt of patchouli in here. Or what she imagined patchouli smelt like. There was a loaded box of tissues on the low pine table between them, and Freddie couldn't get comfortable on her inoffensive cream chair. Amanda continued to gaze at her. *Great.* They were going to play this game again. Amanda – *call me Mandy* – was one of those counsellors who liked to give their clients time to talk. Freddie had had counselling before – *who hadn't?* – but she preferred the proactive CBT approach. She didn't want to talk about her relationship with her hamster as a child, or whatever. She just wanted to be able to sleep at nights. Or during the day. She wasn't fussy. The scar on her head, still spiky with stitches the doctors kept promising would dissolve, throbbed. 'Look, I don't want to waste your time or anything.' God knows the NHS had better things to spend their money on than paying this woman for a staring contest for fifty minutes once a fortnight.

'I'm not a shrink, as you call it, Freddie,' said Mandy.

'Head doctor then. Psychiatrist. Quack.' This room was like her first-year halls at uni. Pine bookshelves stood to attention, proudly displaying Amanda's only redeeming factor: she had some Naomi Wolf books. Feminist icon. It'd lured her into a false sense of security. She should have clocked there were no windows in here and left straight away. Was that a counsellor thing? Nothing to distract you from your emotional trauma? Or nothing for you to jump from? She'd only ticked the box saying she felt suicidal at the GP so they'd hurry up and give her her meds back.

'I'm a counsellor, Freddie. As you know. Do you not want to talk about how you're feeling?'

'Not really.'

'Why are you here, Freddie?'

'You know why I'm here.' Everyone knew. She'd made the front page of every national newspaper: *Social Media Murder Mayhem! Newsnight* had done a special on it.

'I know that you were nearly killed. That you had emergency brain surgery. That since then you've been recovering at your parents' home. And that you haven't been back to London since,' said Amanda. The trump card.

51

Freddie started counting the books, noting the colour of the spines: *one blue, two white, three white, four red...*

'Did you think any more about contacting your old friend, Gemma?' said Amanda.

Freddie rolled her eyes. She knew it'd been a dumb idea. Why would Gemma want to speak to her after everything that happened? *Five yellow, six white...* Did publishers get a cheap deal on white covers or something?

'You did ask to attend counselling, Freddie. There must be a part of you that wants to talk about what happened?'

'I'm only here because my doctor won't sign off on meds unless I show up.'

'I see.' Amanda looked sad. Disappointed.

Freddie sighed. 'Look, I'm not trying to be difficult, I'm sure you're a very good therapist. It's just that I don't need to talk. I just need to be able to sleep.' Something caught the corner of her eye, a dark shadow flashing across the edge of the room. She turned, but there was nothing there. It was just her and Amanda and a box of Kleenex. She casually let go of the cushion she'd clutched in mild panic.

Amanda frowned. 'Does the thought of not having your sleeping pills frighten you?'

Well, duh. Without them, any sleep she got was full of the face she feared. 'It's like I said to the GP: if you found a drug that let you sleep, which let you get up, live, eat, do normal things, then you wouldn't want to stop taking it, would you?'

'And what did he say?'

'She,' Freddie said.

'What did she say?' pressed Amanda.

The ballsy girl who'd worked in Espress-oh's coffee shop, the one who was a promising journalist and walked round Dalston like she owned it, had vanished. A heavy, dusty curtain had been dropped across her life. And she was too frightened to pull it back, in case there was nothing left on the other side. 'The doctor said I had to come here to see you, *Mandy*.'

'And how did that make you feel?'

Chapter 7

Wednesday 16 March

'Thanks.' Nasreen hung up the phone. That decided it then. She didn't have a choice. She was going to have to take a gamble. For that's what it was: a roll of the dice. It could go well, or it could go badly. Very badly.

Saunders had his back turned, speaking on the phone, writing notes in his barely legible scrawl. He didn't trust her. Better to try Chips.

He was sitting at his desk. 'Sir, can I have a word?' she asked quietly, the printouts tucked under her arm.

'Aye, lass.' He didn't look up.

'In private?'

That got his attention. His eyes flicked to Burgone, who was back at his desk. She shook her head: *No, it's not that. We haven't found a body. Yet.*

He nodded, stuck the pen he was using behind his ear, and followed her out of the room.

Chips looked up and down the empty hallway. 'This private enough?' He had a way of softening his voice, and tilting his head so he was looking down at her as he talked, some feat given they were the same height. Gently patronising: it was how she imagined he talked to his grandkids.

She nodded. Not sure where to start. *How* to start. 'You know I worked on the Hashtag Murderer case?'

'We all know that, lass.' A mild look of exasperation spread across his jovial face, as if to say, *Now is not the time for an ego stroke, young lady.*

Chips wasn't a career cop interested in office politics, so no point playing games. He was focused on bringing those responsible to justice. Stick to the facts; get to the point. 'The killer used an alias online,' said Nasreen. 'He called himself Apollyon.'

Chips took the biro out from behind his ear and popped the top off. 'I read the newspapers at the time, and your report when you arrived.'

'Did you?' It was a surprise: he'd never shown much interest.

'I like to know who I'm working with, Nasreen.'

'Yes, sorry, sir.' He'd made her feel childish again. Of course he'd want to know what his new colleagues had worked on before. She thrust the printouts forward. 'Look at this.'

'The suicide notes?' His fleshy hands wrapped around them. The skin of his finger had bubbled up around his wedding ring, fusing the smooth gold band into his flesh.

'The first letter of each of the words of Lottie's, and the letters at the beginning of each line of Chloe Strofton's note. They spell…'

'Apollyon. Well blow me.' He frowned at pages. 'Are you thinking there might be a link between this case and the Hashtag Killer case?'

Yes. And it's me. I'm the link. I'm connected to both these people. 'It's possible. Someone's gone to a lot of trouble to spell these notes out. Would Chloe and Lottie do that themselves?'

'So you're thinking if someone else wrote and sent the note from the other lass's phone as well, it might not have been suicide after all?' He flipped between the pages.

'Exactly. Then whoever did that might be the same person who has Lottie.'

'But there's nothing in the file to suggest foul play?'

'The investigating force had no reason to think it wasn't suicide,' said Nasreen. 'They didn't have the note at the time.' Chips blew air through his teeth. Nasreen pushed. 'If it was your daughter missing, would you follow it up?' His eyes flew up, angry. She'd gone too far. But if her gut was right, and this person was targeting their team because of Nasreen's presence in it, then it could have been *her* younger sister, it could have been Chips's daughter, it could have been any one of them snatched. 'I'd like to go back over the Chloe Strofton case, speak to her family, see if there was anyone new in her life, anyone acting suspiciously. The local force won't have been asking those questions first time round.' Could she really sit across from Gemma and her parents and look them in the eye while she asked about Chloe? *This is your chance to make it better, Nasreen.*

'No. You can't go upsetting the poor lass's family and hinting their daughter's death was suspicious. Not without something more concrete.'

He was right, of course. For a moment she felt relief. Then reality smacked back. Lottie was still missing. 'But I could speak to the girl's friends discreetly, those who received the note. The report said she'd recently broken it off with a boyfriend – I could speak to him? I could go to her school? The teachers would count as responsible adults. See if there's anything there?'

Chips was still looking at the notes, chewing on his cheek. 'You can go, but make it quick. If there's nothing in it I want you back here and helping Saunders and me.'

He was trusting her with this. She knew what she had to do, but the thought of threatening this newfound fragile pact snagged the words in her throat. 'I'm going to need help.'

'Green can go with you. Take a pool car.' Chips straightened; the conversation was over.

What did she think of Green? Could she be trusted? Anything was better than having Morris along. *You're doing this for Burgone, remember.* 'I'm going to need more than that, sir. I need a second pair of eyes: someone else who knows the Apollyon case inside out. To bounce ideas off. I'd like to bring in Freddie Venton.'

'The civilian who worked on the Hashtag case?' He raised his eyebrows. 'No chance. What about your former DCI?'

'I've spoken to DCI Moast.' The call had been awkward: silence on the other end as she'd mentioned the word Apollyon. They both had blood-smeared memories of the case; they both felt they could have done things differently. 'He's in the middle of a trafficking bust. The Jubilee station is full of people smugglers and refugees. Some were being shipped out for the sex trade, small children being sold into slavery. It sounds like a mess. The soonest he or any of his team would be able to help would be the day after next. If we were lucky.'

'And according to the message we've got twenty-four hours,' Chips sighed.

'Twenty-three, now.' And ticking down. 'Freddie could help us.'

'I thought she was brought in as a PR stunt during the Hashtag case?'

57

'Freddie knows Apollyon better than anyone. She was the one who cracked the cryptic clues he posted.' *She'd also been the one who'd goaded him into a response.* 'She's a little unorthodox.' *Rash, confrontational, and prone to erratic behaviour: she'd need to keep a close eye on her.* 'But she has an encyclopaedic knowledge of popular culture.' *Which she'd probably prefer to call Wikipedic.* 'She understands references that are common knowledge online, and could overlay them analytically to the information we have. I think it's worth at least consulting with her.'

'She's too young.'

'She's the same age as me.'

Chips's face suggested that was rather the point. 'We have tech specialists we can consult if need be.'

Irritation toyed with her. 'With all due respect, sir, this is different. The digital forensics team are second to none, I'm not questioning that, but Freddie wouldn't be looking at recovering and investigating material from devices we find. She's a digital native, able to recognise things we might miss. She knows the Apollyon case. Aside from DCI Moast and his team, she's the one person I'd trust to spot patterns.' If she could just get him to understand how important it was to get Freddie on board.

Chips peered at the notes and sucked air through his teeth. 'It's not him is it – the Hashtag Murderer? Apollyon? Doing these?'

The thought was terrifying, but she'd had to consider it. 'I spoke to the assistant chief at his prison. He's in solitary after stabbing a fellow prisoner in the eye with a sharpened pencil.'

'Nice lad.' Chips rubbed his temple.

'He's got no internet access and refuses visitors. The assistant chief was adamant there's no way he could have written this, sent it, or shared it with the outside world.' Despite that there was still doubt in her mind; she knew what the Hashtag Murderer was capable of. But the evidence didn't point to him, not directly. 'If it's not him then someone else is using his moniker. Freddie could just take a look – that's all I'm asking.'

'You came to me because you know Saunders won't agree to some consultant being brought in to a case that involves the guv. Because you think I'm a soft touch?'

Crap. 'I don't think that, sir. I have the utmost respect for you. You're a legend in the force.' She felt her face blush.

'You mean I'm old, lass?' Chips chuckled.

'No, not that. You're not old. I…' The chance of getting Freddie's help was slipping through her fingers. She couldn't tell any of the team she was the link between the two victims. Not until she knew it wasn't some ghastly coincidence. But she could tell Freddie. Freddie could help. 'I just want to find Lottie. Safe.'

'We're already treading a fine line, lass, having Burgone stay. Saunders is jumpy. He likes doing things by the book.' He paused. 'Then again, I thought you did too.'

Her face coloured again. 'I do. I really believe Freddie could help. I'm not asking for her to be brought onto the team. I can show her the intelligence on the notes, see what she makes of it. If this is a copycat, then it's a copycat of a serial killer.'

His face clouded. 'Then this might just be the start.'

The threat hung in the air between them.

'Okay,' he relented. 'She can look at what we've got, but it's got to be off record: there's no budget for this. She can't be expecting money.'

'Not a problem.' She hoped. Freddie may come off rough round the edges, but she had a big heart.

'This stays between you and me. No mention to Saunders, no mention to the guv, okay?'

'Yes, sir.' She reasoned she was merely protecting her source: Freddie.

'I don't want any difficult questions from the CPS. Got it?'
She nodded.

'If we were talking about anyone other than Jack's sister I wouldn't be authorising this.' Chips thrust the notes back her. His face was closed, stern. He was angry she'd put him in this position.

'If it was anyone other than the guv's sister, I wouldn't be asking.' That was the truth. If Nasreen was the link between the two girls then one person was already dead because of her. She had to follow this lead, no matter where it led. Saunders and Burgone couldn't find out about Freddie. Saunders was itching to find fault with her. If he knew about Freddie he might start digging, and then how long would it be before he uncovered that she, Freddie and Gemma had all gone to school together? That they had been the best of friends. That Freddie and she had nearly driven Gemma to her death. She had no doubt he'd use that to leverage her out. It had to stay a secret for her own safety too.

Chips looked at his watch. 'You've got three hours. Max. Make it count, Cudmore.' Three hours to speak to Freddie. Three hours to interview Chloe's friends. Three hours to work out if she really was the link. Three hours to work out if she was to blame for Lottie's predicament. She could hear Chips's watch ticking as she hurried away. This is it. No room for error. 10.55 a.m. T − 22 hours 25 minutes. *Make it count.*

Chapter 8

Wednesday 16 March

11:45
T – 21 hrs 45 mins

Freddie Venton stared at the ceiling of her childhood bedroom. A hairpin crack ran from the top of the rose-patterned wallpaper (her mum's choice) and slithered across the ceiling. Mum had been at the doctors for her blood pressure, she was going into the school late today. Freddie could hear the sound of her work pumps moving across the hallway. She shut her eyes and slowed her breathing, like she used to when she was young, reading late under the covers.

'Love?' her mum whispered. 'Are you awake?'

Yes, I'm awake! I've been awake since blood poured into my eyes. Since sleeping meant the dreams came. And they couldn't come. She couldn't relive it. She couldn't sleep. So she pretended. Her mum had enough on her plate with her dad's antics; she didn't need any more worry.

There was a rattle as her mum put a tray down, not wanting to intrude, but not wanting her daughter to starve either. Freddie could sense her standing there. A broken husband and a broken child – life had not been kind to Mrs Venton. 'Happy birthday, love,' she whispered, pulling the door gently to.

Not long now. Freddie heard the gruff grunt of her father, his articulation lost to the alcohol.

'Do you think we should try the doctor again?' her mum stage-whispered.

Another grunt.

'It's been weeks. She's barely eating. She hasn't said more than a few words.' Freddie heard the worry in her mum's voice. She wanted to tell her it was all going to be all right. But she couldn't. Instead, she began to count the roses on the wall again. 'This can't go on,' her mum was saying. *Twenty-nine, thirty, thirty-one…*

The front door opened and closed, and Freddie heard her mum's Corsa start. She listened for the jingle of the keys. *A whistle for the dog.* The door opened – Dad was leaving for the pub. She waited in case he'd forgotten anything. *One minute, two minutes, three minutes…* Then she threw the duvet off, shuffling across to the tray. Sandwiches. Marmite and cucumber: her favourite when she was little. There were a couple of cards tucked under a present. Freddie picked up the small weighty rectangle, the wrapping paper covered in birds, and read the tag:

Thought I'd get this fixed for you.
Happy Birthday, love Mum and Dad xxx

She knew what it was. Placed it unopened on the tray.

She padded downstairs and into the room at the back of the house. Her father's den: a boxy room, with a raised, jutting windowsill, as if the builder had forgotten to put the bottom part of the wall in. The blue curtains were drawn. Mum didn't come in here. Freddie didn't come in here. The small coffee table and the blue sofa bed were covered in used glasses. Dad slept in here sometimes, when Mum couldn't take it anymore. It smelled stale. *Sour.* Sitting on the sofa, she stroked the grooves where her dad sat. Closed her eyes. Tried to remember what he was like before. The good memories were fainter now. Him swinging her round in the garden, her giggling uncontrollably. Her and Nas cycling up and down the path outside their house. A trip to Thorpe Park. She tried to remember what happiness felt like. But a heavy blanket had settled over Freddie the day she was attacked; she'd felt nothing but thrumming anxiety since.

The doorbell sounded. She froze, as if they could see what she was doing. The guilt of the emptiness.

The doorbell rang again. Longer. More insistent. 'Hang on!' she shouted. When did she last speak that loud? She ran to the door. The dark blur of the person standing behind it was fractured by the geometric glass pattern. She opened it. Fought the urge to dissolve into tears. There on the doorstep in her smart black trouser suit was Nasreen Cudmore.

'Hello, Freddie.'

Chapter 9

Wednesday 16 March

12:20
T – 22 hrs 10 mins

'You going to invite me in?' Nas's face looked as it always had: high cheekbones carved into flawless skin, brown eyes sparkling, dark hair hanging in a velvet tuile from her hairband. Beautiful, but detached. There was something new in her eyes: a nervousness, a quick sweep from one side of the room to the other, as if she was scanning the horizon, checking the exits. Then it was gone, replaced with the face Freddie knew Nas used to greet the general public. Warm, effusive, persuasive.

'What you doing here?' It was the middle of the day. Why wasn't Nas at work? This was a long way from the East End's Jubilee police station. Skyscrapers cut like a bookmark through the pages of her memory. Highlighting moments of pain. *That's far away. You're safe here. Safe.*

'I need to talk to you.' Nas's gaze flickered to her hand, and Freddie realised she was gripping the door handle so tight her knuckles were stretched white. She let go.

'You best come in then.' She led her into the spotless lounge. Her mum's OCD hung in the air, mingling with the smell of polish. Trying to scrub out the stains in her life. 'Bit different from my usual style.' She tried to sound lighthearted, but saw Nas take in the perfectly spaced ornaments on the dresser. Did she remember when Dad broke them all? Smashed them while Freddie and Nas told ghost stories by torchlight under a duvet; Nas scared, Freddie flippant about the shouts and screams coming from downstairs. As if it was normal. In a way it was. That was a long time ago. Different house. Different ornaments. Different life.

They sat on the dark brown leather DFS sofas, facing each other. Nas perched on the edge of her seat, still in her coat, her hands clasped in her lap. Her nails shiny with clear polish. Freddie glanced at her own mismatched pyjamas. Nas looked at her scar. It throbbed in response. *It's all in my mind.* 'Do you want a cup of tea or something?'

'No. Thank you.' Nasreen smiled, but it didn't reach her eyes, as if she were talking to a child. She was uneasy in her presence. 'How are you doing, Freddie?'

'Nightmares, no sleep, I'm trapped in suburbia, you know.' It was supposed to be a joke, but her words were brittle, cracking ice underfoot. A car drove past outside, the rumble of the engine underscoring the silence that engulfed the room. Freddie's breathing sounded loud, a rasping echo of the car's exhaust.

Nas shuffled in her seat, her polished heels squeaking against each other. She cleared her throat. 'I need your help. With a case.'

'No.' Freddie was shocked at the word. She hadn't planned to say it. It felt as though someone was speaking through her, someone she'd forgotten existed. How dare Nas just show up and say that! How dare she just walk in and act as if nothing had happened. She wanted her gone. Standing, she caught the edge of the veneered coffee table with her knee. A weird, unfamiliar feeling spread through her. Pain. A short, sharp stab. She *felt* it. She was thawing. Melting. Her body tried to override it. 'Well, if you don't want a drink, then…' She wanted to shout: *We're done. We're finished. Get out!* But she'd sound crazy. Was she going crazy? Maybe. Maybe she already had. But she didn't want to show Nas that. 'I think I'll make myself a coffee.'

Nas didn't move. Freddie could see what was dancing around behind her eyes when she'd scanned the room: desperation.

She was supposed to be safe here. Hidden. No one would think to look in a suburban backwater. Down a winding country lane. *What's out there?* She could feel the isolation of the house. All four walls exposed to the elements. *Is he back?* 'I can't,' she said, her hand shooting to her forehead. Her scar felt coarse and bumpy: a warning to never get too close again.

Nas produced a brown envelope and placed a photo of a smiling blonde girl on the coffee table. *Don't look at it.* 'This is Chloe. On Friday, 12 March at 8 p.m. she sent this photo of her suicide note via Snapchat to her friends and sisters.' Nas pulled a photo of a printed letter from the envelope. Freddie walked to the bay window; straightened her parents' 1970s wedding photo.

Nas continued, unperturbed. 'The note warned that the body would not be found until twenty-four hours later.' Freddie looked at her mum's smile. So happy. So long ago. Before life had taken all hope from her. 'At just after 8 p.m. on Saturday, 13 March, Chloe's body was found in Wildhill Wood.'

'I'm sorry for the girl, Nas. Course I am. But it's nothing to do with me.' All her edges felt raw, as if every nerve ending had been exposed. She needed her to leave.

The leather of the sofa creaked. 'Chloe was Gemma's sister.'

Freddie spun, catching her parents' photo; it clattered backwards against the windowsill. 'Why tell me this? Haven't you put me through enough?'

'This morning at 9.30 a.m. a second Snapchat suicide note was received from Lottie Burgone.' Nas's tone was calm.

Freddie picked up the photo, slamming the frame down onto the wood.

'We have reason to suspect someone might have taken Lottie. Look at the note. It sounds like a threat.' Nas thrust two photos at her.

She grabbed them so they wouldn't fall. 'I can't.' Her eyes scanned the words. *I feel calmer…. the right thing… the pain will fade.*

'She's eighteen, Freddie.' Nas dragged her palm back over her hair.

The words pulled on Freddie's eyes. *You have 6 seconds to read this and 24 hours to save the girl's life.* Nas said 9.30 a.m. Over three hours ago. *I can't.*

'Lottie's the sister of my new boss.' Nas shook her head, as if it wasn't real.

'I'm sorry.' Freddie handed the photos back. She didn't want to touch them. Didn't want to know this. She just wanted to be left alone. Freddie saw the shadows under Nas's eye make-up. *She saved your life. You owe her. I can't… An eighteen-year-old girl… Gemma's sister. Gemma, who told you never to contact her again.* Her chest constricted, her windpipe closing. The words, the images, started to tumble down on her. Freddie turned away. Stared out the window. *One leaf, two, three, four, five…*

Nas gathered up the photos – *Gemma's dead sister* – and put them back in the envelope. Outside the light started to shift, a slow descent into the shadows. 'You don't need me. You've got cops. Trained professionals.' Freddie wasn't sure who she was talking to. 'I'm seeing a counsellor. She wouldn't like this. I'm not ready.' The fields around her parents' house stretched away from the single-track road. If she listened hard, blocked everything else out, she could just make out the motorway.

Chapter 10

Wednesday 16 March

12:30
T − 21 hrs

Nasreen wanted to grab Freddie. Shake her. Beg her. The devastation on Burgone's face floated before her; jarring with the images of gasped pleasure last night. *His toned, slender torso. His arms around her.* Her heart screamed at Freddie to help. But what could this broken shell of a woman do? She looked awful. She'd lost weight – it didn't suit her. Dark shadows were etched into her face. And the scar. She thought it would have healed. Faded. But it's belligerently, defiantly there. The most real part of her. There was nothing left of the girl she knew. This had been a mistake.

'I'm sorry,' she said. 'I shouldn't have come.' She'd look into getting Freddie some help when this was over. The grim thought of what the next twenty-four hours might hold was destabilising.

Her stomach churned at the thought of explaining this to Chips. So much for impressing him: she'd wasted time and resources, roping in DC Green on a wild goose chase. Her phone had full signal, but no missed calls. No updates from the office. *No breakthrough.* They had twenty-one hours to find Lottie. They needed a lead. Another message. *Something.*

Freddie was silhouetted against the net curtains, hugging herself tight across her chest, her cartoon character pyjama top hanging off of her. Nasreen didn't like to guess when she'd last washed her hair. She should have come sooner. As a friend. She didn't know things were this bad. She would have made time, if Freddie or her mum had called her. Wouldn't she? She swallowed her own doubt and guilt.

'Do you remember the year it snowed and school was closed for four days?' Freddie was staring out the window as she spoke. 'We made snow angels at the bus stop.'

Nasreen's chest pinched. This was her fault. Freddie should never have been involved in the previous case. She was a civilian. Not trained. She had put her childhood friend in the path of danger. It was a gamble, and Freddie had lost. When this was over she'd come back. Try and get her to have a shower, take her out for a walk.

Nasreen tucked the envelope into her jacket: the only clues she had, resting against her heart. 'Take care of yourself, Freddie.' The black leather gloves she'd been issued with when she'd joined the force creaked as she pulled them on and made for the door. She'd call Chips while DC Green drove. This was not going to be fun.

'It's not him, is it?' Freddie asked.

Nasreen paused. 'Who?'

Freddie turned, the faraway look gone, her eyes focused. She pushed her glasses up the bridge of her nose. 'Apollyon.'

Nasreen stared at her. She'd barely looked at the notes...

'It's an acrostic – you know that, right?' She tilted her head to one side, her hair, longer now, falling in jagged corkscrews. Her face had a familiar look: the one that came before she announced some great discovery. *Fish don't have fingers. Grown-ups make babies by sexing. Hayley Mandrake's sister has done it behind Morrisons.* Hundreds of Freddie's revelations cascaded through Nasreen's memory, half of which were declared dud, tossed away as Freddie's mind raced to the next adventure. The light had switched back on behind her childhood friend's eyes.

'Yes,' said Nasreen. 'But it can't be Apollyon. He's inside. Locked up. Solitary. No internet access.'

Freddie nodded. Circuits flashed, connecting above her head. 'Gemma's sister. Your boss's sister. Apollyon.'

It wasn't a question, but she nodded anyway. Keen not to break the chain. She knew what she was asking her to do.

'You told them yet?' Freddie raised her eyebrows.

There was no way she could know about Burgone – could she? Nasreen's ears grew warm. 'Told who what?'

'That you're the link.'

The relief was fleeting. 'I've told them the relevant bits. About the Apollyon link in the notes.' Freddie would never meet the team. They were highly unlikely to bump into each other in a social situation. Chips and Saunders liked pubs, with real ale and loud inappropriate jokes. And Freddie liked... being nocturnal? She'd get Freddie's insight and then get back to the unit, with neither party ever being the wiser. 'The name on the notes is circumstantial, but we could be looking at some kind of copycat.' The idea of another serial killer sloshed through her stomach like acid. 'It's not a pattern. I just want to double check. If the same person is involved in Lottie's disappearance then we might find something in Chloe's case that leads us to them.'

'Apollyon used Twitter, and now he's shifted to Snapchat,' mused Freddie.

'We know the Apollyon case better than anyone else.'

'I am the case!' Freddie pointed at the gouged scar on her forehead.

If these two girls had been abducted, killed, because of Nasreen, then she had to fix it. *Had to.* Freddie was her best shot at that. She was wrapped up in this tighter than anyone else.

'Am I in danger?' Freddie's face shifted, threatening to withdraw.

Of course she'd want to know that! Nasreen should've immediately reassured her. 'There's no evidence to suggest you're at risk.'

'What about the people I know? Mum? My dad?' Freddie folded her arms over her chest.

'There's no reason they should be. You don't know DCI Burgone, or his sister, Lottie. Do you?' The thought that Freddie might somehow know Burgone stung, though she wasn't sure why.

'Don't think so.'

'Okay. If there is any link then, it's me.' It was the first time she'd verbalised it. Suddenly, it was no longer an abstract concern. The events of the last twenty-four hours slipped through her fingers like uncooked rice. Wishing things were different and that she could stay here with Freddie was pointless. 'Perhaps the Apollyon word cropping up in both notes is coincidence, I just…'

'Feel it in your gut?' Freddie had a glint of mischief in her eye. She put great faith in intuition, using it more than once to sanction a bad idea. 'I didn't think you went in for all that wishy-washy stuff, Nas. You're a woman of facts, evidence, procedure. *You* follow the letter of the law.' She gave a mock salute.

'I still think homeopathy is a load of rubbish, if it makes you feel better.' This was more like the Freddie she knew and loved to bicker with.

'Doesn't everyone?'

Freddie was deflecting. Possibly stalling for time. That meant she hadn't made her mind up yet.

'Will you help?'

They stared at each other. The tick of the carriage clock on the mantelpiece filled the silence. *Tick. Tick. Tick. Tick.* Nasreen didn't have anything left to say. She was asking a lot of her friend, knew it was irresponsible. But asking for Freddie's help was the only thing she could think of. T – 20 hours 38 mins. *Tick. Tick. Tick.*

Freddie looked round, as if she were seeing the room for the first time. 'Give me five.' She tugged at her top. 'I need a shower.'

Nasreen could have hugged her. Should she hug her? She stepped forward, faltered, and stopped. She'd taken too long to decide, and Freddie was already at the stairs. That kind of gesture – a hug – belonged to their past. When they were teen BFF's, or whatever it was called now. 'I'll wait in the car.' She felt better. As if just having Freddie on board changed everything. It was a familiar feeling, she realised, one from childhood. From when she'd stood shoulder to shoulder with Freddie in the playground. The mouthy girl had protected her, taught her to fight back, speak up. She'd had this invincibility: a gift. Nasreen now understood it was bravado, bolstered from Freddie's troubled home life. You had to speak up to be heard over a drunken father. You had to fight back. But it was still a powerful feeling: two is better than one. They could do anything together. She wanted to give that reassurance, that same feeling to this Freddie. The pale, thin, damaged one. 'They get better, by the way.'

'What?' Freddie was halfway up the stairs, school photos of her in her grey-and-red uniform on the wall behind her.

'The nightmares.' Nasreen's eyes rested on the image of the eight-year-old Freddie. How old they'd been when they'd first met. Two young girls, skipping in the playground. Eating strawberry yoghurts with plastic spoons. Running with their hoods on their heads, their coats flying behind them like capes. Their whole lives ahead of them.

'Good to know,' she said over her shoulder. And Freddie Venton walked back into the flames.

Chapter 11

Wednesday 16 March

13:05
T – 20 hrs 25 mins

Freddie shook the towel from her hair and opened the wardrobe in her room. Inside, unopened, were all the cardboard boxes that had been returned to her by the police. After what had happened, her room – the living room in her flat – had become a crime scene. Ironic really, given that it was her breaking into a crime scene in search of a news story that had kickstarted all of this. She tried to think back to that person: the one who was a journalist, writing reams of articles – mostly for free – for online newspapers. It was like imagining a character in a TV show or a film. The threads linking her to that person had been severed. And that life, *her life*, had been sealed in boxes and hidden away.

Pulling down the first box, she ripped off the tape, rummaging through sweatshirts, jean shorts, knickers... the detritus of her former self. Nope. Not there. She opened the next: full of paper takeaway cups bagged in forensic plastic. They had to be kidding. Why keep this crap? Bloody police – always so proper. She shoved it aside and opened the next. Finally! She pulled out her skinny jeans. Black. And under them her DM boots. Black. The jeans were loose, so she rolled the waistband to sit low on her hips. She could do with a pizza. She was hungry. When had she last been hungry? Pulling on her boots, she felt the familiar tilt and wear to the leather, shaped on the streets of London. They were made for city streets, not country lanes or, even more insulting, suburban pavements. Was it hunger or was it excitement? There was a strange sensation in her stomach: fizzing. Her body felt different, and it wasn't just that her checked red shirt and purple hoodie hung off her, unexpected gaps between her skin and the material. It was that she felt it at all. It had started downstairs with that warm, damp feeling inside, and it had spread through her, tingling her fingers, wriggling her toes. A switch had been flicked. She'd experienced a surge. Was she ready for this? Could she leave this house? This street? This town? Could she get in a car with Nas and drive back to London? She could – should – call her counsellor. *And do what? Talk about her bloody feelings?* There was a girl out there who needed her help. Who gave a toss about her feelings? She shoved the small present from her mum, still wrapped, into her pocket. Running down the stairs, she grabbed her denim jacket on the way.

The cold March air blew through the flapping fabric of her clothes. No meat on her bones to keep her warm, that's what her gran would've said. The strange car parked in the driveway brought Freddie back to the present. To what she was about to do. *And how does that make you feel?* she heard Amanda's voice say in her head. *Fuck you, Mandy. Fuck you and your feels.* Walking with purpose towards the car, she faltered when she spotted the outline in the driver seat: a woman with red hair. Nas was on the passenger side. Freddie didn't much fancy making chit-chat. Pulling open the back door she slid into the car. It smelt of pine air freshener, and the faint hint of disinfectant that seemed to cling to all police property. Did they buy it in bulk? Or did it just permeate everything, seeping in from stations, cells, hospitals, morgues…

She didn't want to think of Chloe's body lying cold on a stainless-steel slab. Would they have taken her to the same hospital her sister worked at? Would Gemma have been there when they brought her in?

Freddie had always liked Gemma's mum. She didn't do 'the face' when she asked after Freddie's parents. So many adults – teachers, the librarian, other mums and dads – had done 'the face'. Head tilted, lips pursed into a solemn pout, eyes full of false concern. They'd only wanted gossip. More dirty titbits about how terrible her drunk father was. She remembered being eight or nine, walking into the entrance to the village hall for Brownies and hearing Sally Perkins' mum: *Sally says Freddie is always getting into trouble at school. She's disruptive. It's hardly a surprise with a father like that. He's an alcoholic.* Freddie had looked the word up on Ask Jeeves later: she hadn't known what it meant, but she knew it was bad. *She'll probably be a drug addict before she's left secondary. It's genetic, isn't it? I won't let Sally play there anymore.* Tears had stung her eyes. Adults weren't supposed to say mean things. She'd wanted to run and hide, burying her face in her arm to sob, but instead she had decided to get angry. Sally's mum had a big shiny Range Rover; Freddie walked back out and whipped the car with her coat, the zip leaving a white scratch on the black bonnet. The stupid woman thought an animal had done it. Freddie didn't care what anyone else thought of her dad: she loved him.

Nas turned to smile at her. 'Freddie, this is DC Green.' She was back in RoboCop mode, all traces of warmth and personality replaced with a peppy, authoritative tone. Whenever there was another cop present, Nas felt the need to demonstrate either distance from or disapproval of Freddie.

DC Green's face puckered as she took in the hole in Freddie's jacket, and her hair, which was now drying at right angles to her head. Not what she had been expecting. A thin-lipped smile made a fleeting appearance on her pale, upside-down-egg of a face. 'Seatbelt, please,' she said. Her voice carried a South London tinge. No offer of a first name.

'Yes, Mum,' Freddie smiled.

'You don't have to call me ma'am.' Green's face wrinkled in distaste.

'I didn't.'

'I can see why the Sarge described you as not a *normal* consultant.' Green's hazel eyes locked onto Freddie.

Freddie almost laughed: the last thing she wanted was to be the normal kind of person who worked with the police. That measure of normal was probably right wing, judge-y, and power crazed. How did Nas work with these guys every day?

'If we could focus on the job at hand, please,' Nas interrupted.

DC Green started the engine. Nas turned to face the road – she got carsick and couldn't look back while they were moving. Freddie clicked her seatbelt in, watching the house as they turned out of the drive. She should have left a note for her mum. Something to let her know not to worry. 'Where we going then?'

'DI McCain doesn't think we should speak to Chloe Strofton's family without evidence of foul play.'

It made sense that Nas'd want to go speak to the Stroftons. Should she tell Nas about the email? About her failed attempt

78

to contact Gemma? *Never contact me again.* Freddie hoiked her bag onto her lap.

'I want to speak to her friends,' Nas was saying. 'I've spoken to the teachers at Chloe's school – Romeland High, it's in St Albans.'

St Albans, another commuter town, was twenty minutes away by car, a satellite to London. 'God, they didn't move far then?'

A tightness invaded Nas's shoulders. 'From where they used to live, which you saw in the files. That's right,' she said.

Ah. Nas obviously hadn't told her work pal she knew Chloe's older sister. Fair enough. Freddie didn't like thinking about back then either. There was a tiny tremor across DC Green's eyebrows, but it could've been the pot-holed country lane.

Nas stared forwards while she talked, as if transfixed by the stubby hedges that lined the winding road. 'I've spoken to her teachers and they're arranging for us to interview – informally – some of her friends. There was mention of a boyfriend, they split up. Her parents thought she was upset about that.'

'Sounds like they were right, if she killed herself,' Green said. 'I reckon this Snapchat thing with the guv's sister is all a distraction to make us look the wrong way.'

'If that's the case, then the quicker we eliminate any link between the two girls the better,' Nas said.

Nas clearly thought there was a link, or else she wouldn't be here. Silence descended in the car, broken only by the tick of the indicator as they turned onto the main road through Pendrick. Tick-tick. Tick-tick. Tick-tick.

The road widened as they drove through Pendrick's treelined main parade, filled with expensive old-lady shops, a Boots, two card shops, three pubs and a large number of cafes in tasteful Farrow & Ball shades. The homogenous monotony of it all was broken by a chippie up the hill near the station. This morning

79

Freddie hadn't been able to imagine leaving her mum's house, except to visit Amanda, and yet here she was: in a car with Nas, with the police, driving towards the school Chloe Strofton had attended. What had Lottie Burgone thought when she got out of bed this morning? Neither's day had gone as planned.

Taking her mum's present out, she slid a chewed nail under the sellotape and the stiff paper sprang open. She lifted the cool metal phone out of the paper. Her mum, who always strove to do the right thing, would no doubt have ignored the dodgy guys at the market who fixed screens and unlocked phones cheaply. She'd have sent it off to the manufacturer at huge cost. She peeled the protective plastic off. No scratches, no cracks, not even a finger smudge marked it. If only everything were so easy to fix. She hadn't held her phone, touched it, since the day it had got smashed. Since the day she too had cracked from side to side. *Pandora's box.* She couldn't do this without help. She needed the internet. All that information at her fingertips. All that power. She held down the button and her phone came alive. A blur of message alerts filled her screen. Three months' worth of friends, colleagues, contacts, strangers, trying to find out how she was. Angry red spots of numbers covered her apps. 1203 emails. Freddie clicked onto her account, selected all and marked as read, exhaling. *Better.* Clicking into Twitter and Facebook she did the same; it was refreshing to get rid of the new messages. She'd go through them later. *Maybe.* For now, she needed a clear phone and a clear head. Moving through WhatsApp she repeated the same fast removal of anything 'pending'. But as she reached Snapchat, clicking through the pictures, videos and gifs, something caught her eye: something she'd seen before. Her heart sputtered. Her fingers, acting on muscle memory, screenshot the image before it disappeared.

'Nas?' She pushed her phone forwards over her friend's

shoulder. Nas reached up and took it without turning. 'You were right – about the link you suspected.' Freddie glanced at the back of DC Green's head as she turned the car off the dual carriageway and followed the signs to St Albans. Nas hadn't said anything much in front of this woman; she was not a confidante.

'Is that…'

'Yeah.' *The suicide note from Lottie Burgone.* 'It was sent to me, too. I haven't turned it on recently.' She felt stupid. As if admitting she was frightened of her phone. She was digital detoxing; people did that all the time. Last time she'd seen Nas, she *had* been under medical advice not to use her phone.

'How'd they get your number?'

'It's on my blog and my business cards.' Nas was a different story. In all the time Freddie had spent working with her last year, she'd not seen her flirt with anyone. Ever. Getting Nas's number was like getting the nuclear codes.

They passed an art deco cinema, rows of Victorian houses and a growing number of shops; St Albans had the same small market town feel as Pendrick. Ideal for hoovering up the young professionals who were being priced out of the London property market. Though Freddie always wondered who these young professionals were. No one she knew would be able to afford to buy in town, or anywhere. Pendrick was for the poached-eggs posse: suburbanites in their thirties and forties, pushing designer buggies and breakfasting on avo on toast. The Stroftons had relocated to another safe, sanitised place. Pendrick mark two. Except you can't outrun tragedy. A posh postcode and good transport links can't protect you from death.

'Romeland High is by the cathedral,' said DC Green, stopping at a red light. 'We should be there in two minutes.'

Freddie couldn't believe she'd survived bourgeois, bland Pendrick for so long. Bright blue sky opened between white clouds over St Albans' historic rooftops, and she felt overwhelmingly claustrophobic.

Lottie's suicide note was still backlit on her screen. Why had she been sent a copy too? They were being sucked in. Nas was right: they were the link, she and Freddie. They were the eye of the storm that threatened to destroy the missing girl.

Chapter 12

Wednesday 16 March

13:25
T – 20 hrs 55 mins

Freddie had been sent the message too. Nasreen felt sick. The sender wanted them to know this was about the Hashtag Murderer. About Apollyon. There was no reason to think the prison officer had lied about the access the killer had to the outside world; but the prison officer might not know what he was up against. It wasn't unheard of for a sympathetic or bribed screw to take a mobile in to a criminal.

The car turned and St Albans Cathedral, a grand, gothic building, glowed majestically before them, golden in the sun. Along from the abbey was a flint-layered block gateway house, which looked to be part of the grandiose St Albans School.

'It's stunning,' said Nasreen, inhaling the fresh, cut-grass smell of spring and trying to roll the tension from her shoulders. They could be standing in a quad at an Oxford college.

'All right if you're into Hogwarts, I suppose.' Freddie's hands were in her hoodie pockets.

'Romeland School is on Fishpool Street,' said Nas, shielding her eyes from the sun. 'That one.' She pointed at the chocolate box road that wended away downhill.

DC Green shut the car door, her tan suit jacket creased from the drive. She didn't take her eyes from Freddie, who was leaning against the car. 'Can you not do that? I'll be in trouble if the paintwork's chipped.'

Freddie didn't move. 'You always want to be a cop?'

Green stiffened. 'My father was in the force.'

Nasreen knew cops who were devastated when their children joined, not wanting them to have the life they had, the long stressful hours away from family. You didn't get a good work–life balance, and not everyone was happy for their loved ones to take such risks. The first time she'd been hospitalised, her dad had cried and begged her not to return to work. But it wasn't that easy. This was more than a job. Green retreated at the personal question, turning away. No bad thing: the less interaction Freddie had with the team, the better. Nasreen didn't want anything getting back to Saunders or Burgone.

'Green, I'm going to take Freddie into the interviews with me. To observe. I don't want to overwhelm the kids.' Green looked crestfallen. Nasreen had been there: getting palmed off with the dull jobs. She sympathised. 'Why don't you go get yourself some lunch? We can meet you back here in, say half an hour?'

'Oh, get me a pain au chocolat?' Freddie rifled through her pockets. Green sucked her cheeks in. Oblivious, or unbothered, Freddie continued. 'And an espresso, but like a good one, yeah?'

'Now I'm a waitress?' Green looked at her disdainfully.

'You got any cash, Nas?'

Nasreen cringed. 'Sure.' She handed Green, who managed a sarcastic smile, a twenty from her wallet. 'Lunch is on me, yeah?'

'Cheers, Sarge. Do you want anything?' Green's face softened a fraction, placated by the gesture.

The thought of food made her stomach heave – she wasn't sure if it was the hangover or stress. 'Just a smoothie. Something like that'd be lovely. Thanks.'

'No probs.' Green folded the notes into her back pocket. 'I'll see you back here.'

'Right,' said Nas, turning to face Freddie. 'Ready?' The sight of her friend's livid scar jarred again. This was what Apollyon had done to her. And Freddie was lucky: she'd lived.

Freddie caught Nas looking and self-consciously pulled her hair forwards.

'Sorry – I didn't mean to stare.' Nasreen felt her face grow hot.

'Don't wanna frighten the children do we,' said Freddie as she headed down the hill.

Nasreen hurried to catch up. 'I didn't mean…'

'Forget it. It's cool.'

But it wasn't. A muscle in Freddie's neck twitched. She was putting on a brave face. Nasreen always took care to maintain eye contact in interviews with domestic abuse victims; why couldn't she do that with Freddie? *Because you feel guilty.* The scar was a Post-it note on Freddie's face, reminding her of the trouble she'd caused her.

'How long we got?' Freddie asked.

Recovering herself, Nas replied, 'If we keep it swift, thirty minutes.'

'I mean on the clock. How long until Lottie is…'

She didn't need to check the time. 'Under twenty hours.' What would Saunders be doing now? She was away from the main hub of the investigation out here. Perhaps Chips thought that was better. Had she sidelined herself from the search?

'You said Melisha Khan was Chloe's bestie, right?'

'Yes.' She steered Freddie off the cobbled pavement and into the tarmacked entrance of the school. Set back from the winding road of beautiful historic houses, the red-brick, three-storey nineties pimple of Romeland High was at complete odds with its surroundings. Through the upstairs windows she saw pupils in dark blue blazers, moving, chatting, laughing. Lunch time.

'Nice of them to stick the state comp kids in this, when they've got Malory Towers just up there,' Freddie said. Nasreen didn't have time to respond before she fired out a question: 'What's the name of the boyfriend – the kid she broke up with?'

'William Taylor.' A sign directed them to the reception. A reinforced glass door, green and distorted so those passing by couldn't peer in.

'Presuming our William Taylor is the same Will.i.am. T. on Facebook – why do you think Melisha Kahn has written "I know what you did. You killed my best friend. I'll never forgive you" on his wall?' Freddie held her phone up.

'What?' Melisha had posted the message on William's Facebook page on Monday, after the original investigation by the local force had finished. Emojis underneath marked that others had reacted to the post: small red angry faces, crying faces, laughing faces. Nasreen's pulse accelerated. They could be on to something.

'Their profiles say they're at Romeland. You think it's them?' Freddie asked.

'Let's find out.' If they worked out what had really happened to Chloe, they could work out what had happened to Lottie.

The shrill sound of two phone notifications stopped her in her tracks. Freddie grabbed her arm: her phone had pinged as well. The noise of the schoolyard fell away. Blood rushed to her ears. Nasreen's hands were shaking. A new Snapchat. A photo. Her mind conjured up horrible scenarios. Hundreds of crime scene photos fired through her mind. She didn't want to look. Her legs felt weak. Had this been sent to Burgone? Oh god. She had to do this. Be strong. For Jack. She tapped the Snap open.

The first thing she saw was Lottie's eyes. Wide. Terrified. Her forehead was smeared with blood. *Her blood.* Silver gaffer tape cut across her face, sealing in her scream. Her hair was askew, as if she'd been yanked by it. Tears were running down her face. It was a horrific, twisted take on the selfies of Lottie's feed. Over the photo was a message:

You have 20 hours to save luscious Lottie's life. Tick tock.

Freddie lurched away from her and bounced off the red-brick wall, bending double, gasping for air. 'No. No. No.'

Nasreen couldn't speak. Couldn't find the words. Fighting to control herself, gripping her phone. *Stop shaking.* Lottie was still alive. That had to be a good thing. What had they done to her? Her phone rang: *Saunders calling.* They must have got the message too. Poor Jack. Sending Saunders to voicemail, her finger hovered over Burgone's number. Her breath was coming in short, sharp gulps. What could she say? She screwed her eyes shut, shook her head, tried to get rid of the image of Lottie screaming. Crying. Blood streaked down her face. There was no doubt left: Lottie had been kidnapped and the threat to her life was credible. They had twenty hours to save her. Less than a day. *Tick tock, tick tock, tick tock* sounded Nasreen's heartbeat.

Chapter 13

Wednesday 16 March

13:35
T – 19 hrs 55 mins

'I don't think I can do this,' Freddie said. Her whole body felt hot.

'We have to.' Nas's eyes darted around the square reception room of Romeland High, checking all the exits.

'Will they be able to trace the Snap?'

'The tech lads will try. But it was from the same number as before, so my guess is it'll have been rerouted.' Nas's tone was free of emotion, but she was anxiously twisting her fingers together.

The room the kidnapper was holding Lottie in looked dark, abandoned, scary. Freddie kept seeing the petrified eyes of the girl. She couldn't bring herself to look at the photo again. Nas had ignored several calls, finally silencing her own phone. They had to focus on the interviews. She had to stop her teeth chattering.

'What about the photo itself – could they trace that?'

Nas shook her head, approaching the receptionist with thick-framed glasses, who hadn't looked up from her beige computer. Freddie looked around the room. It was surreal standing here. The white-painted walls were yellowing with age. It was like being inside a giant nicotine experiment. Blue felt pinboards punctuated the walls like clots on an x-ray.

'Good afternoon, I'm Detective Sergeant Nasreen Cudmore.' Nas showed her warrant card to the scowling receptionist. 'Ms Bradshaw is expecting me.' The school bell sounded: end of lunch. Freddie could hear shouts and voices, shuffling feet, doors banging and chairs scraping as the kids went back to class. She blinked away images of Lottie gagged with gaffer tape.

The receptionist took the card in her peach-painted nails.

'You're here about *Chloe Strofton*?' She whispered the name as if it were a delicious secret. 'Such a tragic waste.' Her face puckering into faux concern. 'Young people nowadays, they have it all given to them on a plate.'

Student debt, high unemployment, astronomical house prices, environmental destruction, thought Freddie. *Yeah, so much given to them.*

'We never had mobile phones or laptops in my day and we just got on with it. If you ask me, I think they have it too easy.'

'We didn't ask you,' Freddie's horror quickly segued into anger. How could someone like this work with children?

Nas shot her a warning glance.

The receptionist extended a gnarled hand. 'And your ID?'

Oh shit.

'This is my colleague Freddie Venton.' Nas gave the woman

her winning smile. Freddie couldn't even pretend. 'She's a specialised consultant working on this case.'

'Is she DBS checked?'

'No,' answered Freddie.

'I'm not sure I can let her in. She could be anyone.' She glared at Freddie. 'She could be a paedophile.'

Oh yeah, I'm just hanging around looking at photos of kidnapped girls and interviewing dead girls' friends for a laugh.

'Sign in.' The receptionist slapped a clipboard onto the desk. 'She's not to be left unattended at any time. Even if she needs the toilet.' Her dog's-bum mouth twisted into a smile that suggested she'd won. Freddie signed her name as *Jack Hoff*.

A woman entered the reception from one of the far doors. 'I'm sure that won't be necessary, Mrs Smailes.' In her late twenties, she had cropped blonde hair. Black Converse trainers complimented her smart skinny black trousers and neat grey jumper. 'I'm Ms Bradshaw. We spoke on the phone.'

Nas introduced them and Ms Bradshaw shook their hands. 'We're all devastated about Chloe. Such a bright girl. The pupils are very shocked by it all. We're a small school, and I have to say, thankfully, we don't have much experience of this.' Ms Bradshaw's efficient tone couldn't disguise her anxiety. It must be frightening to feel responsible for all these young lives. Freddie thought of Lottie: they were responsible for her life. 'If you follow me, I've arranged for us to use the school nurse's office. She only comes in for vaccinations. Though we have had a counsellor coming in for any pupils who wish to see her.'

The hallway was empty. Voices, mostly those of teachers, drifted from behind closed classroom doors. *Mineral or organic matter deposited by water, air or ice is called sediment… And y equals?* One wall of the corridor was constructed of glass, overlooking a small square of concrete, on the other side of which was the canteen. More felt pinboards lined the other wall, plastered with posters advertising a forthcoming school disco. It was all so… *ordinary*. Chloe had walked down this hallway, gone to class, left, and vanished. What had happened to make her do that?

'We're in here.' Ms Bradshaw pushed open a green door. The room was small, but sunlit, with low, comfortable chairs that were clearly designed to encourage pupils to relax, to talk.

'Thank you, Ms Bradshaw,' said Nas. 'This is perfect.' It felt separate to the rest of the squeaky corridors, with their dark rubber scuff marks. Safer, as if they were retreating from the threat of the investigation.

'Call me Caroline, please.'

'I will need to ask you to sit in on the conversations, if that's okay, Caroline?' Nas's tone had lost the supercharged charm she'd used for the secretary, but it was still warm. How could she detach so quickly from the horror of that image? How could she stop seeing the terror in Lottie's eyes? 'As I explained on the phone, these aren't official interviews, not at this stage, but I will need an independent responsible adult here while talking to minors.'

'I could have done it,' Freddie said.

Nas smiled as if she'd made a joke. 'I'd like to talk to Melisha Khan, Chloe's best friend.'

'Yes. I also requested that Ruby Dawson come and see you. She, Melisha and Chloe were a bit of a trio,' said Caroline, indicating for her and Nas to sit down. Freddie took a chair, its foam not quite as soft as she'd hoped. She pulled her jacket off and slung it over the back.

Nas was still standing. 'I'd also like to speak to a pupil called William Taylor – we understand he and Chloe had been going out?'

It sounded so childish: *going out*. But Freddie could still feel the heat from her own teen relationships. Alfie from her weekend job at Waterstones had been lanky and pale, with fine, floppy hair she liked to push out of his eyes. They'd bonded over their love of The Smiths. He wasn't her first, but he was certainly the first to leave a mark.

'Do you know why they split up?' Freddie asked.

Caroline looked surprised, as if the question had never occurred to her. 'No. So many youngsters form relationships, break up. It's part of growing up. Are the children suspected of something, Sergeant?'

'Please, call me Nasreen. I don't want to put the pupils on edge.'

'You're a cop, Nas. They're not gonna treat you like you're their best bud.'

Nas frowned. 'Freddie, can I borrow your jumper?' Freddie chucked her hoodie at her.

'I'll go and fetch the students,' Ms Bradshaw said.

'Just Melisha and Ruby first,' Nas said. 'I'd like to speak to the girls without William present.'

A slight shadow passed across Caroline's face. Did she suspect Nas wasn't telling her everything? 'I'll find out where William is and get him to come along… in about ten minutes?'

'Perfect.' Nas was so good at making people do what she wanted, Freddie couldn't help but smile. Caroline stepped out, closing the door behind her.

Nas took her suit jacket off. 'Leave the questions to me. When they come in.'

'But what if I've got something to say?'

'I'm already sailing close to the wind by having you sit in on this.'

'It's not like you to break the rules.' She didn't bother toning down the sarcasm. What was the point of being here if all she did was sit like a pot plant in the corner?

Nas pulled the hoodie over her white button-up shirt. 'I didn't have time to set this up properly. I need to extract any relevant intelligence and get it back to the team.'

The spectre of Lottie filled the small room. 'I'll behave.'

'Good.' Nas zipped the hoodie up. 'How do I look?'

'Like a copper wearing a hoodie over her suit.'

'Right.' Nas unzipped it and flung it back at her. 'I'll play to that: authority. Chloe and her friends have no history of trouble. But I want to know what that Facebook message is about.'

Freddie thought of the lies she told. *Yes, I looked for new jobs today. Yes, I wrote a pitch today.* 'Just because they're young, it doesn't mean they'll trust you.'

'This is hardly a hostile inner-city school is it?' Nas gestured at the pastel landscape on the wall.

'And what d'you know about hostile inner-city schools?' She'd meant it as a joke, but being in a school again, with Nas, and talking about concealing the truth gave her voice an edge.

Instantly Nas cooled. 'When I was a DC I worked on a stabbing at a school in Hackney.'

Freddie tried to imagine a younger Nas – the one who'd got lost somewhere between the shy fourteen-year-old girl she'd known and this composed, cool-headed policewoman. It was still odd: Nas, the girl she used to share her penny sweets with, was a cop. She'd thought the police were sexist, racist, homophobic, transphobic dinosaurs. But while she'd seen things that reinforced this view, she'd also seen the drive, commitment, and sacrifice Nas and her fellow officers made. And – she lightly touched her scar – how they put themselves in danger every day. *By choice.* She wanted to ask after Nas's old colleagues, but it didn't feel like the right time. Instead, she asked, 'What happened – at the school stabbing?'

Nas sat in the chair facing the door, then changed her mind, standing up and dragging another so that she could sit with her back to the door, facing two empty chairs, the windows behind them. Freddie thought she wasn't going to answer, then something akin to grief quivered across her face. *This one had hurt.*

'Two boys had a set-up going where they'd sell drugs – hash mostly – to other kids. Then when they'd pocketed the money, they'd pull a knife on the other kid and steal the drugs back. Small time, but they probably would have built on it.'

Would have? Freddie had a hollow feeling in the pit of her stomach.

'The girlfriend of one of the boys had set up a mark. Unfortunately the mark was also carrying a knife. There was a struggle, and the buyer, the one who'd come for the hash, was stabbed. He was seventeen.' Her eyes were distant. Was she reliving it? Did Nas have nightmares?

'Did he make it?'

'He bled out. By the time the paramedics arrived it was too late. The two lads did a runner, but the girlfriend didn't do a bunk with her boyfriend. She cradled the dying lad in her arms. Afterwards she said she couldn't leave him on his own, even though she knew she'd be in trouble.'

'How do you mean?'

'She knew what they were up to. She knew they would rob him, and that they were carrying knives. Under the joint enterprise law, a person may be found guilty for another person's crime if the suspect knowingly assisted in it.'

'But she stayed with a dying boy – that must count for something?'

'The law is the law.'

'But that's not right.'

'It's not our job to prosecute and sentence people. We gather the evidence; we charge them.'

'And you're okay with that?' Freddie believed in justice for victims, but how could Nas think that was a fair outcome? What did she think should happen to the person who'd kidnapped Lottie? Did she even care?

'She was fifteen. And pregnant.'

Freddie started at a knock at the door. Ms Bradshaw poked her head round. 'Okay if we come in?'

Nas banished the detached look from her face, replacing it with a warm smile. 'Of course.'

Behind Caroline were two girls in navy blazers, pleated navy skirts and opaque tights. Freddie immediately recognised Melisha Khan from her Facebook profile photo. Youth clung to her full cheeks, highlighted rather than hidden by the carefully contoured make-up she wore.

'Nasreen, this is Melisha and Ruby,' Caroline said.

Melisha nodded. 'Hello,' the girl behind her said. Ruby Dawson had long hair like her friend, but where Melisha's was jet black, Ruby's was bleached blonde, and worked into curls. She was wearing less make-up, only mascara framing her green-blue eyes. She reminded Freddie of a mermaid.

'Nice to meet you. Do sit down.' Nas indicated the two chairs that faced into the room and Freddie realised what she'd done: the girls wouldn't be able to see Ms Bradshaw, or the window, without twisting backwards. They only had one place they could look: straight at Sergeant Cudmore.

Seconds ago Nas had been talking about a dying seventeen year old and a pregnant girl who'd been convicted for a crime she didn't commit. Minutes ago they'd received a shocking warning from the kidnapper. Yet Nas was smiling at the young

95

girls as though everything was fine. Freddie couldn't do it. The hairs rose on the back of her neck. Sitting in this calm room, in a sheltered provincial school, Freddie was scared. The first Snap from Lottie had been a grenade. This second photo a pulled pin. She'd been here before. Who would get destroyed in the explosion?

Chapter 14

Wednesday 16 March

14:00
T – 19 hrs 30 mins

'Thank you for coming to see me today,' Nas smiled. The girls moved in unison, unconsciously mirroring each other. Freddie recognised the intensity of teen friendships. Ruby was hugging her large purple leather satchel. Now Melisha was closer, Freddie could see that her eyes were rimmed red. She'd been crying recently. And not sleeping.

'I'm sorry for what happened to Chloe.' Nas deliberately avoided the word suicide. 'I understand you were close?'

'We were best friends,' Melisha said. Ruby nodded, still staring down at the carpet tiles.

'You must miss her very much.'

Ruby's lip trembled. Melisha's eyes dropped to the floor too. 'Yeah.'

'I understand Chloe told her parents she was staying at yours on Friday the eleventh of March, Melisha?' Nas said gently.

'She never told me.' Melisha's sentences carried the silent but implied teenage *duh!* This girl didn't see them as equals. Ms Bradshaw: the teacher. Nas: the cop. *Adults.* Melisha and Ruby were in a different generation. She felt old.

'I wondered if you could help me put together a better picture of what Chloe was like before she died. What kind of person was she?'

Ruby's face lit up. 'She was brilliant. Like not just at school, and sports and all that, but, like everything she did, you know?'

Nas nodded. 'What kind of things – I mean apart from school?'

'She had this summer job last year, in the Pepper Pot – the tearoom near the abbey. She started as a waitress, but she was so good at it, talking to all the old ladies that went there and stuff.' Freddie guessed Ruby was the quietest of the three under usual circumstances. *Shy.* 'She persuaded the manager to let her start making and selling gluten-free cakes. Then everyone started going there and wanting to eat these cakes – it's better, like for your weight and stuff.' Neither Ruby nor Melisha needed to worry about their figures. 'The cakes were so good the manager promoted Chloe. Gave her a job at weekends when school started up again.'

Melisha shot a glance at Ruby, whose face dipped suddenly behind her hair again.

Nas caught it but didn't react. 'And was Chloe still working at the Pepper Pot recently?'

'No.' Melisha shook her head.

'That's a shame. Why was that?' Nas asked.

'I dunno. Got bored, I guess,' Melisha said.

'She quit a job she loved?'

'She didn't really talk about it,' Melisha said.

The two girls were sitting so close they were almost touching. They had that tactile ease many teen girls have with each other. They also had that ability to communicate with just a look – she'd seen it pass between them. They knew something else about why Chloe left her job, but they weren't saying anything.

'Did Chloe have friends from the cafe?' Nas pushed.

'Don't think so,' Melisha said.

'What about anyone else outside school – any friends, boyfriends from anywhere else?'

'Don't think so.' Melisha was doing a fine impression of a stereotypical monotone teen.

'What about you, Ruby, did you know of anyone outside of school that Chloe was friends with?' Nas's tone was upbeat, friendly. Ruby shook her head. 'No one new in her life?'

Melisha shrugged.

'And would she have said? Did she tell you her secrets?'

Ruby's face snapped up. 'We didn't have secrets. We were best friends.' Her voice wavered on the last words. Melisha put an arm round her and hugged her friend. Freddie remembered putting an arm round Nas when they were at school, comforting her over some slight. Though their friend, their third wheel, hadn't died. *Just*.

'Did Chloe ever take drugs?' Nas asked.

Caroline shifted so she wasn't leaning against the glass anymore. 'We don't have a drugs problem at this school, Sergeant.'

Melisha twisted to look over her shoulder at the teacher.

'Chloe would never do that – she didn't even like taking paracetamol.' Ruby's face was panicked. 'It made her gag. Tell them about her – *you know*,' she whispered at Melisha, her eyes dropping down to the floor again.

'She got stomach cramps,' Melisha said. 'And she really struggled to swallow tablets. Like it almost made her vom.'

'We used to get her a Maccy D's milkshake – try with that.' A wistful look took over Ruby's face.

'Did anyone Chloe knew take drugs?' Nas said. 'A boyfriend perhaps?'

'She didn't have a boyfriend,' Melisha answered too fast.

'Oh,' Nas said lightly. 'I thought she was going out with William Taylor?'

'That was a mistake.' Melisha developed two pink spots on her cheeks.

Ruby's fingers tightened around her bag. 'It was nothing. You wouldn't call them boyfriend and girlfriend.'

Nas puckered her face in an act of confusion. 'I'm sure someone mentioned in the report – to my colleagues – that Chloe and William were dating? So he wasn't her boyfriend?'

'He wished!' Melisha's pink spots radiated.

Nas lowered her voice and leant forward, as if she were telling a friend they had spinach in their teeth. 'Melisha, why did you say Chloe's death was William Taylor's fault on his Facebook page?'

Ruby flinched and Melisha's mouth clamped shut. Her lips pursed into a sulk. She folded her arms and slumped back in the chair, staring at Nas. Nas waited. Freddie felt the urge to fill the silence, to say something. *Anything.* Nas was trying to draw it out of them. Ruby moved, her mouth open. Melisha put a hand on her knee – a warning? Ruby gave an involuntary shudder, and Freddie saw that she was crying, mascara snaking down her face in black streaks.

'I want to help,' Nas said softly. 'I need to know the truth about Chloe. To build a picture of what she was really like. Any detail you have could be important, though it might not seem it.'

A sob juddered out of Ruby.

'I think that's enough, Sergeant,' Caroline said. 'The girls are clearly distressed.' She passed a tissue to Ruby, who took it and blew her nose.

Nas took cards from her pocket and placed one on the table in front of each of the girls. 'If you ever want to talk to me, about anything, you can contact me here.'

'I think we better get you girls some fresh air. Come on.' Caroline's voice was cool. She turned and looked at Nas. 'Please do not speak to William until I'm back.'

Ruby's eyes went very wide, twisting to see Nas over her shoulder.

As soon as the door closed Freddie hissed, 'When she said you were talking to William, Ruby looked petrified.'

'Why deny William was Chloe's boyfriend? It makes no sense. Her parents are on record saying they'd recently split up.'

'Because they're teenagers?'

'Perhaps.' Nas chewed on the inside of her cheek.

The door opened and Caroline Bradshaw came back in quickly. 'Those young girls have been through a very traumatic experience, Sergeant. They're still in shock. You said this was just a few background questions?'

'We were led to believe, by Chloe's parents, by you, that Chloe and William had been in a relationship together.' Nas's voice was unwavering.

'These children are my responsibility and I will not have them upset.' Ms Bradshaw, perhaps used to dealing with difficult teens, was holding her own. 'I think it's time we put a stop to this. I wouldn't be surprised if we get complaints from the girls' parents.'

You have twenty hours to save luscious Lottie. 'But they were lying!' The words flew out of Freddie's mouth. If she just knew what was at stake.

'I will be sensitive with William, but we do need to talk to him,' Nas said.

101

'No, you don't.' Ms Bradshaw's arms were crossed. Defiant.

She couldn't let this woman stand in their way. Melisha had felt sure enough to accuse William Taylor of killing Chloe in public. What if he was wrapped up in Lottie's disappearance too? They couldn't drop this now. 'This is important,' Freddie said. 'Life or death!'

Ms Bradshaw looked at her incredulously. 'What are you talking about?'

Nas glowered at Freddie, and stepped towards the teacher, her palms open in supplication. 'Ms Bradshaw, another girl has sent a suicide note. Similar to Chloe's. But this time it looks like it might have come from someone else.'

'What do you mean?' Ms Bradshaw asked.

'There is the possibility that the girl has been taken. That the note was sent against her will.'

'Oh my god!' Ms Bradshaw's hand flew to her mouth. 'Do you think that's what happened with Chloe?'

'This information is not in the public domain, and we ask that you keep it that way,' Nas replied. 'I need to speak to Chloe's friends to try and find out if there was anyone worrying in her life. I would very much like to speak to William, please, Caroline.'

Caroline nodded, her face the same shade as the walls. 'Okay.' There was a knock at the door. The teacher composed herself, before opening it with a smile on her face and only the faintest wobble in her voice. 'William. Come in.'

Chapter 15

Wednesday 16 March

14:31
T – 18 hrs 59 mins

William Taylor was instantly recognisable from the profile picture Freddie had shown her. But unlike the bold teen making an LA gangland sign at the camera, this kid looked shrunken, pale under his naturally tanned skin. He had a battered Jack Wills rucksack slung over one shoulder, a play at nonchalant, which was undermined by his eyes hurtling rapidly between her, Freddie and Ms Bradshaw. Melisha had been petulant, but Ruby was a people pleaser – smiling at her and the teacher on the way in. With a bit more time Nasreen might have got her to talk. Though time wasn't on their side. There were eleven missed calls on her phone. The voicemail notification flashed a livid spot on her screen. How many of those were from Saunders? Had Chips given her up when the photo came in? Time was slipping like silk through her fingers. There was something here, something the girls were trying to hide from them. If she could just find out what before she was recalled, before she had to face Saunders. Whatever it was the girls didn't want them to know had something to do with William. They'd become defensive as soon as his name was mentioned.

She indicated for the lad to take a seat and laid her warrant card on the table between them, watching his gaze fix on it. His chest was heaving under his white school shirt, the sleeves rolled up, blazer shoved in his bag in what she guessed passed as a rebellious disregard for uniform in this school. He'd closed one strong hand over the fist of the other, but it wasn't an aggressive stance, more as if he were trying to fold in on himself, fingers first.

'Thanks for coming to talk to me.'

William was still staring at her ID, his knuckles stretched white with tension.

'Nice watch.' She pointed at the expensive designer piece on his wrist.

He covered it with one hand, as though she'd accused him of stealing it. 'Birthday present.'

He'd never come in contact with the police before. Green had done a PNC check on all three kids. 'Shall I call you William, or do you prefer Will?'

'Either.' He cleared his throat. His blond wavy hair was long, brushing his ears, like Harry Styles'. They would have looked a picture perfect pair, him and Chloe.

'I'll call you William, then.' It said Will on his Facebook page. She didn't want him to feel comfortable, she wanted him on edge. 'I asked you here today, William, to see if you can help me with some questions about Chloe Strofton.' His forearms pulsed. 'I also spoke to Melisha Khan.'

His head jerked up. 'What'd she say?' His Adam's apple bobbed.

'Quite a lot.' She let her hand rest on the table, next to her warrant card.

William ran his hand through his hair. Fidgeted. He was rattled.

'She had a…' Nasreen paused, watching as his eyes grew wider. 'Lot of interesting things to say.' His eyes were wide, panic danced across his eyebrows.

'I didn't do it!' he said.

Ms Bradshaw made a small noise, but Nasreen didn't let her gaze drop from the lad. 'Didn't do what, William?'

'The pictures. I've told her. Melisha. But she just won't believe me.' He looked at Ms Bradshaw, as if asking for her help. All credit to her, she didn't move, but Nasreen saw her hand brace against the window behind.

'What pictures, William?'

He looked back at her. 'The ones online. The naked ones. I swear – it wasn't me!'

Ms Bradshaw took a sharp intake of breath. Nasreen saw Freddie's mouth fall open. *Naked photos?* 'Tell me about the pictures.' She leant back as if she already knew what he was going to say; gave him space to talk.

'It wasn't me. I never sent them. I never even seen them till one of the lads on the rugby team showed me.' His words spilled over themselves, as if he'd been trying to hold them in. 'It was fucked up. Sorry, Miss,' he said in the direction of the teacher. 'Shouldn't I have a lawyer or something?' All the sheen of impending adulthood washed away, he looked like a little boy.

'This isn't a formal interview, William. I'm just trying to find out what happened to Chloe in the weeks leading up to her death.' He nodded, relieved. This had clearly been a burden for him. If there were naked photos being shown round of the fifteen-year-old girl then no wonder Chloe had been distressed – why hadn't the local force picked up on this? 'Do you know who your friend – the one on the rugby team – got the photo from?' They'd have to turn this over to the CEOP. Taking, possessing, and sharing indecent images of anyone under the age of eighteen was illegal.

'I tried to delete it – took his phone off him. But there were more of them.'

'More than one photo of Chloe?'

'Yeah. Loads. And the whole team had them. They were all online. I tried to speak to Chloe. Like she was making herself look easy taking pics like that.' Nasreen heard Freddie blow air through her teeth. William was still going. 'But she went crazy. Screamed at me. She thought I took them. But I never. I mean, me and Chloe, we didn't even have sex. I didn't think she was that kind of girl.'

'What do you mean that kind of girl?' Freddie spat the words.

William looked, shocked, from Freddie to her. Nasreen held her hand up to silence her friend, feeling the heat of anger emanating from her. 'Where online were these pictures of Chloe, William?'

'There's this website. It's like a bulletin board. I thought it was like Ask.FM, you know? A laugh, like, it's anonymous – you can post what you want. Rip the piss out each other, that sort of thing. But this was different. It has all these photos. Of, like, hot girls. And there were photos of Chloe on it. Like in her pants and bra, and other ones. Topless, you know? The whole year saw her like that.' He stopped, looked pained.

'What was the website called, William?'

He sighed. 'It's called Are You Awake.'

Nasreen saw Freddie swiping at her phone. 'Ms Bradshaw, could we please speak to Melisha and Ruby again?' She chose her words carefully. 'This has illuminated things. William, I'll need to arrange for you to speak to some of my colleagues. We'll have to notify your parents.' Alarm filled his eyes. She kept her voice low, even. 'You've helped Chloe in telling us about this site. We will find out who was responsible for sharing these images and get them taken down.' He nodded.

If Chloe had posted the images, and it had got out of hand... Nasreen didn't want to think of what'd been going through the girl's mind in the last few weeks of her life. William said Chloe had accused him of posting the images, which suggested she hadn't uploaded them herself. She could imagine the humiliation, how she must have felt. Why had the girl taken the pictures? Why take the risk? Who had she sent them to, and who had repaid that intimacy by sharing them online? There was, she realised, a clear motive for why Chloe would want to take her own life.

Chapter 16

Wednesday 16 March

14:45
T – 18 hrs 45 mins

'You can't just let him walk out of here!' Freddie said as the door closed. She'd heard everything William had said and hadn't bought a word of it. No way naked images of his girlfriend had got out and he wasn't responsible. She remembered with a sting how she'd caught a guy she was seeing at uni showing an extreme close up of her and a roll-on deodorant to his flatmates. Certain people couldn't be trusted. Where else would photos of Chloe have come from? It had to be him. It was obvious. The phone burned in her hand. 'He has to answer for what he's done. He has to pay. He humiliated her because he wanted to brag.'

'Shush!' Nas said. 'He'll hear you.'

'You can't let him get away with this. He circulated private photos of Chloe!' What a scumbag.

'We have no evidence of that,' Nas said distractedly, looking at her own phone.

'This is fairly self-evident!' She thrust her mobile at her. On screen was a photo of Chloe in what looked like a shop changing room. An orange curtain hung behind her. She was holding her phone up, pouting, and the halterneck red top she was wearing had slipped. You could see one pink nipple. Freddie had lost her virginity at fifteen, and she'd always felt confident she was mature enough to take that decision at that age, but this photo shocked her. It wasn't the nudity, it was Chloe's age. This was not a womanly figure. She was in the first flush of adolescence. And she looked young. Really young. *Like a child.*

Nas looked at the photo, zooming out. 'Is this on the website he named?'

'Yes. Are You Awake. They have a disclaimer. Get this: *By clicking "I Agree," you agree not to hold Are You Awake responsible for any damages from your use of this website, and you understand that the content posted is not owned or generated by Are You Awake, but rather by Are You Awake's users.* You just click through, and voilà: stacks of naked images. There's loads of them. All amateur.' Freddie felt grossed out. She'd always thought the prescribed ideals of beauty were manufactured by capitalism: a way to make women feel shit about themselves so they kept spending money on products and crap. That if you actually saw what people wanted, what they genuinely lusted after, then it would be a pic'n'mix of personal pleasure. Sure one guy might like waifs, but another might be into voluptuous curves. But all these girls looked the same: young, slight, flat stomachs, perky boobs, no pubic hair. They were personal photos, done in bedrooms and bathrooms, but they still fitted the model mould. It was depressing: it went against everything Freddie believed about human desire. It also made her feel fat and ugly and old. 'It didn't take me long to find Chloe. There's a whole thread dedicated to her.'

'Are there more photos?' Nas was taking this very well. *Too well.*

'Why aren't you arresting Will.i.am. A. Twat?'

'He's a sixteen-year-old kid, Freddie. This wasn't a formal interview. If we *suspect* he's more involved in the distribution of these images, then we'll need evidence we can use in court. Nothing he said in here was admissible.'

Freddie turned away. She felt boxed in in this room, there was something oppressive, offensive even, about the bland landscapes on the wall after you'd been looking at naked pics of what were effectively children. She was furious on Chloe's behalf. She felt the burn of humiliation. What had she been going through when these images were shared? 'It's revenge porn isn't it? He said himself that they'd split up. He said they hadn't had sex – maybe he wanted it and was cross he hadn't got it. And then he uploaded these photos for the world to see. Melisha thinks it was him, doesn't she? That's what that Facebook message was about.'

'Do you think it was deliberate, this picture?' Nas was still looking at the phone. 'Do you think she meant to flash?'

'Who cares. If she took it herself, she has a right to privacy.'

'She was under eighteen. If she sent, uploaded, or forwarded sexually explicit photos of herself it would still be illegal. She could have been prosecuted,' said Nas.

'That just sounds like another reason to kill yourself! No wonder none of these guys wanted to say anything. How could Chloe possibly be to blame if she was the victim?'

'It's not a question of blame, it's the law,' Nas said.

Again with this questionable faith in the law.

'We'll get tech to look at it. Contact the site. See if we can get them taken down. But I have to tell you it's not a priority, Freddie.'

'But this *proves* it – this is why Chloe killed herself. She was Gemma's sister, for god's sake.' Freddie snatched the phone back, ignoring the anger flashing in Nas's eyes. 'Look – there are more.' She scrolled through her screen. A photo of Chloe in a bikini. A photo of Chloe in underwear, her tiny breasts barely filling the yellow lace bra. Thin. Childlike. Bile flowered in her stomach. In the second photo you could see her hand holding the phone. In front of the mirror, in what looked like a bedroom. A single bed with a corkboard above it – covered in grinning photos, postcards, what looked like a colour-coordinated timetable. *Chloe's bedroom.* But her face was set, not smiling, almost sulky. She looked tired, there were shadows under her eyes. Her hair, unlike the other photos where it was loose and teased into curly blonde waves, was pulled back into a bun. You could see a pair of jeans draped over the bed behind her. *Skinny.* Like the kind Freddie wore.

'It doesn't prove anything, Freddie. We can turn this over to the Child Exploitation and Online Protection Centre. See if they can get the images taken down. This reinforces the theory that Chloe took her own life, but it doesn't help us with Lottie, and she's my focus right now.'

She thought of Lottie's pretty face, those eyes, the blood smeared across her forehead, and the floor wobbled under her feet. But she couldn't just *forget* Chloe. She deserved justice too. She couldn't let it stop at this. 'Look – it's like they're trading images of her.' There were names of the posters: *XXXSchlong: I've got one of her in her bikini.* She pointed them out to Nas. 'And here, look, someone calling themselves Liam says, "I've got one of her tit." That could be Will, posting under a different name?' Freddie was scrolling back through the thread to the beginning. 'Loads of them are from this guy called Liam. He started the thread on the message board. It must be Will.'

'We need to stay focused on Lottie.' Nas was jabbing her notepad with her pencil.

As soon as they were getting somewhere with Will she'd shut the conversation down. Freddie wanted the truth, but Nas was fixated on doing things to the letter of the law. She believed that way would lead to justice. But if what she said about needing to focus on Lottie made sense, why were they still here? 'Why are you asking to speak to Melisha and Ruby again?'

'This is all backwards. We should be doing this properly – with a responsible adult,' Nas said.

'Ms Bradshaw seems responsible to me,' Freddie said.

'We should have spoken to their parents.' She jabbed a hole in the paper. Tore a page off and threw it in the bin in the corner. 'But we don't have time. I don't like working like this.'

'You're doing that thing you used to do when you were stressed!' Freddie said.

'What thing?' Nas looked irritated.

'Talking to yourself. First sign of madness.'

'I am not.' Nas's nostrils flared. 'This is not helping, Freddie.'

'Neither is this if you think these pics of Chloe are nothing to do with Lottie. Why are we talking to Melisha and Ruby again?'

'In case it is. If Chloe didn't send them to William, then who did she send them to? There's a potential boyfriend. Someone who so far has kept themselves out of the investigation.'

Could that person be involved with Lottie as well? There was a knock at the door and Ms Bradshaw walked in with Melisha behind her.

'Ruby's feeling a little unwell after our earlier chat. I think it's best you don't speak to her without notifying her parents first,' the teacher said.

'Are we in trouble?' Melisha's voice was panicked.

'No one is in any trouble,' Nas smiled. It was alarming how quickly she could move from stressed to calm, concealing her true feelings. What else had she hidden? 'We know about the photos. The ones of Chloe in her underwear, and without her underwear.' Nas spoke as if she were saying sorry, as if she were responsible.

The girl's pencilled eyebrows disappeared under a mountain of thick, wavy hair. With no warning she burst into tears. Freddie blinked in surprise.

'It's okay, Melisha.' Ms Bradshaw stepped forward and put a protective arm across her shoulders. The girl buckled, slumped into the teacher, suddenly looking very young, and Freddie reminded herself that in the eyes of the law these were children. And maybe that was a good thing.

'Did you know about the photos?' Nas said softly.

'We didn't want to say,' Melisha sniffed. Nas pulled a tissue from the box in front of her and handed one to the girl. 'We didn't want to get her in trouble. And we didn't want her parents finding out.'

'Did Chloe send the photos to the Are You Awake site?'

'No! Well, not at first,' Melisha said. A sob caught in her throat.

'Not at first?'

'After the first one appeared she tried to get it taken down, but the site said she had to prove she was who she said she was.' Melisha's mascara was sliding from her eyes. She looked at Ms Bradshaw and then back at Nas. 'They said the only way she could prove it was her in the photo was if she took a photo in her underwear and sent it in to them.' Freddie thought of the image of Chloe in her yellow underwear, unsmiling, face grim. *The evil bastards.*

'Let me guess,' Nas sighed. 'They then posted that image on the site?'

113

'Yeah,' Melisha said. 'Chloe was, like, panicking then. She didn't know where the first image came from.'

'The one where you can see her breast?'

'Yeah, it was an accident. It was a new top she was photographing. She said as soon as she saw it she deleted it.'

Nas frowned. 'She didn't send it to anyone?'

'No.' Melisha's gaze dropped to the tissue she was now shredding in her lap. 'But I always thought maybe she sent it to Will. And he put it up there. We had a row about it.'

'When?' said Nas.

'The day before she…' Melisha's body shook as another sob broke free. 'I just wanted her to say it was her – that she'd sent it in. She could be like that sometimes: attention seeking, you know?' Freddie found herself nodding. 'But by then she was going crazy. Like it got way out of hand. Everyone had them. These photos. And she kept saying she hadn't sent them to anyone and…' She broke off, her eyes, wet with tears, looked haunted, frightened. Poor kid: the last conversation she'd had with her friend had been a row, and then her friend had killed herself. Freddie shivered. She and Nas had some idea of what that was like.

Nas spoke softly. 'The best thing you can do to help Chloe now is tell me what happened.'

'He, someone, they put her phone number on there,' Melisha said. Freddie dug her nails into her chair.

'On the website?' Nas asked.

Melisha nodded.

The fuckers. Freddie'd read enough about female journalists who'd been doxxed – had their contact details published online – to know what came next.

'She started getting all these messages from men and stuff. They started texting her. Gross stuff. And nasty stuff.' Melisha wadded the shredded tissue into a ball. 'It started getting worse. She was frightened. Really frightened.'

Ms Bradshaw looked as if she'd been slapped in the face.

'And she didn't tell anyone?' Nas asked.

'No.' Melisha shook her head. 'She was terrified her dad would find out. They're always going on at us not to take naked selfies. Like, we all know that. And Chloe promised she hadn't sent the first one to anyone. That she'd deleted it immediately. She just wanted them to stop.'

And there it was: the gap between the children and the adult world. Teens too frightened to ask the very people who could have helped. Freddie wondered if 'Liam' and the other users of Are You Awake were the same age as Chloe, or older. Grown men sending abusive threatening messages to a teen girl... Her stomach turned at the thought. She tapped her phone to scroll through the thread again. What kind of person would do this to a kid? It had to be a power play: they got off on her distress.

'Thank you, Melisha. You've been very brave,' Nas said. 'Ms Bradshaw has explained that we may need you to go through this again with some colleagues of mine. To see if we can find who did this to Chloe. This constitutes harassment, and we will try to bring them to justice.' Melisha nodded, her face taking on a steely look. Freddie recognised it as love. She would put herself through this, break the code of silence among teen girls, to try and help her friend. Even if it was too late for Chloe. But perhaps it wasn't too late for Lottie? Nas was still talking as something weighty settled in Freddie's stomach. She clicked out of the thread dedicated to Chloe and into the main message board of Are You Awake.

'I have just one more question for you, Melisha. Was there anyone new in Chloe's life, a boy perhaps, someone else you might be trying to protect? No one she mentioned in passing?' Nas pushed.

'No. Those last few weeks, she was… messed up. Paranoid. She kept thinking she was being followed. Because of the texts, I guess. She was obsessed by this white van, but like, there's hundreds of white vans? She had a go at Ruby once. Accused us of putting the photo online. It was mad – we'd never even seen it before it started going round school…'

The girl's voice drifted away as Freddie's eyes locked onto the screen. A new thread. Started by 'Liam'. *Hottie Lottie Burgone.* The heavy lump in her stomach seemed to crack, spreading acid through her. She clicked on the thread: photos of Lottie in tight-fitting exercise tops; photos of Lottie in a bikini on a beach in a yoga pose; a photo of Lottie, pouting, smiling straight at the camera, leaning forwards, the phone visible in her hand in the mirror, angled down, topless.

'Nas?' Freddie said. Nas looked at her, she saw the flicker of a muscle in her friend's neck. *The recognition.* It must be seeping from her very skin: the ominous dread. Freddie pointed at her phone. *You need to see this.*

'Ms Bradshaw, can you make sure Melisha gets back to class all right? We'll be in touch.'

The teacher looked at Freddie as if she might say something. Guessing from the look on her face she'd known nothing about this maelstrom of horror that was right under their noses. 'Come on, love. Let's get you some water. Maybe a cup of tea.'

Nas waited until they'd left and the door had closed behind them. 'What is it?'

Freddie turned the phone towards her old school friend. She saw her look at the screen, take in what she was seeing.

'Is that Lottie? On the same site?'

Freddie nodded. 'She has her own thread. Like Chloe. What does it mean?'

Nas already had her phone out. When she spoke, her tone was flat, like she'd had the life sucked out of her. 'It means we've got a lot of explaining to do.' She held the mobile to her ear, turned away from Freddie and spoke into the handset. 'DI McCain, please. It's Sergeant Cudmore. It's urgent.'

Chapter 17

Wednesday 16 March

14:58
T – 18 hrs 32 mins

Nas stalked out of the school reception, leaving Freddie to sign them out. The receptionist, her face a slapped arse, handed her a pen. Freddie's mind was reeling with images: Chloe in her knickers and bra, looking miserable; Lottie pouting seductively at the camera; Lottie gagged and bleeding. She thought of different photos too, ones she'd taken and sent to others. *Lovers*. She and her mates, Vic and Hannah from uni, they'd had a phase of sending Snaps of their boobs. It was a laugh. A tit-off. Squashed together, nips out in a bathroom, stupid faces. Once, she'd turned her nipples into eyes and drawn a smile in eyeliner on her stomach. Then they'd run out of steam, or found better things to do, or better people to send naked pics to. She wasn't bothered who saw her tits. They were natural. No reason why it was fine for blokes to walk around topless, when it wasn't for women. She'd written an article about the #FreeTheNipple campaign. Grown angry at those who'd shamed women for breastfeeding in public, even though the thought of actually doing that herself grossed her out. She'd been socialised so successfully into believing tits were sexual things that she felt queasy about their real function. Then again, having children seemed an alien prospect. Even when she hadn't been back living with her parents, she'd only made it as far as a sofa in Dalston. Babies, children, having a family of her own… Those felt as realistic as getting a mortgage and paying off her student loan.

Outside, Nas was still on her phone; she'd walked down the road away from her. She was gesturing with one hand as she spoke, but Freddie couldn't hear the words. Just to the right of the gates, sitting on the steps of the kind of twee wooden door that would've made Cath Kidston come, were three girls. Bundled under scarves, she saw the smart casual navy-blue clothes she presumed was sixth-form dress code. They were smoking. She glanced at Nas. She didn't look like she was about to finish, and Freddie didn't fancy heading back to the pass agg DC Green. She walked towards the girls; they were chatting, laughing, each a phone in hand, ciggies tucked in their fingers behind. A world away from the horror she was tumbling around in.

'Good thing I ain't a teacher,' she said.

They stopped talking and looked up at her. One, her face prettier than the other two, even though she had the least amount of make-up on, shielded her eyes from the sun with a small white hand. 'Can we help you?'

Polite, middle-class kids: this was as confrontational as they got. What would it be like to have naked photos of you shown to others in this world? 'Can I bum a cigarette?' She felt ancient standing in front of them. A different tick box: 18–21, 22–25. Jesus, she'd be twenty-five this time next year!

The girl who'd spoken shrugged and pulled the packet from her jeans. Freddie took one. 'Cheers.' She felt the familiar weight on her lips. 'Got a light?'

One of the girls held up a yellow plastic one. Freddie shielded the wind. Inhaled. Felt the warm smoke. Leant back. Exhaled. 'You go to Romeland High?'

'Yeah.' The girl with the fingerless gloves narrowed her eyes. What'd she done to be made Queen Bee of this little clique?

'Did you know Chloe Strofton?'

'The girl who killed herself?' The girl with the lighter sounded vaguely disgusted.

'Yeah.'

'So sad.' Fingerless gloves girl's eyelids fluttered. 'A tragic waste.'

Freddie had the feeling this wasn't the first time she'd said this. She sounded like a government spokesperson after a national tragedy: sympathetic but removed. It was a reminder that teens could be cold, calculating, capable of more than you might suspect.

'She was in year eleven. I didn't know her, but I saw her around.' She touched her clavicle lightly, making it personal. Making it about her. Just the kind of girl who wouldn't give two hoots about Chloe in real life.

Freddie reminded herself that just because she and Nas and Gemma, Chloe's sister, hadn't been in the cool crowd, it didn't mean that Chloe hadn't pulled it off. *Pretty. Popular. Good at school. Boyfriend.* All the stuff you needed to succeed at being a teen girl. Before it all went wrong. 'Did you hear anything about some nude photos of Chloe being circulated?'

To give them credit they looked shocked. 'No,' fingerless gloves girl said. 'Why would someone do that?'

'Rookie error,' said the other girl, earning herself an evil look from the third and resolutely silent girl. Her heart-shaped face was pink, her lips pursed into a look of – what? Distaste? Panic? Freddie settled on recognition.

'Thanks for the fag.' Nas was coming up the road, a look of anger on her face. *Busted. Shouldn't be making small talk with the kiddies.*

'Are you the police?' Fingerless gloves girl eyed the rolled waistband of Freddie's jeans.

'No. But she is.' Freddie nodded at Nas. The girls stubbed their cigarettes out quickly, kicking them away, even though they were legally old enough to smoke. They ducked past Nasreen in a tight gaggle, heads down, looking at their phones. Back to teen world.

'What are you doing?' Nas said.

'Just getting a cigarette,' she said.

'From the children?'

'They were sixth formers.'

'You can't just go speaking to minors about a case,' Nas snapped. The tops of her ears were red.

'Wrong. I'm not police: I can do what I like.'

'What did you say to them?' Nas demanded.

'Nothing. I told you, I just asked for a fag!' She waved the cigarette about in the air.

'I thought you'd quit?'

'Jesus, what is this? Are you my mother? I fancied a fag. I asked for a fag. End of story.'

Nas looking unconvinced and started up the slope at a pace. Freddie had to take two steps at a time to keep up. 'What did your lot say about the photos?' She would've thought she'd be pleased. 'This is another link, isn't it? Between the two girls. Something other than us, I mean.' Nas stopped and it took everything she had not to plough into her suited back, holding the fag out so as not to catch her hair. 'Christ, watch it!'

Nas turned to face her. She'd lost the look of anger that had singed her ears moments before. Her eyebrows were knit together. Her eyes showed her tiredness. She looked like she'd had about as much sleep as Freddie had recently. Freddie sucked on the ciggie. 'Freddie, look…' She faltered.

'You aren't seriously pissed off that I've had a cheeky fag – I deserve one after the last couple of hours.'

'No, it's not that, it's…' She batted the smoke away. 'Look can you put that out a minute and just listen.' The red was appearing on her ears again.

Freddie dropped the cigarette, overzealously grinding it into the floor. 'Better?' Nas was getting annoying now.

'I was just talking to my boss.' She was waving her hands around, palms open, as if she were offering her something. 'And, well…'

'Spit it out, Nas.' Freddie thrust her hands into her pockets. 'It's cold out here.' Nas looked pained. She felt the smile fall from her face and smash on the floor, fear breaking round her feet. 'Has there been another message? Another photo? Is Lottie okay?' *Oh god.*

'No, it's nothing like that.' Nas looked desperate, as if she were willing her to do something. 'It's… Look, Freddie, I haven't exactly been straight with you.'

Freddie sucked her cheeks in. *I knew it.* A chill feeling trickled down her spine. Would she have left the house if it had been anyone else? Been so willing to leave the last few months behind? 'What do you mean?'

Nas had a look of sadness on her face. 'I haven't exactly told my boss about you.'

'What?' She was struggling to fit this together – a minute ago they'd found a link between Chloe and Lottie, another one. Admittedly not a nice one, but it was something. Her fingers closed round her phone. She wanted to check something. But now this, Nas going all weird on her. 'You were just talking to him, weren't you – on the phone?'

'That was DI McCain – Chips. He's my superior, yes, and I told him I was talking to you about the case.'

'So what's the problem?'

'I didn't tell anyone else.' Nas put out a hand to stop her from walking past. 'I didn't tell DI Saunders or DCI Burgone.'

'Lottie's brother?' Freddie frowned. 'Why?'

'He doesn't know I'm – we're – here. Well, he does now. We need to bring in the tech lads to look into the poster calling himself Liam on Are You Awake. See if we can track his IP address. I want to know where he got those photos from, and whether he knew Chloe in real life.'

'Do you think he could be linked to Lottie? I saw his name at least once in her thread.' She pulled the phone from her pocket. 'Let's have a look and see if he crops up any more. My money's still on it being Will though. Do you think he'd be capable of taking Lottie?'

'Freddie, you're not listening. I've really screwed up with this. I took a chance bringing you in.' Her eyes were wide, desperate.

'Yeah, and we found this website.' The photos on Are You Awake were a colourful blur as she shook her phone at her.

'Yes. But now I have to take what I have back in to the team. Saunders has just torn me a new one for going AWOL.' Nas's face was so stretched into contrition it looked painful.

'I?' Was she being given the brush off? 'You can't turn up at my house, with no warning, and just show me photos of dead and kidnapped girls, Nas. And then ditch me. You can't get me involved in something like this and then drop me!'

'It's not up to me.' Nas looked at the ground, at the smeared ash on the cobbled path. 'You've been really helpful, Freddie. I don't know if I'd have got this far without you.'

'Bullshit!' Freddie stabbed her finger towards Nas, whose reflexes apparently weren't dulled by lack of sleep; her hand shot up and closed over Freddie's finger before it connected with her breastbone. 'Ouch! Let go!'

'Sorry.' Nas dropped her hand.

'Sorry? Is that all you've got to say?' Freddie's temper bubbled up and over, words spewing from her mouth before she could catch hold of them. 'You thought I was good enough to help you on this ten minutes ago, when you came to my parents' house and practically begged me. And now, because some idiot in a uniform has said so, you've changed your mind? That's weak, Nas. Really fucking weak.' Nas's jaw was set; she had the feeling she was grinding her teeth. 'This is not school. This is not some stupid thing we did as kids.' She shuddered involuntarily at the mention of what they'd done before. 'This is serious. Lottie is missing, and I can help. Whoever has her sent me her photo, too – did you tell your boss that?'

'No. I…'

'Don't bow to some stuck-up copper because you're a *good little girl*. You're better than that! I'm better than that!' The last words rained out in a hail of spittle that settled on the street in tiny bubbles before they burst and vanished. Freddie exhaled. Nas was still looking at her, her eyes fixed somewhere just beyond hers, as if she were trying to see into her mind.

'You're right,' she said.

'What?'

Nas started off up the hill again. 'You're right. You are an asset to this case. We've got a new link between the victims, a possible lead. And you were part of that.'

'What?' Freddie was trying to keep up. How was she managing to walk even faster than before? Freddie was jogging to keep up, puffs of air coming out in short sharp bursts.

'I made a difficult call and it's paid off. DI Saunders will have to cope.'

As the cold air hit the back of her throat, mingled with the leftover nicotine, Freddie coughed. 'Can you just slow down!'

'We need to get back to the station. The sooner the better.'

She was getting a stitch. 'What time is it?'

Nas flicked her hand out and looked at her watch. 'We have just over eighteen hours.'

Freddie had broken into a full trot by the time they reached the car. Nas, and her long legs, folded into the front, sweeping the tail of her black coat behind her. Freddie threw herself into the back.

'DI Saunders and Chips have been trying to reach you, Sarge.' Green was immediately on them. The car smelt of coffee and sweaty pastry.

'We've had a photo message that confirms Lottie is being held against her will,' Nas said.

'Yes, I heard.' Green screwed up the paper bag in her lap and stuffed it into the door well. 'I put a cheeky call in to a pal on digital forensics – not good news I'm afraid. They can't get anything from it.'

Green jumped as Nas slammed her palm against the glove compartment. 'We need to get back to the office.' Freddie swallowed her rising panic.

'Are we dropping our guest off first?' Green jerked her head towards the back seat, trying to disguise her own apprehension at Nas's outburst.

'No. We're all going,' Nas answered.

Green looked confused, as if she might have misheard her.

Freddie almost felt sorry for her, as Nas snapped, 'Quickly please,' and the cop started the engine.

Freddie's breath calmed enough for her to force the words out. 'I think you're right about the fags.'

Green flicked on the lights, the houses and shops of St Albans splashed with blue flashes. They were going to London. Now. Fast. *She* was going back. Freddie tugged at the skin on her lip. Was she ready? They swung round a corner as the sun disappeared behind a cloud, stealing the bright colours, and washing everything in grey, before it flared blue. *Blue. Grey. Blue. Grey.* The wail of the siren filled the car. Freddie shivered. She didn't know if it was because of the drop in temperature or the nerves. Closing her eyes she saw Lottie's bloodied face. Opening them she saw London rushing towards her. What would be waiting for them?

Chapter 18

Wednesday 16 March

15:15
T − 18 hrs 15 mins

Nasreen tapped her fingers against her knee. Chips had told her, *This stays between you and me. No mention to Saunders, no mention to the guv.* And she'd blown it. Saunders's words rang in her ears. He'd actually snatched the phone from Chips – or at least that's what it sounded like. 'Asking a civilian because you couldn't do the job yourself? Is that what you call proper police work?' She hadn't been able to get a word in as he kept going. 'I don't care what they taught you at your old station, but that's not how we do things on Gremlin. Get rid of her and get your sorry arse back here now.'

She'd managed a 'But…' before he'd torn into her again.

'Just be thankful the guv's under too much pressure for me

to haul you in front of him and make you explain yourself. Try something like this again and I'll personally march you out the fucking building.'

Then he'd hung up. Actually cut her off. She kept replaying it in her mind, growing more incredulous each time. A part of her wanted to believe Saunders was so threatened by her presence in the team that he was behaving like this to drive her out. Or reinforce the hierarchy. But his vitriol was so great, it felt personal. He really did doubt her ability. He really did think she was threatening the investigation. Even though she'd turned up a result: a link between Chloe and Lottie. Together Freddie and she had uncovered explicit images of first Chloe and then Lottie. Both girls were on Are You Awake. She didn't believe in coincidence, she believed in reasonable doubt. Likelihoods. The truth you saw under the lies people told. And could she lie now? She was building her argument, aware that as they got closer to London, closer to the office, she would have to explain herself. Explain why she hadn't only deceived Saunders and Burgone once, but why she was wilfully doing it again. *Get rid of her,* he'd said. But Freddie was here in the car. Eating a croissant on the back seat. She was taking them the very person she wanted to hide from them.

'Did you think Chloe was taking drugs?' Freddie's voice rang out from the back seat, dragging her into the here and now. She was scribbling notes onto a napkin, croissant crumbs everywhere.

Nasreen hadn't seen anything that hinted at Chloe being involved in drugs at all. 'No, did you?' It was nagging at her.

'Will seems the type to buy tea leaves thinking it's hash. I had a mate in uni who...'

'Can I remind you, before you go any further with that sentence, that Green and I are members of the law,' Nasreen interrupted. This was all she needed. Though she caught the faint hint of a smile from Green.

'Well why'd you ask then?' Freddie looked up from her phone.

'*I didn't*. You brought it up.' Nasreen could sense Green listening keenly. She'd been unfair to snap at her earlier: it wasn't her fault Saunders was furious at her. If she could just keep a lid on Freddie's quirkier aspects…

'In the interview – why did you ask the girls about it?'

'Because Chloe Strofton died of a heroin overdose.' Nasreen heard Freddie's pen clatter against her phone. She was starting to feel sick from turning round. She looked at the car in front of them, read the number plate in her mind. That was supposed to help.

'Heroin? Where the hell did she get that from?' Freddie was sounding excited. 'Seriously. I doubt she'd ever even seen magic mushrooms! The riskiest thing those kids do is sniff Pritt Stick.'

Green snorted.

'It doesn't strike me as the kind of school that has a big drug problem,' said Nasreen. 'But you can never tell – the dealers get everywhere.'

'I can attest to that,' said Green, as she signalled to change lanes. 'I did a stint with the NCA.'

'I thought they were basketball? No – wait – that's NBA,' Freddie said.

'I don't think the National Crime Agency would be thrilled with that mix-up,' Green said drily. Nasreen smiled despite herself.

Freddie was tapping her pen against the phone. 'So someone sourced it for her?'

'It's possible,' said Nasreen.

'Someone could have stuck it in her as well?'

She winced. 'The thought had occurred to me, yes.' Freddie didn't mean to sound cruel, but she had a habit of externalising what was going on. A hangover from being a journalist: as if she were seeing it all from two steps back, making it fit a story. It was a good trick to have, one many police officers used. Flippant remarks, black humour: a good coping mechanism. But it was one Nasreen didn't like. It was important not to lose sight of the human cost at the heart of their cases. That was what drove you on, made you look longer, harder, keep trying.

'Our boy Liam's on here 123 times. Chloe's thread goes on for pages, I haven't read it all, though there's plenty of nasty stuff by the looks of it.'

Nasreen braced her hand against the glove box as Green braked sharply at a roundabout.

'Sorry about that, I thought they were going. Think the blue lights panicked them.'

'We'll get them printed when we get to the station.'

'He started it. The thread, I mean,' Freddie said. They curved round the slip road and onto the M1. Thankfully the traffic was moving, things would be better now: *a straight line*. No stopping and starting. 'And Lottie's.'

'Liam started the thread about Lottie as well?' She'd given the website details and the name Liam to Chips. They'd soon know who owned the site, assuming it hadn't been encrypted. It wasn't a dedicated revenge porn site, or at least that didn't seem to be its MO based on the threads she and Freddie had scrolled through. Finding out who this Liam was could be the first serious lead they'd had. Hiding her hunch from Saunders had been worth the gamble; she tried to stoke her resolve.

'He hasn't commented as many times as he has on the Chloe one – twenty-six times by my reckoning. But Lottie's thread is more popular. It's got over 2,000 comments. She's Lottie Londoner isn't she?'

Nasreen twisted to look at her. *Another link?* 'You said you didn't know the victim?'

'I don't. Not in real life. I did a piece once on the rising stars of Instagram. She was on the list.'

'Right. Of course.' That made sense. Last year Nasreen had read back through some of Freddie's published articles: 'Why You Should Send Your Used Tampons to the Chancellor of the Exchequer'. 'Twenty Ways Your Best Friend at Twelve Will Always Be Your BFF'. That one had been about her: them. It made her uneasy that there was yet another connection between Freddie and Lottie and Chloe.

'Can we have some music?' Freddie asked.

'Erm, yes. I suppose. Green, is that okay?'

The DC sighed and nodded.

'How does this work?' Nasreen pressed buttons and the radio blared into life. 'Can't Fight the Moonlight' by LeAnn Rimes filled the car. 'How's that?'

'Awful.' Freddie wrinkled her nose. 'Has this got Bluetooth?'

'That's your department, Green.'

The DC looked irritated, stabbing at the radio to silence it. 'Yes.'

'Aces! Got ya.' Two pips, like the speaking clock, rang out through the speakers. And then a voice, a woman, husky, amused. *We always thought that we were not a rock'n'roll band, but it sure feels like rock'n'roll* – a laugh – *over here tonight.* And then the beat kicked in, filling the car with synth guitar. The staccato lyrics, rhythmic, like a chant: *We don't play guitars.* Green tapped her finger against the steering wheel in time, an actual smile on her face.

'Who's this?' Nasreen asked.

'Chicks on Speed.' Freddie was looking at the gathering warehouses that were starting to blur the edges of the countryside, marking the start of London. Had she really not been back since then? Freddie nodded her head in time to the track. It was shouty. Defiant. Infectious. Just what she needed. Nasreen let the song lift her, inflate her with confidence. They could do this. And then she looked at her watch. T – 17 hours 50 minutes.

Chapter 19

Wednesday 16 March

16:00
T – 17 hrs 30 mins

Freddie's skin was alive, as if it were crawling with a thousand ants: they were in her hair, her nose, her mouth, she couldn't breathe. *A panic attack. Try to remain calm.* What had her counsellor said? *Acknowledge your feelings. Allow them to pass through you.* Fuck that! Her hands groped for the switch to open the window. The car filled with the air and rush and noise of the motorway.

'Freddie?'

It was the same voice that called to her that night. As her blood sprayed against the wall. She could see him: his face misted with her blood. He swung again. Again. She was going to die.

'Freddie, you're having a panic attack.' Nas's hair flew in the wind. Cars screamed past, shunting her from the past to now. To terror. Her ears would explode. Her head would explode.

Try to focus on Nas. Her smell. Clean. Soap. She grasped at the hand on her knee. Her prescription was on the bedside table. Had she taken it this morning?

'Shall I pull over, ma'am?' She'd forgotten Green.

What had happened? She must have fallen asleep. Did she dream, did she cry out? A jagged breath clawed its way into her lungs.

'Do you want to stop, Freddie?'

She could see nothing but Nas now. Her head was tilted so the air from the open window pushed her dark hair streaming away from her face. Like she was standing on a beach. They'd been to the beach as kids. Staying in the Cudmores' caravan. Huddled together in a single bed. Salt in the air. Her shoulders relaxed.

'Freddie?'

The wind dropped: they were turning off the motorway. In her peripheral vision she saw three-storey Victorian terraces; trees, almost as old as the houses, thrusting up out of the pavement. They hadn't even reached proper London yet. They were in the suburbs and she'd already freaked out. Weakening her grip on Nas's hand, she felt a little squeeze in return. The frenzied gulps subsided.

'Sorry.' The words bruised. Her throat ached from the tension.

'It's okay.' Nas's professional voice was back, but she still looked worried.

Freddie nodded. Swallowed, trying to lubricate her throat. 'I fell asleep. I think.' *Typical.* She'd barely slept for weeks and now here, when she needed to be awake, alert, she'd managed to doze off. 'Good timing, huh?'

'Impeccable.' Nas lifted her hand away from her knee, and with it any final lingering hints of the closeness of the past. 'You sure you're okay?'

Freddie remembered Green was in the car and felt her neck grow hot. How to make yourself look like a tool in front of the fuzz. 'Fine. Sit down. Show's over.'

Nas looked like she was going to say something, but thought better of it. She turned, sat back in her seat. She heard her exhale.

'Not long now – ten minutes. Unless we need to stop? My partner gets panic attacks,' said Green, twisting to look at her. Instead of the patronising look of victory Freddie had expected, she looked concerned.

'I'm sorry to hear that, Green,' Nas said.

'Yeah, well, she's got a stressful job,' Green said.

Freddie tried to imagine Green consoling someone, comforting them like Nas had her. 'She a cop as well?'

'No, social worker,' Green said.

'Tough gig.' It was weird to think of Green as a person outside of this nightmare, with a life, a home, a lover. Silence descended on the car, as if they were all trying to reposition after the fabric of reality had been torn with Freddie's panic attack. It was too visceral. Tangible. It betrayed how fragile they all were. Reminded them of Lottie. Of her terror.

'Do you believe Melisha didn't know she was the cover story the night Chloe disappeared?' she asked.

Nas stared ahead. She must have felt sick turning round to talk. 'I can't see why she'd lie about that.'

'To keep out of trouble?' Green suggested.

'Chloe definitely lied about where she was going,' Freddie said. 'She planned it.'

'Or she planned to stay somewhere else,' Nas said.

The traffic was bunching up, vehicles pulling slowly, labouredly aside to let them and their blue flashing lights through. The buildings were growing bigger, the sky disappearing as they stretched upwards, flexing. 'What did she take with her? Did she have overnight stuff?'

'Nothing was found on her apart from her school bag,' Nas said. 'Her parents reported nothing was missing. Her toothbrush, her pyjamas, it was all still at home.'

'She said she was staying at Melisha's, but she didn't take any things? And they didn't notice?' Her belt tightened across her as she leant forward to see Nas's face.

Green muttered at the van in front of them that hadn't pulled far enough over.

'They're good parents,' Nas said too quickly. Her fingers were still drumming against her knee, as if she were counting the beat.

Were they? They hadn't noticed Gemma was distressed eight years ago. Perhaps they didn't pay enough attention to their children.

'Both her mum and dad left for work before she left for school, according to their statement.'

Nas's phone sounded and Freddie felt hers vibrate in her hand.

'It's a Snapchat notification,' said Nas, pulling her phone from her pocket and catching her eye.

'Is it another message?' Green didn't take her eyes from the road. 'What is it?'

Freddie's mouth was stripped dry; her ribs tightened around her, threatening to drag her back under. She wanted to get out the car. To get away. To run. Not to look, not to see. It was a video clip. Across it was a banner message: *Watch me.* She fought to keep control of her breathing, her whole body shaking as she stared at the screen. The camera adjusted to the same dark room as before, focusing on Lottie's flash-lit face. Bleached white. Terrified. Gagged. She was frantically struggling, twisting from side to side. Freddie felt the floor fall away as a gloved hand appeared in the shot, a long silver knife glinting in the light. *No!*

136

'Oh my god!' Nas cried.

'What is it? Shit – there's nowhere to pull over,' Green said.

Freddie's heart was in her mouth, battering against her teeth as the knife moved towards Lottie. *This couldn't be happening. She couldn't be watching this.* Lottie was screaming under the tape. Her face stretched in anguish. Freddie wanted to look away as a second gloved hand grabbed Lottie by her hair, yanking her towards the camera. *No.* The knife blazed like lightning as it swung down towards the captive girl. And the feed cut out. Freddie's mind fought to process what it was seeing. Lottie bleached, terrified, gagged, desperate, trying to escape, the knife flashing through the air – cut. Terror. Desperate. Knife. Cut.

'Jack can't see this!' Nas was saying.

'Can we copy the video?' Green shouted.

'There's an app – I don't have it!' Nas was screenshotting the video again and again, as the counter wound down. 'We need to get back to the office now. The tech lads might be able to retrieve this.'

Freddie was aware of the car lurching forward, that she was being thrown from side to side, that they were powering through the streets. Someone was speaking, their voice trembling, jerky, the words difficult to make out. It was her. She was talking. As the buildings of Westminster rose either side of them, the same question fell from her like tears: *What happened after the camera cut?*

137

Chapter 20

Wednesday 16 March

16:20
T − 17 hrs 10 mins

'Is she dead?' Freddie kept saying it. She was pale with shock.

Nasreen didn't know the answer. She kept a hand on Freddie's back, feeling her shivers, steering her through the double-height reception. The knife sweeping towards Lottie played on loop in her mind. *Watch me*: that's what the message had said. The perp had given them a show.

Green was in front of them, quiet following the video. Chips knew they were on their way up. They'd received the message too: Chips, Saunders, Burgone. The thought of Jack seeing that, of what he must be imagining right now, bit into her and clamped on. It was even more important to have Freddie here now. She'd tell them Freddie had been sent the messages too. That this *was* linked to the Hashtag Murderer case; that the person who had Lottie wanted them all to watch.

Green reached the bulletproof glass security doors that shielded the offices from the reception. She handed her warrant card over to the guard, glancing back to give Nasreen a worried look. Green buttoned her suit jacket before she was waved through the metal detector. As if neatening herself might make sense of the situation.

'Freddie, I need you to listen to me. Are you okay to do this?' She couldn't have Freddie going to pieces. Whoever had Lottie was toying with them. 'If you're not strong enough – mentally – then no one will blame you…'

'I'm okay.'

Her eyes were glassy and her skin felt cold as Nasreen placed a hand on her arm. 'I can't have you having a panic attack in front of Saunders or Chips.'

'Harsh, Nas.' Freddie's eyes met hers for the first time since the car. It was a good sign.

'I know you haven't had any relevant training.'

'There's training for getting a video like that?' Freddie looked incredulous.

Fair point. 'No, not exactly. But I need to know that if it comes down to it, you won't fall apart.' She meant it. This investigation wouldn't make collateral damage of Freddie. Nasreen would keep her safe. Keep her close. 'I need to know you can cope with this.'

'You need to work on your trust issues.' Freddie was warming up, getting angry again. That was good. That was normal.

'*We* need to make sure we handle this properly. I need you to watch what you say. In fact, let me do the talking. DI Saunders will not be thrilled you're here.'

'DI Saunders hasn't met me yet,' Freddie shrugged.

Nasreen tried to imagine what Saunders, with his tailor-made suits and pressed shirts, would make of Freddie's frayed jumper and scuffed boots. 'That message wasn't a ransom note – whoever made it wanted us to see what they were doing to Lottie. They wanted us to watch. You included.'

'Do you think she's… still alive?'

Before she had to answer, a voice called from reception. 'DS Cudmore?' Lorna was sitting behind the huge curved desk, waving like they were old friends.

She forced a smile in return, pulling Freddie with her. 'Lorna, I need to sign in Freddie Venton. She'll need a security pass to get upstairs. She's working as a consultant on an active case.'

'Oh, of course.'

Nasreen watched Lorna's delicate fingers fly over the keyboard. The printer whirred into life and the girl leant down to pull a strip from the machine.

'Is there any news on DCI Burgone's sister?' Lorna's eyes were wide with concern as she slid the printed strip into a plastic lanyard for Freddie.

Freddie tensed next to her. *Don't give anything away.* Case details weren't to be discussed with civilians. 'Nothing yet.'

Lorna gave a little shudder and rallied herself. 'I'll need you to sign in please, ma'am.'

Freddie caught the vase of lilies on the reception with her elbow as she reached for the pen. 'Sorry.' She was too antsy. She scribbled her signature and looked up at the girl. As if she were trying to root herself in the room. She knew how she felt. 'You look familiar. Have we met before?'

'I don't think so.' Lorna looked from Freddie to Nasreen, as if it might be a trick question.

'You need to wear this.' Nasreen gave the lanyard to Freddie. 'At all times.'

'Got it!' Freddie snapped her fingers and Lorna jumped. Nasreen wished she would shut up. They were wasting time they didn't have. 'You look like that YouTuber!'

'Oh no,' Lorna blushed. 'I get that a lot though. I know the one you mean.'

She cut over Freddie's nervous yammering. 'Do you have a message for me, Lorna? You called me over?'

'Oh yes! That's right.' The girl smiled. 'Not a message – a package.' She spun her chair to pick up a large white box from behind her.

Alarm flooded through her. She wasn't expecting anything. No one other than the team knew she worked at this address. You couldn't receive things at work. She hadn't even told her parents what road the office was on. Could the person who'd been clever enough to snatch Lottie without anyone seeing, tenacious enough to source the private numbers of the team, wily enough to evade detection by the tech lads, be capable of finding the office? *What happened after the video cut?*

Lorna turned round, holding the box. It was basketball sized. Wrapped completely in masking tape. Watertight. On one side were printed words that rooted Nasreen to the floor. It must have showed on her face.

'What's wrong?'

'I need you to put that down very carefully, Lorna.'

Freddie stepped away from the desk.

'What is it?' Lorna's lip trembled.

Without taking her eyes from the girl she activated her radio. 'This is Detective Sergeant Nasreen Cudmore. We have a State 14. Suspect package delivered to reception.'

'Oh my god,' Lorna's face was ashen.

'It's from them,' Freddie gasped.

'Lorna, I need you to very carefully place the package down on the desk in front of you.' Nasreen was aware of noise around her. The fire alarm began to scream. An evacuation.

'Help me!' Lorna said.

'Please make your way quickly and calmly from the building,' the security guard boomed.

'You're okay, Lorna, you're doing great. Just put it down – that's it.' The girl's hands were shaking. Nasreen braced. It could be a bomb, or chemical. 'Freddie, I need you to go outside.'

'I'm not leaving you.'

Watertight. Blood-tight. What had happened after the camera had cut? What was in the box? They had to preserve any evidence – if it wasn't about to blow them all sky high. 'That's it. Good girl.'

Lorna put the box down, her fine fingers juddering. Nasreen braced. Nothing happened. Lorna looked like she might cry. If it was an explosive device, it could still trigger. If it was biological, she could have been contaminated. 'I need you to not touch any part of yourself. Can you do that?' The girl nodded. 'You're okay. I just need to get you checked over first, all right? Paramedics will be here soon.'

In the corner of her eye she saw the glass door to the offices swing open. The bulk of Chips running towards them. 'Cudmore?'

The security guard blocked him. 'Sir, I'm going to have to ask you to step outside.'

'Get off me, lad. That's my sergeant.'

'You need to leave the building,' the guard was shouting. 'This is a full evacuation.'

'Secure the cordon, lad,' Chips commanded. 'What is it?' He was at her side. Panting. She still had her hand up, a signal to hold Lorna in place. Keep her calm. She couldn't let her out until they knew any chemical risk had been contained.

'Suspect package,' Freddie said.

'Who're you?' Chips said. Nasreen looked away from Lorna for just a second. Heard the girl whimper and snapped her head back. There were too many of them here. Too many at risk.

'Freddie Venton.' Freddie's voice was shaking.

Sweat pooled on Nasreen's lower back. She itched to tug her shirt free, but didn't dare bring her arm down: it was pacifying Lorna. She'd brought Freddie here; she was putting her life at risk. 'Can you take Freddie outside please, sir.'

'Not until you tell me what the hell is going on...' Chips's voice collapsed as he caught sight of the words, printed in capitals on the top of the package: *WATCH ME*.

Chapter 21

Wednesday 16 March

16:55
T – 16 hrs 35 mins

Nasreen watched as Green flashed her ID at the uniformed officer guarding the cordon and he lifted it for her to duck under. Behind them, the bomb disposal unit were packing their long-armed robot back into their van. The officer who'd investigated the package, resembling a large, threatening mole in his protective overalls and reinforced diving bell helmet, was now stripped of his weighty equipment. He was laughing with his team in an unremarkable t-shirt and trousers. What was it like to spend your life approaching what could be explosive devices by choice? She knew a lot of the unit were ex-army.

'Thought you could do with one of these.' Green held up a bag from Espress-oh's.

'You lifesaver, how did you get past the guard?' As potential contamination risks, Lorna, Chips, Freddie and she had been filed out to a separate area. Swabbed down and scanned in the same way she imagined the package had been. All of them were clean. No traces of explosives. No traces of biological or chemical weaponry.

'I told him you were my boss and diabetic, and if I didn't get this to you, you'd be passing out.' Green opened the bag and passed over a coffee.

Nasreen grinned. 'No wonder he jumped to it: I've already caused them enough aggro.'

'I've got one for Chips, Venton, and the reception girl too.'

Chips and Freddie were sitting on the open back of a van just over from them. They'd managed to find some fags and someone daft enough to give them a lighter this close to a bomb scare. Lorna had proved herself more resilient than Nasreen had given her credit for. Once it was clear she was safe, she had been keen to get back inside. Especially as she'd left her handbag and phone there.

'Any sign of Saunders or the guv?' She knew Chips had spoken to Saunders on the phone.

'Nah, they were stuck round the back I think. They roped off two streets on both sides, had everyone stay inside and away from the windows.'

'And all for nothing, hey? That's going to win me some brownie points,' she grimaced. The money this charade would've cost. Had she overreacted? Two little words had caused all this. But the thought of what was in the box was still frightening. Sealed within all that tape. She didn't want to think what might be that shape and size. *Watch me.* You used your eyes to watch, didn't you? She tried to stem the scenarios that were running through her mind.

Green turned as Matt Snow, a senior crime scene manager,

emerged from inside the building, scanned the small crowd and headed for them. 'Here we go,' Green said.

'Sir.' Chips eased himself off the truck, stubbed his cigarette out and came to join her as they watched Matt walk the length of the street to reach them; a lone white SOCO-suited figure against the empty road and towering buildings.

'The moment of truth,' Chips muttered grimly. Out here they were shrouded in the cold shadows of the buildings behind them. The eerie silence of the evacuated street added to the feeling of unease. Even the pigeons had scarpered.

'McCain.' Matt came to a halt the other side of the fluttering tape. He could only be five foot eight, but he still curled his shoulders towards the ground, as if he were permanently trying to hide. He had a nice face when he smiled, but he seemed to do that rarely. This was the third time she'd worked with him. Each time a serious crime. 'This your party, is it?'

'I radioed it in,' said Nasreen.

'We had reason to believe we were dealing with something nasty, Matt,' Chips said. His hands in his pockets were an attempt to keep things casual; there'd be time to answer questions later. 'You open it up yet?'

'Thought you might want to see,' said Matt, looking at Nasreen, 'as you caused all this fuss.'

'Aye.' Chips stood forward, holding the tape for her to duck under.

Freddie's voice from behind made her jump. 'Can I come?'

'No,' Chips and Nasreen said in unison.

Freddie looked pissed off, but it was better this way. She didn't want to give her any more images to have nightmares over. Nasreen knew she was privileged to be going in with the DI, and tried to feel it. A big part of her wanted to stay far away from the package. 'Green, keep an eye on Freddie and Lorna. Hopefully it won't be too much longer before we can all get back.'

146

'Bloody freezing out here,' Freddie muttered as they walked off – Matt in front, Chips and Nasreen a stride behind; in formation, like flying ducks.

'Sir, I'm sorry about bringing Freddie back without clearing it.'

'I'd be thankful you had half the bomb squad keeping you and Saunders separated, lass.'

'The messages, the original note regarding Lottie, the photo, and the video – they were all sent to Freddie too.'

Chips cricked his neck to look at her. 'Why?'

'Whoever has Lottie, whoever is sending them, they want Freddie involved.'

'That's another link to your Hashtag Murderer case.'

'I know.' The more things stacked up, the more she doubted the prison officer's promises that no communication was getting in or out from Apollyon.

They were nearing the door; the glass front of the building loomed up, opaque from the cloudy sky, a grey marble tombstone.

'The SOCO team get anything off the package?' Chips asked.

'Whoever handled it wore gloves,' Matt answered. The reception had been transformed into a crime scene. The package was still on the desk. A glistening masking-tape hive, around which the suited SOCOs buzzed. Lorna had already confirmed it was a normal courier who delivered it – the one who brought the stationery supplies. It had been sent via a standard firm, picked up from a Mail Boxes in Angel. They had no cameras, and couldn't remember anything about who'd brought the package in. 'There was a hair caught in the tape: long, blonde.'

Nasreen's stomach hardened: Lottie had long blonde hair. The remaining SOCOs stood to the side as they drew near. Matt passed them gloves and masks. She tried to keep her breath

147

steady as she pulled the mask over her face, made sure all her hair was tied back. Chips's gloves snapped against his hands. Black powder marks covered the box where it had been dusted for prints. Matt picked up a scalpel from the reception, and she saw that he'd already cut a careful incision all the way round the top of the box.

'Ready?'

She didn't trust herself to speak.

'Aye,' said Chips. This was it. *Watch me.*

Matt carefully worked the scalpel round the remaining section of the top, disturbing as little of the material as possible. Behind her the SOCOs gathered. Waiting. She was glad her face was covered. Matt placed the scalpel down and with two hands he slowly lifted off the top. Nasreen caught sight of a weft of blonde hair and felt the floor give under her. Nightmares reared up from the box.

'Fucking hell,' Chips said.

'What is it?' someone asked from behind.

Matt had put his hand in and gently lifted out a ponytail of blonde hair, roughly shorn at the top, and still held in place by the pink band Nasreen recognised from the video of Lottie.

'He cut her hair off?' Chips sounded aghast. Angry.

She forced herself forwards and steeled herself to look into the box. Inside was a photo, printed from a normal printer on regular A4 paper – a grainy colour shot of Lottie's hair being held aloft like a trophy. In the background she could see the girl, tears streaming down her face. 'She's still alive.' She held it up to Chips. 'There's still time. We can still find her.'

Chapter 22

Wednesday 16 March

17:30
T – 16 hrs

Officers and support staff were filing back into the building. The excitable hum sounded like children returning to the classroom after sports day. Everyone was whispering about what might have been in the package. No one but the team would be told. Chips had spoken to Burgone on the phone, while Nasreen had arranged for the package to be prioritised at the lab. Matt Snow had packed Lottie's hair into a plastic evidence bag, dehumanising her further. *Who would do such a thing?* The need to look into the person calling himself Liam, who'd published the obscene images of Chloe and Lottie, burned brighter still. If he had her, they had to reach him fast. The photos, the video, and now Lottie's hair – it was escalating.

Nasreen made it to three metres from the office before DI Saunders caught up with her.

'What the hell do you think you're playing at, Cudmore?'

'All right, lad.' Chips indicated the empty meeting room. 'This isn't the place.'

Saunders ignored the door and stepped closer to her. His voice was restrained, simmering, ticking down to Armageddon. The fear of the explosion greater than the force itself. It was an interrogation technique she'd seen him use on suspects. 'You disobeyed a direct order bringing Freddie Venton here. That's a disciplinary offence, Sergeant.'

'Give over, Pete, we've lost enough time on this. I told you I cleared her to speak to the lass.'

'You've always been a sucker for a pretty face, Chips.'

A hot wash of anger poured over her. 'There are valid reasons to talk to Freddie in relation to this case. The suicide notes sent allegedly from Chloe Strofton and Lottie Burgone were both acrostics of "Apollyon." The perp also sent copies of Lottie's messages and videos directly to Freddie. Freddie was heavily involved in the Apollyon case: she could provide intelligence that could be key.'

'She's a civilian. She shouldn't be anywhere near this building,' said Saunders.

Chips folded his arms, his face unmoved. 'I've been around long enough to know that when someone offers you help on a case – especially one like this – you take it, Pete.'

'What help?' Burgone appeared round the corner. Her heart lurched. His tie was loosened at the collar, as if he'd been tugging at it. A hint of red rimmed his eyes. Had he been crying? Had he seen his sister's hair reduced to evidence in a plastic baggie?

Nasreen repressed the desire to reach out and touch him. Instead she seized her chance. 'Sir, I have reason to believe there is a possible link between the Apollyon case I worked on previously and…'

'Lottie?' he said, his eyes wide. 'Are you sure?'

'Not a hundred per cent, but enough to ask Freddie Venton, the woman who consulted on that case, to help us. If she can.'

'Your old school friend?' Burgone said.

This time she felt her ears burn. It sounded preposterous. 'She's a digital expert.'

'I'm not happy about this, guv,' Saunders said.

'They've turned up some good, and relevant, leads,' said Chips. She could kiss him.

'Are we any closer to finding who took Lottie?' His sister's name crashed and broke over his tongue.

'We're following up a number of enquiries,' Chips answered.

All of which had been delayed by the last hour's actions. Was that deliberate? Had the kidnapper sent the hair to slow them down?

'I'd like to keep Freddie involved, sir. In an advisory role. She's worked with the police before. My former DCI, Moast, will vouch for her.' *Hopefully.* They hadn't had the best working relationship, but ultimately she thought he'd been won round by Freddie's commitment, if nothing else.

'Do you think she'll be helpful, Chips?' asked Burgone.

'I think it's worth a gamble.'

Burgone seemed to weigh the options before him. 'Okay. Miss Venton stays.' Nasreen felt like punching the air. Saunders tutted. 'But she's not to go anywhere near the general public. I want her involvement kept on the quiet, and her movements restricted to this building. At no point are the press to get wind that we have anyone other than us working on the case. Do I make myself clear?'

He was looking at her, his eyes those of a boss. It was as if nothing had happened between them. Perhaps that was the way it was going to be. She pushed her hurt and confusion aside. 'Yes, sir.'

'I've just spoken to the superintendent.' Burgone looked uncomfortable. He wouldn't have told her about them? No, she was being ridiculous. 'She thinks it would be best if I stepped down.'

Nasreen felt her stomach drop away.

'None of us want that,' Saunders said. Chips shook his head.

'As things... *progress*,' Burgone said, 'I can't trust myself to make the best calls.'

If anything else was sent to them... As time ticked down to the deadline... It was too awful to think about. They all murmured their dissent. What would she do if it were her sister? Was it possible to be this close to a case and not allow yourself to be compromised? She'd been close to Chloe's parents once. But she hadn't told anyone about that.

'The superintendent thinks that if we catch the *bastard* who did this...' Burgone's words spat and fizzled to nothing on the ground.

Chips reached out and laid a hand on his shoulder. 'We'll get him, Jack.'

Burgone regained his composure. 'Yes, and when we do I don't want my involvement to risk the case in court.' Nasreen tried not to think of the Stroftons.

'I'm not going anywhere, and I'd appreciate it if you keep me up to date on any developments.' They nodded. 'And I'd like you to act up on this one, Pete,' he said to Saunders.

Shit.

'Pete has experience with a number of previous kidnap cases, and I know he'll make the right calls if necessary.'

'Of course,' said Chips. Nasreen felt sick. She might have got Freddie onto the team, but at what cost? Saunders distrusted her, and now he was in charge. Or at least he was for the next twenty-four hours. Again the timeframe loomed before her: a perfect before and after. Except she couldn't picture what the after looked like. Or just how bad it might be.

'Thank you.' Burgone's eyes dropped to the floor, as if he'd spent every ounce of energy he had left. They watched him walk down the corridor.

'Let's get on with finding this Liam lad.' Chips plodded through the office door.

Nasreen quickly went to follow him, but Saunders blocked her path. He put his face very close to hers, the smell of mint chewing gum strong on his breath. Her teeth clenched. He spoke quietly, but the menace in his words ran like cold fingers over her body.

'You may have charmed the boss and Chips, but I'm not such an easy play.'

Every muscle in her body was screaming to step backwards. She daren't breathe.

'I'm in charge now, and I'm watching you, Cudmore.'

Chapter 23

Wednesday 16 March

17:44
T – 15 hrs 46 mins

Green handed her another wad of paper churned out from the printer. Freddie saw the comments broken by the odd photo. *This was going to take time.* She looked at her phone. They had just under sixteen hours left until Lottie would be killed. She didn't doubt it now. Not after seeing her hair. Each time she closed her eyes the video replayed in her mind, the girl's frantic yanks to get away. How scared must she be? Chips's puffy face was puckered into a series of frowns; he'd told her and Green what to get on with. It'd taken all this time to get the reams of threads on Are You Awake printed. Time they didn't have. There was no sign of Nas. Saunders had barely looked at her.

'Is this Nas's desk?' She pointed at the only one with a box of tissues on it. 'Can I sit here?'

'Sure.' Chips's face relaxed into a smile, all the creases now pointing up. He seemed sound.

'You okay with half?' Green asked.

'I'm fast.'

Green raised her eyebrows in amusement.

Had she called her girlfriend to say she'd be late home? Freddie had texted her mum, said she'd gone to visit Nas. It wasn't a lie as such. Perhaps that's where Nas was – speaking to her parents. Or Lottie's brother. This place was a warren. Thank god they'd only been on the ground floor when the evacuation happened.

Nas's desk was spotless, obvs. Freddie opened a drawer, looking for a highlighter, and found one compartment of blue pens, one of red pens, one of pencils. Where were the screwed-up receipts? The chewed pens? The tights? The empty cans of deodorant? Chips's desk was piled high with papers, coffee mugs balanced like a totem pole. That was more like it. She selected two red pens from Nas's drawer, put one on the desk to use on the printouts, and one in the blue pen compartment. Saunders's desk was as regimented as Nas's, the only personal touch a framed photo of him with two other guys, his arm across the shoulder of one. They were all in lycra, gold medals round their necks, sweaty and grinning from whatever sporting event they'd just triumphed at. She shut the drawer as Nas entered.

'How many pages are there in total?' Freddie leafed through the pile of printouts.

Green's computer screen displayed Are You Awake in all its lurid glory, a photo of a woman in what looked like her early twenties, on all fours, naked, was visible from here. '167.'

She was grinding her teeth: still furious at the idiots who felt it was totally fine to share photos of women like this. Nas was crouched next to Chips, their conversation audible.

'The Are You Awake site is being run through Tor software,

which allows for anonymous communication,' Chips said. 'It's rerouting the site's internet traffic through multiple networks, so the tech lads have no way to find the real location or source of the site, or who's using it.'

'I thought that'd be too much to hope for.'

'Whoever hosts that site knows what they're doing. They're also using end-to-end encryption, something like SSL or TLS.'

'Can you say that again in English?' Nas asked.

'Transport Layer Security protocol,' DI Saunders said without looking up. 'They protect privacy between communication apps – it means we can't eavesdrop on any of their messages.'

He knew his stuff. It sounded like 4chan.

'There's nothing we can do to trace any of these posters?' Nas asked.

'Unlikely.' Chips pursed his lips. 'Even if we could, it isn't a job that'll be done in a few hours.'

This couldn't be a dead end. Scanning the printouts Freddie saw that each time someone posted on a thread, that thread would be moved to the top of the bulletin board. Putting the threads, and therefore the victims of Are You Awake, into chronological order would take time. She seemed to have all of the comments and photos that were dedicated to Chloe. Flicking back, she went to the first thread Liam had posted, and read the first comment:

[-] **Liam 17/01 (Sun) 17:55:09.**
Does anyone kno the cute blonde who worked in the Pepper Pot? Chloe was her name. I'd love to see pics of that specimen.

Freddie shuddered. *Specimen?* What a nasty freak: acting as if he was entitled to see photos of Chloe just because he liked her. Posts jumped out as she skimmed the rest of the thread:

[-] **Nostradamuspoo 17/01 (Sun) 17:55:59.**
Shes at my school. Romeland. I'd hit it.
[-] **Dudeman23 17/01 (Sun) 18:09:09.**
I got one in her bikini from her Facebook page.
[-] **Anonymous 17/01 (Sun) 18:09:42.**
MOAR!
[-] **AlexBlack 17/01 (Sun) 19:09:00**
I got better than that, dude. I'll message you.
[-] **Ratmanking 17/01 (Sun) 19:11:57**
Tight booty. Innocent face. Top marks. Yum.

It was infuriating that these guys were hidden behind the anonymity of the message board, while openly calling for photos that *should* have been private. And they got what they wanted: the photos started to appear. First one of Chloe in a bikini at an outside swimming pool with Melisha, smiling at the camera. Then a selfie in a vest top. Each one accompanied by an applause of sexual innuendo. And calls for MOAR. Freddie was fairly clued up on internet acronyms, but she'd had to Google MOAR. It was slang: a mash up of more and roar, used for screaming for more sexy stuff. It made sense she didn't recognise it: she couldn't think of a single situation where she'd use such a dickish term. It was like they were trading Top Trumps cards. Each raising the stakes with what photo they could get hold of, their language growing more gross as they did. When the nip slip picture appeared (posted by Liam, the scumbag) the tone changed:

[-] **Ratmanking 19/01 (Tue) 17:09:13**
Show some self-respect.
[-] **Anonymous 19/01 (Tue) 17:10:21**
She posing. Ho.

[-] SmackMaBitchUpz 19/01 (Tue) 17:10:27
It takes a whore world of slutz.

So it was totally fine for them to wank off over private pictures of Chloe that they stole, but god forbid the girl posed in a sexual way herself? A mist of rage came over her. She wanted to tear these printouts to shreds and ram them down the throats of the spoilt man-babies who'd contrived to make Chloe first an angel, and then a whore. They put their own narrative on her, probably without the girl even knowing. A girl can't even get a goddam holiday job and be left alone! *Wait...* She flicked back. He mentioned the cafe by name – the Pepper Pot. He must have been there. He must have seen Chloe. He knew her in real life. At least from a distance. She shuddered, skimming quickly through the pages: more hate, Chloe's telephone number, the messages where she asked them to remove her photos. There were screenshots of text exchanges between Chloe and these bullies:

> Have some self-respect slut.
> *Who is this?*
> Your friends and family gonna find out what a whore you are.
> *leave me alone. please.*
> You're better off dead.
> Kill yourself dirty bitch.
> Die

Freddie wanted to reach into the messages and pull Chloe out. To block these numbers. Find these men and make them answer for what they'd done. *Chloe was fifteen.* She must have been terrified. They had come at her from every angle. There was nowhere she could hide. Freddie blinked back tears.

Swallowed the lump in her throat. *Don't let this spiteful hate get to you: stay focused.* She was doing this for Chloe. And for Lottie: there was still time to save her. Freddie kept reading. And there it was – a clue!

[-] Liam 25/02 (Thurs) 11:10:35
BORED. Stuk in waitin for a dam microwave from argos.
Need some new frapping fun.

Freddie's lip curled in distaste at his crude pun on the word frap: he could barely write and yet he knew how to make wank jokes. 'I've got something,' she said.

Nas was at her side straight away. 'What is it?'

'Look.' She pointed at the two comments she'd circled. 'Liam mentions seeing Chloe at the cafe she worked at.'

'He's local?' Chips swivelled his seat round to face them. Even Green had looked up from her own stack of papers.

'Possibly,' Nas said. 'Or he's certainly spent time in the area.'

'And here...' Freddie felt the adrenaline rise in her. 'On February the twenty-fifth at 11:10 the idiot says he's waiting in for a new microwave from Argos.'

'There must be a limited number of microwaves delivered that day, after that time,' Nas said.

'Exactly,' Freddie smiled.

'I'm on it.' Nas reached across for her handset, shooing Freddie out of her chair.

'Green,' Saunders said. 'Cross-reference any addresses with the names listed on the electoral register, see if it looks like our guy is using a real or fake name on this site.'

'Sir.' Green's fingers started tapping at her keyboard.

Saunders was staring at her, an impenetrable look on his face. She gave him her best smile. 'Chips,' he said, 'any updates from the Greenwich lads on whether any of Lottie's friends recognise the name Liam?'

'Nothing so far. And we've still got teams out going door to door.'

'I'm guessing it's too much to hope for that someone saw a woman in exercise kit being pulled into a vehicle this morning?' Freddie looked at the incident board: there was a printed photo that looked like it was from a catalogue, and another taken from Lottie's Instagram feed in which she was wearing the same outfit. *So that's what she'd had on when she disappeared.* The old saying about serial killers always targeting joggers popped into her head.

'No one's come forward,' Chips said.

Saunders rubbed his hand over his face. 'Okay. Well they'll have to keep knocking: someone might remember something.'

'Aye,' said Chips. Quietly, he added, 'It's just if it's in time.' He turned back to his own computer. Without looking up he said, 'I've requested the lads at St Albans send us over all the CCTV they've got on wee Chloe Strofton's last twenty-four hours. See if we see anyone we recognise.'

They were taking it seriously that the two cases were linked. Nas must have shared her suspicions about Chloe's ability to source heroin. What did they call that? Reasonable doubt?

Nas appeared to be on hold. Now seemed like a good time to go for a wee. 'Here, Green. Where's the ladies'?'

'Two floors down.' She didn't look up. 'The one on the eighth floor is only for senior officers.' *Handy*, thought Freddie. She wondered at which point the police detectives had detected there were only two sets of ladies' loos in the twelve-storey building?

Waiting for the lift, she took out her mobile phone and went back into the Are You Awake Chloe thread. The lift doors opened and she stepped in. Pressed the button. Scrolled through her phone. Things had escalated fast. There were calls for Chloe to

160

be taught a lesson. For what, she wasn't sure. Taking a pic where her boob was on show? That seemed to be the gist of it. Calls for her to be raped. Freddie looked up as the doors opened. The toilets were opposite. As she walked in, a hand-soap-scented, cream marble cocoon enveloped her. This was better than a standard police station bog. She didn't bother to look in the mirror over the sinks. Inside a cubicle she pulled her jeans down with one hand and sat on the seat. Resting her elbow on her knee, she kept reading her phone. She'd got to the part where Chloe had started to ask for her photos to be removed from the site. And the image of her in her yellow underwear, which someone called 'AB' had immediately posted. They were like a pack of dogs then, falling on her with vitriol and bile. She found circulated instructions on how to hack into accounts: they called it 'the magic key'. And even though they'd tricked a fifteen-year-old girl into sending them an underwear shot, they were the ones condemning her. She paused to tear off some toilet roll.

[-] **Liam 08/03 (Tue) 16:10:23**
I'll cut your tits off and stuff them up your snatch.
[-] **DuneBuggi 08/03 (Tue) 16:10:49**
Bitch be begging to take her nastypics down? Bitch I make you beg. Shove my cock in your mouth so you can't breathe.

No wonder Chloe felt hopeless. Even if you suspected these were just sad bastards at home spanking the monkey while they fantasised about mutilating her, it was undoubtedly scary. And Freddie was an adult. Chloe was a kid. The door to the ladies' opened and she jumped. The sound of heels clicked on the floor: *not Nas*. She stood up, flushed. Standing in front of the mirror was the receptionist, Lorna. She looked surprised to see her. Freddie smiled, focusing on washing her hands. Her phone was tucked in her waistband, gently pressing against her skin. She washed her hands again. She felt dirty after reading the messages aimed at Chloe, seeing the photos they'd stolen and tricked from her. Like she too had been violated. Lorna stood two sinks down, carefully applying baby-pink lipgloss. She couldn't believe some people wasted their time coming to the bathroom just to reapply make-up.

Taking her phone out of her jeans, she resumed her walk and read. They had to get the bastards who'd done this. They were hounding the girl. You could see it building. Press call for lift. Get into lift. Step out lift. Walk back to office. The name on the thread hit her as if it were physical. She felt her chest concave, forcing the air out of her. Her hand was shaking. She stumbled. Stopped. Never taking her eyes from the screen. There was no mistake. It was the same pseudonym used by the Hashtag Murderer. The serial killer she and Nas had put away. Dread spread over her like heat rash. She read the post again:

[-] **ApollyonsRevenge** 08/03 (Tue) 16:15:00
Who wants to play?

Chapter 24

Wednesday 16 March

18:00
T – 15 hrs 30 mins

Running back into the office, she found the printouts still on Nas's desk. Freddie searched for the corresponding pages from the post she'd just seen. Nas was next to Green, who was on the phone. *You're safe. No one can hurt you here. You're in the middle of a secure police building.* Her pen shook in her hand.

[-] **ApollyonsRevenge 08/03 (Tue) 16:15:00**
Who wants to play?
[-] **Liam 08/03 (Tue) 16:15:13**
Apollyon – total dude!
[-] **ApollyonsRevenge 08/03 (Tue) 16:16:00**

A god among mortals. You could be one of his chosen warriors. A.

[-] **BeamMeUpHottie** 08/03 (Tue) 16:16:11

The dude's legend. Saw past all the shit. Played the fuzz for fools.

[-] **ApollyonsRevenge** 08/03 (Tue) 16:17:00

I can teach you the tricks of the master. Help you honour that legend. Bring these bitches to heel.

[-] **Liam** 08/03 (Tue) 16:17:14

The destroyer, man!!! Genius plays.

[-] **ApollyonsRevenge** 08/03 (Tue) 16:17:41

I can help you be great too, Liam. Rise.

Was it him? Nas had promised he was locked away, no access to the internet. But still the name clung like icy rain. It couldn't be a coincidence that both Chloe and Lottie's suicide notes spelt out the word Apollyon, and here was a poster calling himself Apollyon's Revenge? *And he was talking to Liam.* Liam, who'd been obsessed with Chloe, stealing intimate photos of her and sharing them on this site. She'd read of batshit women who'd married serial killers in prison, but this was mad. She couldn't believe these guys were excited by Apollyon. Sad scrote-monkeys who sought private images of their crushes as frap fodder; of course they'd revere a killer who'd caused a mass media frenzy and led the police on a merry dance across the internet. They probably thought he was the serial killing version of a computer game hero. *Fanboys.* This was all getting a bit *Natural Born Killers*. Would they progress to fan fic? It was ludicrous. Laughable. And chilling. What did Apollyon's Revenge mean by *teaching them tricks*? Were they emulating the serial killer? She looked up for help, but everyone was on the phone. On the board the smiling photo of Lottie stared back at her.

'We've got him!' Nas shouted. 'Liam Schofield, aged eighteen. Registered address 103 St Albans Road, Watford. He lives there with his disabled father, Martin Schofield, aged forty-three. And on the twenty-fifth of February they received a new microwave ordered from Argos, and signed for at 1.30 p.m.' Nasreen waved a bit of paper in the air.

'I rang the cafe Melisha said Chloe helped out in, and guess who had a trial day at the Pepper Pot last summer? Our Liam Schofield, though he didn't make the grade,' said Green triumphantly, smiling at Nas. Freddie felt a stab of jealousy. They were work colleagues. *This is their thing. Let them have it.* 'The owner, Mrs Peterson, said he was difficult and, I quote, "made her feel uncomfortable".' Green made speech marks with her fingers.

'Good work.' Chips grabbed his jacket from the back of his chair.

'And he's on the system,' Nas said. 'Cautioned for voyeurism two years ago after he fell out a tree while watching a girl he went to school with getting changed in her bedroom. He was picked up when her parents called an ambulance. He broke his wrist.'

Freddie scoffed. 'Hardly a master criminal.'

'The cops who took him in at the time didn't think so,' said Nas. 'I spoke to the PC. He laughed when I reminded him of the case. They thought he was an over-exuberant teenager. I think they thought his broken wrist was punishment enough.'

Freddie felt uneasy. Saunders had finished his call and turned his chair to join the conversation. 'That sounds like an escalation to me. Started out a peeping Tom, graduated to a stalker. Wanted what he couldn't have: hence the obscene photos.'

What a creep.

'Time we had a chat with Mr Schofield, I think,' said Chips.

'We'll get onto the local force and request an interview room there. Green, how long will it take to drive us?'

'You want me to come, sir?' Nas had hope in her eyes. Always the eager beaver. Freddie couldn't think of anything worse than spending time in this creep's presence.

'Aye, I think having a pretty girl there might bring the best out of Mr Schofield,' he said, raising a questioning eyebrow at Saunders, who nodded in return. *Bait: charming.* Nasreen's ears tinted pink.

'About forty-five minutes, sir,' Green said.

'I'll call ahead and get the local force to send someone down and take a peek to check our lad's in,' Chips said.

'Get them to stay below radar,' Saunders said. 'We don't want them to tip him off, so he's got time to get rid of anything.'

Or anyone, Freddie swallowed. Chips took his mobile to the corner of the room to make the call.

Freddie looked her phone: 17:36. If the Snapchat threat was to be believed, they only had fifteen hours left to find Lottie. The clock was ticking down. 'Do you think he's got Lottie?' Her fingers were sweaty round the printouts in her hands.

'It's another reason to go to him,' Saunders said. 'See how he reacts when he sees us. If he's nervous when we're at his house.'

'He set up the message boards about both Chloe and Lottie,' Nas said. She was looking through her notepad. 'And, according to what Freddie saw on Are You Awake it looked like Liam was the one who obtained and posted the first intimate photos of the girls.'

'Chloe was only fifteen, that's enough to hand him over to the Child Exploitation lads. But we want a crack at him first,' Saunders continued. 'Chips can call it in – he knows them.' Saunders was leaning his elbow on his chair arm, scratching at his stubble with his thumb and forefinger. He reminded her of a monkey. *Planet of the Apes.* 'Cudmore, you said Chloe's mates said she thought she was being followed?'

'They said she was paranoid about it,' Freddie said.

'Let's find out if he made a habit of following women. If he's been to Greenwich recently. Can he drive?' Saunders nodded his question at Green. She rolled her chair back so she was at the computer.

Freddie raised an eyebrow at Nas. 'What else you got on your database?'

'The PNC – Police National Computer – lists driving licence holders and DVLA registered vehicles, as well as details of those who've been convicted, cautioned and arrested,' Nas said.

'Cool,' said Freddie. 'Like a criminal Google. Can I have a go?'

'No,' Saunders and Nas answered at the same time.

'He does have a driving licence,' Green said. 'And he's listed as the owner of a Ford Transit Connect.'

'A van?' Freddie's voice was high. 'With, like, back panels? No windows?' She couldn't get the words straight.

'Perfect for transporting pallets, tools, and eighteen-year-old girls you've snatched off the street,' Saunders said. Freddie's stomach flipped. Had Lottie been forced into the back of Liam's van? Shaken around in the back, bumped and bruised, no windows, no idea where she was being taken. Had she hammered against the side, desperate for help?

'He's there.' Chips waved his phone. 'One of the local CID constables lives two roads down. He was off duty – popped over pretending he was collecting for charity. Our Liam told him to eff off. The DC's at a car garage down from his now, waiting for back-up. Liam hasn't left the house. And he thinks there's someone in the upstairs bedroom. He saw shadows moving.'

Suddenly they were all on their feet. Saunders pulled on his blazer: 'He'd have had time to get her out from Greenwich. Straight onto the A12, then the North Circular. It'd be what, an hour's drive, give or take, that time of the morning. I'll take my car. Cudmore, you can ride with me. I like someone to hold my drink while I'm driving.' He clapped her on the back. Nasreen looked less than thrilled.

'What about me?' Freddie didn't want to be left behind with the missing girl's brother. A dude she hadn't met, who might be about to find out what had happened to his sister. *No, thanks. Too stressful.*

'You can stay here and keep going through those printouts.' Saunders flicked his hand dismissively.

'You'd leave me on my own? In the office. With all this top-secret police stuff?' she said.

He pulled his wallet from his back pocket, lip curled, and checked his warrant card. 'You're not coming in my car. You can stay in Green's – going through that lot.' He tapped the papers she was holding. 'Make yourself useful.'

Freddie looked at the printouts. 'What if someone else is helping Liam?'

Nas pulled her jacket aside, checking her telescopic baton was in its holster. 'Why'd you ask that?'

'Look.' She held out the highlighted excerpt from the Apollyon conversation on Are You Awake.

'More Apollyon references,' Nasreen frowned. *It kept coming back to him.*

'He's talking to Liam about it,' Freddie said.

'Sick fucks like sick fucks,' Saunders shrugged.

'There's more, I haven't had time to go through it all yet.' *I can teach you the tricks of the master. Bring these bitches to heel.* They sounded like sinister promises. What was still to come? She shivered as she picked up the other pages from the desk, skim

168

reading them. 'Here – look. Apollyon's Revenge says he'll send Liam instructions on how to "unlock the treasure trove of other people's computers". She pointed at the post.

'Does he mean instructions to hack?' Nas asked.

Freddie flicked forward. 'The first image of Chloe – the one where you can see her nipple – was posted by Liam not long after.'

Green grimaced. 'Nice guy.' *Nice guy, indeed.* Freddie thought of the internet slang that described men who hung out with women, pretending to be their friend and then getting angry when they didn't get the sex they felt entitled to for being *a nice guy.*

Nasreen was still looking at the printouts. 'I think we should ask Liam about the Are You Awake poster calling himself Apollyon's Revenge. See if he knows who he is in real life.' Nas was marking the side of the sheet with indents of her nail.

Freddie skipped forwards a few pages. '*Shit*. It gets worse.' She shuddered. 'Here Apollyon's Revenge says he has a special present for Liam. Next post from Liam is Chloe's phone number and home address.' She held the page up. 'Bastard gave him the details to dox her!' Green looked disgusted.

'Quit squawking like bloody mother hens,' Saunders snapped. 'And let's get up there.'

'Oh goody: road trip,' Freddie said. 'I've only just escaped suburbia and you're taking me back.'

'With a bit of luck we'll be leaving you there,' he said, heading for the door. She caught Nas trying to suppress a smile and mouthed *traitor* at her. She'd forgotten how good it was to talk to other people. Even if they were psycho cops.

Chips opened his desk drawer, moving the mountain of crap inside until he found a half-eaten packet of mints, the silver foil a curled apostrophe. He dropped them into his pocket. 'Doubt we'll have time for afternoon tea on the way.'

Saunders was outside the door. 'Move it, people.'

Freddie grabbed her rucksack from the floor, stuffing the papers and a couple of pens inside.

They packed into the lift like the worst game of sardines ever. Saunders's solid arm was pressed against her shoulder. He was a fan of citrus aftershave. It made her thirsty. He scowled. 'Cudmore, I want you to put a call in to Morris and the team at Greenwich. Tell them what we've got and get them to do some digging on this Apollyon's Revenge guy. We know the tech lads won't be able to lift anything from Are You Awake but get them to see if the same name crops up elsewhere.'

'Sir.'

The car park was cold, and smelt faintly of petrol. Nas and Saunders headed in one direction, and Freddie trudged behind Green in the other, Chips beside her. 'Do you think Liam has her?' she asked.

'Possibly,' he said, as Green unlocked the car they'd driven down in.

This could be it. Liam's posts about both Chloe and Lottie were sexually explicit. She felt sick at the thought of what that might mean.

Chips paused, the front passenger door open. 'You okay in the back?'

'Sure.' She pulled the door open and scrambled in. He was all right – for a cop.

'You know how DI Saunders drives?' Chips said to Green.

'Fast, sir.'

That'll be great for Nas's travel sickness.

'Aye. I think this warrants the lights.'

Green smiled and flicked them on. The siren started up and

they sped away from Westminster, hurrying towards Watford and what they might find there. Freddie thought of Lottie, trapped somewhere against her will. Was she shouting for help? Trying to escape? *Her fingers scraping against a wall, a door, a floor.* They wove between cars and buses, Green expertly navigating the masses of vehicles that seemed to stand between them and Lottie. She'd seen Apollyon's name: Freddie knew every second counted.

Chapter 25

Wednesday 16 March

18:55
T – 14 hrs 35 mins

The siren was switched off before they reached St Albans Road. A row of 1930s semis, painted white and dotted with satellite dishes, were set on a slip road, back from a large grass oblong roundabout. The last of the rush hour thundered past on the thoroughfare. The streetlights from the roundabout and nearby petrol station provided plenty of light. Was there a back entrance? It'd be hard to get someone inside the house unseen, unless the busy comings and goings of the main road prevented any one event from standing out. They pulled into an adjacent car dealership, large stickers on the car bonnets advertising the prices. A bald guy wearing jeans and a North Face jacket waved them over. Saunders and Nas were already parked up and waiting. Chips wound the window down. The bald guy came over, followed by Nas, who had her hands in her coat pockets and her collar turned up against the biting wind. The sky was heavy with grey clouds, merging into night. Saunders, apparently impervious to the cold, bounced over to join them. He was hyper. *From nerves or excitement?*

'DS Ahmed, sir,' the bald guy introduced himself through the window. 'We spoke on the phone.'

Chips shook his hand. 'Any more sightings of the suspect?'

'We've got two officers round the back. There's been no comings or goings,' DS Ahmed said.

'What about that figure you saw upstairs – is it our girl?' Chips said.

Freddie crossed her fingers. She was shaking from the cold wind that was billowing into the car – at least she thought it was from that. 'Nothing conclusive,' DS Ahmed said. He had a nice face, shiny and creased, like he smiled a lot.

'How d'you want to do this, Pete? I don't fancy dragging him all the way down that road to the car if he's difficult.' Chips indicated the row of houses that stretched away from them, on the other side of a Chinese takeaway.

'We'll drive down,' said Saunders. 'Green can go round the back, Cudmore down the side passage, me and you can knock.' Freddie assumed she was to stay in the car. 'Sergeant,' he said to Ahmed. 'You got a van for this arse?'

'Round the back where it dropped the boys off, sir,' Ahmed smiled. 'I'll radio them to follow you round.'

'Good man.' Saunders tapped the roof of the car. 'Now get out, Green, I'm driving.' PC Green obediently got into the back, followed by Nas. The police van was waiting by the slip road, just out of sight of the houses. The car was hot, and Freddie could hear PC Green breathing, see her chest rising and falling quickly. Nas drummed her gloved fingers on her knee, sitting

173

bolt upright. It must be a rush of adrenaline doing this. Though it was making her feel queasy. Saunders accelerated, pulling the car swiftly onto the slip road and stopping outside number 103. Wordlessly they opened the doors at once, and closed them quietly. PC Green went past the house and disappeared down the side alley of the semi two doors down, to join the others out the back. Light flickered at the downstairs bay window: the television was on. There were heavy curtains at the upstairs window, and she couldn't see through them. Freddie lowered her window a fraction; the noise from the passing road and the swirl of the wind filled the car. She wanted to hear what was happening. The police van was still waiting, out of sight, behind them. Nas, her coat billowing behind her, walked quickly with Saunders and Chips to the front of the house. At a nod from Saunders she headed down the side path as the two male officers reached the front door. Freddie reminded herself that Nas had her baton. Though that didn't feel like much. The guy could have a knife. Or maybe even a gun, if he'd managed to snatch Lottie?

There was a pause, a collective intake of breath to allow everyone to get into position, and then Saunders rapped on the door. The flickering light in the lounge stilled: live pause. A shape approached the patterned glass door, making a Picasso out of whoever was behind it. A young guy with dark, stringy hair, wearing a long sleeved t-shirt and jeans, opened it. His eyes widened at the sight of Saunders and Chips in their suits. *They were obviously cops.* He slammed the door shut. 'Runner!' Saunders shouted. A radio in the car crackled to life, Chips echoing his sentence, making her jump. 'Don't be an idiot, Liam!' Saunders shouted, kicking open the door. Instinctively Freddie got out of the car. Saunders and Chips barrelled into the house. The curtains next door twitched. 'Liam Schofield,'

Saunders's voice carried from inside. 'You are wanted in relation to… *Shit!*'

'Don't run lad, you'll only make it worse!' Chips boomed. Freddie's heart was racing. The police van revved behind her, squealing to a stop as a uniformed officer jumped out and ran into the house.

There was a crash from inside. Breaking glass. Splintering wood. Yells. 'Green, he's headed your way. He's got a baseball bat,' the radio screamed. A blur that could have been Nas shot past the open front door.

'Stop!' Green's voice was further away. *Feet on wood. A thump onto concrete.* 'He's gone over the fence!'

More sounds of scrabbling feet on wood.

Liam burst out the side alley, the baseball bat pumping like a piston as he ran straight at her.

Freddie saw the keys in the ignition. She tried to let go of the handle. *To run. To do anything.* But she was frozen in front of the car.

Saunders charged out the house, but Liam was already level with the semi next door. Nothing would stop him from taking the car. He swung the baseball bat back. Freddie braced for the blow. *It was happening again. Blood.*

Nas, her black coat a cape behind her, her legs long, streaked from the neighbour's passageway and jumped for him. Liam slammed into the side of the car, and went down like Jenga. The baseball bat bounced with an aluminium ping. Nas pinned him under her knee, wrenching her handcuffs from her belt. Blew her hair off her face. 'Liam Schofield, I'm arresting you for attempted assault of a police officer…'

Freddie looked at Saunders, open-mouthed. 'He took a swing at Green. And missed. He's going to have to repair the fence though.'

Freddie looked down: she was completely untouched. *Nas had stopped him.*

'Great job, Cudmore.' Chips arrived, swiftly followed by Green and the uniformed coppers. Three great, hulking guys in bulky stab vests. Nas pulled Liam to his feet and shouldered him forwards. Freddie finally let go of the car door handle, and stood aside as a wincing Liam was escorted into the waiting van. Freddie shook her head in disbelief. Timid little Nasreen Cudmore, who used to hide in the toilets during break time and cry if people called her names, had grown up to be a certified badass.

Chapter 26

Wednesday 16 March

19:20
T – 14 hrs 10 mins

'I can't believe it's on a road called Shady Lane!' Freddie laughed.

'What?' Nasreen took her eyes off the prison van carrying Liam, and glanced at the Georgian, yellow-brick Watford police station. It had the traditional blue police lamp suspended over the entrance. 'Oh right. Yeah.'

As she got out of the car, she kept the van in her sights. Lottie hadn't been at Liam's house. The person they'd seen at the upstairs window turned out to be his father.

'You going to let me out?' Freddie tapped on the window. Without taking her eyes from the van, Nasreen opened the back door. She couldn't believe it. Couldn't believe he would be so stupid. So selfish. Anger bubbled under her skin.

'I'll go park up,' Green called.

'Bet you're pleased to be out of Saunders's car,' Freddie whispered.

Stiffening, she saw Chips drop down from the back of the van, helping the handcuffed Liam behind him. The suspect's hair fell over his sallow face like a drab curtain. 'Why don't you wait inside?'

Freddie didn't move, watching as Liam tripped over his Converse trainers as the bigger of the two constables escorted him past them and up the steps into the station.

Nasreen walked to Chips, her heel clicks quickening in indignation. It violated protocol. 'Why did you travel in the van with the suspect?'

Chips held his hands up in mock surrender. 'Whoa, lassie. I haven't had my coffee yet, shall we get in out of the cold?'

You don't get to patronise me now. 'I saw you get in the cage with him. You put something in front of the camera.' She was aware Freddie was standing behind them.

'If debris obscures the camera it's not my fault.' Chips's voice shifted and his words became cold. Hard. 'May I remind you I'm your senior officer, Sergeant.'

She wouldn't be intimidated. 'Did you touch the suspect? Sir.'

'Enough.' Chips grabbed her arm roughly and pulled her away from the station.

'Let go of me.' She shook him off.

'Hey!' Freddie ran towards them.

Nasreen thrust her finger into his chest. Her ears burned hot. It was outrageous. 'If he files a complaint the whole case could be thrown out!'

'Calm down, Cudmore,' Chips hissed, looking around to see if anyone could hear them.

'Don't tell me to calm down. I have every right to report you to the DCI.' She couldn't believe he'd put her in this position.

Couldn't believe he was that kind of cop. Regardless of what Liam had done, might have done, Chips couldn't just do whatever the hell he liked. 'Why'd you go in the cage? No one but the suspect should be in there.' With her heels back on she just had the height advantage over Chips.

Chips lowered his voice. 'We are not alone. Remember your pal is listening to every word of this.'

If this got out it could threaten the CPS case against Liam. *Dammit*, she should have forced Freddie to go inside. 'Freddie, I need you to not repeat this conversation.' What if she took up reporting again? 'You can't write about this. Even later, okay?'

'In case you hadn't noticed I've not got much journalism on at the moment,' said Freddie, looking uneasily between them.

'You have my word I didn't lay a finger on the lad,' Chips said. Nasreen watched his face for telltale signs of lying. He looked genuine. Maybe.

Freddie cut in. 'I would've put the baseball bat in the back of the van. Taken a picture of his tiny dick and sent it to all his man-baby mates.'

Chips burst into laughter. 'I like this one, Cudmore. Can we keep her?'

She refused to smile. 'Did you threaten or assault the suspect, sir?'

'Jack Burgone is more than just my boss, lass.' Chips leant closer to her, his voice low, friendly, like he was explaining the meal options in the canteen. 'He's my mate. I just wanted a quiet word with the lad to find out where the guv's sister is.'

Her pulse quickened, despite herself. 'What did he say?'

The click of brogues on concrete behind them interrupted Chips's reply. Saunders's voice boomed. 'Can we stop with the mothers' meeting and get on with this?'

'Course lad.' Chips beamed and walked towards him.

Rage fired Nasreen after them, up the concrete steps into the station's reception. Plastic chairs lined the back wall. Posters advertising the dangers of drink driving hung in Perspex frames on the walls. Two male uniformed PCs looked up with fascination from behind the desk. Until she could be one hundred per cent sure what had happened in that van, she had to keep Chips out the way. 'I want to be in on the interview.'

Saunders stopped and looked first at Chips and then her in surprise.

She needed to be in that room. She wanted to find out what she could, properly. Legally. 'We've seen his posts online. I would guess he's not massively used to talking to real women. I can use that.' She could do this. She could help.

'Here, lads, what do you think?' Saunders called to the uniformed guys behind the desk. 'Would you rather be locked in a small room with Chips or pretty little Nasreen here?' They guffawed.

'What the hell?' Freddie rounded on Saunders.

Nasreen felt her face flush. She wouldn't give him the satisfaction of looking away. She held a hand up to silence Freddie. 'I'm a trained interrogator, I know how to exploit a nominal's weaknesses. Sir.'

'You gonna flash him your nominals?' Saunders smirked.

One of the uniforms wolf whistled. She spun towards them, making sure her voice was even, not hysterical. 'Mind your manners, Constable.' As she turned back the other snickered. She wouldn't let them bully her.

'Wish we'd cracked on to this years ago, hey, Chips?' Saunders led them past the smirking uniforms. Chips refused to meet her gaze. 'Think of how many we could've banged up if only we'd worn a pair of high heels!'

'That's enough. Sir.' Nas dug her fingernails into her palms to mask the anger in her voice. Chips looked abashed. They were in a corridor, recessed light panels sitting among the ceiling tiles. It smelt faintly of bleach.

Saunders turned to grin at her. 'We all gotta make sacrifices, Cudmore. Lie back and think of England.'

She would not rise to it. Wouldn't give him the pleasure. 'What do you think, Chips?' She held his gaze as Saunders turned back: *I will tell him what you did if I have to.*

Chips didn't react to her look. 'I say give the lassie a chance.'

Had she forced his hand or did he really believe in her? Nasreen had to believe in herself. Had to believe that she could get the truth out of Liam.

'Fine. Let's see what you've got, Cudmore,' Saunders said without bothering to turn. She felt a tingle of adrenaline. 'So far the SOCOs have found no trace of Lottie at the house, or in Schofield's van.'

She caught Freddie glancing at Chips. *What had Liam said to him?*

'What about Liam's laptop and phone?' She kept stride with Saunders, Freddie puffing behind them.

'Computer's on the way to the local lab, but I had one of the SOCOs take a look. Brain of Britain here didn't use a password. He had a folder, helpfully named "Chloe," which contained the images that were posted online. And he had a photo of the suicide note from the first girl, which looks mighty similar to the one that turned up on Snapchat.'

'Does it have the banner across it?' Freddie interjected.

'Nope, and it was saved to his machine before Chloe's Snapchat was sent.'

Nasreen was running through the timeline in her head.

Freddie was completely out of breath now. 'What does that mean? He sent the note to Chloe? As a suggestion?'

She'd been thinking the same thing. It didn't add up.

'That's what I want to find out.' Saunders came to a stop outside a door. 'Chips, you and Civvy Longstocking can watch the interview on the live feed in here.' He opened the door to a small beige staff room.

'Oh goodie – coffee,' Freddie said.

Nasreen saw a kettle and microwave on the side. It must double as the officers' mess. A number of chairs were grouped together, facing a flat-screen television. On the screen she saw Liam, shot from above, sitting at a table in a small, white interview room. He was leaning back, picking his nose. 'He doesn't want a lawyer?'

'You'll like this, Cudmore.' Saunders smiled at her as he might a child. She was sick of them treating her like a useless kid. 'He wants a brief, all right. He gave us a specific name, a Mr H. D. Cooper of Webb and Cooper. A pretty fancy-pants London lawyer for a kid who lives next to a Chinese takeaway.'

'Where'd he hear of a lawyer like that?' Chips folded his arms and leant against the wall.

'Very pleased with himself as well, when he told us,' Saunders said.

'We have to wait till Mr Cooper arrives from town?' asked Nas in dismay. That could take an hour. Maybe more. She looked at her phone. It was nearly half seven. They were into the evening. The deadline was gaining on them

'No, the dingbat's happy to go ahead before he gets here. I think he thinks lawyers are like magicians, they just stroll in, click their fingers and poof! You're home safe again.'

'Lucky for us,' Chips smiled. *Had he really not touched Liam?*

'So let's be quick.' Saunders winked at her.

This was it. This was their chance. 'Was there anything else of relevance on his computer?'

Saunders frowned. 'There was a "Lottie" folder as well. A lot of images I don't think we want the guv to see.' She swallowed her wince.

'And the suicide note?' Freddie asked.

'Not this time.'

Could that mean the kidnapper was someone else? That Liam didn't have anything to do with Lottie's abduction? But the evidence suggested he was involved, at least in some way.

'He did have a folder with instructions on how to hack into someone else's network,' Saunders said.

'Genius,' muttered Chips.

'The Scene of Crime Officer is sending over copies, and they're printing it for us here.' He looked up as a woman in her fifties, with dyed black hair and heavy eye make-up, hurried towards them. 'Right on cue. Thanks, Barbara.' The woman passed him a folder of printouts.

'There you go, pet,' she said. 'And I'm seeing if we can shake up some rooibos tea for you.'

'You angel.' Saunders gave her a hundred-watt grin. Barbara walked off in a warm glow. He dropped all pretence of charm in a second. 'Ready to smile for Daddy, Cudmore?'

She ignored his leer. 'One sec.' Pulling the band from her ponytail, she shook her hair down. 'You got any lipgloss, Freddie?' It didn't matter what Saunders had lewdly suggested, she knew what Liam had posted on Are You Awake. She was fairly certain he hadn't had much interaction at all with females. Hating herself, she undid three shirt buttons.

'Do I look like I'm packing MAC?' Freddie crossed her arms over her chest.

Nasreen ignored the judgement in her tone. Whatever it took, she would get the information they needed. She would prove herself to Saunders and Chips. This was the same as going undercover, she reasoned, feeling a bit sick as she put her hand inside her shirt and hiked her breasts up. Chips had the good grace to find something incredibly interesting to look at on the ceiling. 'Okay?'

'Better than your usual repressed headmistress look,' Saunders said. 'Who knew you had those babies?'

'God, you're a dick,' said Freddie, shaking her head.

'I'm only doing this because it's the guv's sister.' Her voice was flat.

'Whatever lets you sleep at night, Cudmore,' Saunders grinned. 'Ready?' She nodded. 'You play good cop, Cudmore. And I'll play better cop.' In two strides he'd opened the door to the interview room. Nasreen followed him. Liam's face lit up like an Apple Store window when he saw her walk in. The clock was ticking. This was it.

Chapter 27

Wednesday 16 March

19:40
T − 13 hrs 50 mins

Freddie gripped her half-drunk cup of coffee, staring at the screen. On the chair next to her she'd spread out her printouts. On the other side sat Chips. He'd eaten most of his Polos by now and the air smelt minty fresh. Green sat behind them.

'We've got your laptop, Liam.' Saunders casually sat back in his chair while Nas sorted the photos and papers they had. Her hair was tumbling over her shoulders and she kept shaking her head as if to flick it back. Liam, who was fidgeting in his chair, kept looking up at her, then back down at his hands. 'We've seen the photos. No point lying anymore.'

Liam didn't respond.

Nasreen's voice fluttered through the mic. 'It was quite something how you managed to get hold of all these images, Liam.'

She looked straight at him. 'I'd have no idea where to even start!'

'Did she just giggle?' Green said.

'Yeah,' Freddie said, aware her coping mechanism was kicking in. *Make jokes. Draw attention away from the frightening reality.* 'It's like watching Police Barbie. Saunders is Ken.'

'More like GI Joe,' she said. Freddie laughed.

'It's working though.' Chips looked impressed.

Liam's tongue was practically on the floor. His eyes were wide and the words were falling out of him. 'It's not hard once you know how to do it.'

'But how did you even know where to start?' Nas was breathy.

'You just have to know the right people.' Liam was pleased with himself. A sour taste filled Freddie's mouth. She took a gulp of coffee.

'People who know big fancy-pants London lawyers?' Nas giggled. Did she just quote Saunders? Brilliant.

'It doesn't impress me,' Saunders sounded petulant.

'Shush!' Nasreen flapped a hand at Saunders. Her voice sing-song Disney, 'I wasn't talking to you, silly.' Chips spat his coffee out. Freddie laughed. On screen, Saunders scowled, and folded his arms over his chest in a sulk.

Liam looked like he might burst with pride. 'Bet he wishes he was on Mr Cooper's list,' he said, quickly glancing at Saunders to check he wasn't about to get punched. Saunders simply glowered.

Nasreen put her elbows on the table and leant on her hands. Channelling Marilyn Monroe. 'How did you get on the list, Liam?'

'Jesus, are all men this easy?' Chips said.

'You'd be surprised, sir,' Green said. 'She's doing a great job though.'

'The lad will need a cold shower after this.'

186

'So will Nas,' Freddie shuddered. She felt soiled just watching.

'The chosen get a special little black book.' Liam had pride in his voice. 'I'm one of the chosen warriors.'

'I've heard that before,' Freddie said. 'On the website. That's what Apollyon's Revenge said. Hold this.' She pushed her mug at Chips and rummaged through the papers.

'That sounds cool,' said Nasreen.

'It's like an elite special force,' Liam said. *It sounds like a cult*, thought Freddie, the Apollyon fanboys springing into her mind.

'How'd you get selected?' Nas asked breathily.

'You have to prove yourself. Complete a task.' Liam could've been talking about an honourable act, not sharing revenge porn online.

'What did you have to do?' Nasreen sounded enthralled.

'You're looking at it.' He tapped the table in front of him.

'What did he touch?' Freddie looked up.

'The photo of the suicide note,' Chips said. '*Christ*. Someone else told him to do it.'

And Freddie thought she knew who. She was leafing fast through the pages now. There were countless mentions of 'chosen warrior'. 'He's telling them what to do. Look. Here he says he's chosen this dude for a special task. A few posts down and the dude posts instructions for how to inject heroin!'

Green grabbed her shoulder. 'That's how Chloe killed herself.'

He was orchestrating the whole thing from this website. 'He got this guy to send Chloe instructions on how to kill herself!' Freddie slapped the paper.

'Wait a minute,' Chips said. 'Slow down. Who are you talking about?'

'Apollyon's Revenge,' Freddie said, her words echoing in the room as Nas said the same name on the television.

'You don't know who he is though?' She was teasing, flirty. 'That must be an awfully big secret.'

'I know who he is,' Liam said confidently.

Nas exhaled. 'Have you met him?' They were all leaning in towards the screen now. *Come on. Come on.*

'He's not the type to do personal appearances,' Liam smiled.

'But you've spoken to him?' Her voice light and fluffy as candy floss.

'He only communicates online. He comes to you.' He paused. 'But I know his name.' Liam was loving his moment in the Nas sunlight.

'You don't!' Nas reached out and lightly touched his hand. *Bet he won't wash that for a week.*

'Alex Black,' Liam said.

Got ya.

Nas pulled her hand back like he was dog shit. Straightened. Started doing up her blouse. All trace of sugar gone from her voice. 'If you have a contact for Alex Black – a number, or an email – we'll find it on your computer or phone. The Child Exploitation and Online Centre are very excited to meet you.'

'Wait, what?' He looked bewildered.

'Do you know what they do to paedophiles in prison, Liam?' Saunders said.

'I'm not a kiddie fiddler!' Liam looked from Saunders to Nas frantically. Trying to work out what had happened.

Nasreen leant across so she was close to him again. This time she was in his face, her voice cold, hard, and clear. 'Chloe Strofton was a fifteen-year-old girl. A minor. You stalked her. You stole personal photos from her. Photos you had no right to have. And then you published those photos online. You shared her home contact details and encouraged others to threaten and abuse her. You sent her a scripted suicide note. You may not have pressed the plunger on the heroin syringe that killed her, but you as good as did. I will see that you go down for every last bit of it, you pathetic little boy.' Nas pulled the photos from under him, slammed the folder shut and stood up. *Yes!*

'Interview terminated. Nineteen forty-nine.' Saunders flicked the machine. And they stalked out.

Chapter 28

Wednesday 16 March

20:00
T – 13 hrs 30 mins

'High five!' Saunders held his shovel palm up.

'No, thanks.' Nasreen didn't want to encourage any physical contact after the way he'd humiliated her in the reception. He'd made it clear he was in charge now, and that this was a series of tests. Trials to put her through. This was as close as she was going to get to a well done, or even just a thank you.

'Suit yourself.' He wound his hand back and *pop*! Punched the air. He was pumped from the interview, his energy levels increasing as the day drew on. Nas was exhausted. She put the folder between her knees to tie her hair back up. She'd have to try and get some sleep in the car. If she could stop seeing either Lottie or Burgone every time she closed her eyes.

'Cheer up, Cudmore.' Saunders clapped her on the back. 'We got a prize idiot there. Like taking candy from a baby.'

'Easy for you to say,' she said, her voice thin. 'I did all the work.'

Saunders stopped bouncing and smiled. A dark, uncomfortable smile. 'We found your use, Cudmore.'

This was just another form of resource management. *Cudmore's female, she can handle the educational work and the flirting.*

'You're riding with me,' he added.

Great: more dance anthems and racing line bends. So much for that power nap. Saunders leant into the staff room and slapped the wall. 'Chips, we need to get back to the station. You all right to come with us? I want to cross-reference what we've got on the Alex Black guy.'

Chips was pulling his jacket on. 'Yup.'

'There's a load of it in here.' Freddie held up the printouts from Are You Awake. Her face was flushed and her voice fast. 'At one point he tells another of his "chosen warriors" that he'll send them details of "a present Chloe can pick up at the Galleria." That must mean something?'

'The Galleria is the shopping centre Chloe stopped at on her way to Wildhill Wood, the day she killed herself,' said Nasreen. That had to be a reference to the heroin. 'Nothing used to cook the heroin was found at the scene – she could have been picking up the drugs?'

'She's on the security cameras at the shopping centre isn't she?' Freddie was stuffing the papers back into her bag.

'The footage has been sent over to us,' Nasreen said. 'I could get Morris to get onto it?' If they could trace the drugs back, they might be able to work out who this Alex Black is. The name *Apollyon's Revenge* tugged at her again. There were too many links. These instructions were all being sent online. Again she thought of the Hashtag Murderer's prison officer's denials that communication could be getting out.

'Where's Green?' Saunders sounded irritated. He was swinging his car keys round on his finger.

'Gone with one of the constables to put Alex Black through the PNC,' Chips said. 'Give us a bit of a head start.'

Saunders caught his keys in his palm and pointed at Freddie. 'Civvy Street, you're with us. I want to know what else is on that site. Just make sure you wipe your shoes before you get into my car.'

Freddie rolled her eyes. Nasreen tried to smile. She was pleased they'd caught Liam, and he'd given them vital intelligence, but an end still wasn't in sight. The Alex Black lead might go nowhere. It might not even be a real name. She'd been here before with investigations: teetering on the edge of what felt like a major breakthrough, only for it to all crumble to dust. In her mind she wrote the word Apollyon in the dust.

'He's like a Svengali. Or a cult leader,' Freddie was saying. 'All this chosen warrior crap – he's manipulating them into doing what he wants.'

'Not getting his own hands dirty, more like,' Saunders grunted.

'Looks like he might have supplied instructions on how to inject heroin to one of his goons,' Chips said. 'The kid then boasts about sending it to Chloe's phone.'

Poor Chloe. A fresh wave of anger rolled over her. They'd made the girl's life a living hell. They'd harangued her into killing herself. And it all led back to the mysterious Alex Black. 'I'd like to talk to the prison guards of the Hashtag Murderer again.'

Freddie made a small gasping sound. Turned it into a cough.

'Too many links for your liking?' Chips asked.

'Something like that. I think we should speak to him.'

To her left Freddie emitted a small 'No'. Nasreen talked over it. Covering up for her friend.

'I want to make sure this isn't him. Sending these instructions, puppeting this from inside.'

Saunders looked thoughtful.

'Worth it to definitely rule him out,' Chips said. 'Otherwise we've been looking in the wrong direction.'

'Get on it when we get back,' Saunders said. 'Let's focus on Alex Black for now.'

Outside the sky was dark, weighty. The first drops of rain fell. Freddie pulled her hood over her head and Saunders kicked up a light jog to the car. Nasreen pulled her gloves from her pocket and fell into line with Chips.

'You did a good job, lass.'

The praise took her so by surprise that she forgot what she'd been meaning to say. 'Thank you, sir.' Had he been telling the truth before? Liam hadn't accused anyone of assault. With a new lead there was no time to rake over it again. She had to trust Chips. 'I'm sorry about before. I know you were just doing the best by the guv.'

'And you were just doing your job. I see why he brought you in now.' Chips kept his eyes fixed ahead. 'You're a straight arrow. Diligent. A good choice.'

Tugging at her collar, Nasreen felt very hot. The focus was shifting to Alex Black, but Saunders and Chips now wanted to know all about Chloe's case. She knew they'd be looking for similarities, links that could tie the two girls and the shadowy Alex Black together. She knew what the link was, or she had a fair idea: it was uncomfortably close to pointing right at her and Freddie. The discovery of the Apollyon's Revenge account reinforced that. The name couldn't be a coincidence; she had to eliminate him for herself. 'Have you spoken to the guv?'

Chips nodded, his lips pursed. 'He's holding up. His parents less so: the doctor's had to give his mother a sedative.'

Nas couldn't imagine what it was like to know your daughter had been taken by someone who planned to hurt her. You'd feel powerless. She felt powerless. *Thrust the painful thoughts aside.* They were almost at the car now. She had to do it before she'd be overheard. 'Sir,' she said quietly and quickly, 'I'm sorry to ask this, but do you mind if I sit in the front? I get travel sick.'

'Course, lass.'

'And do you mind if this is our little secret?' There was no way she wanted DI Saunders to know.

Chips raised his eyebrows, but it was playful. 'He's all right you know. He just likes to push people's buttons.'

'I noticed.' He enjoyed it. It was a game. He was like a bored cat, toying with you till he'd had enough. Then he'd leave you eviscerated to die slowly. Any hint of what had happened with Burgone and she had no doubt he'd destroy her. Saunders liked finding a person's weakness and exploiting it. Nasreen wouldn't let him see hers. Not when they were so close. Not while there was still a chance they could save Lottie.

Chapter 29

Wednesday 16 March

20:30
T – 13 hrs

Rain was hammering against the car, the windscreen wipers swooshing in time to the space-disco beats of Lindstrøm. Saunders jiggled to the music. He reminded Freddie of a puppet she'd seen operated by a dude off his tits at a festival. Manic, jerky twitches. And she'd not seen him have a single caffeinated drink all day. Nas, by contrast, was still and aloof in the front seat, staring at the hypnotic oscillations of the windscreen wipers on the glass. Once or twice Freddie had seen her head loll. But she'd jerk awake moments later. Was she thinking about *him*? The Hashtag Murderer? She'd promised it couldn't be him. She'd lied.

Chips was sitting next to Freddie in the back, reading through the printouts. The occasional grunt was interspersed with announcements of information he thought the rest should know. They were collecting countless examples of what a twat this Alex Black was. Like Hamlet's dead dad, he popped up like a portent to impending crap. He was there, again and again. Before images were stolen. Before girls were doxxed. Always alluding to information that would help his 'chosen warriors' achieve their dreams. And their dreams were usually to see photos of girls without their pants on. Was Nas right: could it be *him*?

'Surely if he's sending them hacking instructions we can trace it?' she asked.

'He refers to sending them private messages,' Chips said. 'Chances are those are encrypted. If it's part of the site we ain't going to get it.'

They were going round in circles. Apollyon's Revenge sometimes signed his posts with an A, or an AB, but there wasn't a single revelatory thing in any of them. The same phrases cropped up again and again:

Who wants to play? You could be one of Apollyon's chosen warriors. I can teach you. I can help you be great.

His language was grandiose, removed from real life. He spoke like a character. He didn't boast, as Liam had; the focus wasn't on his ego. It was outwards: he was explaining, building a myth, reeling them in, and manipulating them. Just like the tweets the Hashtag Murderer had sent. It was an avatar. He wasn't going to slip up like Liam. There were no personal details. The closest he'd got was suggesting that Chloe might 'prefer to leave this realm', before they started calling for the girl to kill herself. They had nothing at all on Alex Black. Freddie was getting a headache. She dropped the pages onto her lap and stopped to think. It was 20:36. *Thirteen hours to save Lottie's life.* They'd already lost half a day. This wasn't working. Her neck felt cold with sweat: clammy. She tried to wipe it away with her hand.

Picking up her phone, she Googled Alex Black. The first search results were for an American teen actor, and a funeral director in Maryhill, Glasgow. After that were links to Are You Awake. Following them, images appeared along the top. One of a woman on all fours, naked, smiling suggestively at the camera. Another young woman who'd had her private images stolen. The same image appeared again; this time there were two men in the shot. You couldn't see their faces, their penises were erect and ejaculating into the woman's face. They'd been retouched onto the first image.

'There's a girl in here who's had her photos retouched to make them look like porn shots. We should let your mates on the paedo unit know that,' she said.

Chips leant over to look at her phone and wrinkled his nose. 'The Criminal Justice and Courts Act 2015 for revenge pornography doesn't include retouched images.'

'What?' Freddie was stunned. 'It makes her look like she's in bloody *Debbie Does Dallas*!'

'Aye. Chances are, with an image like that, it's an abusive ex looking to humiliate and punish the lass.'

'That's awful! Why the hell doesn't the law cover that?'

'The revenge porn laws are fairly recent. We managed to close down almost all of the dedicated revenge porn sites that were registered here in the UK. And the CPS have made a number of convictions for individuals. It's often easier to get the ones that are ex-partners.' Chips pointed at Freddie's phone. 'They're known to the victims. We can do them for harassment. When they're people like Liam, who just take a shine to a lass, it's a hell of a lot harder to trace them. Think of the resources we've got on this.' He indicated the other police in the car. 'If we didn't think this was linked to the kidnap investigation we'd be struggling to find the manpower to do it. Revenge porn peddlers have gone underground, onto anonymous message boards like Are You Awake. If the women don't know who posted it, there's nowhere to start.'

She stared at the photo on the phone. 'Is it always women?'

'About twenty-five per cent of reported cases involve men,' Saunders answered from the front. 'Their images tend to revolve around gay iconography.'

'It's just another form of control,' Freddie said.

'Before we cleared out most of the dedicated sites there was a case of a young Muslim lass.' Chips glanced at Nas in the front seat. 'They'd mocked up some mucky images like that and sent them to the local imam.'

Freddie felt sick. 'The images were fake, right?'

'But the elders didn't know that. She was cast out of the community. Family cut her off. The lot.' Chips was staring out the window now, as if he were reliving it. 'Brave girl: her testimony got the site closed. They asked her for money to take the images down so we got them for extortion.'

An entire life decimated by a fake photo. It wasn't fair. It wasn't right. These people were deliberately trying to hurt others. Girls like Chloe. Alex Black had to answer for the pain he'd caused.

'No one's asked for money on Are You Awake, have they?' There were no references to blackmail at all. So why were they doing it? For fun? Freddie closed her eyes and leant her head back. Wished she were back in her room, in her bed. Wished this horrific corner of the world hadn't been brought into her life. But life wasn't fair. Chloe hadn't asked for this. Lottie hadn't asked for this. They had no choice, so neither did she.

Freddie looked at the screen again, scrolling down and past

the other Alex Black search results. The next hit led to a site called the Maleosphere. She clicked through. A corporate-style 'The Maleosphere' logo spun repeatedly round on the home page. What was this?

> The Maleosphere's mission is to propagate information exposing misandry at all levels of our society. We will educate men and boys about the threat from feminist governance and fight to end that despotism. The current institution of marriage is dangerous for men, and we seek to provide the tools men who are already married need to protect themselves. We demand an end to rape hysteria and false allegations.

Oh god. Freddie scanned through the forums underneath. She recognised the juvenile terms straight away: 'Mangina' – a male feminist. 'Incel' – involuntary celibate. That's what American mass murderer Elliot Rodger described himself as, before he went out and shot six innocent people because he wanted to punish women for not sleeping with him. This was an MRA site. Full of Men's Rights Activists. And there was Alex Black's name: again and again.

Alex Black
Senior Member
I can help you get revenge on your cheating wife. Who wants to play?

Alex Black
Senior Member
I can help you discredit your ex and get your kids back. Who wants to play?

And he'd do this, Freddie knew, by either stealing their ex's intimate photos, or creating fake ones to share online and send to everyone they worked with. All his posts linked back to Are You Awake. It was a recruitment drive. He was building an army.

'Alex Black is all over the MRA sites.' Her voice was heavy with disgust. 'He's basically advertising his services as someone who can destroy women's lives.'

'Email me the link.' Chips rummaged in his pocket for a card. 'I'll get the tech lads to add it to the list. These websites tend to be fairly security conscious, but we might get lucky and find a link to him.'

'Why don't these people understand that feminism is about equality regardless of gender?' she snapped.

'Because fun-suckers like you bang on about it so much it sounds like a drag,' Saunders said, turning the car.

'That's a load of crap and you know it,' said Freddie. She could feel the white heat of anger searing through her.

Saunders seemed to think it was a big joke. 'I'm totally in touch with my feminine side, tell her, Cudmore.'

'Your comments in front of the officers at Watford station were pretty derogatory,' Nas said. Freddie blinked.

'I was only having a laugh.' Saunders was still grinning.

'I would prefer it if you didn't make sexual references about me in front of other people. Or at all.' Nas's ears were pink.

'Do you think I pulled off a convincing performance, Chips?' Saunders winked at him. *Smug git.*

'What does that mean?' Nas glared at him.

'Oh for god's sake, Nas!' Freddie said. 'He's gay!' For a detective she could be pretty slow sometimes. He had a photo of his boyfriend on his desk: the only personal item on it.

Chips laughed.

'What?!' Nas's mouth was open.

'You've not got a problem with me shagging men have you, Cudmore?'

'No… I… Of course not.' Her face flushed.

'We'll have to send her on diversity training, won't we, Chips?' Saunders was drumming along to the radio with his fingers. Chips was chuckling. Nas looked like she wanted the ground to open up beneath her.

'Phone's ringing.' Chips pulled his mobile from his jacket pocket, stretching as he did so and nearly filling the entire back seat. Freddie tilted her head to avoid catching a stray elbow. 'It's Green.' He put it on loudspeaker.

'Hello, Green,' Saunders said. 'We were just discussing Cudmore's homophobia.'

'We were not! I mean I am not. I do not have a problem with gay people.' Nas was wriggling in her seat. Poor Nas, trying so hard to say the right thing. Freddie felt guilty for finding it funny, but it was so rare to see the perfect Nas put a foot wrong. She was usually the one doing that.

'*Right*,' Green said, clearly confused.

'What you got for us?' Chips said.

'Not much, I'm afraid. Alex Black is a fairly common name, so hundreds of hits on the DVLA and electoral register, but none that jump out with criminal records. Unless you count a sixty-seven-year-old guy done for poaching on Skye?'

'Probably not our guy,' Chips said.

'He could be using an alias.' Saunders scratched the stubble on his chin. 'Can you narrow it down by area? Go through those who live in a one- to two-hour radius of both Chloe Strofton and Lottie Burgone.'

'It'll take time, sir,' Green said. *Just thirteen hours to save the girl's life*, thought Freddie. *Thirteen: unlucky for some.* She realised she was scratching at her wrist, deep red grooves cutting into the skin. She sat on her hands.

'Do it,' Saunders said. 'Then check against what we have on both girls, go back again and see if anything pops.'

'Yes, sir.'

They sat in silence after the call. Freddie could feel it in the air: despondency. Apprehension. Each of them was lost in their own thoughts. Everything was taking too long. Chips was reading through pages. Tilting her phone so it was turned away from him, Freddie clicked into Are You Awake. She selected 'new post', and typed:

Hey bro, a mate said you could help me get some pics of this chick?

She entered 'Farvers4Justice' as the username. Suitably MRA. Maybe she could draw him out, get him to send her something privately; something they could use. She pressed send. The post appeared on the message board. Her right leg was jiggly, drumming her fingertips against her knee. A reply! She refreshed so the message would show. Her stomach fell away. The floor reverberated. Her breath caught in her throat. She gripped a fistful of denim in her hand, trying to steady herself. No. This couldn't be happening. She blinked. Swallowed. Focused on the words:

[-] **ApollyonsRevenge** [Date -recent]
Freddie Venton, I wondered if we'd have the pleasure of your company. I assume Sergeant Cudmore is with you? Welcome to the party. *Who wants to play?*
    Alex Black.

Fuck. He must be monitoring the IP address on her phone. Was it him? The Hashtag Murderer? Freddie dropped her mobile. Dread flicked its glacial tongue over her. No. This couldn't be happening. Outside, the buildings were growing more concentrated, taller, London folding in on them, pressing down. She felt her breath accelerate. She gripped the handle next to the window. Chips glanced at her. She had to keep calm. Had to say something. She opened her mouth but no words came. Her lungs were being squeezed. He knew who she was. He knew she was here. What did it mean? She had to warn them. He knew too much. He was too close. He was monitoring them. He was watching.

'Nas!' Her voice came out as a squeak. A breath. Not loud enough.

'You all right?' Chips reached towards her with a big hand and she recoiled.

'She has panic attacks,' Nas was saying. 'You're okay, Freddie.'

'Oh perfect!' said Saunders.

'No,' Freddie said. It wasn't a panic attack, it was real panic. 'No, I'm not okay.'

'Put your head between your knees, lass.'

Her hands were slick with sweat, fumbling for her phone. She had to show them. She had to warn them.

Chips's phone rang. He pulled it from his pocket.

'DI McCain,' he grunted into it.

And Freddie saw his face sag, give, roll away into defeat. The others sensed it too. Nas had stopped talking to her and was staring at Chips, her face growing pale. Saunders turned the radio off. They all knew. *Who wants to play?* This wasn't a game you won. The odds were stacked against them from the start: he was watching. He knew it was her posting the message. He knew she was here.

Chips hung up the call, took a deep, heaving breath. 'A body matching the description of Lottie Burgone has been found near Greenwich Deer Park.'

'No!' It was Nas who shrieked. Freddie just crumbled. They were too late. He knew who she was. He knew where they were. He was two steps ahead. Lottie had never stood a chance. Tears fell from her eyes. Game over.

Chapter 30

Wednesday 16 March

20:50
T – 12 hrs 40 mins

Nasreen's feet felt like clay as she stepped from the car. They'd arrived in sombre silence at the edge of the park on Maze Hill, Saunders slowing as they'd reached a parked squad car, its portentous blue light flashing and disappearing among the gathering trees at the edge of the woodland. He'd held his warrant card up to a uniformed PC she didn't recognise, and they'd been waved in alongside them.

'No need for you to come, lass,' Chips was saying. For a moment Nas thought he was talking to her, but when she turned she could see him bent down to the car, talking to Freddie in the back. He was holding out an old-fashioned white cotton hanky. She imagined his wife lovingly ironing it for him, so he'd be smart at work, and a new deluge of horror crashed over her.

She didn't think she could do this. She was too frightened of her own voice breaking to try to offer words of comfort to Freddie who was snivelling on the back seat. She'd brought her here; she'd brought this tragedy into her life. Nasreen thought of how the suicide notes spelt out Apollyon, of how she knew both victims by extension, of how she could be the link. Of how she could have brought this heartache onto the Stroftons, onto Burgone and his parents.

'DI Saunders?' The uniformed PC had come over to introduce himself. 'PC Palmer, sir.' She tried to focus on his pained face. On what he was saying. 'The pathologist is with the body now. The park warden spotted her. She's been hidden behind some trees, away from the pathway. The park's locked up for the night you see, no one would have found her before the morning.'

'When does it open?' Saunders looked grim, but was holding it together. He was still in charge. This had happened on his watch. Would he have to tell Burgone?

'Six a.m., sir. That's what the warden said.' PC Palmer looked nervous. Finding the body of a DCI's younger sister was not a position he'd ever thought he'd find himself in.

'Not nine thirty then,' Saunders said.

'No, why?' PC Palmer tugged at his collar.

'Is she this way?' Saunders pointed at a pathway that could be glimpsed weaving through the trees.

'Dr Anderson doesn't want anyone up there till the SOCOs are done, sir.' PC Palmer was taking panicked sidesteps along with them.

'Dr Anderson can tell me that himself,' Saunders snapped. Under normal circumstances she'd have offered a comforting word to the PC, but as the trees closed overhead she still couldn't bring herself to speak. Chips had joined them, and she could see Freddie standing outside Saunders's car, gripping the door, her fingers pale and tiny in the streetlights.

A car screeched and she looked up to see a black Ford Mondeo forcibly mount the kerb behind Saunders's sporty model. The front door opened and her heart leapt as Burgone threw himself out. 'Where is she? Where is she?' he cried.

Chips made a start towards him but Saunders was there already. He had a hand to Burgone's chest.

'Sir, you don't want to do this. You don't want to be here.'

The passenger door opened and DC Morris ran out, his face a mix of confusion and shock. *He'd told Burgone about the body.*

'I tried to stop him, but he wouldn't listen!'

Rage boiled in Nasreen. *Of all the irresponsible things to do.*

'Jack,' Chips was saying, 'you shouldn't be here.' Nasreen's heart was lodged in her throat, she couldn't move her feet. Burgone's face was twisted in agony.

'I'm not leaving her out here on her own,' he said, flinging off Saunders's arm.

'Is that Jack the Lad?' PC Palmer whispered next to her.

'It's his sister,' she said, as if that were enough, her voice hard and alien. It was like she was watching all of this unfold from above.

'Okay,' Chips was saying. 'But you've got to get a hold of yourself.' Morris hung back, looking at the floor, no doubt in case anyone asked how the guv had found out about the body. 'You can't go in there like this, Jack.'

Saunders was scowling; his reaction to emotion seemed to be one of anger. And Burgone was shoving his hands through his hair. *Last night she'd had her fingers in his hair, overwhelmed by desire for him. She'd kissed him, pulled him forwards and they'd consumed each other in hasty, longing bites.* And now everything was broken. *He* was broken. Tears welled in her eyes. She reached her hand out towards him, and let it drop back. PC Palmer was too busy staring open-mouthed at the guv to notice. She swallowed and pushed it all down inside.

They walked in silence, PC Palmer leading the way, along the path and then cut away into the trees. A white van, used by the SOCOs, was parked up, its back doors open. She could see the yellow crime scene tape; hear it fluttering in the breeze. A canopied tent had been erected over the body, and for the first time she noticed there were spots of rain in the air. She looked at the fine mist of droplets that had settled over her coat sleeve: had it been raining all this time? A petite blonde SOCO in her protective all-in-one suit came out of the tent, clutching plastic tubes and bags of evidence ready for the lab. She looked at them all standing there, her eyes widening.

'Kelly, isn't it?' Saunders said. 'Can you get Anderson?' He stopped at the edge of the tape. This was not their territory. *Yet.*

The woman's small snub nose seemed to wrinkle, but she nodded when she saw Burgone standing just behind them, Chips at his side, close enough to grab the guv if he did anything stupid.

The SOCO disappeared into the tent and they could hear murmured voices. Anderson appeared, taking his plastic gloves off and putting them in a bag he'd pulled from his pocket. He was an older man, with thick grey hair cut close to his skull. Nasreen had encountered him before, and knew him to be professional and fierce, not frightened of putting any detective that tried their luck in their place. 'We have not finished clearing the scene yet,' he said.

'Special circumstances, this one, doc.' Saunders had his hands in his pockets, and he turned slightly so Anderson could see Burgone. Nasreen risked a look at him: Burgone's eyes were glassy, distant, as if he were somewhere else.

Anderson's face was unmoved, but then he let out a sigh.

'Okay. You've got two minutes. But I want you all suited up.' His words echoed off the trees surrounding them. Nasreen found herself nodding.

Kelly handed them protective suits from the back of the van and they pulled them over their clothes. She also gave them plastic covers for their shoes, face masks and gloves. 'Hoods up, please,' she said. 'We don't want any of your hairs showing up in the lab.'

Pulling her suit over her trousers, Nasreen couldn't help remembering how she'd got dressed next to Burgone's sleeping body this morning. The last twenty-four hours were meshing and mixing in an impossible and sickening way. But there was something about being in the clinical suit that pulled her back from the edge. She looked back the way they'd come. They were quite far from the path, and PC Palmer was right: you wouldn't see the body from there. A knotted clump of trees spread over them, the grass neat and clipped either by a lawnmower or the deer. Did deer eat grass? She wasn't sure.

Saunders was obviously thinking the same thing, as he said, 'Do you think the victim was killed here or elsewhere, doc?'

'Too early to say.' Anderson had rounded up his SOCO team, who stood behind him blinking at them all. Like they were two different tribes. 'But it looks like the victim suffered a blunt-force trauma to the back of the head, followed by a number of sustained blows to the head and torso.' Burgone made a tiny sound as he flinched. *Not an overdose this time.* Anderson cleared his throat and looked at the ground. This was all wrong. Why would the perp give the deadline, the threat, if he was going to kill her anyway? Though with no ransom, or other apparent motive, perhaps it was part of a game, part of the thrill for him? Nasreen felt her lip curl in disgust. Maybe he had thought the body wouldn't be found until 9.30 a.m. There were no cameras in the park, and she hadn't seen any where they'd parked up. This spot wasn't overlooked, and the weather hadn't been great today. It would have given the perp an uninterrupted spot to act. Would anyone hear you scream from here? The road would drown out much of the noise.

She clung to the analytical police side of her brain, her suit rustling in her ears, her skin growing warm in the plastic. Saunders held the tape up for Burgone to pass under, and she saw him take his arm in case he fell. She swallowed and faltered.

'You all right, lass?' Chips was at her side. She could only see his eyes above the mask, and she wondered how much of her killer Lottie had seen. Had he been wearing a mask, or did he show her his whole face? Knowing she would never tell anyone what he looked like. She nodded, and took big strides to reach the tent. Morris remained behind, one less person to disrupt the crime scene. Nasreen wished she could swap places with him. She'd seen plenty of bodies, but she didn't know if she could cope with this one. It was too close, too personal, too painful.

Burgone and Saunders stepped aside to let them into the stuffy tent, the smell of blood, like freshly cut meat, magnified by the plastic walls. Nasreen felt a bubble of sick burst up her throat and lick the back of her tongue. Saunders still had a firm grip on Burgone. She could feel the heat of him next to her. Could hear his breathing fast, sucking in and out through his face mask. The dead girl was in the far corner, her body curled away from them in a foetal position, her blonde hair darkened from blood at the crown. The slowly stiffening muscles of her back visible under the racerback bra top. Nasreen thought of Chloe, curled dead on a different forest floor. *They'd failed.* Two young girls were dead and all they had was a name. *Alex Black.* They didn't even know if it was an alias.

Burgone started next to her, his voice unfeasibly loud in the silence. 'It's not her.'

'What?' She turned to stare at him. Her pulse crashed. Was he in denial?

'It's not Lottie,' he said. Saunders's eyebrows were meeting, and she could see his hand was tightening on Burgone's sleeve.

Chips was already at the girl's body, round the other side, bending to look. 'It's not her. He's right.' The floor undulated beneath Nasreen's feet; she took a big gulp of air.

'Thank god,' Burgone whispered. '*Thank god.*' Saunders dropped his arm, and Burgone staggered back. Turning, he pushed past her and ran from the tent, leaves and twigs snapping under his feet. There was a shout from outside – probably Anderson – and she closed her eyes as they heard him retch. *It's not Lottie.*

She and Saunders stepped towards the body at the same time. As they looked from above, she could see Chips and Burgone were right. This girl was the same age as Lottie, but up close she could see her hair was a neat bob. Not shorn by a knife. Her eyes had been closed, her arms bent in front of her, hands up, bloodied, as if she'd been protecting her face. Her mind was racing, filled with relief and sadness. This was still someone's daughter, someone's loved one, killed and left on the cold ground.

'Poor lass,' Chips murmured.

'Do you think she was jogging along here when she was attacked?' she said.

'A bop and drop?' said Chips. 'Could be. Opportunistic rather than planned. As the doc says, it looks like she was hit from behind first. Then he finished off the job.'

She thought of the rain, and whether it would have washed away any forensic evidence from the pathway. Under the blood and bruising on her body, the skin was puckered. Faded red circles: four working their way down to the waistband of her leggings. 'They look like cigarette burns. Old ones.'

'Aye. Good spot. Could be a history of domestic abuse. I'd be wanting to talk to her partner if it was my job.'

Nasreen looked up shocked. 'What do you mean *if it was my job*?'

'Okay, that's enough. Let's get out of here,' Saunders said. Chips pushed his hands against his knees and straightened.

What? 'We can't just leave her!' Nasreen's voice betrayed the hysteria she'd been fighting for the last hour.

'She's not our case, Cudmore,' Saunders said. 'MIT will take over.' He held the entrance of the tent open.

'We can't just turn her over to the murder squad,' she said. A minute ago they'd thought this was Lottie and they'd been ready to throw everything they had at it to catch the killer. 'It's not right.' Chips's forehead creased under his hood.

'There's nothing to suggest this is linked to our case,' Saunders said.

'I know,' she said. 'But we can't just leave her here.' The blood-soaked grass under her head, her bruises, spoke of a vicious and frightening death.

'This isn't our patch,' Saunders said. He sounded tired, as if the last hour had taken everything he had out of him. 'We have to focus on Lottie.' He eyeballed her, daring her to disagree.

She tore her eyes away from the woman at their feet, nodded, and made to follow them out. 'They'll do a good job, lass,' Chips said quietly. 'They'll get whoever did this.' She nodded again. And left the tent without looking back.

She knew the MITs would do their job on this one. When this nightmare twenty-four hours were over, she'd find out which detective had been assigned to it, and make sure she could help in any way she could. She'd do it in her spare time if necessary.

212

But now, right now, she had to give her all to finding Lottie. Her head swam with images of the dead blonde, curled on the floor in her exercise gear. *Please don't let the same thing happen to Lottie.* Lottie's face mixed with that of the dead runner in her mind, her bloodied blonde hair framing her pretty features. She shook her head, trying to dislodge the scene.

It was now after ten o'clock. They had to make up for the time they'd lost on this. There were only eleven hours and thirty minutes left to find Lottie. Burgone was nowhere to be seen. Anderson and the other SOCOs were headed back for the tent, Saunders filling them in, Chips talking to PC Palmer. Nasreen closed her eyes to compose herself, inhaling the scent of wet pine from the woodland. She couldn't – *wouldn't* – see another dead girl. They would find Lottie. But no matter how much she promised herself, the dead runner lying metres from them told her you couldn't count on anything. If someone wanted to hurt you, they could. If someone wanted to hurt Lottie, they could.

She passed her suit and gloves to one of the waiting SOCOs and started back towards the road. Someone needed to tell Freddie: she would still think this was Burgone's sister. Saunders and Chips were following her. She walked back to the path, through the dark trees, imagining what the last frantic moments of the running girl's life had been like. Had she recognised her attacker? Was she still awake, groggy after the blow? Did she know she was being dragged? Did she fight back, scratch at her assailant, lodge their DNA under her fingernails? That made her think of Lottie, and the signs of the struggle they'd found mere streets away from here. Two girls, two runners, snatched in the same twenty-four hours. Was it possible this case was related after all? She turned to watch Chips and Saunders emerging through the trees behind her.

A cacophony of beeps sounded. *Their phones.* She wrenched it from her pocket.

'What the hell?' Chips had his phone already in his hand.

An angry red circle denoting a new text message flashed accusingly on her phone. Trepidation smashed against her. She tapped the message.

'What's going on?' Saunders was saying.

No, please no. It was another photo.

'Oh shit,' Chips said. And then they were sprinting, all three of them, along the path, towards the car. She was ahead of the others. She flung herself out onto the roadside. Burgone's car was gone. Freddie was standing outside Saunders's car. She had her phone open and was staring at the screen. She was shaking. *She'd got the message too.*

'We need to get on to Jack right now!' she heard herself shout. *If he'd got this – if he'd seen this…* The memory of him flinging himself towards them when he thought *this* was Lottie flashed through her mind. When he thought it was her dead under the trees. They had to reach him. They had to help him.

Saunders powered past her and then they were all in the car, squealing away from the park. Panting and condensation filled the vehicle. Saunders was speeding – but was it already too late? Nasreen stared at the phone in her hand, the photo backlit, jolting as Saunders flung them round corners. She felt sick. Her mouth drowning in saliva.

It was a close up of Lottie. Tears in her eyes. The gloved hand pressed the knife into her throat. Blood dribbled down and over the sign that had been taped to her chest. Scrawled on it were the words *watch me die.*

Underneath was a message:

You won't get so lucky this time,
Nasreen Cudmore. You have 11
hours & 30 mins to save Lottie
Burgone's life. Happy Birthday,
Freddie Venton! Who wants to play?
   Apollyon's Revenge

He'd addressed her. It was aimed at her. It was her fault. Both
Chips's and Saunders's phones rang. The car was full of noise.
She could hear Freddie's teeth chattering. Her name was there
too; her birthday! He knew who they were. He knew all about
them. There was nowhere to hide. Apollyon's Revenge had found
them.

Chapter 31

Wednesday 16 March

22:20
T − 11 hrs 10 mins

Everything moved fast around Freddie. Lottie wasn't the body in the wood. Lottie wasn't dead. Lottie was hurt. Lottie was in danger.

They were at the office in what felt like minutes. But time was speeding up. They only had eleven hours to save her. Nas, Chips, and Saunders were all shouting into their phones. The message and the photo of Lottie hadn't just been sent to them, it had been emailed anonymously to every newsroom in the UK. The same message and photo had also been posted on Facebook, Twitter, Snapchat, Google+, Instagram and Vine: all from accounts called Apollyon's Revenge. Each of them linking back to Are You Awake. The name and link of the site was everywhere. It was trending worldwide. And Lottie's terrified face was being shared across hundreds, thousands, tens of thousands of social media pages. Freddie had trained as a journalist and knew the UK press operated a blackout on reporting on active kidnapping cases, but the internet had smashed straight through that. Lottie's disappearance, who she was, who Nasreen was, who Freddie was, was public knowledge. Statistics ran through Freddie's head. *Fifteen million Twitter users in the UK. Three hundred and ten million users worldwide in a single month. Thirty-two million Facebook users in the UK, and 1.6 billion Facebook users worldwide per month.* All those people. All those screens. All those eyes. It was incomprehensible. Uncontainable. They couldn't stop the news spreading. They couldn't catch hold of it. It snaked away from them, exploded, reformed, re-shared, re-tweeted, reborn. The horror of what was happening to Lottie – an Instagram star, an internet sensation – was magnified in devices across the country, across the continent, across the world. The fear in her eyes had become a commodity. It was picked over, passed around, commented on, joked about. Viral. Apollyon's Revenge had released a virus: Lottie's terror transmitted from phone to phone. An airborne disease of fear. Wildfire burning through everyone's hands.

Lottie's kidnap was now headline news. The photo of her bound and gagged would be reproduced in grainy print on the front pages of the early editions. Breaking news on the ten o'clock show. Her face a permanent fixture on the rolling news channels. Freddie knew the story: attractive blonde kidnapped in sensational social-media-based plot. Possible links to the Hashtag Murderer. Apollyon's Revenge hadn't just brought the circus to town, he'd brought every clown on the globe. Everyone's eyes were on them. Everyone knew what was happening. They'd lost control of the press coverage. They'd lost control of everything. The office was full of police. Ringing phones. Shouting. People were running in and out. And Freddie couldn't do anything. She was useless.

'How did he do it?' Nas was saying.

'The text message version was only sent to us and the guv,' Saunders barked. 'The newspapers and channels got an email instead. The texts were sent from an automated computer account – not another phone. We can't trace it. It's bounced between here and – fuck!' He flung his hand up in frustration.

'But how did he get our numbers?' Nas was saying. 'And Freddie's?'

'A hack,' Chips was saying. 'Or a leak? He could have someone on the inside.' They looked around the room with alarm: it was swimming with people. Freddie didn't know any of these people. She didn't trust any of them. And there was something else: something Nas had said when she'd appeared out of the dark, ghostly trees. Something was very wrong, but she couldn't find it among all the noise.

'We can't get anything off the email address that sent the message to the media either,' Chips said. 'The whole lot's gone via Tor: it's anonymous. The Twitter account, Instagram, and all the social media accounts that posted the same message look like they've been hacked. They're all registered to a handful of stupid buggers who had easy-to-guess passwords. It's simple enough to do and means we've got next to no way of finding out who really posted that message.'

'Dammit!' Saunders slammed his hand onto the nearest desk.

'The photo's not geotagged,' Nas said. 'But I'm getting it blown up. There's something in the background. If we can see what it is it could give us a clue as to where he's keeping her.'

Freddie put her head in her hands and took a deep breath. It was like the room had no air left. She had to get out. Keep breathing. *One, two, three…* She stumbled into the corridor.

Took the stairs. *Thirteen. Fourteen. Fifteen.* Her breath fast now. *Too fast.* Her heart hammering to get out. Then she was out the ground floor fire escape. Out the back of the building. Gasping. Taking a huge greedy gulp of air. Her chest heaved. Slowed. The noises around her started to come back. A car beeped in the distance. A taxi drove past. Two people walked along the street laughing, a drink after work. *She was okay.* She was in London. She was okay. She was scratching her wrist again. Fuck it. She'd needed something for her hands to do. Checking her back pocket for her cash card Freddie walked down to the shop with the Lotto sign outside. A man stood behind the till, looking up at a small television on the wall. On the screen was the news. A photo she recognised from Lottie's Instagram page. Then a stock image of DCI Jack Burgone in uniform – it was difficult to tally the composed, smiling man on screen with the distraught man who'd run into the woods to be with his dead sister. What did it feel like to think a person you loved was dead? Murdered? What did it feel like to then have hope, and then this? She thought of the sickening photo of Lottie. How much could one person take?

On screen a photo of Nasreen appeared. It must have been taken at a crime scene – she was outside a building, walking across camera. Her hair was scraped back into a ponytail and she had a look Freddie recognised as 'pissed off' on her face. She still looked like she was in a movie. Freddie would've looked like she'd been dragged through a hedge backwards. And as if to prove the point the image shifted and there she was – a photo from her Facebook page, taken at a 1980s fancy dress party. She was wearing a shoulder-padded jacket that made her look like a Michelin man, and her smile was lopsided, as though she was drunk. Which she had been. It must have been about one in the morning when they took that. The shop assistant turned to glare at her, as if it were her fault she was on the bloody television.

He had an excellent monobrow. 'Ten B&H? Ta.' Freddie held out her card for contactless. Outside she cupped the cigarette against the wind and inhaled.

As soon as she turned the corner she realised she'd made a mistake. She thought this was a secure building. Didn't that mean it was a secret? She should have stayed round the back.

A woman on the edge of the scrum, dark hair hanging over one side of her face, her microphone in her hand, smiling at the camera, caught sight of her. *Fuck.* 'Freddie! Freddie Venton! Do you know who has Lottie Burgone?'

They surged towards her. Journalists, twenty at least. Lightbulbs flashing. Blinding her. *Shouting.*

'Is Lottie Burgone dead?'

'Is the Hashtag Murderer back?'

'Has the kidnapper demanded money for Lottie's return?'

'Is the message board site Are You Awake involved?'

'Should these sites be closed?'

'Is this personal?'

'Happy Birthday, Freddie!'

It'd be further to turn back. Putting her free arm up in front of her face she pushed on for the building, the rising shouts mirroring the rising dread she felt. Lottie was out there: trapped, tied up, terrified; and the whole world had an opinion on it. *A tweet. A share. A thinkpiece.* Any illusion that they had control of the investigation had been shattered into thousands of unfixable pieces the moment the photo of Lottie had been sent to the press. There would be crank calls, panic and the general public to deal with. They had eleven hours to find her. *Less than half a day.* The clock ticking down with each camera flash. How could they possibly reach her in time now?

Chapter 32

Wednesday 16 March

22:41
T – 10 hrs 59 mins

Chips handed Nas a cup of coffee. She took it gratefully, looking away from the blown-up versions of the photo Alex Black had sent them. She couldn't look at the girl's eyes. Every time she caught a flash of Lottie's terrified expression she was back in Greenwich Deer Park, the blonde hair of the runner splayed on the ground. The background behind Lottie was dark, the light limited. The wall behind the girl, and it did look like a wall, was dark brown – discoloured maybe?

'How you getting on?' Chips perched on the edge of her desk, which creaked under his bulk.

'It could be a disused building? Looks damp.' There were what looked like green water marks over the dark brown walls. The room had a low ceiling.

'What about the wall hanging?'

She showed him the zoomed-in section of print. To the left of Lottie's head, behind her by a metre or two, was something hanging on the wall. White, or at least once that colour. They could only see a section of it. 'I can't tell what it is. A print of a drawing maybe?' Four long, thin lozenge shapes were visible, pointed loops marked their ends, as if four asparagus stalks had been laid next to each other at a fifteen-degree angle. 'What do you think these are? Fingers?'

Chips held the print away from him. 'Pencils, maybe? Or bananas?'

This was all they had to go on. Her heart was racing after seeing the body. She couldn't see another. Lottie couldn't end up like that. She hadn't seen Burgone since they'd arrived back, but she knew he was here: his car was downstairs. Chips had been to speak to him. The sound of Burgone retching in the wood in relief, or horror, juddered through her. It was a visceral response; he'd been stripped by this, robbed of his professionalism, his dignity. The brilliant cop was gone, and instead he was just a man. A victim himself. And the message had been addressed to her: she was doing this to him. She shook it all off. Looked again at the blown-up image. She wondered if Freddie might recognise it. 'Where's Freddie gone?'

'Guv!' Morris, his voice near hysterical, was pointing at his desktop. He had the news on. The cameras were outside the office. *Oh shit.*

'Found her.' Chips nodded at the screen as Freddie rounded on the poor person behind the camera. Nasreen recognised that look all too well. *Red mist.* 'What's she doing?'

'They've pissed her off.' Nasreen shook her head. The woman worked as a journalist: you would think she'd know better than to take the bait.

'Put the sound on,' Saunders barked. *Please don't.* Morris, ever accommodating, whacked the volume right up.

The room hushed as a chirpy female voiceover said, 'And we're getting reports of a live comment coming from Freddie Venton, the consultant we believe is working with the police on this case, right now.'

'Consultant!' Morris scoffed. Nasreen winced.

A plummy male voice off camera could be heard saying, 'Is this a warning to silly girls not to take obscene photos of themselves?'

Crap.

Freddie's nostrils flared as she spun to face the guy. Her voice crackled and sparked with unsuppressed rage. 'Every woman, every person, has the right to take whatever photos of themselves they like, without having to worry about twisted, entitled idiots stealing them or sharing them without their consent. The ones at fault are those who circulate intimate images to humiliate, embarrass or coerce others.' White-hot spittle rained. 'No one is responsible for Lottie Burgone's kidnap other than her kidnapper.' Nasreen's heart leapt. 'The person calling himself Alex Black.' And it crashed back into her chest. *You couldn't just quit while you were ahead?* They shouldn't be commenting on this.

Freddie looked straight at the camera. 'I am sick of being told what to wear, how much to drink, where to go, where not to go, to be nice, to smile, interrupted, dictated to, blamed, lectured, trolled and patronised. *We've* had enough.' There was a cheer in the background and a few people laughed. The camera zoomed in, so Freddie's face filled the screen. 'We are not victims. You don't get to blame us for the things *you* do. You're screaming into the wind, you and your man-baby pals, Black. You've already lost. We run the game now.'

The camera cut back to the chirpy woman in the studio, her eyes wide. 'Well, that was quite some statement,' she said. Her co-presenter had a rictus smile on his face. 'I think we can all agree that was...'

'Really quite unexpected,' the co-presenter guffawed.

Chirpy's head snapped to glare at him. 'I haven't finished, Simon.'

Nasreen smiled and shook her head as Morris cut the volume. The room dissolved into excitable chatter. A couple of people were clapping. *She'd stuck up for the guv's sister: that made her a hero.* There was a whoop. *Only Freddie could lose it and deliver a political diatribe during the middle of a police investigation.* And she knew just who was going to get blamed for bringing her in... It was over. Burgone had said Freddie couldn't interact with anyone outside of this office. And she certainly couldn't speak to the press. Saunders would never let her stay on the team now, but when she looked up he had a smile on his face, and he was still looking at the screen. He turned and his face fell into a hard scowl. 'Okay, people, settle down, that's enough,' he snapped. Hush descended on the room.

'Remind me never to play Scrabble with Freddie,' Chips said, standing up from the desk. He looked sympathetic, as if he were at a wake.

Saunders was powering towards her. 'You and me need to have a little chat, Cudmore.' His voice was low and threatening – his favoured style. She was aware the whole room was listening, hushed in anticipation of the fireworks. A dissonance of mobile tones sounded. *Oh god, not again.*

'We weren't the only ones watching.' Chips had his phone out.

Saunders was frowning at the screen, his eyes widening, a look of what? Shock? He stared at Nasreen.

'*Cudmore?*' Chips's pudgy face gaped at her.

There were murmurs round the room; people were pushing themselves away from their computer screens. *Had he emailed it again?* People were turning to look at her. 'What? What is it? Another photo? Is Lottie okay?' The eyes of the room were on her. Dread tingled over her whole body. Chips turned his phone round, shaking his head as he held it out to her. And she knew straight away what it was.

To: JonathanBurgone@police.uk
From: NCudmore@btinternet.com

I'm sorry I left without waking you. I didn't know what to say. I know we haven't worked together for long, but you need to understand that I'm not like this. This is the first one-night stand I've ever had. I drank too much. Way too much. I can't undo what happened, but I can take responsibility for my actions. I admire you greatly. Maybe too much, maybe that was the problem. And if there's any way we can forget this ever happened… I want to fix this, sir. I'm committed to the team. I promise nothing like this will ever happen again.

Chapter 33

Wednesday 16 March

22:51
T – 10 hrs 49 mins

Freddie's heart was thumping in the lift. *Bastard. Bastard!* She'd let him get to her. She could just hear her mum now: *Freddie, you've got to watch that temper of yours. It lands you in hot water. And couldn't you have run a brush through your hair?* It'd be all over the news now: her threatening a kidnapper! Would he retaliate? Had she endangered Lottie? Her stomach lurched at the thought. Her fingers tapped frantically at her phone. She had no signal in the lift. The screen was frozen on the last Alex Black search result she'd been looking at in the car. It wasn't an MRA site or another display of awful photos. It was text heavy: a blog titled 'Cynthia Warner.' She scanned the menu tabs:

The lift doors opened. She clicked on the Alex Black page, looking up just in time to avoid walking into a pinch-faced woman in a grey skirt suit. 'Sorry. Do you know if there's somewhere I can go for one of these?' She rattled her fag packet at her.

The woman didn't smile. 'There's a balcony on the next floor. Next to the fire exit.'

'Cheers.' Freddie looked back down at her phone. The page had opened onto what looked like a blog. She pushed open the door to the back staircase and ran up. On the next floor was another fire door. Freddie tested it gingerly. Evacuating the building by setting off the fire alarm wouldn't be a good move right now. But all that greeted her was the rush of cool air from outside and rhythmic hum of London drifting up from below. It was comforting to know life was still normal for other people out there. That they weren't trapped in a Kafkaesque nightmare of reoccurring internet criminals. Her phone beeped.

'You're not supposed to be out here.' She jumped. At her feet was the man she recognised from the park: DCI Burgone. He looked different with his face composed: quite hot. He had a touch of Tom Hiddleston about him. He was leaning against the stone wall of the building, elbows resting on his knees. Ornate brickwork shielded them from the outside, so she couldn't see the road below, only the twinkling towers of the London skyline. 'Freddie Venton, I presume?' He held a hand out for her to shake. The moonlight picked out his cheekbones like they were made of cut glass. And he was bloody posh. As if she'd stumbled on a character from *Brideshead Revisited*.

'Fag?' She put one between her lips and offered him the carton.

'You're not supposed to smoke up here,' Burgone said.

'Some woman just told me I could,' Freddie said, sliding down the wall to sit beside him. She didn't really want company, but the guy's sister was missing. And she'd potentially put her in more danger by messaging Alex Black.

'Which woman?' He was a typical policeman, asking a load of questions.

Freddie sparked up as she replied. 'Thin, dark hair piled on her head, grey skirt suit, face like a smacked arse.'

'Ah,' Burgone said. 'That'll be the superintendent.'

'Bollocks,' Freddie exhaled. 'And I was just getting settled in.'

'Can I have one of those?' he said. 'I've changed my mind.'

Freddie handed him the packet and the lighter.

He coughed as he inhaled. 'I haven't smoked since Eton.' Freddie raised her eyebrows. 'Did that make me sound like a twat?'

'Yup.' She blew smoke up into the air, noticing the faint rings of red around his eyes.

'I'm a bit out of sorts.' He looked at his phone. The screensaver was of him and Lottie. She with her arm round his shoulder.

'I should take up vaping really.' She leant back and looked at the sky. 'Makes you look like such a tosser though.'

She caught a slight smile in the corner of her eye. 'I can see the risk,' he said.

She paused for a moment. It hung in the air between them. The weight of the situation. The fate of his sister. 'She seems like she's really nice,' she said, nodding at the photo.

'She is,' he smiled. 'This was on Sunday. We met for brunch. I get busy at work, so we don't always get to spend time together.' Freddie snatched the phone from him. 'Hey!'

'What's that?' She pointed at the watch on Lottie's wrist. *She'd seen one before.*

'A smartwatch,' he said. 'It was a gift, I think.'

'It's a FitSpo,' she said. 'Some cockblanket I went to uni with has one.' He looked offended. '*Sorry*. Look, the point is it tracks your movements. He's always posting his stats. His running routes and stuff on it.' Burgone was already on his feet. 'It works in tandem with but separate to your phone. These babies beam out a whole stack of info. I read a piece about it: advertisers suck it up and half the time people don't realise they're sharing all this data about themselves.'

Burgone pulled her arm up. She dropped her cigarette. He ground both of them underfoot. 'If we can access her account...'

'Then we can pick up her GPS.' They were running. Down the stairs. They burst into the office – she panting, Burgone fine. Everyone stared at them. Something was wrong. Where was Nas?

'Jack...' Chips came towards them, solemn. Freddie felt sick. Her outburst: what had he done to Lottie?

'What is it – have you found her?' Burgone's voice grew anguished. It twisted inside Freddie.

'No, nothing like that,' Chips said quickly.

'Then tell me later. We need to get onto FitSpo – it's a smartwatch company. Lottie has one. It has a tracker in it.'

'On it!' Saunders shouted from the far desk. He was standing with his phone tucked between his ear and shoulder, and typing with a look of extreme concentration on his face.

'Her route might be on her Facebook page. Some people share them automatically,' Freddie said. Her heart was thudding. Chips was at the desktop.

'This is DI Peter Saunders. I need to speak to your IT department now. It's urgent. Thank you. I'll hold.'

'Nothing on her Facebook page that looks like it.' Chips pressed his lips together.

'My mother always moans about her doing it – she thinks running is unladylike,' Burgone was gabbling. Pacing.

'They've given me her login details!' Saunders shouted. They crowded round his screen as he typed. The dashboard opened.

'There – routes!' Freddie pointed at the menu tab. *This could be it.* If the FitSpo had picked up Lottie's GPS then it would know where she was. They could find her. They could save her. She looked at the time: just over ten hours to go. Her pulse increased.

Saunders clicked and scrolled. Each route was the same: a green line, wobbly, as if it had been hand drawn, snaking round Greenwich in a loop. 'Looks like she ran the same route every day. These have been shared to Instagram,' he said.

'Stupid girl.' Burgone's voice was tight. 'Anyone would know where to find her.'

'Here, look.' The last route started out like the others, before it veered off track. 'That must be when he put her in the vehicle.' The line veered right.

'That's the Blackwall Tunnel!' Chips said.

'He took the North Circular, then the M11,' Saunders said, following the line as it snaked out of the city. And then it stopped.

'Where's that? Is that where she is?' Freddie said. *This was it. This was it!*

'It looks like it's on the M11 – but just stops,' Saunders said.

'There's nothing there.' Chips was shaking his head. 'After Loughton it's just fields, pull it up on Google Earth. He must have realised. He tossed it.'

'No,' Freddie said. 'No! She's *got* to be there!' Burgone sat heavily onto the chair.

'We'll call traffic. Get the helicopter and heat-seeking over there,' Saunders said, squeezing Burgone's shoulder.

'Chips is right,' Burgone said.

'We'll do it anyway,' Saunders said. 'If we find the watch it might have something forensics can use.'

'He was headed for the M25,' Chips said. 'Let's cross-reference this with what Green's got on her list of names.'

Freddie stepped backwards from them. *They were just going to give up. To stop.* 'What if she's in one of those fields?'

'She's in a building,' Chips said kindly. 'We know that from the photo he sent. There's nothing in that area it could be. But we'll get the helicopter out – double check.' It wasn't fair. They'd been so close. 'Look,' Chips said gently. 'I know Nasreen wanted you to look at the blown-up photo.' *Why did he call her Nasreen? He always called her Cudmore.* 'Why don't you go help her with that? She's in the meeting room.'

'Are you trying to get rid of me?'

'Have you seen what he sent?' Chips asked. *The text message.* She scrabbled at her pocket, her fingernails catching on the hem.

'What is it?' Burgone said.

Chips's face flushed. 'It's a personal email, Jack. Between you and the lass.' The final dregs of colour in Burgone's face drained away. Freddie was already out of the door, her phone shaking in her hand. Alex Black had lashed out at Nas and she was to blame.

Chapter 34

Wednesday 16 March

23:21
T – 10 hrs 19 mins

She had known something was off. Known there was something Nas wasn't telling her. She'd called him Jack when they got the photo of Lottie – she would never normally use a superior officer's first name. It all made sense now. Nas's desperation over this case. The way she'd lost her cool. The way she'd gone rogue. Freddie had never been more proud of her in her life. The meeting room was empty, Nas's jacket hanging forlornly over the back of the chair. Freddie knew where she'd be. It was easy to hide in a building where the majority of the staff were men. She pushed open the ladies', bending down as she walked past the stalls. Only one was occupied and Freddie recognised Nas's polished shoes. Spotless as ever. She leant back against the sink.

'You can't stay in here forever,' she said. She heard Nas's feet shuffle on the floor. But there was no reply. She waited. 'I know it's you, Nas.' *Nothing*. She crossed her arms. This wasn't the time for a pity party. They had just over ten hours to find Lottie. Sweat formed on her brow; she blew at it with her breath. They had to get back to it. 'I can't believe you slept with a public school boy! *Bleurgh*. Must have been like shagging the Chancellor of the Exchequer.'

There was a sigh. 'I just need a minute.'

'It's not as bad as you think. I screwed my boss at work once. In the stationery cupboard. Two colleagues found us when they were looking for printer paper. No one blinked an eye.' She had still been finding paperclips in her hair a week later.

'This is the police, Freddie. It's different. Superintendent Lewis bans relationships between colleagues.'

'You're not having a relationship. You had sex,' Freddie said. 'It's not a big deal. People will judge you, but so what? They do that anyway.' Nas emitted a small noise – something like a snort. 'I bet Saunders had a field day.'

'He was angry,' she said.

'I'm sure.' *He would've loved that.* The perfect opportunity to stick the knife in. The guy was a musclebound Machiavelli.

'Not like that. He was angry at him.'

'Burgone? Did he think he took advantage – because reading between the lines in that email I would've said you were pretty up for it?'

'Freddie!' Nas flung the door open and glared at her.

'You not going to flush?' She raised an eyebrow.

'I didn't go.' She stomped out and leant against the sink next to her, like she used to as a teen. 'I meant he got angry at Alex Black. Saunders was furious because he said he was trying to divide and conquer. He was so caught up in that that I think he forgot about me.' She turned and rinsed her hands under the tap. Apparently Nas's hygiene standards were drummed into her hard.

'He has a point,' Freddie said. 'Much as I hate to admit it.'

Nasreen sighed. 'Everything's such a mess. I can't help thinking that if it wasn't for me and Jack, then Lottie wouldn't have been taken.'

'Whoever's done this has been planning it for ages. And she was already gone by the time you sent that email. You just gave him an extra tool to whack you with.' Nas nodded, though Freddie knew she was trying to convince herself at the same time. She watched as Nas checked under her eyes for mascara. She looked tired. Freddie knew what a hypocrite she was being, given that she pretty much hadn't left the house for the last three months, but she pushed on. 'Hiding away won't help anything. Lottie needs you.' *I need you.*

'What about Jack?' Nas whispered. 'I don't want to get him into trouble.'

Freddie looked in the mirror, using her nail to free a bit of food that was stuck between her teeth. 'No one's worrying about that now. We need to keep our eyes on Lottie. Don't let this fucker win: he's trying to derail you.'

'I wish you hadn't gone on the evening news.' Nas shook her head.

'Not my finest hour, admittedly. Another one to worry about later. We need to stay focused.'

'Thank you.' Nas looked at her as if it were just the two of them versus the world. 'When did you get so clever, Freddie?'

'I'm a late bloomer. Now, Chips said you wanted to show me some photos?'

Nas nodded her head. Looked once more in the mirror, and tugged the cuffs of her shirt sleeves down so they were straight. *Ready.*

'Attagirl,' said Freddie.

She glanced at her phone. Ten hours to go. Precious seconds were ticking by. Alex Black had successfully got under Nas's skin. Destabilised her. Shaken the team. What more was he capable of? What else did he know? She thought of her fear in the car, when he'd known it was her posting on Are You Awake. She felt like they were being watched. Was he in their phones? Their emails? In here? She glanced behind her, as if a shadowy figure might be lurking in the corner. But the bathroom was empty.

Chapter 35

Wednesday 16 March

23:40
T – 9 hrs 50 mins

'Pencils? Maybe? I don't know. Sorry, Nas.' Freddie handed the blown-up photo to her. It felt important, but she couldn't work out what it was. Couldn't see it. She rubbed her gritty eyes. It was twenty to midnight. Nine hours and fifty minutes left. They were into single figures. Nearly into the next day. *Deadline day.*

'Worth a shot,' Nas said. 'We're narrowing it down. The info you got from the smartwatch tells us which direction they were headed in. We know we're looking for a building. Small. Disused by the looks of it, and Green's working through the names she has on the list. The net's closing in.'

Freddie looked at the time on her phone. But would it be quick enough?

'I'm gonna take a break and grab a coffee. Do you want me to grab you one?'

'Please,' Freddie said. Her body was dog tired. Nas must be exhausted – she was doing all this on a hangover. 'Do you want to grab a few minutes kip?' She'd seen a couple of the officers curled up on chairs, under jackets. But she couldn't stop. Couldn't just lie down and go to sleep while Lottie was out there, her life ticking away. Saunders and Chips showed no sign of stopping, and she doubted Nas would either, but she had to ask.

'I'll stretch my legs and I'll feel better,' said Nas, picking her jacket back up.

'You okay if I use your laptop?' she asked. They were in a weird, standoffish place since they'd had their heart to heart in the toilets. Struggling to fit back into – *what?* The normal routine? She wondered if all female friendships were like this. Just as complex as those between romantic partners, with moods and rhythms, moments where you pulled together and moments when you fell apart. Apart from her relationship with her parents, Nas was by far the most continuous presence in Freddie's life. They'd even weathered an eight-year 'break', after Gemma tried to kill herself and Nas had been homeschooled. But where there were countless articles on romantic relationship dos and don'ts, and how-to dating guides, there was nothing on friendships. They had so much history it dominated every space they stood in. Nas made her who she was. Freddie would go to the ends of the earth for her. She'd do more for Nas than she would for any man, regardless of how long she'd been shagging him. But she didn't know if Nas felt the same. Or if it even mattered.

She typed in the address of Cynthia Warner's blog and read the Alex Black page. It gave details of Are You Awake and what to do if photos of you were shared on it. The page also documented posts by Alex Black across the internet. It read like she was amassing a case file: compiling evidence. She leant towards the computer, feeling hope lift inside her. There was a huge amount of detailed work in here. It included a plea for more information.

Freddie clicked back to Are You Awake and typed in 'Cynthia Warner'. Was she a victim herself? A number of hits appeared. No skin shots, but photos of what she assumed was Cynthia Warner's face photoshopped onto images of Jabba the Hutt, hippopotamuses, slugs. There was a theme. There was also a link back to an MRA site, and an article called 'Is Feminism Making Women Fat?' which contained references to Cynthia Warner. Was it so personal because Cynthia was getting close? Her stomach fluttered in excitement: this woman could be the key to finding Alex Black.

Nas walked back in, holding two mugs. 'You need to look at this. We should speak to this woman. She's been monitoring Black for months. She might be able to identify him.'

'Agreed,' Nas said. 'I'll run it past Saunders and go call her.'

Freddie moved between Cynthia's site and Are You Awake. Nas hadn't mentioned the possibility of speaking to Apollyon since they'd been back. Everything had moved so quickly, had she just forgotten? The thought of her friend talking to that monster set her teeth on edge. Her chest compressed. There had to be another way. If they could trace Alex Black through this woman, Cynthia, then they could find Lottie. If there was a link, if the Hashtag Murderer was orchestrating this somehow, let them worry about it later. Let someone else talk to him. But the more she tried to reason with herself, the more she felt his grip, tightening over her ribs. Closing over her mouth. She shook herself. She had to stop this. She was tired: it was playing tricks on her mind.

The building had grown quiet over the last few hours. The

majority of the workers had gone home. Where was that for her? Her parents' house, steeped in its misery? Somewhere she had yet to find? She didn't know anymore.

Nas leant into the room, making her jump. 'Cynthia Warner's on her way in. She's based in London. A squad car's picking her up from Islington.'

Freddie nodded. Took a moment to hope, pray, that this woman would hold the answer. That she would lead them to Lottie. Opening her eyes, she saw the steady stream of new comments on Are You Awake. Each sentence a line of hate. Each word a slap. It was time to stem the flow.

Chapter 36

Thursday 17 March

00:43
T – 8 hrs 47 mins

Nasreen was heading down to reception to collect Cynthia Warner. Morris stepped out of the gents and an ugly sneer spread across his face. 'Can we all have a go, or do you only shag DCIs and above?'

Anger and shame burned through her. 'Fuck off, Morris.'

'Touchy!' he laughed.

Pushing past him into the stairwell, she was relieved to find herself alone. She could punch Morris in his smug, disgusting face. Where was Jack? Was he angry? Upset? Did he blame her for the leaked email? This was a total disaster, and she hadn't even had to face anyone senior yet.

It was Thursday. *Deadline day.* Under nine hours to go. Sliding ever closer to 9.30 a.m., when what was left of Nasreen's life would be detonated. Lottie would be killed. Jack's heart would break. Her heart would break. The horror of the situation threatened to rear up and throw her off course.

Cynthia Warner was standing in reception, a visitor lanyard round her neck. Short, with a wide torso, she was swathed in various dark layers of clothing. A large handbag hung from her shoulder and in a fabric shopper she had a collection of files tied together with what looked like red legal ribbon. Nasreen had taken some time to look into Cynthia and discovered she'd been arrested for breach of peace at a Greenham Common rally in the eighties. She'd not crossed paths with the law again, but Nasreen had noted a litany of campaigning causes across the woman's social media – Amnesty International petitions and lots of articles from the *New Statesman*. She was the kind of busybody do-gooder that used to clog up her old station's reception, shouting about parking rights. It would be like sitting in the room with two Freddies.

Nasreen touched her ID against the barrier. 'Mrs Warner, I'm Sergeant Nasreen Cudmore, thank you for coming in so quickly.' She held out her hand to shake.

Cynthia's round face separated into an efficient smile as she dropped her phone in her bag and grabbed Nasreen's hand with a force that belied her diminutive stature. '*Ms* Warner. Pleased to meet you, Sergeant Cudmore, I'm a big fan of your work.'

A fan? Her work? 'I just do my job. Thank you.'

'Nonsense.' Cynthia whirled the lengths of fabric that hung from her and waddled towards the security barrier. 'It's vital that we have an increasing number of diverse faces representing the police force in this country. Time we broke down some of these barriers.'

Diverse? 'My ethnicity has nothing to do with my placement in the force, Ms Warner.'

Cynthia turned and smiled warmly at Nasreen, her small rabbit eyes twitching. 'Of course, dear. I'm just saying you're a beacon. A role model. I did a talk at a school in Hackney the other week and showed them photos of you at the arrest of the Hashtag Murderer.'

Nasreen felt a chill go through her. The Apollyon Hashtag Murderer case had been front-page news for weeks. Her face, her photo and her actions had all been part of that. She still couldn't get used to strangers who thought they knew her. Inwardly she groaned as she imagined what the Hackney kids had thought of this woman's slideshow. 'As I'm sure you're aware, we're working on a pressing case at this minute. Thank you for coming in so swiftly.' She steered Cynthia Warner towards the lift.

'That poor girl. I feared this would happen,' Cynthia sighed.

Nasreen needed to stay away from the subject of Lottie. 'We appreciate your discretion on this matter, Ms Warner.' The doors opened. 'If we could take a look at your research and ask you some questions about the suspect named Alex Black that would be great.'

'That man is depraved.'

'We can talk discreetly here,' said Nas, leading the woman into the meeting room. The phone on the desk was already connected so DI Saunders, Chips and Freddie could listen in. 'Please: have a seat.' Cynthia manoeuvred her hips into the chair and placed the folders she'd brought with her onto the table between them. Hopefully she'd agree to leave them behind.

Nasreen kept her manner clipped. They needed to find out fast if this woman did have any relevant info. 'Cynthia, do you know who Alex Black is? In real life? Do you have any contact details for him?'

'No,' she said.

Nasreen felt her shoulders droop. 'You've clearly been researching him for quite a while. You've never seen anything that would lead you to guess where he's based?'

'No, I haven't.' Her eyebrows knitted together and she frowned, as if she hadn't thought of this before. 'I contact the girls, or try to.' She tapped the files. 'So that we have everything ready for prosecution.'

'You've spoken to the girls featured on the site?' This sounded more promising.

'Most of them. I either contact them when they post themselves – trying to get the images taken down – or when *they* post their details.'

'Do you mean when they dox them – share the girls' telephone numbers?' How many had they done it to?

'Yes. And sometimes they post their work addresses, or their home addresses,' she said.

'Do they dox them all?'

'No,' she said. 'Some don't even know their photos are there until I contact them.' A look of sadness hooded her eyes further. *Would it be better to remain ignorant?*

'And you've never spoken to the police about any of this?' Nasreen asked.

'Oh, I've tried.' She sounded accusatory. 'There was a woman officer at my local station – honestly, I thought she was on my side. She took me out for a cup of tea at some greasy cafe and said there wasn't anything they could do about all these poor girls being victimised like this. They didn't have the manpower. She suggested I turn my research over to the Internet Watch Foundation. But I wasn't going to do that unless I knew they'd act on it.' She rapped her ringed fingers against the folders. 'Some of the girls in here are only fourteen.'

Nasreen sympathised with the officer who'd dealt with this

prickly woman. The Are You Awake website was encrypted. The policewoman would have quickly found herself at a dead end. The way Alex Black had sourced the team's mobile numbers, her email account, potentially breaching the police's own intranet, showed how Cynthia Warner was trying to fight an opponent she could never beat. She was hopelessly out of her depth. 'I'm sorry you were told that, Cynthia. I can promise we'll look at what you have now.'

'Now it's too late. He's got that poor girl!' Her face coloured in angry raspberry-coloured blotches. 'I knew something like this would happen!'

'Why do you say that?'

'He's evil!' she spat.

'There's nothing else you've seen, something you might not have thought important at the time, that could suggest where Black is based? Alex has never posted photos that show him, or the place he is?'

'No.' Cynthia shook her head. 'He's too wily for that.' She was so vehement, it was like she knew him. He was clearly real to her, very real. But she knew nothing more than they did.

Nasreen tried not to sigh. This was a waste of time. 'Can I ask when you first became aware of Alex Black, Ms Warner?'

The woman seemed to deflate, her bosom collapsing down onto her stomach, her layered scarves drooping like the petals of a dying flower. 'My daughter. One of his henchmen hacked into her computer. She'd never even sent the photo to anyone.'

Nasreen didn't remember seeing a victim named Warner in the list of names they'd uncovered. 'Did you get him to remove the images?'

'Oh no.' She shook her head. 'The more I tried to reason, the more things he posted. Images that were fake, but awful. He told his disciples how to target Laney: she started getting texts.' *Like*

244

Chloe. 'And then they sent fake photos of her, disgusting photos, to all the governors at her school. She's a teacher.'

Nasreen put down her pen. 'Did you report this, Cynthia?'

'Laney wouldn't let me. She just wanted it to stop.' She had tears in her eyes. She wanted to comfort her, but she had to ask. 'What happened?'

Cynthia took her glasses off and rubbed at her eyes; a smile touched her lips, but there was no joy in it. 'She didn't kill herself, if that's what you want to know. After the photos were sent to the governors she was let go by the school. The headmaster was a lovely man, you could tell he felt dreadful about it, but he had no choice. Even though the photos were fake, the governors wouldn't believe it, or they didn't care. They said they couldn't have her teaching children after that. That it had "compromised her professional authority". The last words came out bitter. She paused for a moment, swallowed, and Nasreen had to lean closer to hear her. 'She had a breakdown.'

'I'm so sorry.'

'He's a monster. Manipulative, controlling. He gets under the skin of those boys. They think he's the messiah.'

From what Freddie had shown her it was more like recruitment: Black targeted disillusioned young men. 'Like a cult?' Nasreen asked. She thought of the frenzy the Hashtag Murderer had inspired.

'Alex Black inspires obsession. Evil!' Cynthia jabbed the tortoiseshell glasses in her hands towards her. No wonder she was so emotional on the matter. It must be awful to see a person you love go through that. With a twinge, she thought of Burgone. Cynthia was a hurt and upset woman, but she'd amassed a huge amount of information on Alex Black – there must be something she knew, something he'd done that would tell them where to find him. Cynthia summoned the energy, or maybe the courage, to speak again. 'Laney never went back to work. It was six years ago.'

Nasreen made a note to go back through Are You Awake to find Laney's thread, to study it, to match the online with the real-life timeline. If there was anything she could do to bring this man to justice she would. She would try to help Cynthia and her daughter. 'The site must have been in its infancy then?'

Cynthia nodded. 'Yes, Laney was one of the first.'

'Does Laney use the same surname as you?'

'No, she uses her father's surname: Gardem.'

That explained why Nasreen didn't recognise her from the list Freddie was compiling. 'She was only the second girl he targeted.'

Nasreen felt her heart quicken. 'Do you know who was the first?' They were combing through the threads, but it would take them hours, possibly days, to sort all of the posts into chronological order. Any time someone posted something new, that thread was elevated to first position on the message board.

'Yes,' Cynthia said with a sad smile. 'A girl called Daisy Jones. She was only sixteen, poor thing.'

If Daisy was the first target, was it possible she had been known personally to Alex Black? If they found Daisy Jones, was there a chance they could trace him? But it was a common name. 'Did you ever speak to Daisy Jones during your research?'

'I tracked her down. Alex Black posted her contact details next to the photos of her.' Cynthia made a noise like a laugh. 'But she'd moved. Her whole family had. They emigrated. He forced them out of the country.' Anger dripped from Cynthia's voice. *How many lives had this man destroyed?*

'Do you have contact details for her now? Where does she live?' Nasreen was taking hasty notes. Saunders or Chips would already be running the name through the PNC.

246

'The States, I believe.'

Nasreen caught the word and felt her hope fade. 'You believe? You haven't spoken to her?'

'She wouldn't speak to me. I found an email address. Her father replied: he said they'd done the best they could to forget what had happened. To move on.' Cynthia looked angry again. 'They refused to talk to me.'

But they might speak to me, thought Nasreen. *To the police.* This was important. 'When was this, Cynthia?'

Cynthia pulled one of the folders towards her and undid the ribbon, moving her glasses to the end of her nose so she could peer through the bifocals as she flicked through the printed sheets inside. Small transparent coloured tabs stuck out from between the pages. 'Here it is.' Her rings creaked as she placed the other pages down. 'I received the email on Sunday the seventeenth of November, five years ago. I have an email address for her and her father.'

Nasreen nodded. They could use that to try to source a number. Try to get hold of Daisy Jones. See if she could identify Alex Black. 'And Daisy's father: he gave no indication who Alex Black was?'

'The message was short: he only said what I've told you already.' She turned the printout to face Nasreen. She scanned the words: Cynthia had recited it almost perfectly. 'Parents get like that sometimes. It's happened before. They blame the girls for taking the photos in the first place. Think it's best to leave it well alone. Brush it under the carpet and forget about it.'

Nasreen felt anger on behalf of Daisy. To go through something like that and have your own family hold you responsible; it was awful. She bit her cheek to stop it from showing on her face and in her voice. 'Thank you. Do you know anything more about Daisy? You said you had her previous address – when the family lived in the UK?'

'Yes.' Cynthia turned back a few pages and Nasreen guessed each coloured marker denoted a different girl. *A different victim.* 'Here you go.' She turned the page to face Nasreen. Next to a photo of a pretty blonde with long wavy hair was a screenshot of a post on Are You Awake. And underneath was a typed catalogue of the victim: name, address, place of work and/or school. The words jumped out at her.

'You're sure this is right?' She rested her finger on the paper.

'Yes,' said Cynthia, nodding. 'Why?'

Nasreen felt her heart rate increase. *This was it.* Everything had been connected right from the beginning. 'I'm going to need to take this, Cynthia, if that's okay?' The woman nodded, her face blotchy with emotion. 'You've been very helpful, Ms Warner. Thank you.'

'Please,' Cynthia reached out and grabbed her hand, the cold metal of her rings pressing into her fingers. *'Please get him.'*

'I will do everything I can,' said Nasreen, looking into her sad eyes. She pulled away. DI Saunders, Chips and Freddie were already waiting in the corridor. Nasreen held the page up. 'Daisy Jones went to Romeland High. She was the first victim. She was sixteen. What's the betting there's a personal connection and that's where our Alex Black went too?'

Chapter 37

Thursday 17 March

01:40
T – 7 hrs 50 mins

'I'll get onto the US State Department and see if we can track Miss Daisy,' said Chips, taking the papers from Nas's hand. Freddie looked at her phone screen: it'd taken time to interview Cynthia Warner and get to grips with the information she had. They had less than eight hours left. Less than a working day. Her heart was hammering against her ribcage. Her palms were sweaty. If Alex Black had been at Romeland School then they could find him. They could find Lottie. But something was niggling at her, something Cynthia had said about Black inspiring obsession.

'This must be more than coincidence.' Nas's cheeks were flushed, and Freddie recognised she was excited: this was their big breakthrough. 'If we keep digging through the threads and find where the heroin came from, we might be able to trace that back to him. The CPS would have enough for assisted suicide, manslaughter or maybe even murder for Chloe? The links between the two girls' cases show Black's criminal activity has been increasing. For whatever reason, he's got bored of engineering things from the sidelines. But there are enough similarities between the two girls that suggest we're looking at the same guy. And that gives us an advantage.'

Saunders was nodding his head, but his mouth was turned down, as if he still wasn't sure. Nas looked at her: she wouldn't confess about the link between the Stroftons and them would she? Nas held her gaze for a second and then kept going. 'Chloe went to Romeland High. The first victim of Alex Black's website was Daisy Jones, who also went to Romeland High. I think that's where this all started. This could be our chance to get him.'

Saunders nodded. 'It makes sense. Get onto the school and see what you can find out.'

'I'll see if there are any previous jobs at Romeland High on the PNC: if they've ever reported a burglary, vandalism or anything, then there should be contact details on the system.'

'And try the alarm as well. If we know which alarm system they use, we can speak to the company – they'll have keyholder details,' Saunders said.

'Great,' Nas nodded.

'When you get through, get a full list of students in the same year as Daisy Jones. And the ones either side, in case Alex Black is an alias,' Saunders said. 'I'll brief the guv and let him know what we've got. Let's cross-reference this with Green's work from the PNC. The tracker was picked up heading for the M11. She could have easily been taken to North Hertfordshire from there.'

'Freddie, could you show Cynthia Warner out – is that okay?' Nas said.

'Sure.' Freddie felt them gearing up around her; she'd keep

250

going through the printouts, see if there was anything that linked back to Romeland High.

'Thanks.' Nas looked relieved to have it off her list. They were assembling the pieces of the puzzle. Aligning everything. Closing the net. *They could do this.*

Something was bugging her and she couldn't place her finger on it. *Finger. Fingers.* She was sure it was something to do with that. She opened the door to the room where Nas had left Cynthia Warner. The woman was staring at the wall, a distant look on her owlish face. Freddie coughed. 'Hi!'

Cynthia looked up, startled. 'Hello.'

Freddie looked at Cynthia Warner's hands, which were covered in tarnished silver rings; her fingers looked like stacks of coins. Something was making Freddie uncomfortable. What was it? Cynthia Warner was looking wary. Freddie forced a smile onto her face. 'I'll show you out.'

Cynthia pulled her leather handbag towards her as she stood. Freddie kept smiling, willing her not to ask what was going on. The woman scuttled through the open door.

'You don't have to see me out, I'm sure I can find my way,' she said.

'Security's tight.' Freddie's face was aching.

Spots of colour appeared on the woman's cheeks. Freddie didn't trust herself to say anything else. The horror of it all pushed up from under her skin. They rode in silence in the lift, Cynthia merely nodding goodbye to Freddie, lost in her own thoughts about Alex Black.

'Ms Warner!' Lorna the receptionist called. 'PC Goldstein is waiting outside to give you a lift.'

Cynthia didn't turn. Outside there were still photographers. As soon as the woman stepped out the flashbulbs started. Freddie tried to breathe normally. Her jaw hurt. Lorna was still staring at her. She held a palm up in acknowledgement and the girl smiled and waved back. And Freddie saw it: *fingers*. She fought to keep the smile on her face, she fought not to run, but as soon as she was out of sight she pressed the lift button agitatedly and reached for her phone. She knew she'd seen that ring before. She pressed play on the video. What was it Cynthia had said: *Alex Black inspires obsession*. The screen sprang to life. *Oh shit*. They were making a mistake. Freddie sprinted from the lift. She had to warn them. Now.

Chapter 38

Thursday 17 March

02:15
T – 7 hrs 15 mins

Chips was trying America again; Saunders had his broad, V-shaped back turned away from them as he spoke into the phone. Nasreen had found the school caretaker's mobile number from a previous burglary reported at the school. She had the phone in her hand when the door flew open and Freddie careered in. 'I knew it! I knew I recognised her!'

She didn't want to deal with Freddie's impulsiveness right now.

'She's the YouTuber!' Freddie collided with her desk, and the pile of papers she'd been looking through tipped and scattered across the floor.

'Careful!' She bent to pick up the papers. It was like having a Labrador puppy in the office. Her back ached.

Freddie was right in her face. 'Nas, will you listen to me.'

Nasreen screwed her eyes shut, willing herself not to shout. 'Sure.'

'Look!' Freddie thrust her phone at her again. 'Recognise anyone?'

Chips let out a sigh. 'Still no answer.'

Nasreen took the phone. It was a video. A young, slim girl with blonde hair and quite a lot of make-up — false eyelashes, red lipstick — was talking to the camera in an animated way. Behind her was a bookcase strung with fairy lights. 'What is this?'

'A vlog,' said Freddie. She felt like she'd seen the girl in the video before. 'It's Gracie Williams.'

Chips joined them. 'She's the spit of Lorna.'

That's who she reminded her of: their receptionist.

'Lorna *is* Gracie Williams.' Freddie stabbed the screen with her finger.

'What?' Nasreen and Chips said at the same time.

'Look at this.' Freddie took the phone back and froze on a shot of Gracie Williams squeezing her boobs in what Nasreen assumed was a playful, flirtatious manner. *Lorna would never do that.* 'Recognise that?' Freddie zoomed in on the freeze frame of the girl's hand. On her right hand was a large jade and gold ring.

'So? They look alike and they own similar rings?' Nasreen's throat felt dry.

'Not similar,' said Freddie. 'It's unique. It was gifted to her after she hit two million viewers. A jewellery house made it for her specially.'

'I'm in the wrong game,' said Chips.

'She did a whole post about it.'

Freddie flicked between screens and pressed play on another video, turning up the sound. There was Lorna, all blonde hair and make-up, bubbly and loud, talking to the camera: 'Shout out to the amaze Klass Jewels for this beaut of a ring. They said one of a kind for a one-of-a-kind vlogger! Sweet. Thanks, guys!'

Peppy, thought Nasreen. The dryness spread to her mouth.

'I'm not seeing the problem,' Chips said. Nasreen's mind was whirring. Lorna had changed her hair colour. Worn minimal make-up, almost retro clothing – completely different from the overt, cutting-edge style she wore in the videos. She spoke quietly, barely making eye contact. She was as quiet as a mouse. And moved around just as freely. Unnoticed.

'She's loaded,' Freddie said. 'Made a fortune from advertising and stuff. Look, here's a *Daily Mail* article on her house in Dulwich. It cost £1.2 million.' Chips took the phone, frowning.

How many times had Lorna used the ladies' at the same time as her? What about when they were at the pub? Had Nasreen ever left her handbag by the sink while she was in the cubicle? Had her phone been in her bag? 'So why the hell is she working in a minimum-wage admin job?'

Nasreen picked up her receiver then put it down. What was the best way to handle this? 'You're thinking she's our leak?'

'What's she even still doing here – it's gone two in the morning,' Freddie said.

'She was asked to stay late because of the press outside,' Chips said. 'An email went round.' Nas had seen that but skipped straight over it. It wasn't high on her list of priorities.

'Who sent it?' Freddie asked.

'Lorna did. It said she'd been asked to stay on…' His voice shifted. She saw the idea take hold. '*Oh Christ.* Does she have any known links to Alex Black? We need to get onto tech about this straight away. Jesus, she's been in here: in the office!'

'She's been everywhere in the building,' said Nasreen. Had she really pulled this off? Got their mobile numbers, got access to her personal email? It'd be easy for her to pass the whole building's email addresses on – she had them on her computer, she used them for work. And then it would be easy for someone to send everyone on that list the email exchange between her and Burgone. But she must have had help.

'She did a vlog a few months ago reaching out to the MRAs,' Freddie said. 'I think it was the first time I watched her: it went viral. She'd been on their sites, asked them to start a dialogue. To try and help young, disaffected men. She was trying to tackle the high suicide rate. Men between twenty and forty-nine are more likely to die from suicide than anything else in this country.' She shrugged. 'The MRAs are dicks, but they're also a symptom of a wider problem. They've just got their wires crossed: they think feminism is the issue, when it's the solution. The current system is failing young men as well.'

'Alex Black could have met Lorna on the MRA site? Somehow convinced the wee lass to do... *this*?' Chips said. He had YouTube open on his browser.

'Or he's blackmailed her?' Nasreen suggested. 'We know he's capable of lifting information from other people's servers.'

Black was capable of many things. The level of detail that had gone into this was extraordinary. If Black had persuaded Lorna to give him information, who knew what he could do. The thought that this could be the Hashtag Murderer reared again.

'Perhaps he's got photos the lass doesn't want seen? We need to tread carefully. We don't want her doing a runner.'

'It's like Cynthia Warner said: he inspires obsession,' Freddie said. 'She might be loony tunes.'

'She could know who Alex Black is. Where he is.' Nasreen felt violated. Lorna had had access to all the team's telephone numbers. Burgone's next-of-kin details would be listed on the HR system. A quick search and you could easily trace Lottie to him. Nasreen thought of her sisters. Her parents. The girl could have their telephone numbers as well. Bile flowered in her stomach.

'Aye.' Chips puffed air out his cheeks. 'Green, dig into this Gracie Williams. See if she's on file. Run Lorna Thompson too. See what we can get before we show our hand. Get onto her phone provider and get copies of her messages. See how she's communicating with him. See if we can get to him that way.'

Lorna had always been friendly. All those questions about how the case was going… Had she been gathering intelligence to feed back to Black? 'She could be updating him. Do you think that's why she's stayed late?'

'Aye. So keep communication about the case verbal – make sure you're not being overheard.'

Nasreen shivered. She felt like they were being watched. *Maybe they were?* She took a pad and wrote on it, passing the message to Chips: *What if she's bugged the office?*

He nodded, took the pen and wrote back: *Then she'll know we're on to her.*

Nasreen took the pen and hurriedly scrawled a reply: *I'll check.*

She took the back stairs – less chance of being seen. She couldn't risk the lift alerting Lorna to her presence. Reaching the ground floor, one level above the car park, she took her shoes off. Carrying them, she walked softly out of the stairwell. The building was largely quiet, apart from their floor. She could see the press still gathered outside, only a handful now, in North Face jackets and clutching steaming takeaway coffee cups. They were doing the same thing as them: waiting, chipping away at the story. She didn't want them to catch sight of her, bring her to the attention of Lorna. If she'd been listening in on what they'd said then Chips was right, she'd be long gone.

She walked along the edge of the wall that led from the lift, which allowed her to peer round the corner. Lorna was at her desk. She wasn't typing, but Nas could see that her desktop was open on the live news. She was staring at Lottie's face on the screen. Nasreen could see the ring from here. She'd been fiddling with it in the bathroom this morning. That felt like a lifetime ago. Everything had been shaken and thrown upside down since then. Did Lorna know where Lottie was? She wanted to grab her; make her talk. But Chips was right, blundering in now could cost them. So with great restraint, Nasreen headed back upstairs. This could be the first proper advantage they'd had over Black and she wasn't going to waste it on an impetuous response. It was nearly three in the morning. *Tick tock.*

Chapter 39

Thursday 17 March

04:05
T − 5 hrs 25 mins

Chips hung up the phone, a look of resignation on his face. 'Still no answer from the States. I'm beginning to think they're ignoring me.'

Saunders stretched his muscular arms up and back, and rotated his head to loosen his neck. 'How about you, Cudmore?'

Nasreen sighed. 'Not much, I'm afraid. I got hold of the caretaker, but it turns out he left Romeland about a year ago. He said he'd see if he could find the number of anyone still there and call me back. But he hasn't so far.' She looked at her watch. It was after 4 a.m. They had less than six hours to go. *Lottie's terrified eyes were pleading with her to save her.* She felt her heart squeeze. 'He wasn't best thrilled to be woken up. I could hear a baby crying in the background.'

'What about you, Green?' Chips asked.

'Sorry, sir: no good news.' Exhaustion had rinsed Green's face of colour; even her freckles seemed subdued. 'I can only get hold of customer services in India – they need clearance from above and no one will be in until eight thirty.'

They couldn't wait that long. Nasreen felt like she was trapped in some horror film of déjà vu, repeatedly calling people and getting no answer. Everyone they needed to speak to was asleep. She took a gulp of the now cold coffee on her desk. Freddie had managed to make espressos from the machine they had, joking that her previous job as a barista was finally coming in handy. They all had them: anything to keep going. Saunders was interspersing cans of Diet Coke with his. Each bitter sip of coffee that hit her stomach seemed to knot it tighter. She felt under her shirt: it was swollen and hard. She was stiffening from the inside, turning to stone like petrified wood. Fear spreading like wet concrete through her, setting solid until there was nothing alive left. They couldn't just sit here getting nowhere. 'I think we should have a chat with Lorna. She won't know we don't have her phone records.'

Saunders was nodding: they didn't have much option. 'Worth a try. PC Goldstein is still monitoring her downstairs. She's done nothing but stare at her computer for the last hour or so.' Nasreen thought of the photo of Lottie from the news she'd seen on Lorna's desktop. *Was she pleased with herself?*

'I've Googled Gracie Williams.' Freddie sounded full of energy. She was using the spare desk behind her and had quickly cultivated a collection of papers, mugs, glasses and used tissues. One of the floaters had found her some Berocca, which she'd been dropping into glasses of water with fizzy regularity. Neon orange rings sat at the bottom of her disposable cups.

'Anything useful?' She'd need leverage, something to make the girl talk.

'Turns out she did that MRA reach-out because of her younger brother.' Freddie unplugged her phone from its charger and passed it to her. It showed a photo of a smiling lad, about seventeen, pale, with mousey hair, and a shyness you could feel through the screen. 'He has a history of mental health issues,' Freddie added.

'So she's interested in the mental health of young men – that makes sense,' said Nasreen. That was a way Alex Black could have got to her – if they were right and she was involved. There was still a part of her that wanted to believe they were wrong. That it was just a case of mistaken identity.

'I don't see how that's of use though,' said Saunders. He was standing up now, bending to touch his toes in a stretch that doubled as a boast at his flexibility. The damp creases in his shirt by his lower back betrayed his show of calm. He was sweating about the time, too.

'She also has a problem with the police.' Freddie passed forward a printout. 'I'm surprised I haven't come across her before.' Nasreen ignored the reference to Freddie's former anti-police blogs and hoped no one else caught it either. Nasreen scanned the article before passing it to Saunders's waiting hand: 'Campaign Against Police and State Violence. Family and Friends Unite.'

'This wasn't on her vlog…' Saunders was squinting at the pages and passing them to Chips, who'd swivelled his chair to face them.

'Nah.' Freddie's face was animated. The sleeves of her hoodie were pushed up her arms, causing the fabric to fray more. This hour of the morning suited her. 'She obvs didn't think it was suitable for her YouTube channel. I bet her agent quashed it.'

'*Her agent?*' Chips said disbelievingly. Nasreen herself found it hard to understand how both Gracie Williams and Lottie made money from sharing photos and videos of their lives online. It seemed pointless.

'What's the name of the brother?' DC Green asked.

'Harry Williams,' Freddie answered. 'I think it says how old he is on that one.' She pointed at the printout Chips was reading.

'Seventeen according to this,' Chips said. 'It says we've been harassing him.'

'*We?*' Saunders raised an eyebrow.

'The force,' Chips said.

'He's got form.' Green was reading from her computer. 'He's on the PNC. Priors for breach of peace and drunk and disorderly.'

'Seriously?' Freddie said. 'No one drinks anymore. It's too much bother. Jobs are too competitive – you need the edge.' Nasreen felt herself blush at the memory of last night. Freddie was right: she didn't normally drink, and look what had happened when she had. The thought of everyone reading that email hit her afresh.

'There's more,' Green said.

Nasreen was relieved the conversation was moving on. The more tired she got, the harder it was to maintain her defences against the unrelenting feeling she'd messed up.

'He made a complaint to the Independent Police Complaints Commission,' Green said.

Freddie let out a slow whistle. 'What did you guys do?'

'That's enough, Freddie.' Nasreen's words came out harsher than she'd meant, but Freddie just rolled her eyes.

'If she has a problem with the force, that could be a motive for her doing this,' Chips said.

'Agreed,' said Saunders. 'Time we had a little chat.'

Nasreen's brain crackled. 'I'd like to have a crack at her, sir.

She's tried to ingratiate herself with me, she asked me to go for a drink before last night. She might think of me as a friend.'

'Or a weak link in the chain.' Saunders's face was emotionless.

Nasreen swallowed. 'Possibly, but then she might feel like she's in control: I could use that.'

'I've seen her talking a lot to Sergeant Cudmore, she does seem to have taken a shine to her,' Green said. Nasreen shot her a grateful look.

Saunders sniffed. Nasreen realised why he'd never been won over by Lorna's feminine charm: *of course*. She glanced at the photo on Saunders's desk: him and his boyfriend. 'What do you think, Chips?' he said.

'Worth letting the lass have a go.' Chips crossed his arms. 'I'm still getting my head round it.' None of them liked thinking they'd been fooled.

'Okay. It's you and me, Cudmore. But if we're getting nowhere, I'm bringing in Chips,' Saunders said.

Nasreen felt a pathetic rush of thankfulness. Despite her liaison with Burgone getting out, she was still seen as a useful member of the team. Perhaps she could survive this. She looked at her watch: the word *survive* jarring in her mind. Just over five hours for them to find Lottie. Would *she* survive?

'Green,' Saunders said. 'Get the interview room ready. I'll let PC Goldstein know you're on your way, Cudmore, in case she makes a break for it.'

Nasreen checked her ASP was in its holster, though it felt absurd to be doing this for Lorna, or whatever her real name was. She too had to pass through security to get in and out of the building; there'd have had to be a mighty cock-up if she'd managed to get a weapon in. But then it was a mighty cock-up that she'd got the job in the first place. Nasreen thought of Lottie and what the girl was going through: anger buzzed around her.

She swatted it away, knowing the best way to make Lorna pay would be to get the truth out of her. 'Are we arresting her?'

Saunders frowned. 'Let's just ask her a few questions at this stage, I don't want to caution her till we've got more evidence. Let's treat her like a witness. See what she lets slip.'

She nodded. A caution would mean they'd have to find a lawyer, and at this time of night that would take time they didn't have. Take time Lottie didn't have. T – 5 hours 30 minutes. They had to move cleverly – and fast.

Chapter 40

Thursday 17 March

04:31
T − 4 hrs 59 mins

Lorna was still at her desk and Nasreen wasted no time approaching. She wanted her to run. Wanted to chase her. *Wanted to slam her into the floor.* PC Goldstein was by the door, under the pretence of keeping the journalists out. There was still a small knot huddled outside. Lorna had her coat over her shoulders, keeping off the cold. Nasreen was metres from her.

'Gracie?' she said.

The girl's head snapped round and she looked up at her, her face pale, eyes wide. She made a slight nod of her head. She wasn't even going to try and hide it.

'We'd like a word.' Nasreen's voice was cold, and calmer than she felt. Gracie looked bewildered. She turned to look at PC Goldstein, who had his sights trained on her, and beyond that to the photographers outside. 'Don't make a scene.' Nasreen stepped back and signalled with her arm that she should walk in front of her. The girl rolled off her chair like a stroppy teen. Nasreen put a hand on her lower back. She could feel her shaking. 'Into the lift, please.'

They both got in and Nasreen pressed the button to go up. Gracie was staring at the floor. They were alone. She thought of Chips in the back of the van with Liam. She thought of the dead runner lying in Greenwich Park. She thought of Lottie's pleading, desperate eyes. No one would blame her if she grabbed Gracie. If she *made* her talk. But she knew she could never do that. Never be that kind of person. No matter what Gracie had done, she wouldn't hurt her. That would make her one of *them*. That would make her as bad as Alex Black. And no matter what he did, he could never have that.

The lift doors opened. 'This way.' She pushed Gracie towards the interview room. The girl stopped at the door, a small mew coming from her lips. 'Drop the act,' Nasreen said, irritated. 'We've seen your videos – we know you're no wallflower.' She opened the door. Saunders was inside already, leaning back in his chair in a deliberately relaxed posture, designed to imply he couldn't care less what about what they were about to discuss. Gracie faltered and turned her face up at Nasreen, her eyes still pitifully wide. She looked scared.

'It's okay. Have a seat.' Nasreen shut the door behind them and took the chair next to Saunders.

Gracie sat opposite, her jumper sleeves pulled down over her little hands, staring into her lap.

'Do you know why we've asked to talk to you?' Saunders said.

Gracie looked up, her eyes were wider again. She looked panicked. Different. All traces of timid Lorna were gone. This wasn't social ineptitude; this was fear. 'I didn't know he was going to do this!' Her voice was loud, frantic. 'I didn't know he was going to take that girl. The DCI's sister.'

Nasreen thought of the way Gracie had been staring at the news. 'She's called Lottie.'

Tears fell from her eyes. 'I didn't know until I heard this morning. I never thought he would do anything to hurt anyone. He told me he was just using the email addresses to expose malpractice.' She was gripping the table now. 'I only got the job – I only got the telephone numbers and stuff because he said I'd be helping. I thought I was doing the right thing. You have to believe me! I never would have helped him if I'd known.' She'd broken so fast, it must have been pressing against her to get out.

Saunders exhaled. 'Do you want a lawyer, Gracie?' She'd admitted she'd deliberately got the job to source personal information and contact details of those in the force.

'He gave me a name – a lawyer I should call if I got into trouble: Webb and Cooper.' *The same lawyer Liam gave.* 'But I don't want him. I need to answer for this. Oh god.' She was babbling, tears falling down her face, cutting streams through her foundation. She let out a big sob. 'I thought I'd be a whistle-blower.'

Nasreen looked at Saunders. He raised his eyebrows: *get back in there.* She passed Gracie a tissue.

'Thanks,' she said, blowing her nose.

'Gracie...' Nasreen kept her voice light. They didn't need her to clam up now. 'Who told you to get a job here?'

Gracie looked up from her tissue. 'Alex Black.'

'You know him?' Saunders said.

'We met online. He contacted me about a sting: said I was the perfect person to do it. He'd seen some of my vlogs where I play two parts – it's like a conversation between me and my psyche. He said he admired my acting.'

Jesus. Nasreen thought of Are You Awake. Had Gracie's name appeared there? People wanting obscene photos of a famous YouTuber? Did Alex Black look into her, find the stuff about her younger brother, see her impersonation skills and recognise a twisted opportunity? 'You live in London, don't you?'

'Yes,' she said. 'Like twenty minutes away.' She was close to their offices. Did that mean Alex Black wasn't, or just that he didn't want to get his own hands dirty? He couldn't be here and taking Lottie at the same time.

'Do you have contact details for Alex?' Saunders had abandoned his calm stance in favour of writing down what Gracie was saying.

'Only an email address,' Gracie said. 'He contacted me via my website.'

'Where do you meet him?' Nasreen asked. They could see if there was CCTV. If he selected the locations it would give them an idea of his potential patch; they could compare it to the GPS results from Lottie's FitSpo.

'I've never met him,' Gracie said.

'What?' Saunders sounded disbelieving. 'You expect us to believe you created a false identity, took a job with the police force and then shared sensitive information with someone outside – all for some guy you've never met?' The final words were a growl.

Gracie blinked, her lip trembled. 'He told me it was better this way, that I wouldn't get into trouble if I didn't meet him. That I'd have deniability.'

'You stupid girl.' Saunders shook his head.

Nasreen couldn't believe what she was hearing. 'Why, Gracie – why did you do it?'

The words hiccupped out of her. 'You hurt Harry!'

She didn't understand. 'Your brother?'

'You hurt him.' She stabbed a finger towards her.

'I've never even met him,' Nasreen said. Had Black lied to her? Lied about her? Why would he do that? Why was he fixated on her? She tried to remember if she'd ever met anyone called Alex, ever arrested an Alex, but there was nothing.

'Cops like you!' Gracie was sounding hysterical. 'He's ill, but they arrested him anyway, they hurt him. He was bleeding. It was Gross Misconduct! But no one wanted to listen. Society isn't interested because he's a young white man. You should be answerable for your actions!'

Nasreen's heart was racing, Gracie's words felt personal; she was directing them *at her*.

Saunders sounded calm. 'The IPCC takes all accusations of misconduct seriously. Believe me.' Had there been previous complaints against Saunders? Chips, she could believe: he clearly favoured the old-fashioned ways when they were necessary, but Saunders always felt squeaky clean. His face betrayed nothing. He sighed. 'So you thought you'd go on a one-woman spy operation, is that right?'

Gracie stared at him.

'What exactly did Black say to you, Gracie?' Nasreen tried.

'He said he had proof, but that he needed someone on the inside to help him with the exposure. And that it had to be a woman.' Gracie seemed to have exhausted herself with her crying, her words now landing flat and hard from her mouth.

'Did you follow me into the ladies'?' Nasreen said. She daren't look at Saunders.

Gracie nodded. 'I could see when you were going from the security cameras.'

She knew it. 'Did you look at my phone, Gracie?'

'Yes.' The girl nodded.

Black had used this girl to get information on them and they still had virtually nothing on him. 'And you never communicated with Black in any other way? Did you ever speak on the telephone? Text? Anything?'

'No, I told you...' Gracie sounded exasperated. 'He said we had to keep contact between us to the email address only.'

'We're going to need that email address, and to look at your phone and your computer at home,' Saunders was saying. But Nasreen knew they wouldn't be able to track the email: every form of communication he'd used so far had been encrypted.

'And you didn't know he was planning to take Lottie?' Nasreen asked.

At the sound of Lottie's name, Gracie started sobbing again. 'I didn't know what to do. I emailed him, but he's not replied. I thought... I don't know. I hoped it wasn't how it looked. That, like, maybe she was in on the sting as well?'

'Jesus,' Saunders said. 'What do you think this is – James Bond?'

'I thought it'd be like WikiLeaks – a whistle-blower. DCI Burgone seems nice, like maybe he was involved and this was to draw someone into the light? I don't know. I didn't know what to think.'

Nasreen couldn't believe what she was hearing. He'd got inside Gracie's belief system. Convinced her she was doing the right thing. So that even when Lottie was kidnapped she still thought it might be part of the plan. She thought of her staring at Lottie's face on the news. She would have seen the frightening message of her he'd sent: it was everywhere. The blood. The tape. Her eyes. 'Why didn't you say something when he released the photo of Lottie – you must have known then that something was wrong?'

Gracie started to cry again. 'I didn't know what to do. If I told you what I'd done I knew I'd be in trouble.'

Nasreen's heart hardened. If Freddie hadn't spotted the ring, made the connection, they might not have realised. Presumably 'Lorna' would have just stopped turning up to work. Even if they'd found compromising things on her computer, it could have taken them weeks to find the evidence linking Gracie to Alex Black. 'You chose to save your own skin.'

Gracie didn't reply, she just cried harder, the sobs racking her body. *Another victim of Alex Black.*

'I'll get an external officer – one who's not known to you, to formally charge you,' Saunders said. 'PC Goldstein will sit with you till then.'

Once they left the interview room, Nasreen leant against the hallway wall. Gracie didn't know who Alex Black was. They hadn't been able to reach Daisy Jones. No one at Romeland High School would be in until later that morning. They were running out of options and time. She took a deep breath. There was one thing left to try. But it was the very thing she feared the most.

Chapter 41

Thursday 17 March

06:00
T – 3 hrs 30 mins

Gracie would be charged with conspiracy, as she'd signed part of the Official Secrets Act when she joined the admin team. She had found herself collateral damage in the faceless Black's plan. Freddie shuddered at the thought that he might not be a stranger at all. That it was his face that haunted her nightmares. She dug her fingers into the car seat, the brushed fabric pushing under her nails. She couldn't believe this was happening. The sun had risen orange and angry, turning clouds into vivid gashes over the neat grass verges of Thamesmead. White flats and houses clumped together as if for warmth. What was it like to live so close to a category A prison: where they kept killers, rapists, terrorists? Where they kept the Hashtag Murderer.

Nas'd hoped for a Skype interview, but when his chief prison officer had woken him, the Hashtag Murderer had said he'd only talk if they came in person. Both of them. Nas and her. Her skin crawled with the memories of what he'd done: the terrifying messages posted online, the ticking clock, the slaughter. With only four hours left to save Lottie from a similar fate, what choice did they have? Every fibre of Freddie was screaming to run as Green turned off the dual carriageway into Belmarsh prison.

There were barriers, roundabouts, no-entry signs, and spreading away from them were the yellow-bricked squares of the prison complex. It could have been a nineties university, were it not for the high fences and mounted CCTV cameras. It echoed images of concentration camps Freddie had seen. Had *he* known they would come? Had *he* engineered all this?

Green pulled into the hedge-lined car park.

'You all right to stay in the car?' Nas opened her door.

Green loosened her grip on the wheel, but didn't take her eyes off the blue, sloped visitor building in front of them. 'With pleasure, Sarge.'

Freddie's heart quickened. She wanted Green with them. She wanted as many people between her and *him* as possible.

'We won't have our phones with us inside,' Nas said. 'So make sure you're ready with updates as soon as we're out.' Green nodded.

'Why won't we have our phones? What if we need help?' Freddie's voice betrayed her panic.

'We're in a high-security unit, we'll be perfectly safe.' Nas sounded normal, but the tension in her face said otherwise. Freddie's blood was hurtling round her body; she could hear it. *Thump. Thump. Thump.* Sweat pooled in her lower back. *He* would know. *He* would smell fear on her. She touched her scar.

In the reception, a tall, white prison officer who looked to be in his fifties, his square face riven with wrinkles, met them.

'I'm Detective Sergeant Nasreen Cudmore and this is Freddie Venton. We have a Visiting Order, in relation to an active and time-sensitive case. I rang ahead.'

'We've been expecting you. We aren't used to receiving visitors so early.' He sounded surprisingly friendly. 'You're here to see our James. You're the first visitors he's accepted.'

Every muscle in her tightened. *He* wanted to see them. *He* wanted them here.

'I'll need my colleague to pat you both down.' The officer indicated a po-faced woman behind him. Neither offered their name. What was it like to work here? To be with these people every day. Her mouth went dry and she felt her breath quicken; she wasn't sure she could do this.

Nas held her arms out while the female officer worked along them with gloved hands, then down her back, round her bra. Freddie swallowed a joke about over-friendly welcomes and airport security: it wouldn't go down well.

'And your ID, please. We ask that you remove mobile phones, electrical items and watches, and leave them in a locker.' The officer was reeling through a practised speech. 'Do you have permission to use a Dictaphone?'

'No, there wasn't time to obtain written authorisation,' Nas said. 'I have two pens and some paper.'

'Fine. Keep hold of them at all times and do not pass anything to the prisoner.'

Freddie thought about what the Hashtag Murderer had done the last time he'd got hold of a pencil: he'd stabbed it into someone's eye.

'Two officers will be with you at all times in the interview suite. No other prisoners will be allowed out of their cells while you're in there.' The officer smiled.

She couldn't even nod. Her legs automatically followed behind

274

Nas while the woman took their fingerprints, made them stare into a camera and added their information to the system. A UV stamp was pressed onto their hands, like they were about to enter a club.

She had to get control of her breathing. *He'll* know. She saw again his hand swinging down towards her. Blood. Lottie. *Breathe: one, two, three.* They passed through the metal detector.

'He's in the HSU,' said the male officer.

'The what?' Focus on questions. Talking was better.

'The High Security Unit. It's separate to the main prison,' Nas answered.

'Home to the country's most dangerous criminals,' the officer said with pride.

'How many are there?' *Most dangerous.*

'We can house up to forty-eight.' The officer was almost four times the width of Nas. And taller. A solid giant of a man.

They reached a gated door and waited while another uniformed giant unlocked it from the other side. They stepped through and it was locked immediately behind them. *Clunk. Clink.* Freddie swallowed. It was hot in here. Oppressive.

'How many prisoners have you got now?' Nas asked.

'That's confidential. But I can tell you we get the high-profile ones: those who make the front pages.'

Another gated door. *Clunk. Clink.* There were cameras everywhere, watching them. They reached another locked door. *Clunk. Clink.* Another. *Clunk. Clink.* They were getting deeper into the prison. The air felt heavier. Old. It smelt of bleach and metal. And dry sweat. They hadn't passed a window for some time. No sky. No views of the outside world. What if they had to get out?

'Do they share rooms?' Nas was making small talk, keeping the conversation going. Trying to act normal, but her hands were gripped tightly together behind her back.

'No. There are four "spurs" to the block.' The officer pauses for another door, still smiling. *Clunk. Clink.* 'Each spur has twelve single-occupancy cells. Your boy has a whole wing to himself.' *Clunk. Clink.*

'Why?' The white walls are bleaching Nas out, making her paler, as if she's fading.

'We had some issues when we first moved him in. He's been deemed too violent to encounter other prisoners.'

Freddie's ribs squeezed around her. 'I thought this place housed the most dangerous criminals in the country? It's not nursery school, is it!'

'Too violent and too troublesome. He got a couple of the inmates to do things for him. To attack the others.' *Clunk. Clink.* Fourteen gated doors.

The hot air caught in her throat. What else had he got people to do? The image of the knife slashing towards Lottie played on loop as they reach a double-height crossroads. This must be the centre of a spur. Four walkways stretched away from them. Green-painted floors. White bars like the teeth of a comb slice through her vision. Somewhere else, someone is moving. The *clunk clink* echoes through the halls.

'What about officers?' Nas asked. 'He could manipulate them too.'

'We cycle them out of the HSU. Move them to the main prison. No one does longer than three years. And we don't use names. If you don't know my name you can't accidentally use it in front of him.'

Not knowing a name wouldn't be enough to stop him. They had let him talk to other prisoners: did they really know what they were dealing with?

'Is it normal for a prisoner to have the whole wing to them-selves? *Clunk. Clink.* Fifteen doors.

'It's only happened once before.' The officer stopped in a small, carpeted reception area. 'With Charles Bronson.' *Britain's most notorious and violent prisoner.* What illustrious company to be in.

'Okay, ready?' he asked.

'Yes.' Nas was rigid.

No. No, no, no. I can't do this.

'Look up at that camera please. The lads in the office just need to match your faces against the biometrics we have of you on the system.'

The cameras whirred as they zoomed in. Freddie's eyes darted about the room, looking for an escape. Fifteen locked doors between her and the outside world. Her breath was so loud the others must be able to hear it.

When she was little they'd taken a family holiday to Jersey, visiting the underground German war tunnels. It smelt of death and decay. Despite the disinfectant, and the state-of-the-art security software, this place smelt the same. As if the air was running out and they'd all slowly suffocate in here. The biting throb of her scar sliced across her face and down her spine. Nas gave her arm a quick, comforting squeeze. *Think of Lottie.* Blood trickling over skin. *Think of Lottie.*

Freddie's thoughts were speeding up, spiralling away from her. The floor squeaked. Too clean. As if spilled blood had just been wiped up. What was on the other side of these walls? There were doors. Small Perspex windows showed cells; a man in maroon jogging bottoms leaning back, watching a small telly. A metal toilet – no seat. A window that looked at a brick wall. Another. And another. They were inmates. Locked in their little boxes. One turned and caught sight of Nas, who was walking with purpose. Showing no fear. He hammered against the door. 'How come my lawyer don't look like that!'

'Keep walking, please.' The officer directed them to a small room at the end of the hallway. A table and three chairs: like the interview room at a station, except everything was screwed to the floor.

Nas took a seat and Freddie followed suit. Instinctively she wrapped her ankles around the chair and tried to move it away from the table. Away from where *he* would be. A camera purred above: everyone was ready.

They had said there would be two officers with him at all times. In case he did anything. What if he'd got one of them onside? What if all this – Chloe, Lottie – was a ruse to get them here? This small locked box inside a myriad of other locked boxes. There was nowhere to run. Nowhere to hide. What if he had designed this? What if this was his revenge?

A noise rippled towards them. Voices. A roar. Growing louder. She gripped the chair. The room reverberated with the sound of forty-eight men jeering, chanting, banging on their cell doors. The walls felt woefully flimsy. *Jesus.*

'Here he comes.' The officer smiled. 'Always causes a bit of a fuss with the lads. Bit of an enigma is our James.' The roar mushroomed, then fell away. The silence was worse. *What's happening now? Clunk. Clink.* The officer took a few steps away as the door opened.

The atmosphere in the room changed. Her ears popped. *Breathe: one, two, three.*

He walked in.

Chapter 42

Thursday 17 March

06:30
T − 3 hrs

The Hashtag Murderer was wearing maroon jogging bottoms and a sweatshirt, like the man Freddie'd seen in the cell. Two broad officers flanked his movements, like bouncers from a dodgy club. They'd obviously picked those who would tower over him, but it made no difference. He didn't need bulk or muscle: his presence filled the space, sucking all the oxygen out, like a vacuum. Nas inhaled.

As if he were out for a stroll and had decided to pause on a park bench, he took the chair opposite. His skin was flat, like he'd been moulded from putty. He'd been without sunlight, fresh air, for a while. *Prison skin.* Effortlessly he held Nas's gaze, and then slowly, swivelling like the camera, he turned to look at her. His eyes roamed over her. A fingernail on her right hand punctured her palm.

'I need water.' His voice dominated the room.

The officer behind them exited quickly. Nas could hear his hurried steps outside. The Hashtag Murderer stared at her. She didn't blink. Couldn't move.

The officer came back with a small plastic glass of water and placed it on the edge of the table. *Why isn't he in handcuffs? Why isn't he restrained?* He picked up his drink and brought it to his thin lips. His Adam's apple bobbed as he swallowed. He gave a refreshed sigh. A smack of his lips. Vomit threatened her throat.

Nas started next to her, like she'd had an electric shock. 'Are you communicating with anyone outside of the prison?'

He smiled, resting his finger in the condensation ring left by the cup. Five pairs of eyes were trained on him. He wiped his damp finger along the table, staring at Freddie. Her molars reached for each other. He was making a shape, a jagged line. *He's drawing my scar.* With each movement she could feel him working his finger into her, probing, peeling it back, pulling her apart.

'You sick fuck,' she said. The officers bristled.

'Someone is using your name.' Nas's knuckles were transparent from gripping her pen and paper.

He looked at her languidly. 'Which one?'

'Someone is using Apollyon. On suicide notes. On threatening notes.'

He lifted his finger to his mouth, sucking the water drop.

'Is it you?' A tiny tremor shook Nas's words.

Heat accelerated through Freddie. There wasn't time for games. Somewhere out there Lottie was being held, tortured, her life in danger. 'An innocent girl is missing: stop fucking around!'

He turned his head very slowly, savouring the view, until he was looking straight at her. Into her. His eyes burned through her skin. Slashed at her. Tore her to ribbons. *Red red ribbons.*

280

The room thrummed with anxiety. A nervous laugh gurgled out of her. He didn't look away.

Nas tapped the end of her pen on the table. The sound was cannon fire in the silence. They had no power in this room. No leverage. 'If you know anything about this, this is your chance to act. Don't condemn more families to suffering.'

He dropped Freddie's gaze and she exhaled. Tried to swallow but her mouth was full of dust.

He looked at Nas and licked his tongue slowly over his teeth. Freddie longed to protect her from this. 'Did you bring me any photos?' he asked.

Nas recoiled. Freddie felt the room tilt. Disbelief and disgust burned like fireworks over Nas's face. 'I'm not showing you photos of the victims.'

A trickle of sweat ran between Freddie's shoulders. The thought of bringing pictures of Chloe or Lottie into this place, this room, was repulsive.

'This interview is finished.' Nas pushed herself up and away from the desk. The officers looked startled. This wasn't the plan. They were supposed to remain seated until he was removed.

He leant back in his chair; the two officers flexed, ready.

Nas thrust her finger forwards. 'If I find out that you're responsible for the disappearance of these young girls, I will see that you're tried for it. You will never, ever get out of here.' The tops of her ears were red. Time seemed to slow. The officers exchanged glances. Freddie's stomach flipped. *We have to get out of here.*

He brought a hand up and the officers leapt forwards. Nas stumbled back, her legs colliding with the immovable chair. He turned his palm into a stop sign and they all froze. Obeying his command. He gave a small, amused smile, and ran his hand through his hair.

281

'I wanted photos of you, Nasreen.'

Nas's mouth fell open. The heat of the room was extinguished as ice exploded in sharp crystals through Freddie.

'This has been fun.' He stood. The officers immediately stepped alongside him. The Hashtag Murderer left the room. *Clunk. Clink.*

Chapter 43

Thursday 17 March

07:30
T – 2 hrs

What did he mean? Freddie asked the same question over and over in her head. Had he done all this to get photos of Nas? Had he put out a request on Are You Awake for pictures of her friend? Escalated it from there? Or was it just him toying with them? Making them squirm? Nas had only said one thing since they'd left: *we shouldn't have come.*

She'd checked her phone on the way back, watching as the morning news beamed through the country, the world. A fresh wave of despair came from those who'd just seen the photos of Lottie. A missing eighteen year old. Had she seen the sun rise where she was being held? Or did she have her eyes screwed shut, longing for safety?

They drove into the underground car park, avoiding the journalists out front. Green's phone rang as they stopped. 'DC Green speaking.'

Nas got out and Freddie followed, listening to her friend's heels echo on the concrete. *What did he mean? Now what did they do?* Nas pressed the call button on the lift repeatedly.

Green was still on her mobile, walking quickly to catch up. Nodding as she spoke. 'I see. Yes. Thank you.' She hung up, adding quietly, 'dammit.'

Freddie swallowed. *More bad news.*

'I got hold of someone at Romeland, Sarge. The current caretaker had the number for the administrator and I've just spoken to her.'

Freddie wondered if it was the same belligerent receptionist she'd met just yesterday. 'But that's good isn't it?' Freddie could hear the desperation in her voice. They needed a break. It wasn't the Hashtag Murderer. They'd wasted their time. Given him a cheap thrill. Now they had to find a chink in Alex Black's armour. There were only two hours to go. 'Did she tell you how to get hold of Alex Black?'

Green's face clouded. They got in the lift. 'She's only been at the school a couple of years. And guess what? All of Romeland High's records are computerised, and about two months ago they had some kind of computer virus. They've lost everything – the whole lot.'

Freddie's breath was coming fast. 'It's him: it has to be. He did that. He must have hacked their system. Sent in a Trojan or something.' The lift doors pinged open and Nas was out and running.

'Chloe's thread appeared on Are You Awake two months ago. He must have destroyed the records to hide the link back to him.'

Saunders looked up as they came in. He was on the phone. Chips was down to his shirt sleeves, his tie abandoned over his chair.

'We think Alex Black may have taken out Romeland's online records,' Nas said.

Was this part of the game? *This has been fun.* Is this what the Hashtag Murderer had meant? It had been easy to track Lottie: to hunt her. *I wanted photos of you.* Were they the next target? His prey.

'They suffered a cyber attack two months ago,' Green added.

Chips was up. 'I don't trust coincidences. There must be another way to confirm if he was there.'

'What about the teachers? They must know?' Freddie looked at Saunders, who was still talking on the phone. He looked disappointed. Another dead end.

'Apparently a few years ago the headmaster was accused of having an affair: emails between him and one of the teachers were leaked to the governors,' Green said. 'The lady said it was quite the local scandal. He denied the allegations. A number of teachers resigned in support of him. And when the new head came in she replaced pretty much everyone.'

'Jesus. Black again?' How long had he been planning this for? He'd systematically removed all trace of himself.

'I bet he's responsible for at least some of that, but I doubt we'll ever prove it.' Nas rubbed at her eyes with her thumb and forefinger, then pulled a tissue from the box on the desk, swiping under her eyes. 'He knew we'd come. He's invisible.'

'So there's no one at the school who was there when Daisy Jones was there?' asked Freddie. Frustration mingled fast with panic. How long would it take to track down the teachers who had been there and speak to them? Did they have that long?

'There's a Mrs Agnes Wilshire who apparently runs the alumni on a voluntary basis,' said Green. 'She's retired but she did work in the school at the time Daisy Jones was there.'

Hope inflated like a balloon. 'Then let's speak to her!'

'I'm waiting for the administrator to call me back with her number. She needs to get into the school to get it.' She looked at her watch. 'She should be there within forty-five minutes.'

Freddie's heart was hammering. 'Forty-five minutes? We can't wait that long!'

'Get onto the local force,' Chips said. 'Get them to go to Agnes Wilshire's registered address. See if we can get hold of her sooner.'

Nas picked up the phone. Freddie was pacing. *Thinking.* Staring at her phone. Agnes Wilshire wasn't on Facebook. She Googled her. She couldn't find details of Agnes online. *Not a silver surfer.* Was it a coincidence that she was the last thread that linked to Romeland School's past: a woman with no digital footprint? A local newspaper piece covered the 'much-loved' teacher's retirement five years ago. If she had been sixty-five then, she'd be seventy now. They needed more. She started going through the printouts from Are You Awake again from the beginning.

'Cudmore, West Herts force on line one,' Saunders shouted.

Nas picked up the phone. They only had one hour and fifty-five minutes left. *Come on, come on.* She crossed her fingers.

Nas's face fell and she hung up. 'Agnes Wilshire isn't answering. The neighbours say she often goes out to walk the dog first thing in the mornings. There's been a major RTA on the motorway, so the constable can't stay. They'll try and pop back in thirty minutes or so.'

No. Freddie's stomach was fizzing. The phone rang and Nas grabbed it.

'Detective Sergeant Cudmore… Great! You can speak to me. Thanks for getting back to us.' She grabbed her pen, mouthing *admin* at Green.

There was a knock and a male staff member popped his head round the door. 'Call for the DI.' Chips looked up. 'DI Saunders, sir.' Saunders replaced the receiver and swung his chair round to face them. 'Line two, sir. They want to speak to the person in charge of the investigation. They said they'd hold.' Saunders nodded and picked the receiver up. Could it be a *Crimestoppers* lead? A member of the public who'd seen something and realised the importance? Freddie's heart was racing.

Nas hung up the phone and started pulling on her jacket. 'Agnes Wilshire isn't answering her phone and she doesn't have a mobile. Apparently she doesn't like the things,' she said.

'Very sensible.' If anything could put you off technology, then it was this case.

'We need to get over there. She's due in today; every Thursday she does their alumni newsletter. She told her colleagues she'd be in late as she has a dentist appointment. They've promised they'll get her to call us as soon as she gets in.'

In the corner DI Saunders had stood up, still on the phone, gripping it tightly. She caught the words. 'I'm sorry. Very sorry.' He wasn't the type for contrition. The hairs on her arms stood to attention. Chips, Green and Nas turned to look. There was something in his tone, a warning, his legs jiggled. She could see his face colouring, but he was still apologising. *Something's wrong. Very, very wrong.* Freddie tried to steady her breathing. It couldn't be Lottie? Not yet: they still had time. Unless Black had changed the rules? Had visiting the Hashtag Murderer set something in motion?

'I can promise you measures will be taken. Thank you,' DI Saunders was saying. He held the receiver slightly away from his ear as if the other person was shouting. And then nodded, replacing it on the cradle.

His face was contorted with rage as he turned to glare at Nas. 'Cudmore, do you want to explain to me why the fuck Chloe Strofton's parents have just given me an ear bashing? They want to know why an officer who bullied their daughter is now asking questions about their other daughter's death?'

Nasreen inhaled so fast she squeaked.

'What?' Chips looked aghast.

'They want to know why I've let *her*,' he pointed directly at Freddie, his face puce, 'also ask questions. When she also bullied their kid.'

'Sir, I can explain,' Nas said. Freddie felt panic rise in her. Gemma. Gemma's mum and dad. *Never contact me again.* She should have told Nas. Should have said something.

'You know the family. You and *her* were accused of bullying one of the Stroftons' other kids and you thought you wouldn't fucking mention it!' Saunders's face was beetroot. He marched at her.

'It was eight years ago…' Nas said.

Saunders was leaning over her, his hands braced on the arms of her chair. Chips was up now. 'I don't give a fuck!' he snarled in her face. 'They could be called as witnesses for this case. If the defence lawyer sniffs out any relationship between an officer and a witness they'll say you're compromised: the case could collapse.'

Oh god. She hadn't known that: why hadn't Nas said?

'I don't have a relationship with them. And I haven't spoken to Chloe's parents,' Nas managed.

'No, but you and your little buddy here have been all over

the kid's school! You've spoken to her friends! Her teachers! Do you know how this looks?'

Chips pulled at Saunders. 'That's enough.'

Freddie saw Nas's eyes glisten. 'I thought I could help.'

'You thought you could help?' Saunders flicked a hand towards her face, almost as though he might hit her. Freddie jumped up and Chips put a hand out. 'Like you thought it would help to screw the boss!' Saunders screamed.

'Fuck you,' Freddie said.

'Come on now, Pete,' said Chips, pulling Saunders back a pace.

'No.' He shook him off. 'She's lied from start to finish!' He jabbed his finger towards Nas. Freddie could hear her own breath; she was panting.

Nas was flushed, and blinking furiously. 'I'm sorry, sir,' she said. 'I did what I thought was best for the investigation. I thought my inside knowledge of the family might help.'

'Your behaviour has brought the unit into disrepute, Cudmore.' Saunders turned his back on her.

'*No.*' Nas sounded like she couldn't believe it.

'I want you out of this office.' Saunders didn't look at her.

Panic surged through Freddie. This was wrong. He was making a mistake. Nas had only been trying to help – surely he could see that?

Nas looked desperate. 'Sir, I…'

'Enough. You're suspended, as of now. You're gone.'

Nas looked at Chips for help. He looked at the floor. Freddie's heart ached for her.

'But what about Black? What about Lottie? I can help.' Nas's voice was panicked. 'There are links between me and the victims. We're so close to finding him.'

'I'm not having you compromising anything else. Get your

stuff and go home. You too,' he said, jabbing a finger at Freddie. Freddie felt heat pass through her. 'Neither of you should have been near this case in the first place.'

Nas stood staring at Saunders, pleading with him silently. He turned away. Nas took her handbag and coat and stalked out, wiping a tear from her eye. *What had she done?*

Chapter 44

Thursday 17 March

07:35
T – 1 hr 55 mins

Freddie grabbed her bag from behind the desk, not caring that she sent papers and a mug spinning to the floor as she went. Saunders had his arms crossed, watching her as if she might be about to nick a laptop or something. She stopped in front of Chips. He looked pale, his face sagged, like he was in shock. 'Thanks for nothing,' she said.

She eyeballed Saunders as she walked out. 'Cock,' she said, loud enough so they both heard it, and slammed the door behind her. The walls vibrated, and she ploughed straight into the back of Nas. The impact seemed to spur Nas into motion and she started away, picking up speed down the corridor, her coat flung over her arm. 'Nas, wait. We need to go back in there. They can't do this.' Could they speak to Burgone? He probably wouldn't be thrilled at their little lapse in honesty either. 'We can't walk away now!' But Nas didn't stop, she burst through a door next to the lift. *The stairs. Shit.* Freddie started to jog to catch up.

She could hear Nas's heels clicking down the concrete stairs at speed. *What was this? The fire exit?* 'What's wrong with the lift?' Nas didn't reply. She could see her pulling on her coat, the tails fanning behind her. 'You need to make them understand that you're the link. That you're the one who connects Chloe and Lottie,' she shouted. Freddie thought of the anger in Saunders's eyes. From the first moment she'd seen him she'd known he didn't like Nas. He wanted her out of the way. Should Nas have just told her colleagues that she knew Chloe's family from the beginning? Would it have made any difference? It was difficult to untangle the pointless police protocol from what was truly dicey. Nas wouldn't do anything that might risk Lottie's life. Would she?

Freddie had never had to question any of this, any of Nas's behaviour, before. It had been Nas who'd confronted Chips when he got in the van with Liam. Nas who had immediately told the rest of the team what they'd found out from interviewing William. Nas was the one who always did things by the book. The sound of her heels was getting further away. She had to decide: *whose side was she on?* She thought of Lottie's petrified eyes, Saunders's angry stance, Chips's gormless shock… *Fuck it.* She started running down the stairs. Light shone through the distorted windows, strobing as she tried to catch up. 'Can you just stop a second?'

There was a noise below and she craned to see Nas disappear through a door. *Fuck.* She jumped the last few steps, pushing open the fire door into the car park. 'Where are you going?'

Nasreen was walking across the expanse. She turned, and Freddie saw for the first time that she had something in her hand. *Keys.*

'Romeland High.' Nas pressed the fob and a navy car beeped into life.

Freddie was so shocked she stopped. 'The school?'

'I want to talk to Mrs Wilshire, find out if she knows who Alex Black is. She's our best shot.' She opened the driver's door.

'I didn't know you could drive.' Freddie ran the last few metres and let herself into the passenger seat. 'Is this your car?'

'No, it's a pool car.' Nas fiddled with the ignition and adjusted her seat and mirror.

'Right,' Freddie nodded. She couldn't believe she was going to say this. 'Are you sure this is a good idea?'

Nas turned to look at her. 'I may very well have lost my job, Freddie.'

Freddie saw the pain on her friend's face, reached out and gave her hand a squeeze.

Nas shook her off. 'But I'm not losing Lottie: I owe Jack that much.' She started the car.

'Seriously, I can't believe you never said you could drive?'

A smile flickered across Nas's lips. She pulled a pair of black boots from her handbag and replaced her high, spiked heels. *Better.* She stopped the car as they reached the barrier to exit the car park and turned to look at Freddie again. Nas's mascara had smudged under her right eye. Just a small amount, but enough to tell Freddie she'd been crying on the way down the stairs. 'You heard what DI Saunders said.'

'He's a prick.'

'He's my boss. And he's suspended me. I've already compromised myself, but *you* don't have to do this.'

Freddie almost laughed. It was absurd: the rebel Nasreen. How had they got here?

Nas took a big breath. 'I won't blame you if you choose to walk away.'

'I can't just forget Lottie.' It was ten past seven. The thought of the girl out there in danger, the clock ticking…

'You're sure?' Nasreen said. Her eyes searched Freddie's face, looking for what: fear? Freddie was shit scared, but that didn't mean she was about to abandon her friend. She nodded.

'Good,' said Nas, but she didn't look pleased. Determination coloured her face. She edged the car forwards and the barrier lifted. And then they were out on the street, driving away from Westminster, from London. Driving towards St Albans. Instinctively Freddie reached for her phone, gripping it like a comforter in her hand.

Chapter 45

Thursday 17 March

08:35
T – 55 mins

Again Agnes Wilshire's landline rang out. Freddie Googled St Albans dentists: there were twenty-seven of them. 'What about if I start calling local dentists – see if we can find out where she is?' She braced as Nas sped past cars on the slip road off the motorway. She'd stopped looking at the speedometer when she saw it break a hundred.

'Patient confidentiality. They probably won't confirm if she's there,' Nas said.

She had to try. She dialled the first number; an answerphone clicked in. 'You've reached the Maltings Dental Practice. Our opening hours are 9 a.m. until 5.30 p.m. Monday to Friday.' Dammit. She tried the next, ringing off as she heard another machine click in. 'Why does no one get up in the bloody mornings!'

They were passing gaggles of school kids now, bustling towards their day. They'd made record time, but it still might not be enough. Freddie felt sick thinking of Lottie. They had less than an hour.

Nas drove straight up to the modern school building, beeping the horn to move the blur of school kids.

'Pigs!' a lad shouted, and there was a clap of laughter. Nasreen gave them a cold stare as she slammed her door.

Kids had their phones out and were taking photos of the car, its blue lights still flashing behind the grille. Up ahead a woman in a long dark skirt and coat turned to look at the commotion. Freddie did a double take. Was it just wishful thinking? No: she recognised her grey hair and glasses. 'Oh my god! That's her! That's Agnes! I saw her photo online!'

'Mrs Wilshire?' Nasreen jogged towards her.

'Yes?' The woman looked from the car to them.

'I'm Detective Sergeant Cudmore and this is Freddie Venton. We're investigating a case and we wondered if we could ask you some questions?' Was she allowed to say that if she'd been suspended?

'Oh, of course. Won't you come in?' Mrs Wilshire stood aside as they filed into the reception area.

'We wanted to ask you some questions about a pupil called Alex Black. We believe he would have been here six years ago,' Nas said.

Freddie's heart was pounding. Mrs Wilshire looked thoughtful. 'Alex? That's quite a popular name. Alex Black, you say?'

Nas nodded.

'I'm not sure. I think I remember. Short boy. Dark hair. You remember some children so well. It can be for all kinds of reasons, but there are so many of them. People stop me in the street to say hello, and I have no recollection of them at all. I just ask them how they're doing.' She smiled sweetly. Freddie felt her heart drop. Possibly short with dark hair wasn't much to go on.

'What about a Daisy Jones? Blonde girl. She might have been in the same year as Alex.'

'Oh, now Daisy I remember. Such a pretty thing. One of those always surrounded by friends. She had such a lovely smile.' Mrs Wilshire looked worried. 'Nothing's happened to her, has it?'

'No she's fine, as far as we're aware,' Nas said.

Freddie looked around at the felt boards on the walls. The displays had been changed since they'd been in the day before.

'Do you remember anything happening between Alex Black and Daisy Jones?' Nas said.

'I'm not sure, dear. I'm sorry,' the lady said. 'But I do remember some upset in her final year. I can't remember what it was over. A boyfriend, probably. You know what teenagers are like.'

Freddie was staring at the board in front of her, which documented a biology field trip. There were sketches of trees and animals, graphs and pie charts, printed fact sheets and photos. It was a wood. She leant in to read one project: 'Biodiversity in Wildhill Wood.' The wood Chloe's body had been found in. 'Is this Wildhill Wood?' she said. Nas's ears pricked. 'Do the school go here frequently?'

'Why, yes it is,' smiled Agnes Wilshire. 'We take the Year Elevens annually. It's a beautiful place, great fun for the kids.'

Nas's voice had quickened. 'Would Alex Black have gone there? And Daisy Jones?'

'I would expect so. They were probably the last year we camped: it's so hard to get parental volunteers that we just go for the day now.'

'Is there a campsite in the wood?' Nas said.

Freddie was staring at the sketches. Bats. Birds. A badger.

'There is an education centre,' Mrs Wilshire was saying.

Freddie took her phone out. Flicked through her photos. 'It was used as a hide and the children used to sleep there. They'd stay up and observe bats and owls in their natural habitat.'

Owls.

'Nas!' Freddie held her phone against the board. She'd taken a photo of the blown-up section of the wall hanging behind Lottie's head, the elongated loops they thought might be a drawing of bananas or pencils. She held it next to a student's drawing of an owl mid-flight. The owl's wings were in full span, the feathers on the end forming a row of elongated loops. 'It's a wing.'

This is it.

'Mrs Wilshire, do they have drawings of animals on the wall?' Nas asked quickly.

'How did you know that?' Mrs Wilshire asked. 'They had all these lovely scientific diagrams. But they lost funding and closed it a few years ago now.'

'It's the wing tip of an owl,' Freddie said. Her voice sounded far away as blood rushed through her ears. 'He's got her in Wildhill Wood. In the education centre.' She looked at Nas and they started for the door.

Chapter 46

Thursday 17 March

08:45
T − 45 mins

Freddie was running for the car. Nas was already there. On her phone calling it in. 'Suspect is believed to be in Wildhill Wood. We are in pursuit. Suspect has one hostage and he may be armed. We have reason to believe the hostage's life is in danger. This needs to be immediately relayed to DI Peter Saunders on the Gremlin taskforce at the Met.'

Freddie wrenched open the door as Nas did the same on the opposite side, throwing herself into the driver seat. The radio in the car crackled. Nas started the engine. Freddie pulled her belt across her. Nas flicked a button and a siren and flashing light sprang to life. 'The controller said their full team is at the road traffic accident on the motorway. It's a multi-vehicle pile-up. About forty minutes away.'

Forty minutes? Freddie looked at her phone. 'They're not going to get there in time.'

'They're going to try. They've put in a request for an armed response unit.'

'We've got forty-five minutes to the deadline,' Freddie gasped. 'Go now!'

With the blue light flashing and the siren blaring, Nas's unmarked police car squealed away from the kerbside. Freddie had directions to the wood up on her phone. 'Turn left!' she shouted.

They powered down the road, Nas circumventing cars in front of them. Freddie's heart was slamming against her ribcage.

Their phones beeped in unison. 'It's him! It's another message.'

'What does it say?' shouted Nas.

She stared at the phone, her hands shaking. 'You have thirty minutes to save the girl's life. Shit!' The image opened on her screen: a photo of a syringe and a burned spoon. 'Is that heroin?' She held the phone up for Nas to see.

'Same as the syringe found at Chloe's crime scene,' Nas said.

He's going to inject Lottie, like he did Chloe. He's going to kill her. 'Drive!' Freddie screamed. She was flicking between screens. They weren't going to make it. 'There's a turn-off, coming up on the left. Fuck. No. It's one way. The wrong way.'

'Show me.' Nas grabbed Freddie's hand and pulled the phone into her line of sight. *God, don't get car sick now, Nas.* Her own stomach somersaulted as they powered past a black car.

'Twenty-seven minutes!' shouted Freddie, her voice as high as the siren.

Nas exhaled as she flipped the indicator and swung the car into the one-way street. A car was coming directly at them. Freddie closed her eyes and braced. There was a jolt as they mounted the kerb. She opened her eyes just in time to see them narrowly miss a lamppost as Nas turned the car back onto the road. 'Fuck! Now I know why you don't drive often!' The driver behind them leant on his horn. The loud honk ripped through Freddie. 'We're the police, you idiot!'

'Time!' Nas's eyes were fixed ahead.

'Twenty-five minutes!' They were doing nearly ninety miles per hour. Houses blurred past, then Nasreen suddenly took a right and they were at the edge of the wood. It was huge, stretching on in front of them. The car bumped onto a mud track. Less than fifty metres ahead of them was a gate. Nas slid the car to a stop. Freddie was already out and running. The gate was padlocked. She shook it. *No way through.* 'It's locked!'

'We haven't time, go!' Nas's car door slammed shut behind her.

Freddie gripped the cold damp metal, one trainer on the slippy bars as Nas vaulted the gate and headed into the wood. Freddie scrambled to get up, over, slipping on wet leaves as she came down on the other side. Her breath was coming in frantic puffs of condensation. She ran down the path after Nas, the trees rising high above them. The path was narrowing, and they had to jump puddles and dodge stinging nettles. The forest was so dense you couldn't see far in either direction. 'Eighteen minutes!' she shouted. They'd been sprinting for ages and all they were doing was getting deeper and deeper into a forest. This was the perfect place to hide someone. It was dark, damp and difficult under foot. She could no longer hear the cars on the road behind them. How the hell were they going to find her? Mud was splashed up both their legs. 'Shit!' Nas said.

She just stopped short of skidding into her. The path in front of them went in three different directions. 'Which way? We could split, but that's only two options covered,' Nas said.

Freddie pulled out her phone. Signal was dropping in and

out. One bar teased and then vanished. 3G and then nothing. She Googled 'Wildhill Conservation Centre' and found a photo of a squat single-storey building, with a lip of a hide running along the front. It looked like a portakabin. All the photos were tightly cropped; there was nothing to tell her where it was. All the trees looked the same. She looked over her shoulder. Nothing but more trees. She was disorientated.

Freddie scrolled down the images. Searching. Looking. Anything. *Anything.* 'There!' A photo of an old wooden sign pointed to Wildhill Conservation Centre. It stood at a three-way fork in the track. A sign that wasn't here anymore. It pointed left. 'That way!' *Fourteen minutes left.* 'Go!' Freddie screamed.

And Nas did; her legs powerful and strong, she soon stripped past Freddie. Freddie fought to keep up, her legs screaming, her chest burning. Suddenly the track opened into a clearing and there it was: the shell of the building. Smashed windows. Dark inside but for the bare, eerie glow of technology. A blue screen. Freddie thought she might vomit. Nas hurdled over a fallen tree, she was metres away from the building. 'Alex Black!' she shouted. 'This is the police. We know you're in there.' Freddie's throat closed in panic. Nas signalled for Freddie to stop. 'He doesn't know we don't have the whole team here,' she whispered. 'Show back-up where to come.'

She couldn't leave her.

Nas took her baton out of its holster and shook it to extend it. 'Go!' she hissed.

Freddie turned and started to run. She had to get help. Blood thundered in her ears. A tree root grabbed at her foot. She tripped, skidded on wet leaves and fell forwards. Her hands shot out to break the fall. Her phone flew and smashed onto the ground, splitting apart. Her hands pummelled into sharp sticks. Pain radiated out from her knee. She must get help. She pushed herself up as a muffled scream came from within the Wildhill Conservation Centre, and she looked back to see Nas disappear inside. In the distance she heard the faint wail of a police siren. And Freddie Venton ran like she never had before.

Chapter 47

Thursday 17 March

09:21
T – 9 mins

Nasreen bent and stepped through the once glass-panelled door. The building was dark, with a low ceiling. She was in a corridor that smelt of piss. The floor was littered with brown leaves, fag ends and beer cans, strewn amongst the roots of trees that pushed up through the decaying wooden floor. She kept thinking of the runner's body lying under the tree in Greenwich Park. More trees. Another forest. Another body? She listened. She could hear movement. A low murmured voice. She glanced back over her shoulder. How long would back-up take to arrive? She glanced at her watch. Ten minutes for Freddie to reach the road, ten minutes for them to reach the building. T – 9 minutes. There wasn't time to wait.

Heading away from the smashed glass side of the portakabin,

she walked lightly towards where the noise was coming from. The scratched wooden door was heavy with graffiti and swollen from water damage; it lay ajar, the catch no longer biting. She could hear movement on the other side, breathing. The sound of a door closing? She paused, held her own breath. The voice was no longer audible. Everything was still. T – 8 minutes. Nasreen gently pushed the door open a crack. There was Lottie, still in her pink running kit, arms and legs bound to a chair, a gag in her mouth. Her head hung low to her chest, her shorn hair hacked patchy at the back of her scalp, but she was breathing. Still alive. A twig snapped and Nasreen looked up. A woman, blonde hair, also in running gear, fell forwards onto the ground. *There's another one? Another victim?* She looked familiar. She was in her early twenties: the same as Nasreen.

'Oh my god, help me! Please!' She crawled towards Nasreen across the rubbish-strewn floor. Lottie's head snapped up and she screamed through the gag, squirming to break free. 'Please! He's coming! Please help us!' The woman stumbled up to her feet. *Daisy?* Mud and what looked like a scratch sliced across her face.

'Don't worry.' Nasreen kept her eye on the far door; they didn't have long. There were no signs of weapons or traps. A shelf ran the length of the front window, marking where the hide once was, and on it she saw a number of syringes. Lottie was still violently squirming, fear in her eyes. What had he done to her? 'I need you to remain calm, Lottie. Help is on the way. You're safe now.'

The woman on her hands and knees gave out a sob. Struggling up, she took a shaky step. 'Thank you,' she said, and tripped. Nasreen rushed to catch her as she crumpled, dropping her baton. Her blonde hair fell forward; Nasreen put her weight on her back foot, levered her up. She'd have to carry her out. 'Thank you, thank you,' the girl was saying. Tears were falling from her eyes. 'Thank you, Nasreen.'

A cold chill ripped up Nasreen's calves. The hairs on her neck stood to attention. 'How do you know my name?' The girl shifted from slippery liquid sack to solid strength, her hand in her hoodie pocket. Nasreen saw her baton on the floor and went for her pepper spray. Too late. She saw the girl's eyes: clear, focused. The syringe flashed through the air. Lottie was screaming through the gag. Nasreen felt the needle punch into her chest, the plunger being pressed. Air forced its way out of her mouth. 'Who are you?' She stumbled backwards, wrenching at the plastic handle.

'I'm Alex,' the girl said. And then everything went black.

Chapter 48

Thursday 17 March

09:28
T – 2 mins

Grit. In her mouth. Pressure against her teeth. Gums. A finger. Her head was being held. Nasreen coughed. Tried to move. Someone had hold of her chin. She tried to push them away. Kick. Her ankles and wrists strained against tape. She was strapped to a chair. Someone was crying. Muffled sobs. *Lottie?* The room came back into focus. The damp walls, dark green mould spreading like oil on water. She was groggy. She bit at the fingers that were pushed inside her mouth.

'Whoa there!' The woman who'd stabbed her pulled away.

Nasreen spat. 'What are you doing?' Her voice was slurred. The woman appeared in front of her, squatting down and resting her elbows on her knees. She was blonde. Pretty. Athletic. The room wobbled. 'What did you give me?' The grains were sweet in her mouth.

'Jeez, it's just a bit of sugar.' She turned as if she were talking to Lottie. 'Some women are just nuts about avoiding sugar, aren't they, Lottie? Cray cray!'

Nasreen blinked, tried to focus. *Sugar?* Lottie still had silver gaffer tape stretched tight over her mouth, tears falling down her face. Was this another Lorna? Another girl obsessed with Black? 'Who are you?'

The woman laughed. Her mouth a sneer of perfectly straight, white teeth. Like fresh marble gravestones. 'For "the Met's rising star" you're a bit slow, aren't you?' she said. What was going on? Nasreen shook her head, trying to clear it. The woman leant towards her, her eyes sparkling shards of glass. 'I'm Alexandra Black, but most people call me Alex. Or Apollyon's Revenge.'

Nasreen felt the fine hairs on her arms and neck stand up. *But what about Liam? The men on Are You Awake? All those girls?* 'You're a woman?' Her words were thick, clunky. She tried to grasp what was happening.

'Gold star for observation,' Alex said drily.

'But how?' Her mind was swimming. 'Apollyon's Revenge, the warriors, Lorna – they all think you're a man.' *They'd* thought she was a man.

'I don't do meet and greets, Sergeant Cudmore. I prefer to keep my communication online. If people assume they know anything about me, they're fools.'

No wonder Mrs Wilshire couldn't remember a boy called Alex Black. 'Is Alex your real name?' Nasreen managed.

The woman smiled. 'Of course. I don't need a fake name: no one can find me anyway.'

'I found you,' Nasreen said. The broken door had been pulled to, trapping them inside.

'And how's that working out for you?' Alex pointed to the

tape that bound her wrists. This was a trap, and she'd walked straight into it. Nasreen could see that Lottie's eyes were ringed in red. Her nose snotty, blocked. She must have been like this for hours. She was struggling against the tape to get enough air to breathe. 'It's okay, Lottie. I know your brother. It's going to be okay.' Her tongue felt sickly sweet. Her head felt like she'd been hit. 'What did you give me?'

'Insulin,' Alex said. 'Induces hypoglycaemia in those who aren't diabetic. Plus you can inject it subcutaneously – so much easier than trying to find a vein.' She walked slowly towards Lottie. Lottie's breathing became more frantic. She was trying to shout against the tape. 'Worked a treat on this pretty little one as well.' She stroked her hand down Lottie's cheek. The girl strained to get away.

'Stay calm, Lottie. Look at me.' Nas tried to push the chair back so she could see her better. Make eye contact. Lottie's eyes were frantic, flicking from Alex, who was slowly and deliberately stroking her face, to Nasreen and back again. What did she know about insulin? Hypoglycaemia? 'How could you be sure I wasn't diabetic?' Nasreen asked. She had to get her away from Lottie.

Alex jerked towards her; Nasreen turned her face away and braced for the hit. But the woman laughed and grabbed the chair leg instead, scraping it along the floor, almost tipping it over, yanking it so Nasreen was turned to face Lottie. '*Better?*' Alex's breath tickled her cheeks; she smelled of Marmite. 'Front row seats for the show!' She walked away to the far corner, her neon pink trainers sure-footed.

That's how she did it? She looks like a runner. Nasreen could picture her jogging alongside Lottie and then swiping at her with the needle. One quick plunge and the girl would've been incapacitated.

'A child could hack into the NHS system.' Alex picked up a dark rucksack, which was resting on an old table. 'I've seen your medical records. I know all kinds of things about you, Nasreen.'

'I'm flattered,' Nasreen said. Alex placed a video camera on the side. Whatever she had planned, she was going to record it. 'Why are you so interested in me?' She needed to keep her talking. Alex had her back to them. If she could get closer to Lottie she might be able to loosen her tape. Nasreen tried rocking the chair from side to side, pulling with all her weight against the restraints. One chair leg went forwards, then the other.

Alex turned to watch her. 'Pathetic,' she scoffed. She crossed her arms and leant against the window ledge, raising an eyebrow at Nasreen as if she were an amusing puppy. '*You're* the great Sergeant Cudmore who took down the Twitter serial killer?'

'You admire him: Apollyon? Is that what this is about?' *Notoriety*. The media hype had made him famous, like American killers who gunned down innocent school children and had their names and faces splashed all over the news: other people wanted that infamy. It bred shootings.

'He wasn't really up to the job, was he?' Alex said. '*You* managed to arrest him.' She made it sound like an insult.

Nasreen rubbed her tongue along her teeth. Had she spat all the sugar out? Was there some left? 'Why call yourself Apollyon's Revenge then?' It would take Freddie ten minutes to get back to the road, to flag the local force down. Ten minutes for the team to reach them. How long had she been out for? She couldn't see her watch. She'd have to keep her talking.

'Apollyon made a convenient bait,' Alex was saying. 'All those man-babies lap that crap up.' She looked smug.

Nothing was as they'd thought it had been.

'What about the men's rights guys – you tried to help them?'

Nasreen's voice sounded normal, but her heart was beating double time.

Alex's laugh was joyous. 'Those MRA whingers? They only *thought* I was helping them.' She was delighted with herself. 'Crying because life didn't give them their own supermodel to shag? *Pitiful*. I enjoyed using those losers. It was a gratifying bonus. If they'd known they were talking to me, to this…' Alex ran her hands over her breasts and her taut waist. 'It would have blown their minds. Instead I used their dirty little desires for my own ends.'

'Why use them to go after other women?' Nasreen was trying to piece it all together. There was something she was missing. In the broken sunlight that filtered through the grimy window, she could see three syringes lined up on the shelf behind her. *Heroin*. And lying next to them: a long sharp knife.

'I wanted the MRAs for their numbers,' Alex smiled.

'I don't understand.' There was an empty water bottle at Lottie's feet, but no signs of food. Her trainers and leggings were caked in mud on one side, as if she'd been dragged into here. Despite the odd brown splash, Alex was unmarked. She should have noticed that. She should have known.

Alex sighed, growing bored of the questions. 'I work for money, the same as anyone else.'

Extortion. Of course: that made sense. 'You blackmail the girls to take the images down?' Nasreen began to work at the edge of the tape round her right wrist, making tiny tears with her fingernail.

'That would be illegal, Sergeant Cudmore,' Alex laughed. 'I make my money from advertising. Are You Awake gets 2.2 million unique visitors per month, and 200 million page loads per month. That's a lot of traffic to pimp to. It's a bulletin board. I'm not responsible for what people put on it.'

'All this is about money?'

311

Alex's face clouded. 'Money is easy. I wanted more of a…statement.' She straightened the needles. 'One for Lottie Londoner; one for our friendly policewoman,' she sang softly.

'You don't have to do this, Alex. You've got what you want: money, fame. Everyone's talking about you.' She saw the girl smile. 'Let Lottie go – you don't need her now. She's done nothing wrong.' Nasreen kept one eye on the door. Help would arrive soon.

'Oh no, girls like Lottie never do anything wrong, do they?' Alex sprang towards her. Away from the syringes.

'She's not Daisy,' Nasreen said. Keep her talking.

'Don't you use her name!' Alex ran at her, hitting her hard with the back of her hand. Nasreen felt her lip split; blood pooled into her mouth. She spat. Speckled phlegm hit the ground, merging into the dark mess of the floor. 'Tell me what Daisy was like. You were at Romeland together?'

'Very clever, Nasreen. Brains and beauty. Aren't you blessed? You're all so fucking blessed!' she screamed. Lottie flinched and starting snivelling again.

'Did Daisy hurt you, Alex? Is that what this is about?'

Alex lunged and grabbed hold of her jaw, her cold fingers digging into her skin. Nasreen struggled, but Alex was strong. She brought her face level with hers. 'You're very pretty, Sergeant Nasreen Cudmore.' Her voice was almost a whisper. Nasreen tried to move, but Alex Black held her still as she ran her tongue up her cheek. *Tasting her.* Bile rushed up her throat and instinctively Nasreen tried to wipe her face, but the tape pulled tight against her skin. Alex laughed. *Stay calm. Don't show you're frightened.* She was millimetres from her.

'That's what all the papers said at the time, wasn't it, Sergeant Cudmore?' Alex purred. 'When you arrested Apollyon? How brave. How pretty. How smart you are.'

Nasreen flexed her fingers. Her hands were losing circulation. Her toes felt cold in her boots. She fought to control the tremor in her voice. 'Why did you target Chloe Strofton?'

'When I saw that idiot Liam mention her name on Are You Awake it was a gift. It was just what I'd been waiting for.' Alex's grip tightened. 'You pretty girls don't know how hard life is for us. You get *everything*. Attention, adoration, money: it's all handed to you on a plate. You're *nothing* if you're an ugly woman.' Nasreen forced herself to look at Alex's attractive face. This made no sense. The woman smiled. 'I didn't always look like this: the Are You Awake cash has paid for a lot of cosmetic surgery. Fixing my *flaws*. Making me fit. Making me visible. I used to be fat. NHS glasses. Bad skin. Bad bones. *Ugly*.' Her grip tightened and Nasreen's jaw creaked under the pressure. 'I got the highest grades in my year at school, and guess whose photo they put in the local paper? Three blonde bimbos jumping!' Spittle peppered Nasreen's skin. She flinched and blinked. Tried to pull away. But Alex wasn't done. 'I was in line to get a scholarship for uni, until some lithe little waif caught the professor's eye. I was passed over for jobs, promotions, everything I ever wanted, because being clever *isn't enough*. Being the best person for the job *isn't enough*. Girls like Chloe and Lottie and *you* come along and steal it.'

She was squeezing her face so hard, her lips were squashed together. Nasreen forced the words out. 'It's what's on the inside that counts.' *And what's inside you is rotten.*

'Bullshit!' Alex shouted. She smelt of cigarettes too. And behind that was something stale. Something dead. 'If you're *hot* you get away with anything. You know that, Nasreen,' Alex's voice fell calm again. Low and threatening. For a second Nasreen thought of Saunders – what she'd give to see him right now. 'I saw your photo in the news, Nasreen: they called you a hero

313

when you arrested the Hashtag Murderer. And I saw straight through it.' Alex smiled, though it was devoid of warmth. She was enjoying this. 'It didn't take long to find evidence.'

Nasreen swallowed. What was she talking about?

'Nasreen Cudmore is an unusual name. You have a fan site, do you know that?'

'What?' Nasreen tried to move her face. Her own sweaty hand was still working at the edge of the tape round her wrist.

'They think you're *hot*,' Alex smirked. 'They share photos of you.'

What photos?

'But they don't know what you're really like, do they Nasreen? Tell Lottie what you did to Gemma Strofton.' She forced her head round so Nasreen was staring at Lottie: the girl's eyes were wide and anxious.

Nasreen's heart was thumping. She felt sick. She thought of Jack: what would he think of her? 'I don't know what you're talking about.'

'Don't lie!' Alex shouted. 'I read the newspaper reports. I spoke to the editor on the local paper. *You* bullied Gemma Strofton. You hounded her until she tried to kill herself.'

Alarm flooded Nasreen. 'It wasn't like that. I made a mistake.' She tried to pull her face away. She couldn't meet Lottie's eyes.

'You thought you got away with it, but I'll make you pay. A life for a life. And I wanted to select someone close to your team to make sure the message got through: Lottie Londoner with her bragging Instagram seemed perfect.' Alex's nose was almost touching hers. *She's unhinged.* 'Did you work that out, clever Nasreen? That this was my masterpiece?'

Gemma's face, her parents, poor Chloe curled up dead on the forest floor; it all rushed through Nasreen's mind.

Alex kept going: 'Gemma may have survived what you did,

but Chloe died because of you. *You are responsible for all of this.*

No. Alex looked eerily calm. Nasreen's breath was coming too fast. She could feel hysteria banging on the door. She had to get control of the situation. '*You* bullied Chloe, Alex. You published naked photos of her. You bought her heroin. *You* killed her.' Lottie made a noise, she was looking at the syringes, struggling.

Alex just smiled. 'You don't win this time, Nasreen.' She let go.

Nasreen's skin was clammy where she'd touched her. The line of saliva tightened as it dried on her face. Alex headed for the needles. Lottie was jerking against her binds, desperate to free herself. 'You bullied Daisy too,' Nasreen called. Alex froze. *Keep her talking. Distract her.* Her mind was racing, piecing together everything she now knew. Alex was angry: vengeful against girls she thought were pretty. Women she thought had cheated her. But why? How had she become so full of hate? It was something to do with Daisy. 'Daisy didn't deserve what you did to her.'

Alex whirled to stare at her. Despite herself, Nasreen recoiled as much as the chair let her. Alex's eyes were slivers of hate. 'Daisy was my friend,' she said.

'Then why humiliate her?' She had to keep her away from the needles.

'She humiliated *me*,' Alex shouted. She ran her hands through her hair, agitated.

'Everyone says she's a nice girl.' Blood was rushing in Nasreen's ears. She kept working at the tape round her wrist. Keeping her eyes fixed on Alex at all times. Lottie was sobbing, bubbles of snot blowing from her nose. If she could just keep her calm a little longer.

'Daisy was like pretty, famous Lottie here,' Alex snarled. 'Spoilt. Beautiful. Used to getting everything she wanted. She was

315

supposed to be my friend. But the other girls – the popular ones – they hated me being near her. As if my ugliness might contaminate them.' Her voice was rising. Her cheeks were flushed. She was animated in a way Nasreen hadn't seen so far. 'They treated me like an animal. A freak!'

'What happened?' Nasreen pushed. Something had caused Alex to change; to change herself, what she looked like. Something that had turned her into this monster. 'What did they do?'

'They held me down.' Alex's voice became tiny. Nasreen could hear Lottie's strangled breaths. 'They pulled my pants down – took photos of me.' She crumpled in on herself, her hands instinctively covering her breasts, her groin. 'I was fifteen. Fifteen!' Her voice became an angry sob. 'I'd never even kissed a boy. I didn't like undressing in front of other people. *They* thought it was funny.'

Fifteen. The same age as Chloe. Nasreen could imagine the young girl: stripped, humiliated. *How could they do that?* 'Was it here, Alex?' she said softly.

Alex seemed to remember where she was, looking around the cold dark room. She nodded morosely. Her voice barely above a whisper. 'A school trip. They'd been drinking cider. One of them smuggled it in. Telling stories about their boyfriends.' She looked like she might be sick. 'Daisy promised she would throw the photos away. But she didn't. *She* printed them.' She closed her eyes as if she were reliving every painful second. 'They handed them round at school. Put them in my locker. *Everyone* saw.'

'What about the teachers?' Nasreen said. 'They must have helped you?'

Alex gave a mirthless laugh. 'The teachers said they'd expel the girls. But then Daisy's father gave the school a large donation for a new library. Did you see it? An extension on the back: double-height ceiling. They weren't even suspended. I had to see them every day. *Every day.* I dropped out after that. Like all pretty girls, they got away with it. The teachers did *nothing*. Because I was nobody: because I wasn't beautiful, I didn't matter!'

Cynthia Warner's daughter, the second victim of Alex's campaign, was a teacher. Nasreen exhaled. 'That shouldn't have happened. I'm sorry, Alex.'

She watched the woman harden in front of her eyes, all traces of the traumatised child gone. 'No. You're as bad as they are.'

Alex had chosen to hack and share intimate images of other girls. Popular, attractive girls who resembled Daisy: she was repeatedly getting her back. Embarrassing Daisy hadn't been enough. Humiliating strangers hadn't been enough. Like a junkie, Alex needed another hit, she needed more. She wanted them to pay. She needed them to *die*. 'You can't do this,' Nasreen said.

Alex was picking up and flicking the syringes. 'I'll kill you and Lottie, and I'll die too. And it'll be Daisy's fault. She can't hide from this in America.' She was going to kill herself: a final swan song. Nasreen thought of the American school gunmen going down in a blaze of bullets.

Alex turned her attention to Lottie. 'I watched Chloe die. It doesn't hurt.' She put the needles down and straightened the camera next to them. Picked up the knife. Its blade glinted against the dark walls. 'But this will.'

Lottie let out a muffled '*No!*'

Nasreen pulled her wrists and feet against the tape. 'Don't do this, Alex!'

Alex was walking towards Lottie. 'I'll show you what it feels like when you can't look at yourself in the mirror. What it's like when the world thinks you're ugly.' She grabbed Lottie and held the knife against her cheek. Lottie's yells grew shrill under the tape.

'Stop!' Nasreen commanded. But Alex ignored her. She tried again, frantic. 'This won't make up for what happened: it won't make you feel better.' She could feel the pulse in her wrist under the tape. Lottie was twisting in her seat, her oblique muscles tensing and jerking, trying to get away.

'You're wrong: this *will* make it better.' Alex slowly ran the knife up the side of Lottie's face. Angry red blood sprang up around the blade. Lottie screamed. 'Oops.' She gripped the girl's head tighter, pressed the knife into the other side of her face.

Lottie's blue eyes locked onto Nasreen's, pleading. *Help me.*

Nasreen threw her hips from side to side, rocking the chair. One leg clunked forwards, then the other. She clawed at the ends of the tape, her raw, sweat-soaked fingertips sliding off. And then she shouted; screamed as loud as she could. 'Help! We're in here!'

Alex let go of Lottie and rushed at Nasreen. 'I should have gagged you too.' She grabbed Nasreen's hair, yanking her head back. The knife gleamed.

Nasreen felt like her skull might pop. Blood pooled somewhere behind her eyes. Her neck went slack, her head lolled, her eyelids fluttered. 'The insulin,' she murmured.

Alex cupped Nasreen's chin. She felt her face close to hers. 'Shouldn't have spat the sugar out, should you?'

The blade was against her cheek. Nasreen reeled her head back, and with all her force she headbutted Alex.

Alex's face exploded with blood. 'My nose!' she screamed. 'That cost a fortune, you fucking bitch!' She swung the back of her hand hard against the side of Nasreen's head, knocking the chair off balance. Nasreen slammed into the floor with a jolt. Pain shot up her right shoulder. Her ears were ringing. She yanked at her wrist, and the frayed tape, pressed against the floor, gave. Before she could react, Alex's foot swung into her stomach, flicking the chair backwards. Pain tore through her gut. She was on her back. Two ankles and a wrist still attached to the chair. 'You spoilt fucking bitch!' Alex screamed. Nasreen saw the knife swing down towards her. Her arm shot up. Cold seared through her forearm. A wave of nausea crashed over her. Blood dropped onto her. She flung her closed fist back against Alex, connecting with the broken bone of her nose. Alex howled, and rolled backwards.

Her heart pounding, her lungs screaming, Nasreen yanked at the tape on her other wrist and freed her ankles. She lurched. The room was shaking. Her shirt was sodden with blood from her arm. She ran to Lottie. She had to get her out. Lottie was hyperventilating; she couldn't get enough air. Nasreen ripped the tape from the girl's mouth. Her screams filled the room. She tore one of Lottie's wrists free.

Alex kicked her back. Air whooshed out of her. Nasreen reached for the tape round Lottie's ankles as her knees slammed into the floor. She fell forwards; her whole body felt like it'd been compressed. Squeezed. She was gasping. *Get up.* Pain spread from her back – her kidneys? *Get up. You've got to get up.* She could feel the cut on her arm now: hot, burning, deep. Her fingers scrabbled uselessly as Alex grabbed her ankle. She was being dragged backwards. She couldn't catch hold of the floor. *Must turn over.* The blood-spattered swoosh of Alex's pink trainer ground down into her arm. There was a scream: *her* scream.

Nasreen reached up and back, as Lottie pulled herself free from the chair, sobbing, and staggered towards them, her hands outstretched to help. She dredged every bit of authority she had left. 'Run, Lottie! Run!' The words shook at the edges. The girl's eyes were wide, blood was running over her face, she took two steps back. '*Go!*' Nasreen managed. Lottie turned and stumbled towards the door, wrenching it wide, sunlight pouring in. She was free. *Safe.*

Nasreen turned to see the sole of Alex's trainer stamping down towards her face. *Hands up. Get up.* Groaning, she tried to lift herself from the ground. Alex kicked her arm away from her. A fresh wave of agony. She landed on her back, a broken bottle digging into her. She grabbed at the slippery neon-pink leggings. *Get up.* Alex's face was close, screaming. *Two of Alex.* There was a searing pain in her shoulder. She tried to swing her arm up, out. Alex fell onto her, blood smeared across her face, her blonde hair wild. *Get up.* Alex's knees pinned her to the floor. Pushing into her cut arm: Nasreen's vision swam. *Get up!* Black's hands were round her neck, tightening on her windpipe. *Get...* The room wavered. Blood and panic bubbled up in her throat. Dark spots formed at the side of Nasreen's vision. *Get air.* She clawed at Alex's fingers. Her feet kicked helplessly across the floor. *Must breathe. Can't. Can't...*

As her arms fell to her sides, her legs stilled and the darkness came, Nasreen thought of her parents: they'd be sitting on the old, squishy, brown leather sofa, watching telly, when they got the knock at the door.

Chapter 49

Thursday 17 March

09:30
Time's Up

Far away she heard a shout. Her eyelids fluttered. A woman? Lottie? *No.* A blur of black jeans. *Freddie!* There was a crack. Air rushed down Nasreen's throat; she grabbed at her own neck, trying to force more into it, protecting it, her lungs greedy, gasping, coughing. Colour poured into the room. Alex was lying across her, legs sprawled. Freddie, a log in her hand, had hit her. 'Get off her!' Freddie was screaming, pulling at Alex.

Nasreen blinked. She watched as Alex pushed against the floor with her hand, springing up, knife raised. Nasreen tried to cry out but her throat was raw. Freddie swung the log at Alex, cracking her wild, blonde head. Alex dropped the knife, staggered. It was all Nasreen needed: she was up on her feet and launching herself at Alex. They crashed onto the floor.

She grabbed for Alex's hands and wrenched them back. Freddie kicked the knife away. Alex bucked, but this time Nas was ready, forcing her knee down into her spine, pinning her wrists back. 'Ah…' She coughed. Her voice squeaky. Gasped. Croaked. 'Alex Black, I'm arresting you for the kidnap and attempted murder of Charlotte Burgone. For the harassment and manslaughter of Chloe Strofton. For the false imprisonment and attempted murder of a police officer…' She broke off to cough again, Alex squirming under her weight. There were shouts outside. *Back-up.*

'In here!' Freddie shouted. 'We're in here!'

Nasreen spat out the blood that was gathering in her mouth and tried to blow her plastered hair away from her face. 'Thanks,' she said, nodding at the log Freddie was still holding.

'Some people just don't get the sisterhood, do they?' Freddie grinned.

'Cudmore!' Saunders kicked past the door. His face panicked. Mud up his suit legs. He took in Freddie, Nasreen and Alex, squirming under her. Then he was on Alex with his handcuffs. Chips appeared seconds later, followed by a surge of uniforms. Someone helped Nasreen up.

'It's her. Alex Black is a her. She,' Nasreen coughed.

'Bloody hell,' said Chips.

Saunders hauled Alex Black to her feet.

'You okay, lass?' Chips caught hold of her shoulder. She was gripping her arm: blood oozing between her fingers. 'Looks like stitches to me.'

She wiped the gunk that was gathering under her nose. 'Where's Lottie?'

'The wee thing's safe. The guv's here. We found her outside. She told us you freed her. She told us where to find you,' Chips said.

'Thank god.' Relief flooded through her. She touched her hand to her throat.

'Forget god: thank fuck you got here in time.' Chips was shaking his head, a look of shock working across his forehead. 'You took her down single-handedly.'

Nasreen looked up as Freddie shrugged off the blanket a paramedic was trying to wrap her in. 'Not single-handedly,' she said. 'I had a little help.'

Chips raised his eyebrows as he took in the log Freddie was still trailing from one hand. 'The paperwork for this one's going to be tricky.'

Chapter 50

'Someone's taken my swabs. I'll be right back,' the short nurse tutted, flicking the cubicle curtain with her wrist so she could duck through without opening it. Nasreen leant back on the treatment bed, the disposable paper hygiene roll rustling under her, and took in the yellowing ceiling tiles of the hospital. It was nice to have a minute alone. The paramedics had caught her in a silver shock blanket and bundled her into an ambulance as she was trying to get to Lottie. She'd had no chance to speak to Saunders, to apologise for going against him. No chance to even try and explain why she hadn't told them about the Stroftons. She closed her eyes. *I did this for you, Chloe. I got Alex: I stopped her. You can have peace now.*

She swallowed the lump in her throat. She'd write to Gemma and her parents, tell them the killer had targeted Chloe because of her. How she knew the only way to save Lottie, to stop that happening to another innocent family, was to act in secret.

How she'd tried to protect them, and bring Chloe's killer to justice. Ask for them to confirm that she'd had no contact with them in over eight years. Declare her a stranger. Ask for their forgiveness all over again. Alex Black would stand trial for what she did. She would be made to answer for her actions. And Nasreen would be called to the witness stand. She too would have to answer for her actions. Would she still have a job then?

She heard the curtain rings shake as the nurse came back in. 'Sorry, I was just taking a moment,' Nasreen said.

'Don't worry.' It wasn't the nurse, it was the DCI. It was Burgone! Her eyes sprang open and she sat up, forgetting that they'd cut her shirt away from her injuries. She scrabbled to grab the edge of the ripped cotton, to cover her lace bra, the round of her breasts. *Shit.*

'Sorry.' Burgone, whose hair had been combed into place, coughed and turned to look at the wall. She could see he was wearing a clean shirt: there was going to be a press statement, possibly already had been one. He looked pulled together, professional. The sheen of his status restored. Jack the Lad was back.

Her cheeks flamed. 'Sorry, sir, I didn't realise it was you.' She wanted the bed to snap shut with her in it. He looked serious, his expression that of her boss. Her boss that she'd slept with. Her boss that she'd lied to. She didn't know if she could do this: have this conversation now. She was swinging between exhaustion and the adrenaline comedown. She ached all over. Her shirt was torn and she was covered in blood. Not just hers, but his sister's too. They both spoke at once:

'How's Lottie?'

'How are you feeling?'

She laughed at the absurdity of it all. And he did too, the

familiar sparkle returning to his blue eyes. She bit her lip and looked at the floor. 'Is she hurt?'

'Superficial damage,' Burgone said. 'Cuts and bruises, dehydration. They're keeping her in for observation, but she should be released tomorrow.' A shadow of what had happened darkened his face.

Her mind galloped with everything. 'Sir, do you know if there have been any arrests in relation to the body of the runner found in Greenwich Park?'

He looked momentarily wrongfooted. Then nodded. 'PC Goldstein filled me in: shortly after the body was discovered, a man, believed to be the victim's partner, walked into a local pub, covered in blood.'

'Oh god.' It was a domestic abuse case. She'd been right.

'Apparently he ordered a double whisky and then asked the barman to call the police. The story's spread across the force fast.'

'That makes the MIT's job straightforward.'

'If only every job were that easy.'

The poor woman's family and friends. Nasreen wondered if they knew about the abuse. Lottie had been lucky, by comparison. 'Have you spoken to your parents? Do they know Lottie's okay?'

She could feel him looking at her. 'They're on their way from France – Chips volunteered Saunders to pick them up from Heathrow.'

That explained why she hadn't seen him yet, why she'd been spared that confrontation. But not this one. Did Burgone know this was her fault? Had he spoken to Saunders before that? What had Chips said? Had Lottie told him what Alex had said? That all this was punishment for Nasreen's former actions? God, what did Burgone think of her? She felt more scared than she ever had in the woods. 'I'm so sorry, Jack.' Her voice cracked. 'She took her because of me. She killed Chloe because of me.' A tear dripped onto the mud-smudged black of her trousers and she placed her hand over her mouth, as if she could stem the despair.

He stepped towards her, wrapping his arms around her and pulling her into him. 'It wasn't your fault. You saved Lottie. If you hadn't have got there, if you hadn't had risked your own life…' His voice was shaking too. 'I can't ever thank you for what you did.'

She buried her head against his chest, letting herself inhale his amber fragrance. His touch permeated her like air, blowing away her dandelion seed layers. Every part of her was aflame with desire for him. She wanted to kiss his warm mouth, pull him onto her. Gently she pushed herself away, her body screaming, until she was sitting, her legs dangling over the edge of the bed, facing him. This was the hardest thing she'd ever had to do.

'I lied to you and the team. I didn't tell you that I knew the Stroftons personally. That I was involved in an incident that led to Gemma Strofton, Chloe's older sister, trying to take her own life. Freddie too.'

The shock on his face told her Lottie hadn't said anything. That she'd tried to protect Nasreen. Saunders, presumably, hadn't had a chance to fill him in yet. She wanted to reach for his hand, but she couldn't. Not now. Not after this. She forced herself to continue. 'DI Saunders and DI McCain know. They received a complaint from Chloe's parents. DI Saunders has suspended me, pending investigation.'

'What?' He pulled away. 'Chips dragged Saunders away. I thought… I thought he was just trying to give me some time. I didn't think this… No.' Jack's face broke in disbelief. 'You tried to kill Chloe's sister?'

'No, we teased her – bullied her. We were fourteen.' She saw the age register on his beautiful face as he started to draw the lines between what had happened then, and what had happened in the past twenty-four hours. 'We drove her to it. It was inexcusable. I'm ashamed of my behaviour.'

'You were a child,' Jack said.

'Then, yes. But not now.' She forced herself to look him in the eye. 'I knew that if I flagged my personal link to the case then I would be removed. And I couldn't do that. I had to be there for Lottie.' *I had to be there for you.*

His face shifted. She felt him withdraw. '*You* are the connection between Chloe and Lottie – that's what you meant when you said this was your fault?' His face twisted in disgust. 'If you'd said something earlier, we could have worked it out: we could have found her sooner!'

The thought filled her with horror. No! 'I never imagined that… I didn't know Black. I couldn't be sure.' It was too awful. She shot her hand out towards him, and he took a step back. 'I would never have done anything to risk Lottie's safety. You have to believe me.'

Burgone ran his hand through his hair, shaking his head. Her heart pulsed in her chest. Pain stabbed into her side. 'I don't know what to say.'

'I'm sorry,' she said.

'I need to think. This is a lot to take in.' He blew air out his mouth, wiping his hand down over his face. 'Has Saunders started formal suspension procedures?'

'I don't know.'

He paced back and forth, his face tense with concentration. She could hear his laboured breathing. Was he fighting to control his anger? Deciding what he was going to say to the Independent

Police Complaints Commission? 'When did this happen – him dismissing you?'

'Seven oh three this morning.' It was branded onto her mind.

'Only two hours before you found Lottie?' he said. She nodded dumbly. He was building the timeline in his mind, slotting this new information into place. 'I know they were flat out at that point: everything was focused on finding her. I was in the office. I was there. He can't have had a chance to speak to them yet.'

She felt sick. Did he hate her so much he wanted to oversee her discipline personally? Make her pay.

'I'll stop him,' Burgone said.

'What? Why?' He wasn't making sense. 'I breached protocol. I brought the force into disrepute. I deserve this.'

'Cudmore,' he said, his voice stern, 'you kept information from the team. You went against a direct order. You pursued a suspect when you'd been removed from active duty. You entered a situation you knew to be dangerous, without back-up. In short you did everything you shouldn't have done.'

She hung her head in shame, misery mixing with the blood on her clothes.

'But…' She looked up, her mouth open, aware she must look gormless. 'If you hadn't had done that, then Lottie wouldn't be here. Then I would be telling my parents that their daughter was…' He looked away for a moment, as if he could see it all, just over her shoulder. When he looked back his jaw was set, his voice steady. 'You may have breached procedure, but you also worked out where the victim was being held. You got to her and you saved her life. You nearly got yourself killed, and it sounds like there's going to be one hell of a mess to sort out, but when it came down to it, you never stopped being a police officer, Cudmore. You did what you had to under extremely difficult circumstances. You might not have made the ideal call at each stage of the investigation, but I trust that you did what you thought was right. I will speak to Saunders, and the superintendent if necessary.'

'Are you sure?' She sounded like an idiot.

'You saved the life of my sister, Nasreen, I'm not having you punished for this.'

'You still want me on the team?' She couldn't believe he was saying this.

He sighed, a heavy sadness tugging at his face. 'I want you in the team, Nasreen. You're a brilliant sergeant, and I've no doubt you'll make a fantastic DI one day.' He smiled at her and she smiled back, gripping the bed tight. 'But there's only so much I can do to smooth this over with the superintendent.' When he lifted his eyes to hers, she knew what was he was going to say. She felt as if she were falling. He was trying to find the strength to speak. 'I can protect you, but not if...' He stopped: the words choking his throat.

He felt the same. 'But not if we're together,' she said quietly. All her hopes blazed brightly in front of her, before they were incinerated. This time he didn't pull away when she took his hand in hers. She stroked his smooth skin. Brought his fingers to her lips and kissed them one by one.

'I won't strip you of your place in the force, Nasreen.' He cupped her cheek and gently pushed her hair away from her face. If she left the Gremlin taskforce mere months into her post, people would assume she'd screwed up. She'd be tainted. It would kill her career before it got started. He knew it, and she knew it. And DCI Jack Burgone *was* the Gremlin taskforce. Neither could walk away and survive. The road ahead was already

330

looking bumpy; the superintendent wouldn't bend the rules any further.

His fingers were warm against her cheek. She tried to smile though tears gathered in her eyes. She should speak up. She should say she didn't care about her career, that she'd forget it all to be with him. But she didn't.

'People like you and I…' he said. 'This isn't just another job: it's our calling. We do it because if we don't…'

She nodded, thinking of Chloe, and the dead woman lying in Greenwich Park. Out there were the families, people who'd lost loved ones, people who'd lost their own lives, people who deserved justice. She rested her cheek against Jack's shoulder. He stroked her hair, his voice barely above a whisper: 'You'd grow to resent me if I took that from you. And I couldn't bear that.'

A tear rolled down her cheek and she wiped at it with the back of her hand. 'I know,' she said, though it hurt more than the knife. She held him there for a second, knowing now that it would be the last time. Willing the clocks to stop, time to stand still. He hugged her back, both of them desperately trying to hold on. And then she sniffed, straightened away from him. Banished emotion from her voice. 'Thank you, sir.'

The curtain rings whistled, and the short nurse appeared, her face clouding at the sight of Burgone. 'You shouldn't be in here. You need to leave her alone until we've finished. Thank you.' She held the curtain aside for him, her eyebrows a challenge to argue.

'My apologies,' he said. 'Take the rest of the week off, Detective Sergeant. Get some sleep. I'll have one of the team call you to see how you're doing on Monday. Manage your return to the office.' If he hadn't held her stare just a second too long, you would never have known anything had happened at all.

331

'Sir?'

He paused, his sad eyes looking at her, while the nurse tutted and tapped her watch.

'It was Freddie who worked it out. She realised the wall hanging behind Lottie was a drawing of a bird; she realised Alex Black had been on a school trip to the cabin in Wildhill Wood. She put it all together.'

Burgone raised his eyebrows slightly and then nodded. 'I see.'

'I know she's looking for a job right now, sir.' She couldn't believe she was even saying this. Couldn't believe she sounded so calm. But Freddie had helped her when she needed it, and she'd helped Lottie. Nasreen looked at him: *do this one last thing for me.* It was too late to help Gemma, but she owed the three young girls they'd once been before everything broke apart: she could help Freddie.

Burgone nodded, as if he were reassessing the last twenty-four hours afresh. 'You say she was the one who worked out the location of Black?'

'Yes,' Nasreen nodded. 'And she worked through intelligence from the Are You Awake site. She found the link to the website in the first place. And the information that led us to Cynthia Warner. Which led us to Black.'

'Hmm. She also came up with the idea about tracing Lottie's smartwatch.' He put both his hands in his pockets. After everything, he was still rational and fair.

'Ahem,' the nurse coughed loudly. 'Enough now.'

'Yes, sorry.' Burgone smiled at her and she saw the nurse visibly soften. He had that effect. 'I'll give it some thought, Sergeant. Don't worry.'

'Thank you, sir.' He ducked through the curtain, turning to catch her eye as the fabric fell, along with her heart.

'You all right, dear? You've gone quite pale.' The nurse bustled towards her, grabbing her wrist to monitor her pulse.

'Yes.' Nasreen stared at the grubby blue curtain. At where he'd been. If she closed her eyes she could still feel his touch, his heartbeat. His warm scent slowly fading beneath the smell of antiseptic. 'I'm fine,' she said. But it was a lie. She wasn't sure she'd ever be fine again.

Chapter 51

'I'm okay, I told you.' Freddie wanted to get out of here. She wanted to find Nas. They'd got separated: Freddie being driven by Green to the hospital, who'd fired a million questions at her. *How did they work out where Lottie was? How had they found the portakabin? Why had she turned around before she reached the road?* Freddie didn't need emergency treatment herself, but Chips had appeared and hustled her into a cubicle, then spent ages asking her to go over everything in detail. *Again.*

The nurse looking at the cut on Freddie's knee tutted. 'Just let me clean this up,' she said, swiping a wet swab at the stinging cut.

'That hurts more than it did doing it!' She'd have to write and sign a statement, they said. Irritation raged through her. She was knackered. She just wanted to go home and order noodles from the Vietnamese. She caught herself: the Vietnamese was at her old flat in Dalston. She didn't live there anymore.

'Okay, all done.'

'Thanks. Do I get a lollipop?' Freddie hopped off the bed, her leg cool where it was still damp. The nurse ignored her, busying herself by collecting all the bloody gauze into a cardboard kidney tray to take away. 'Do you know where they took my friend – she came in in an ambulance with a blonde girl?'

'Are you next of kin?'

They were just as good as sisters. Nas was certainly the closest she'd ever had to a sibling. 'No,' she said, pulling her hoodie back on, the cuffs mud-stained from her fall.

'Then I'm afraid I can't tell you anything.'

'I'm not press, I promise,' she said. *Well, not anymore.* Journalism felt distant, odd: the idea of sitting and typing up stories was like something from another life. She didn't know what she would do next, but it wouldn't be that.

'Sorry: that's what we've been told.' The nurse pulled the curtain back and left. Just outside, leaning against the corridor wall, was Jack Burgone. Freddie grabbed a roll of surgical tape from the table.

'Freddie,' he nodded.

'Checking I don't make a break for it?' He looked tired, but relieved. His face was soft and she realised he must have been taut with worry when she'd seen him before.

'Not at all. Sergeant Cudmore has been asking after you.'

She had the parts of her phone out of her pocket, holding them together as she wound the tape around. 'Where is she? They wouldn't tell me anything.'

'Getting stitches. She's fine, though she's going to be off work for at least a month,' he said.

'She won't like that.' She held the power button down. The phone blinked into life. A line bisecting the screen. She could live with that.

He smiled. 'No, I don't suppose she will.' His suit and shirt were straight. He looked completely normal, apart from a tiny smear of blood on his tie.

'How's Lottie?'

His smile faded. 'She's okay. Physically, I mean: they've checked her over. She's had a couple of stiches on her cheek. They say they'll be able to fix the scar with a bit of light cosmetic surgery.'

'Scars add character,' she said, tapping her head.

He smiled. 'Yes, they do.'

'And that's it, she's okay other than that?' Lottie's screams for help had made her turn back before she reached the road. She'd never forget seeing the girl: her hair matted, tape trailing from her ankle, her face a mess of tears and red as she ran towards her.

'They want to monitor her blood sugar levels overnight. Black injected her with insulin to render her unconscious.' The muscles in the front of his neck spasmed and pulled tight. *Anger.*

Lottie had fallen on her, saying she had to help the police-woman, and Freddie had gone ice cold, fear exploding in goosebumps over her skin. She hugged herself at the memory.

'You okay?' Burgone placed a hand on her arm.

'I'm fine.' She'd run then. Faster than she ever thought she could. She had to help Nas. 'It's been a crazy day.'

He smiled then. 'It has.'

'How're your folks?' Freddie thought about the faces of Lottie's parents on the news. And then thought of Chloe's parents. Of Gemma.

'They're on their way. Saunders is picking them up from the airport.'

'That'll be nice for them!' She raised her eyebrows.

Jack smiled. 'He's a good man – and a great cop.'

'If you say so. I'm going to see if I can find a coffee in here. I think I saw a Costa on the way in.'

'I can have PC Green drop you home,' he said. 'It's the least I can do.' He reached out to catch hold of her arm. She looked towards the waiting room. She just wanted to sit down. Have a moment to herself. Try and make sense of what had happened in the last twenty-four hours.

'Freddie, I want to thank you for what you did. For helping us find Lottie.'

'No worries,' she said. 'Besides, it's not like I can say no to Nas. She's very persuasive.' He smiled. What would happen between them now all this was over? She didn't want to rub it in about the email. Burgone's eyes were kind, even if his posh voice was irritating. She hoped the cafe had toasties as well. She was ravenous. Grilled cheese would hit the spot right now.

'Shall I get PC Green to meet you outside?' Burgone was keeping pace, his brogues clicking along the floor in time with the squelch of her rubber-soled boots.

She'd like a bath. And then a beer in front of the telly. 'Nah, it's all right. I'll wait for Nas. I want to see her before I go.'

'Of course,' he said, though he showed no signs of leaving her side.

'You want me to get you a bacon bap or something?' How much money was in her current account? Hopefully enough for a couple of sarnies.

'I'm vegetarian,' he said, and she stopped in the middle of the hallway. He raised his eyebrows. 'You okay?'

'You've got to be kidding me! Does Nas know?'

He looked confused. 'Does Nasreen know what?'

'Vegetarian! Brilliant!' Freddie was trying not to laugh. 'Her parents think she's veggie, like the rest of the family – has she told you that? But she can't say no to a Maccy D's.' Burgone was obviously an eat-clean freak like his sister. Classic.

'I haven't been able to eat meat since I worked on a homicide case where the killer set fire to his victims,' he said.

Freddie stopped laughing. Thought of the smell. Decided she wasn't so hungry after all.

'Freddie…' Burgone's tone was serious. 'Have you thought about what you'll do next? Nasreen told me that you're currently on a, err, career break.' He looked embarrassed.

'So?' The bright lights and noise of the hospital corridor were giving her a headache.

'Well, there's a role coming up on my team that I thought you might like to consider.'

Her mouth hung open. 'I'm not a copper, and I certainly ain't about to become one.'

He smiled as if the idea was amusing. 'No, and I'm not sure you'd be happy doing that. But I watched you during this investigation; I know what you did. You have an interesting insight into things. You were instrumental in bringing Lottie home, and I will always be grateful for that.'

'I'm not really the admin type though, mate.'

He smiled again. 'I was thinking more along the lines of an analyst role. I have the budget for a criminal intelligence analyst. You're good with data, we've seen that. You have a good eye for detail, and spotting patterns. I think it might be a good fit.'

Freddie stared at him. She didn't even know what a criminal

whatsit was. Then she thought of her parents' house, back down the deserted lane in deepest darkest suburbia. She thought of how few jobs there were out there, how before she'd had to beat off four hundred other applicants just to make sodding coffee in a cafe.

'You could train on the job,' Burgone said. 'I'd make sure you got the support you need to get back into the workplace.' His eyes flicked over her scar.

'I don't need no sympathy job.'

'I wouldn't offer you the job if I didn't think you'd be good at it.' She caught the whisper of something at the edge of his words, but he shook it off fast. 'There will need to be a probation period, understandably.'

Freddie thought of her bedroom at her parents' house. 'How much does it pay?'

Burgone smiled confidently. 'Take a few days to sort yourself out,' he said, glancing at her ripped jeans, 'and then I'll set up a meeting with HR.'

'Nas is going to be livid!' She could just imagine the look of disapproval on Nas's face.

'Oh, I don't know,' Burgone said. 'I think she'll quite like the idea.' He raised a hand to a uniformed PC who was lurking in the reception, and then held his hand out to shake hers. Freddie rolled her eyes and took it. His grip was firm, his hand warm and smooth. 'Thank you, Freddie. For everything.' He turned towards to the cop. 'PC Thompson, what have you got for me?'

Freddie caught sight of the Costa and her heart leapt. Skirting round the busy waiting room, she made a break for it. No more claustrophobic Pendrick. It was time to go home. Taking her phone out she pressed on Safari, her fingers agile, intuitive and natural across the screen. She opened SpareRoom.co.uk, selected the 'Where would you like to live?' search box, and typed: *London*.

Acknowledgements

This book wouldn't have been possible without the dedicated support, insight, expertise, and occasional cupcake administration of agent (provocateur) Diana Beaumont. My thanks must also be extended to Aneesa Mirza, who keeps on top of the admin, manages a mountain of incoming post, and always has a smile on her face at United Talent Agency. Thank you also to Juliet Mushens, Sarah Manning and all at UTA.

Thank you for the time, skills, and patience of editor Kate Stephenson, and all the luscious lovely hardworking, uber-talented, sell-billions-of-books blinding team at Avon. Special thanks to Phoebe – The Fixer – Morgan, Helena – GIF slinging – Sheffield, Hannah – Tescotastic – Welsh, Natasha – The Editor – Harding, Louis – Boom Knockout – Patel, Natasha Williams, Kate McKay, Katie Reeves, Julie Fergusson, Jo Marino, Oli Malcolm and Helen – Killer Smiles – Huthwaite. You guys are seriously aces.

Thank you to brilliant author and former cop Rebecca Bradley, and the incomparable Amy Jones, and Amy Jones' (a different one: keep up) partner Garry Jones, for letting me pick their police brains. All errors are totes mine. Obvs.

Aaron Ross for tech support and the microwave from Argos idea (criminally genius).

Chris Clarke for knowing way more about Silk Road and the FBI than a brother ought to.

Dr Hayley King, for her suggestions of various ways to effectively kill people. And for having the conversation while avoiding all the bad words, because her two young children were in the room. If they start asking about heroin, tell them you said herons. (Massive heron overdose – still my best typo EVER.)

Thank you to Dr Erica Williams and Dr Nick Williams, for twenty-four-hour callout (via text) medical knowledge, and, most notably, the intracutaneous insulin. (I REALLY want to work sarin into a future project now.) See how brilliant the NHS is? Not only do they save lives, they also save the arses of crime writers. They're basically super heroes. #supportjuniordoctors

The first rule of thanking the secret group of CSers, is not to mention the secret group of CSers. Well cockblankets to that. You are a font of information, support and filth. And I'm very lucky not to be allowed to mention you.

Thank you Graeme Cameron (see above).

Thank you to the incredible book bloggers who love books as much as authors do. I don't know where I'd be without you. A special thank you to Anne Cater and all at Book Connectors, Tracy Fenton and all at TBC, UK Crime Book Club, Crime Book Club, Facebook Book Club The Book Club, and UK Book Club. All excellent people to hang out with.

Thank you to Wendy, Paul, Julie, Beth, (Miranda), and all at Orchard physiotherapy for keeping me writing. Without you guys I'd be stuck in bed. Or the bath.

Thank you to the brilliant Kate McNaughton for excellent calm words, and for letting me bounce plot issues off of her first thing in the morning (you should all buy her book). Thank you to smart, funny, joyous Fleur Sinclair, who has done the impossible and managed to make herself even more impressive by running an indie bookshop. Visit her in Sevenoaks Bookshop and tell her how dazzling she is. (They also serve cake.) Thank you to Lucy Peden for cheerleading, philosophies, pun times, puff support and the best laugh in the business (I can't wait to read your novel). To Jake Kerridge and Gareth Rubin for answering all my random questions, and suggesting excellent books to read. And to Eleanor Dryden for believing in Freddie and Nas to begin with: without you there would be no *Watch Me*.

Thank you to James Harvey and Rosemary Harvey for continued support, buying and voting – you guys go above and beyond, and I'm very grateful.

Thank you to Li Wania and Jenny Jarvis for still listening to me talk about myself, even though you now have much more important things to do, like raising your children (cuddles).

To my partners in lime Claire McGowan and Sarah Day: you guys read, listen, contribute, and take the piss perfectly. I couldn't get through the next twenty-four hours (and/or bottle of Prosecco) without you. May our stream be deleted from history, but our books live forever. (Everyone should buy the Paula Maguire books and *Mussolini's Island*.)

Thank you to mum and dad for putting up with me still. And letting me ask you a million questions. About everything. Always. I love you very much. Thank you to Guy, Hannah, Ani, Bertie, the Ewyas Harold Massive, and the Clarke Crew for being a warm and loving family (and for letting me bang on about feminism after wine). And to my perfect Sammy, who puts up with it all and still, miraculously, seems to like me (I promise I'll try and be more tidy).

Thank you to everyone who voted for *Watch Me*'s forerunner *Follow Me* for the Dead Good Reader Page Turner Award short list 2016, and the Crime Writer's Association's Dagger in the Library long list 2016. And thank you to all those who have bought, read, tweeted, posted, shared, messaged, reviewed and enjoyed both *Follow Me* and *Watch Me*. It makes a huge difference. I've been overwhelmed by just how lovely book readers are. (Though, we all know that they're the best sort of people.)

Q & A with Laura Higgins,
Online Safety Operations Manager
of the Revenge Porn Helpline

What is revenge porn?
This is the term given to someone sharing personal sexual images
or videos of an individual without permission.

Why do people create revenge porn?
There are many motivations; sometimes as the name suggests it
is a personal vendetta, often perpetrated by an aggrieved
ex-partner. Sometimes the relationship between victim and
perpetrator is not a personal one, for example neighbourhood
disputes and even workplace bullying can involve RP. Generally
the common theme is to cause embarrassment and shame to
the person in the images.

How much of a problem is revenge porn in the UK?

Since launching the Revenge Porn Helpline in February 2015 we have received over 4000 contacts to the service. We still feel that this is the tip of the iceberg and there are many more victims out there ...

What should someone do if they are a victim of revenge porn?

Firstly, talk to someone you trust. It is incredibly upsetting to find that you have been a victim of this and you will need support. Then come to an organisation like the Revenge Porn Helpline for help! It is helpful to keep evidence, if you have screenshots of any threats or accounts for example. You may wish to involve the police and they may require this information.

Are there main sites that host revenge porn?

There are dedicated sites that host this content, many encouraging the behaviour with financial reward and they make it very easy to upload content. We choose not to name them so we don't accidently draw further attention to them! Sadly though, revenge porn content can be shared anywhere...

Can't websites that host revenge porn be shut down?

Unfortunately not, the website hosts are not breaking the law, only the people who upload the content are committing a crime. Many also fall outside the jurisdiction of the UK and can claim their right to 'freedom of speech.'

What if the website hosting the images is based abroad?

It may make it challenging to request that content is removed, however we wouldn't let this stand in the way. UK court orders may not apply though, so victims are somewhat at the mercy of the websites themselves.

346

Do only images that are shared online count as revenge porn?
No, images can be shared via mobile, printed off as hard copies or purely shown to someone to fall foul of the law.

What if someone just shows a private sexual photo to someone else – is that illegal?
See above!

If you retweet or share a private sexual image of someone else, are you guilty of revenge porn?
Technically you could be, however there has yet been a case involving this. We would advise that if you see any content you believe shouldn't be there, you should report it.

Are images which are photoshopped to look sexual illegal?
They are not included in the Revenge Porn Legislation, but could still be prosecuted under Malicious Communications or Harassment. The harm caused by these images can be just as serious as with genuine images; sometimes they are very realistic and unless the person viewing them was aware they were fake they could easily assume they are genuine.

What kind of people are most at risk of revenge porn?
Anyone can be at risk. The media portrayal is often of a twenty-something woman who sends selfies to a boyfriend, who then shares them on the internet to humiliate her if the couple break up. The reality is that we have supported victims of every age, many in their forties or fifties. Around a quarter of our clients are men, and many come from professional backgrounds: teachers, police officers, civil servants...

What are the implications if the victim is under the age of eighteen?

We try not to confuse RP with images of minors. It is illegal to produce, download or distribute images of those under the age of eighteen. Anyone who shares them is breaking the law and websites are legally required to remove them when they are reported.

What do you think of people who take naked photos of themselves?

Any adult has the right to take pictures of themselves. We live in a technological world now, where devices and the online environment are part of our everyday. It is natural to assume they are also now part of our romantic or sexual lives. Many women find it empowering to have a few 'feel good' pictures of themselves, and if they are naked or partially dressed, why not? Sadly there are a minority of cases where there has been a level or coercion or the images are taken without consent. These need to managed very sensitively. And of course, no-one ever has the right to share that image with anyone else; if they have been trusted by someone with this personal image, it was meant for them alone.

How many people do the Revenge Porn Helpline help?

We have taken thousands of calls and emails since we launched in February 2015. Sometimes the caller is another support worker, for example a domestic abuse worker or a police officer, but on the whole the calls come from victims. We hope that through our awareness work, and liaison with services to help them understand the issue, we are reaching many more people who many never have contacted the helpline directly.

How many people work for the Revenge Porn Helpline? Who funds the helpline?

There are three of us who manage cases, but we don't all work full time. We are a really small charity but we do have a broad team of specialists we can call on which includes a couple of seconded police officers, social workers and online safety experts. We are currently funded by the Government Equality Office, but we are in desperate need of continued funding post-2017. In addition there are so many areas of work we would like to grow but are not yet funded to do so; this includes providing a limited course of counselling to help our clients manage the emotional fallout until they get back on their feet.

How did you become involved in tackling revenge porn?

I have been working in online safety for five years, and over that time we have seen an increase in issues affecting women and girls. We realised that RP was a growing concern and started investigating the issue. As soon as we started talking about it publicly and in the media, the flood gates opened! We were able to make a case for a service that would provide bespoke help for clients and were lucky enough to pitch to a government representative who really understood the issue. She helped us get the start-up funding we needed for the pilot project and the rest is history!

What legal or social changes would you like to see to help fight revenge porn?

Sex and relationship education in schools is essential. It needs to start much younger and should include conversations about respect and consent. Generally I think we have reached a depressing point in human evolution, where we feel this type of behaviour is acceptable, and I would like to see more work done to challenge disrespectful language, misogyny and harassment, both online and off. Legally I would like the police to have better training and more support in managing these cases.

Can you ever get over being a victim of revenge porn?
Most people are able to move on once the content is removed. The dust does settle. Sadly though for a minority of people, even after counselling and police involvement, they cannot get over what has happened to them. We have heard from several clients that they have been treated for post-traumatic stress disorder after being a victim. That is why it's so important for us to be there for the people that need us.

About the Revenge Porn Helpline
The Revenge Porn Helpine can be reached at help@revengeporn helpline.org.uk or via 0845 6000 459. The website also contains some useful advice and can be found at www.revengepornhelp line.org.uk. The helpline is open between 10am – 4pm, Monday to Friday.

Laura Higgins is the Online Safety Operations Manager at South West Grid for Learning, lead partner of the UK Safer Internet Centre, where she established and currently manages two specialist helpline services. The Professionals Online Safety Helpline has established itself as a lifeline for professionals who work with children and young people experiencing issues with digital technology and online safety. In February 2015, SWGfL launched a brand new service specifically to support victims of revenge porn, the only service of its kind in Europe. The helpline has received thousands of calls in its first year of operation & provides regular guidance to policy makers, government departments, media and law enforcement.

Laura has significant experience in public speaking on all matters relating to internet safety, revenge porn and the online abuse of women & girls, and was honoured to speak at the 'Commission on the Status of Women' event at the United Nations in New York in 2015. Her background is in operational management across different sectors of social care. She was a Committee Member for BBC Children In Need and has a very unhealthy interest in Social Media. You can follow her at @laurahiggins_

LIKE. SHARE. FOLLOW . . . DIE.

Before *Watch Me* there was *Follow Me*.
Discover book one in the
Social Media Murder series,
an Amazon Debut of the Month.

Dark, gritty and always edge-of-your-seat: the No. 1 bestseller is back with a standout new heroine . . .

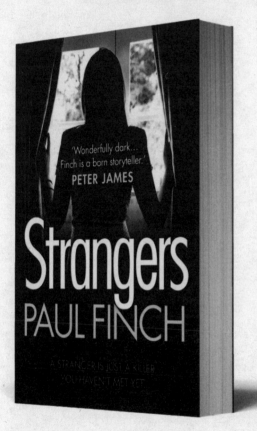

Always gripping. Always gruesome.
Paul Finch will leave you gasping for more.

First he takes them . . .
Then he breaks them . . .

First he
takes them...

Then he
breaks them...

Perfect Remains

A DI CALLANACH THRILLER

HELEN FIELDS

The first in a nail-shredding
new crime series, *Perfect Remains*
will be THE book of the year.